A
PURSUIT
of HOME

Books by Kristi Ann Hunter

HAWTHORNE HOUSE

A Lady of Esteem: A HAWTHORNE HOUSE *Novella*
A Noble Masquerade
An Elegant Façade
An Uncommon Courtship
An Inconvenient Beauty

HAVEN MANOR

A Search for Refuge: A HAVEN MANOR *Novella*
A Defense of Honor
Legacy of Love: A HAVEN MANOR *Novella* from *The Christmas Heirloom Novella Collection*
A Return of Devotion
A Pursuit of Home

3

PURSUIT
of HOME

KRISTI ANN HUNTER

BETHANYHOUSE
a division of Baker Publishing Group
Minneapolis, Minnesota

© 2019 by Kristi Ann Hunter

Published by Bethany House Publishers
11400 Hampshire Avenue South
Bloomington, Minnesota 55438
www.bethanyhouse.com

Bethany House Publishers is a division of
Baker Publishing Group, Grand Rapids, Michigan

Printed in the United States of America

Library of Congress Cataloging-in-Publication Data
Names: Hunter, Kristi Ann, author.
Title: A pursuit of home / Kristi Ann Hunter.
Description: Minneapolis, Minnesota : Bethany House, a division of Baker
    Publishing Group, [2019] | Series: Haven Manor ; 3
Identifiers: LCCN 2019020777| ISBN 9780764230776 (softcover) | ISBN
    9781493420933 (e-book) | ISBN 9780764234835 (cloth)
Subjects: | GSAFD: Christian fiction. | Love stories.
Classification: LCC PS3608.U5935 H39 2019 | DDC 813/.6—dc23
LC record available at https://lccn.loc.gov/2019020777

Scripture quotations are from the King James Version of the Bible.

Cover design by LOOK Design Studio
Cover photography by William Graf, New York

Author represented by Natasha Kern Literary Agency

19 20 21 22 23 24 25   7 6 5 4 3 2 1

To the Ultimate Example of Love
1 John 3:16

And to Jacob, who has shown me the true meaning
of service and sacrificial love.

Prologue

*S*ometimes stories are more about the one doing the telling than the tale being told. The true magic is the heart in the words, the emotion in the pauses, the depth of the conviction.

That was why Jessamine Beauchene always asked her father to tell it again, even when the request made her older brother groan.

"You've got it memorized by now," he complained as he dug his toe into the dirt in front of the log he, Jessamine, and their father were sitting on. They'd escaped into the night to give Mama a bit of space. Some days were more difficult for her than others.

Jessamine could hardly remember the large rooms and enormous gardens of the palace. This small farm with its four-room cottage and large barn had been home for half her life. It was different for Mama, Papa, and Nicolas. They remembered the grand parties and the fancy clothes.

Mama said they'd go back someday, and it was important to remember what that would be like. Sometimes she would have their cook, Ismelde, make an elaborate meal in the rudimentary kitchen. Jessamine would help, even though that made Mama frown.

7

Jessamine and her mother would dress in their finest worn, outdated gowns, and they'd simper and saunter the way Mama said people did at court. Jessamine always felt silly but it made her mother happy, so she did it.

Tonight had been one of those nights. It hadn't made Mama happy, though. It had made her cry. Lots of things made her cry lately. Ever since Jessamine's uncle, the king, had been forced to flee the capital a few months earlier and go into hiding with the rest of the family, Mama had despaired of ever getting to go home.

She tended to hurl blame when she was in despair, so they'd learned it best to let her have the back bedchamber to herself on evenings like this. Once she was asleep, they could all creep back in and find their own beds.

"It never hurts to hear the story again," Papa said, patting his son on the back. "Remembering your legacy is essential to finding your destiny."

He shifted his position on the log, and Jessamine's heart beat a bit faster as the energy crackled through the air. It was like a fairy tale to her, recollections of memories so vague and distant they might have been a dream.

"Many centuries ago," Papa began in a grave voice, "Evrart the Wanderer set out to establish a land of his own. Through the mountains and along the rivers he wandered, sleeping under the trees and in caves, refusing to even pitch his tent until he'd found the perfect place.

"Then one day he topped a mountain. A spring bubbled forth from the rocks atop that mountain, creating a steady stream of water that flowed down the rocks and joined other streams until it became a river rolling across a lush countryside. In the distance was the sea, a barely visible line on the horizon."

"Verbonne," Jessamine whispered.

"Yes, my child. He pitched his tent on the mountain and named the place Verbonne. From the mouth of the spring he pulled an opal. Large, smooth, nearly translucent in its perfection. He called it the waterstone and considered it a sign that he was meant to rule over this land.

"He built a fortress out of stone and declared himself king. He was anointed with water from the spring, poured over the waterstone and onto Evrart's head. Soon others came to join him and his kingdom grew into a powerful land."

"Not powerful enough," Nicolas grumbled, though without much conviction. He always made this observation at this point in the story.

"There is power beyond might and strength, my son," Papa said, just as he always did. "Evrart did everything he could to make Verbonne a place of intellect and culture. His children and his children's children continued that very legacy. A university was formed, filled with minds to rival those in any other country. Our art was renowned, with even the Italians coming to study our creators. Verbonne became the jewel of Europe.

"But jewels are sometimes coveted, my children, and others wanted Verbonne for themselves. Though strength of arms could not withstand the onslaught, strength of mind and heart prevailed."

"Not yet," Nicolas grumbled.

"Persevered, then," Papa said with a good-natured shrug. He didn't care which words he said; it was the heart of the story he cared about.

It was all Jessamine cared about, too. The way his voice would rise and fall, the reverence that coated his words. Sometimes he would whisper certain parts because he cared too much to say them any louder.

"With the threat of war looming, our queen took it upon herself to save the heart of Verbonne. She took everything that represented King Evrart's legacy and stole away with it in the night. Even if they conquered the land, they would never lay claim to the true Verbonne."

Jessamine sat up a little straighter at this part. She'd been named after that courageous queen.

"Alas," Papa said with a sigh, "she was not to see her country reborn. Her life passed on, and our king, who had been reduced to acting as little more than governor of his beloved land, was forced to take a second wife if he hoped to one day restore the crown to its full glory.

"Others have threatened that tenuous hold, claiming to be the rightful heirs to what little power remains, but the descendants of Evrart have remained steady. Your uncle, along with you, my dear children, and your cousins are the latest in that line of steadfast leaders who maintain the hope that one day the heart of Verbonne will return to her. She will thrive in knowledge and culture again, in her own power and freedom.

"One day we will unlock the key sent to us by the queen mother, who fled that fateful night with Queen Jessamine. We are the trusted keepers of the secret, which will be revealed to us at the proper time, when Verbonne is ready to rise again."

Jessamine sighed and laid her head on her father's shoulder. She loved how Papa always said that last part. There was always such deep hope in it. In that moment, he didn't sound tired or worried or frightened or all of those many other things he often seemed. It was the reason Jessamine loved this story so much. When he told it, he became the Papa she remembered from the palace, in her dreamlike recollections.

"I'll help you make it happen, Papa," Jessamine said.

"It's not for us to do," Nicolas said with a shake of his head. "When all of this is over it will be our uncle who pulls Verbonne from the ashes, or maybe Prince Audebert."

"We will all play a part in the restoration of Verbonne. It is close, my children. I can feel it—" Papa stopped short as a small light appeared in the distance. One light became several, all moving quickly and growing larger.

"Inside. Now," Papa said harshly, pulling Jessamine up by her arm and dragging her toward the house. He barged through the door of the cottage. "Someone is coming."

Everything happened so quickly, as if everyone besides Jessamine knew what they were supposed to do in this situation. She'd never been told, never been warned. What was she to do other than stand in the middle of the room and stare?

Her uncle Gerard, King of Verbonne, was still decorated with the court robe he'd worn during dinner. He shifted the heavy leather curtain hung across the window in order to peer outside. "We must get to the barn and the safe room there. Get the bag."

"Is there time?" Jessamine's mother gripped her hands tightly in her skirt, wrinkling the faded silk.

"We have to try," Papa said as he shoved the largest piece of furniture in the room—a sofa, brought from the palace in the early days of their asylum, but now showing the considerable wear of many years of country living. He pried up one of the wide floorboards as Mama and Ismelde ran for the door at the back of the cottage.

Beneath the floorboard was a dug-out area from which he grabbed a small sack. He handed it to Jessamine. "Hold this for me, *mon oisillon*."

He was about to slide the floorboard back into place when the first scream cut through the air from behind the house.

For one breath no one moved, and then everyone did. Gerard, Nicolas, and Audebert ran toward the screams as Papa grabbed Jessamine's small shoulders. Despite being fifteen years of age, she'd yet to grow much bigger than a child.

"No matter what you see or hear, my precious girl, you stay silent. Carry on the heart of Verbonne for me." He glanced over his shoulder to the other side of the room, where some of the close personal servants and royal advisors who had become Jessamine's hidden little village stood pale and frightened. When he turned back to her, his face was grim. "Carry on for us all."

Then he shoved her into the hole, dropped his gaze to the bag clutched to her middle, and put the floorboard back in place.

Jessamine didn't move, barely breathed. There was a small crack through which she could see, but only the front door was visible. Mere hours ago, she and Papa and Nicolas had escaped through that door, laughing about how Mama was in one of her moods.

Now the door shook from the force of blows that would soon render the wooden bar braced across it useless.

The pounding of feet returning to the cottage and incoherent yells filled the pit as surely as the smell of dirt and wood. The front door burst open and a man entered, lantern held high. For a moment, his face was framed by the crack Jessamine peered through.

He had a beard, dark and curly, and a scar slashed across his forehead. She couldn't look into his eyes, but she didn't need to in order to know he was a hard, mean man.

"Gather them all," he said in a voice that was most decidedly not French, "and search the entire place. This line of interlopers will cease sitting on the throne of Verbonne."

More shuffling of feet, more screaming, more everything assaulted Jessamine's senses. Pieces came to her, bits of phrases, pleas, and cries. The sofa was tossed on its side, partially blocking the crack Jessamine peered through. The rip of fabric followed. Her family was ushered out as the entire place was searched.

"I think we found it," someone said in French, and a trunk was carried out the front door.

It was the trunk her uncle had brought with him. It held the king's scepter and crown and all the most important government documents.

The man with the curly beard stepped into the edge of what Jessamine could see. "The line will be corrected and the proper head anointed. Burn this place. Start the fire in the crops so by the time it reaches here and attracts attention the blaze will be too much to fight. When I am finished, there will be no trace of their line."

Then he was gone.

And it was dark.

The loud pounding of Jessamine's heart was all that broke the total silence.

They were going to burn the cottage.

With her still inside.

She began to fight and scream and push, but the sofa was stretched across the floorboards, and her slight body, scrunched into a pit with no way to move, couldn't budge it.

It wasn't until she heard a man say, "What's this?" in a voice bearing the same accent as the man with the curly beard that Jessamine considered the dire consequences of the noise she was making. What if the fire had been a threat to get her to reveal her location and that of the bag her father had deemed so important?

"We're too late," another voice said. "They've taken them all, and if there was anything to be found, it's already been gotten."

"Search the barn one more time," the first voice said.

"The fire's coming. There's no point."

"Search it."

After a sigh, footsteps receded, and a soft grunt preceded the scrape of the sofa against the floorboards.

Jessamine wriggled and twisted until she could shove the bag beneath her stomacher. She normally hated the stiff dress bodice her mother insisted formal gowns still needed, despite the flowing fashions that had begun appearing before they ran from the palace, but at that moment, Jessamine was grateful for it.

With the bag shoved into a space that was already tight, though, she could barely breathe. Something sharp poked her in the stomach and that, combined with her fear, sent tears coursing down her cheeks. The sudden sobs made breathing even more difficult.

The board lifted, and the light from a single small lantern revealed a pair of grey eyes. They didn't look like the eyes of a particularly nice man, but they looked kind and capable.

"What's your name?" he asked.

"Jess—" hiccup—"Jess—" sniffle. Panic welled. She couldn't find enough air to say her full name.

"Well, Jess," the man said, "I'm here to rescue you. How do you feel about going to England?"

CHAPTER ONE

MARLBOROUGH, ENGLAND
1816

*S*ometimes, despite time, distance, and a significant amount of ignoring it, the past never quite went away.

Over the past two days, everything Jess had run from had spilled over the wall of the past and covered her present like gravy. Lumpy, bitter, burnt gravy. Every emotion she'd worked hard to bury had risen to the surface, making her mind a muddled swarm of incomplete thoughts and sharp colors.

After one sleepless night, she'd done what she did best: shoved every modicum of mind-numbing emotion into a trunk, locked it, and set about determining how to solve the problem at hand.

A second sleepless night allowed irritation to trickle out of the locked trunk and fill her until she wanted to stab something. Of all the feelings she'd felt over the past two days—elation, fear, grief, excitement, hope, despair, really any emotion that could be elaborately overdone in a gothic novel—irritation was the one she most knew how to deal with.

People were often rather irritating, after all, especially when you were trying to extract secrets from them.

What wasn't so easily determined was what part of her current situation irritated her most: that someone had been able to locate her to deliver the letter, that she'd been able to decipher the old code without the slightest bit of trouble, or that she was going to have to ask a very bothersome man for his assistance.

No, it was the last one. Definitely.

She'd known her days of hidden isolation were numbered, and no one could expect nearly ten years of living in the shadows of intrigue and danger to disappear with a few well-placed country breezes. Needing help was an annoyance, though.

Having to ask for it was an aggravation.

Having to ask *him* was almost nauseating.

There was nothing else for it, though. If the letter she'd received was true—and she had complete confidence in the man who'd written it, so she had to assume it was—then she didn't have a choice.

She needed Mr. Derek Thornbury's help.

To get it, she was going to have to ask him, which required talking to him, which required being in the same room with him without taking her knife from its hidden sheath and stabbing him in the leg. A tall order, as the man was simply too vexing for words.

He was a walking, talking reminder of everything she wasn't good at, and he pointed it out to her constantly. The man couldn't open his mouth without making Jess feel like a veritable idiot.

Unfortunately, those skills were exactly what she needed.

He knew how to read and interpret old texts and he knew art. Jess knew tactics, strategy, and intricate disguises. Her current plan had her in the kitchen, preparing a tea tray with all his favorites. It had been a while since she'd cooked them, as she'd avoided making any dish he seemed to favor.

Subtle, petty revenge was also a skill Jess held in great abundance.

Voices broke the solitude of the kitchen that had been Jess's refuge for the past three years as a pair of maids passed through on their way to the washroom. They were just two of the many people who now filled the home that had been a perfect hiding place for so long. Even though all of the servants hired within the last two months had been born and raised in the local area and couldn't possibly know of her past, Jess found herself watching them with constant vigilance, seeking the slightest hint that they might not be who they said they were.

Not that it mattered if they'd been the ones to reveal her location. Jess had known this secretive, sheltered house would eventually become exposed. Despite the danger, she hadn't been able to bring herself to move on.

She'd stayed, even as the others stepped out of hiding and got married, even as she went from the kitchen's solitary inhabitant to having authority over a small kitchen staff, even as guests started coming and going.

Or coming and never leaving, in some people's cases. She frowned at the tray she was putting together.

In all fairness, he'd been hired to assess the enormous amount of art in the estate, but he was also close to the owner and taking an awfully long time to complete his task. He hovered somewhere between employee and friend.

Rather like herself.

Jess had come to care about the people she'd been in hiding with. Despite knowing that it made her vulnerable, she'd exposed part of her heart.

Now she'd been found.

It was, actually, a good thing. The regret that would have risen from learning the contents of the letter after it was too late would have slowly eaten her alive until she was nothing but a pile of misery and guilt.

She didn't have to worry about that, though, because she *did* know the contents, *did* have what was needed to potentially solve the problem, and *did* have a plan.

Of sorts.

It was more of a notion, really.

Actually making a workable plan required Mr. Derek Thornbury's help, which required a peace offering of syrup-infused Naples biscuits.

Jess went to the larder for flour and turned an ear to the conversation two maids were having. One of them was stuttering a bit, something she did only when she slept poorly the night before. On the way back to the worktable, Jess took a slight detour to nudge a bucket out of the way of another maid crossing the room with her arms piled so high with linens that she couldn't possibly watch where she was going.

Soon the biscuit dough was mixed, including a little syrup to make the final product soft and cake-like. The suggestion of the additional ingredient had been the first thing *that man* had ever said to her. Jess hated to bake, or cook for that matter, hated the memories attached to the skills, but she knew she was good at it. Very good. An art scholar shouldn't have known more about it than she did.

When she'd tried to prove him wrong, the result had been delicious. Jess had thrown them in the fire and refused to make any more. Until today.

One transgression wouldn't have been enough to make Jess hate the man. Probably. He made it excessively easy, though, by continuing to be a pompous font of knowledge and suggestions. Well, perhaps not pompous.

The man was often too focused on what he was doing to care about lording his exceptional brain over everyone else in the room, but that didn't change the fact that he knew facts others didn't and felt the need to broadcast it on a regular basis.

With any luck, however, she could get him to display his brilliance one more time in a way that benefited her.

With the tea steeping in the steaming pot and the plates of food as prettily arranged as she could manage, Jess took the tray up the servants' stairs. She got a few strange looks, but then, people tended to look at whatever was different. It was the first rule of disguise. Try to look as normal as possible for the surroundings you're in. No one paid attention to normal.

Unfortunately, there was nothing Jess could do about the fact that before now she'd rarely showed her face abovestairs, and she almost never hand-delivered a tray. Sometimes there just wasn't time to set up a proper scene.

Once out of the servants' domain, she faced a problem. Where in the world was her target? As far as Jess could tell, there was no rhyme or reason to Mr. Thornbury's path through the house as he catalogued the abundance of art and antiquities. She could only hope the records he was keeping were more organized than his methods.

Ten minutes later, with the steam no longer curling as nicely from the teapot, she found him in the upstairs private parlor.

"Good afternoon, Mr. Thornbury." She pasted a smile on her face, reminded herself that she'd done worse in the name of necessity, and set the tray down on a little side table.

He looked up from the notebook he was forever scribbling in and tilted his head as he looked at her, making the overgrown flop of brown hair droop over his eyebrows. "Good afternoon."

"I brought you tea."

"I see that." He crossed the room and lifted the top of the pot to gaze into the depths of the brown liquid. "Is it poisoned?"

Jess gritted her teeth but didn't let her smile drop. One single time she'd threatened to put foxglove in his tea if he didn't stop leaving paintings and sculptures spread out on the dining table, and now he looked at every drop of liquid she prepared as if he expected a sea creature to jump out of it.

"No, it isn't poisoned. In fact, I was wondering if I could presume to share a cup with you."

"You want to have tea." He placed a hand on his chest, making the dull brown coat he'd left unbuttoned fall open. "With me."

Jess silently counted to three before speaking. "Yes."

He glanced down at the tea and then back to her, his hazel eyes narrowing a bit behind his round black spectacles.

She couldn't fault his suspicions. Their situation was a strange one. Officially, she was the cook of this country estate and should never approach a gentleman visitor, even if he was, technically, also an employee of the marquis who owned the place. She was, however, a friend of the new marchioness, and before the marquis had come to live here she'd been much more than just the cook, so the social hierarchy was more than a little muddled.

There was also the fact that she'd done nothing to hide how much he irritated her. They'd yet to have a conversation anyone would consider pleasant and proper.

Finally, Mr. Thornbury cleared his throat and nodded before gesturing toward a chair beside the low table. "As you took the trouble to make the tea, I see no reason why you should not partake in it."

Once Jess was seated, he lowered himself onto the sofa that sat at an angle to the chair and table, watching silently as Jess fixed the tea and served plates of food.

He gave the cup she handed him one more contemplative glance before sipping it. "There's a fascinating Caravaggio piece in this room. Just over there. It's hanging in the corner, as if it's trying to hide. A rather odd place to hang such a masterpiece."

Jess took a deep breath and reminded herself that there was more to life than book knowledge. "I don't know anything about Caravaggio."

"I know," he said slowly. "Which does make me wonder why you'd want to have tea with me."

Jess had to give him credit for not being a coward. He'd never had any problem saying what he thought. If only he didn't have such smart thoughts, she might admire that ability.

Carefully, she set her cup to the side and clasped her hands in her lap before raising her eyes to his. Even though she wanted to keep her gaze steady, she was forced to blink away the grittiness of two sleepless nights before she could focus on him properly. She knew the words she needed to say, knew that to continue on with her efforts alone would mean significant delay and possibly even failure.

Knowing this didn't make the task any easier.

One hand slid against her leg, and the slight sound of paper crinkling reminded her of the letter nestled in her pocket. Her brother was alive and doing everything he could to restore the family legacy. Someone—presumably the same someone she'd been hiding from most of her life—wanted him to fail. She held the key to ensuring her brother's success . . . only she didn't know how to use it.

If she wanted to prevent her father's life work from fading into the war-torn lands of Europe, she would have to allow Mr. Thornbury deeper into her life.

She straightened her shoulders and looked him in the eye. "Mr. Thornbury, I need your help."

❧❧

Derek Thornbury didn't know a lot about people, at least not living ones—and he knew even less about females—but he did know one thing: this particular female didn't like him.

It didn't require advanced skills in observation, which he admittedly didn't have, nor an abundance of knowledge in the ways women had interacted with men throughout history—which he *did* have. No, it was fairly obvious that she didn't like him because the last few times they'd had a conversation, she'd said, *"I don't like you."*

That was the type of social indicator even Derek couldn't quite miss.

Yet here she was, sitting down to tea with him, and, if his ears could be believed, she was asking for his help.

Carefully, he set his teacup down. He set the biscuit down, too, though with more reluctance. Jess might confound him on more than one level, but he did very much enjoy her cooking skills. "What?"

He'd meant to ask more, really he had. Perhaps, "What do you mean?" or "What do you need?" or even "What would make you desperate enough that you would willingly seek me out and spend more than a modicum of time in my company?" But since he wasn't sure which question to ask, it simply came out as "What?"

She sighed, releasing a longer breath than he would have thought her petite body capable of holding. "I need your help."

That didn't answer any of his questions.

He picked up the biscuit and put it back down again without taking a bite. "What do you need my help with?"

"I have a diary of sorts, an old one written by an ancestor of mine. It's in Italian."

"You speak Italian." In fact, she spoke it very well, with a flawless accent and the fluency of a native. They'd argued in the language more than once, though his verbal skills were decidedly less eloquent than hers. He rather thought that was why she chose to use the language.

Pink stained her cheeks, and for the first time he could remember, her golden gaze refused to meet his. "Yes." She cleared her throat. "I speak it, but I'm afraid reading it is a bit of a slow endeavor. I have to sound everything out and say it aloud. Even then I don't always know what it's talking about. Translating the diary would take me weeks, possibly more. I'm afraid I don't have that kind of time."

Derek leaned back on the sofa and tilted his head as he considered her.

She rubbed one hand over her skirt before continuing. "There's . . . well, for lack of a better word, this diary holds a message about where this ancestor hid something of great value."

He picked his tea back up, more than a little disappointed even as he was intrigued. She wouldn't be the first person to try to pull him into a bit of potential thievery by glorifying it as some sort of treasure hunt. "And you would like to get your hands on it?"

"Yes. No." She sighed again. "It isn't for me."

That was new. "Who is it for, then?"

"Someone I thought was dead but apparently isn't."

There was a slight lilt to her words, an accent that almost sounded French but wasn't. A tone that had been buried underneath a proper English sound for years. He'd heard it before, when she was especially upset about something he'd done. It was thicker today, though.

"As interesting as a real-life Lazarus would be," he said, "I'm going to need a bit more than that. I've a job I've committed to do, after all."

"You've been here for months," she growled. "How much more could there possibly be?"

"There's a great deal of art that has been amassed at Haven

Manor over the years. The original owner was a consummate collector."

"It isn't going anywhere."

"Presumably neither is whatever you're looking for, if you intend to locate it with a long-dead ancestor's diary."

Her lips thinned and her finely arched blond eyebrows pulled in until a fierce frown covered her face. It looked wrong on her features. Everything about her was petite and delicate, perfect like a porcelain doll or a Botticelli painting. "I have reason to believe the item is now vitally important."

"And you want it before anyone else?" Wasn't that always the way of art? Let one person indicate an interest and everyone would proclaim it a masterpiece.

The actual quality mattered little when determining a piece's value. It was all about who else wanted to possess it.

Saddened, and in truth a bit intimidated by the little woman, he dropped his gaze to her feet. Sturdy, worn leather boots poked out from beneath the forgettable skirt. A long pale scratch cut across the surface of the left toe.

Had she accidentally done that with one of those knives she was always threatening to throw at him whenever he dared to venture down to the kitchens?

He should probably start sending a servant to fetch whatever he needed from belowstairs, but he found an odd sort of enjoyment in aggravating the tiny woman. Like a child taunting a dog on a chain, he got the thrill of danger with the security of knowing she wouldn't actually do anything.

At least, he didn't think she would.

"I already told you it isn't for me," she said. "But yes, I need to find it first."

Derek brought his gaze up from her feet, refusing to have this conversation with the floor.

Jess—he didn't know her last name, and it seemed much too strange to call her Cook—flicked one fingernail gently with the other. She moved in no other way. Her breathing was even, her posture calm, but her little fingernail tapped restlessly against her thumb.

Derek was a scholar of antiquities. He worked with things created by dead people. Well, things that had been created by people who were now dead. Important distinction, that. When he was working, he might go days without a significant interaction with anyone who drew breath.

Living people, quite inconveniently, required him to recall his manners and finish his sentences.

Jess wasn't merely an inconvenience, though. She was a massive complication, a mystery that was constantly changing, frustrating him to no end even as it kept enticing him closer.

Right now she was offering him an opportunity to get close enough to potentially solve the profound mystery she represented. Curiosity had proven to be an undeniable nag over the years, and frankly, anything—or, in this case, anyone—who was intimidating enough to inspire Jess to seek out help must be fascinating.

Of course, it was probably best if said person continued living in ignorance of Derek's existence.

Still, he couldn't resist curiosity's siren call. "Why do you need it first?"

She took a deep breath and straightened her shoulders, sliding into a proper posture that would meet the approval of even the strictest governess. "Because the fate of a country might rest on who finds this treasure first and when."

A country. Not *the* country. He'd suspected she wasn't from England, but that rather confirmed it. Considering the war that had only recently subsided in the French-speaking part of the world, that slight lilt in her voice encouraged skepticism. "Which country?"

Her frown deepened. "Are you going to help me?" She pulled an old leather-covered book from the pocket of her apron.

That was a bit unfair. Resisting the entire thing in concept was much simpler than denying his hand the chance to reach out and touch history, to open the pages and delve into the mind of someone who had lived before him.

The book was worn and frayed at the edges, with darkened spots where hands had held the book over the years. Diaries were incredible windows into the past. People wrote things in diaries that never touched the pages of official historic documents—life, love, the stories behind the scenes depicted in paintings and sculptures.

He wanted that diary. The only question was, did he want it badly enough to deal with *her*?

She turned the book enough for him to see a crest branded onto the cover of the book. The curling flow of lines looked like leaves, but he was willing to bet they were waves crashing against rocks because in the center of those curls was a shield bearing the image of a horned beast, something like a unicorn with paws. One foot was raised with a sword pointed to the sky, while another paw tucked close in to the body, holding a cross. Other parts of the branded image had faded over time, but he knew that horned beast. He'd seen it in books.

"How long ago was it written?" He swallowed hard, staring at the book as if it would disappear. If that diary was from the days before the fall of the monarchy, he wouldn't be able to sleep without having seen it with his own eyes.

"Only the first entry is dated. It says 1660."

Derek licked his lips. He'd like to think he had enough sense to keep his fingers from being burnt by meddling in the affairs of others, but he was already leaning forward and reaching toward the book.

"Very well," he said as his fingers extended toward her. "Where do we start?"

CHAPTER TWO

*J*ess held her breath and tightened every muscle in her body in an attempt to keep the hand holding the diary from trembling. She'd reduced three taper candles to puddles of wax the night before trying to read it herself and learned nothing beyond the fact that the writer had a great affinity for art.

Time was a luxury she didn't have. An art expert who knew Italian was.

Were Mr. Thornbury a starving man, the diary would have been a meal from the king's table. Behind his black-rimmed spectacles, his eyes were wide and unblinking, while his shoulders shifted a bit faster as his breathing grew heavier. It emphasized the fact that his plain woolen coat wasn't quite as tailored as it should have been.

His eyes were locked on the Verbonnian crest on the cover. Did he recognize it? The country had a rich artistic heritage, so it was likely he'd encountered it at some point, but had he studied enough to recognize the difference between the country's crest and that of the royal family?

"May I?" He flipped his hand over, palm outstretched in patient inquiry.

Jess let the corner of the diary fall against his palm but couldn't bring herself to let it go. This book was the only tie she had to her past, to her childhood. She'd protected it with everything she had for years. It had been her father's last request.

She'd kept it a secret. Everything else she'd shared with the man who rescued her, in case it was relevant to the war, but the diary was different. She'd shown it to no one.

Except for Mr. Thornbury.

"I can't read it if you don't let go."

Jess was being sentimental and foolish—two things she tried never to be. They always caused more problems than solutions.

Frustration at herself for succumbing to the weakening emotions gave her the push she needed to press the book into his hand and remove her own.

As he lifted the cover she had to sit on her hand to prevent herself from snatching it back. "Italian," he murmured. "Verbonne spoke French back then."

English and German could frequently be heard in the country as well. Despite its small size, its turbulent history had brought a variety of languages and cultures into its borders. Jess had grown up among them.

How much of that remained? She had no idea.

Mr. Thornbury was correct, though, that French was the main language. They'd spoken French at the country's inception, and many of the governmental communications had remained in French, even when it came under the power of German overlords. A tiny nod of defiance that helped retain the hope of eventual renewed independence.

Fear curled through her middle. Jess was well acquainted with the feeling, knew how to identify it and its source. It was a useful tool in subterfuge, allowing her body to alert her to the potential dangers around her. As long as fear remained a tool and wasn't allowed to take over her mind, it was a good thing.

Personal fear, like the kind currently urging her to shift in her seat, was harder to contain and direct. There was no imminent physical danger for her to brace for or prevent.

All she could do was wait while a man she couldn't stand read her only remaining secret.

A secret so well kept even she didn't know what it was. For all she knew it could lead to the family recipe for *mille-feuille.* Yes, her father had been told otherwise, but what if it wasn't true? What if the vague legend that had been passed down with the diary was nothing but a fairy tale created to keep hope and a passion for freedom lit through the generations?

If that legend weren't true, Jess wasn't sure what she would do. People were so desperate to believe the legend that they were willing to die for it. Or kill.

"Hold this for me, mon oisillon. Carry on the heart of Verbonne for me." She'd lost so many memories of her papa over the years, but those words and his grim face held fast. She knew now, with the experience of someone who had walked long in the darkness of political intrigue, that Papa had not expected to survive the night.

But he'd made sure she had. She and this worn family heirloom.

Mr. Thornbury turned the pages carefully. On the third page he paused, becoming as still as one of the statues he was forever examining. Until that moment, Jess hadn't realized how constantly in motion he was. Lifting a hand, tilting his head, shifting a foot. For all the time he spent staring at statues and picking over paintings, she'd never have described him as constantly in motion, but now that he was still—so still she wasn't even sure he was breathing—she realized how often he moved.

"Who did you say wrote this?" he asked.

Jess leaned forward a bit so she could angle her head to see his face behind the hair that had fallen forward as he leaned over the book. "My great-grandfather's grandmother, or so I was told."

"Who told you that?"

"My father." Jess bit her lip to keep from cursing. She'd heard plenty such language during the war but had managed to refrain from falling into the habit herself. It had been the one refinement she could hold on to, the last remnant of the person she'd been before the world had collapsed around her.

She understood the temptation, though. Times like now, when a pair of hazel eyes were peering at her with suspicion and accusation, she had to fight the desire to use an expletive as defense against the firm set of his thin frown.

"Who was your father?"

What was in that diary? It had taken Jess nearly all night to get as far as he'd gotten in a few minutes, but she couldn't recall anything that would inspire this sort of reaction. Most of it was about water and color and paint.

Jess pointed at the diary. "What does it say?"

"Where did your father get it?"

A growl simmered in the back of Jess's throat. Her determination to be polite and civil to this man was wearing very thin. "From his father. Mr. Thornbury, I am not seeking an inquisition. People are depending on me, and the only way I can help them lies somewhere in that diary. If you are not going to help me, kindly return my property so I can find someone who can."

There were always other options, even if the only ones she could think of were even less appealing than working with Mr. Thornbury. She may not like him, but she trusted him.

Or at least she trusted her ability to control him.

His lips pressed into a thin line as he sat back against the sofa and carefully turned to a section in the middle of the book, his eyes jerking back and forth as he read the pages with an ease that made Jess grind her teeth.

"If this account is accurate," he said slowly, "and indeed written by your"—he waved a long-fingered hand—"ancestor, it is an incredible revelation for the art world."

For the . . . had he just said a revelation for the *art world*? Not for England or France or the world at large or the emerging political dynasties?

Jess contemplated and discarded several possible responses. What would be the most beneficial here? Surprise? That would certainly be genuine. On the other hand, pretending she knew what he was talking about might gain her more information. When in doubt, let silence win out. She'd wait to see what direction he tried to take the conversation.

Except he wasn't talking. He'd flipped back to the beginning and was reading through some of the early entries. "'*Passaggio segreto.*'"

"The secret passage," Jess said.

He glanced at her over his spectacles. "I know." Then he turned his attention back to the book. "'*Affogare in un bicchier d'acqua.*'"

Jess waited.

Once more he cut his eyes toward her over his wire frames. "I don't know that. I mean, I know she's said she doesn't want to drown in a cup of water." He frowned. "Or maybe tea. What I don't know is what it means."

"That she was trying not to lose heart over every small setback."

"Ah, yes, you *speak* the language. Know the slang."

Jess shrugged. Her knowledge was considerably more limited than his was. While it might be practical, it was hardly as respectable as his formal education. Much to the distress of her mother, Jess's life and education had been nothing like what it was supposed to be.

If Mama knew what Jess had done over the past decade, she'd faint.

Mr. Thornbury hummed as he flipped another page. Then, with the sigh of a man about to hand over his last shilling to the debt collectors, he closed the book and handed it back to her.

Would the man ever do what she expected him to? He had once convinced Lord Chemsford, the owner of the house and Jess's employer, to rearrange his dinner schedule so that Mr. Thornbury could have time to inspect the serving platters in the kitchens in search of some rare form of pottery. Now he was going to pass up something that might be of vital importance to the history of art?

"You aren't going to help me?" Jess asked.

"Do you take me for a fool, Miss . . . er, Mrs. . . . er, I say, what *is* your name?"

"Jess. Or Cook, if you prefer."

He brushed that ridiculous flop of hair off his forehead as he slid the spectacles from the slope of his thin, pointed nose. Then he removed a handkerchief from his pocket and started to clean the lenses. "Is that what the other servants call you? Cook?"

Actually, they tried not to call her anything if they could help it. Jess didn't exactly court camaraderie. "What do you wish to say to me, Mr. Thornbury?"

He sighed. "That book"—he pointed at the diary—"is from Verbonne."

Jess's heart thudded a bit harder. Only years of experience allowed her to refrain from breathing hard and fidgeting in her seat. Instead, she tilted her head and waited for him to continue, ignoring that her lungs were burning with the desire to pull in more oxygen.

He slid the spectacles back on and continued to stare at the book as if he could read it while it was closed. "Given the timing, it would seem your ancestor was intimately linked to, if not a part of, The Six. That's all she wrote about in the passages I glimpsed."

The pounding of her heart grew as anxiety gave way to excitement. She had to allow her breathing to increase or risk passing out. This was new information. She didn't know what to do with it because she had no idea who The Six were, but it was a place to start.

Had they been part of a dangerous expedition? Perhaps a plot to assassinate the emperor and stop his overtaking the country? "Who were The Six?"

"A group of artists. They studied under the master Aldric Fournier. His style, his perfectionism was unique. Many sought to study beneath him, but he refused them all until suddenly he came to England and started presenting the work of six apprentices. They became so good that it is sometimes close to impossible to distinguish the master from the student. Still, no one knew their names."

Artists? The stories from childhood, the hopes of a nation fighting for its sovereignty, her father's last free act, his final request had been about a group of artists?

How was that going to help her brother or her family legacy?

Yes, Verbonne had always prided itself on being a center of culture and education, but that wasn't enough to rebuild a nation, particularly not when other, more powerful parties were panting at the chance to carve the country up and absorb it.

If anything, an increase of valuable art or knowledge would only make the area more desirable.

Mr. Thornbury folded his fingers together and gave her that thin frown again. "They are some of the most valuable paintings in the world. I will not help you steal one."

A laugh burst from Jess. Sharp, dry, and crackling around the edges. "I assure you that a painting will not solve the problem. I was told this book held the path to the secret that would restore history. A painting cannot do that."

He lifted his brows until they were visible over the tops of his spectacles. "I once saw a man offer the owner of a Fournier masterpiece four hundred pounds. The owner would not hear of parting with it."

"Then both men are fools," Jess bit out. This couldn't possibly be about a painting. Even if funds were what was required, at the time Queen Marguerite had written this, the paintings would have been worth little or even nothing. Jess thrust the book back toward him. "You mumbled about a secret passage. What does that part say?"

Grudgingly, Mr. Thornbury took the book back and turned to the page he'd been on before. "It says 'the heart is a secret path to the head, though some would think it otherwise. Without understanding the passion of . . . ' heart? Possibly love or emotion? The writing is a bit smudged."

"Heart will work. Please continue," Jess whispered, an idea niggling at the back of her mind. She tried to relax, tried to stop her conscious thought and just listen for what wasn't being said.

Mr. Thornbury cleared his throat and continued. "'Without understanding the passion of the heart, the head will never properly reign, the hand will never properly rule, and the land will dry up into chaos.'"

Air whooshed from Jess's lungs as she collapsed back into her seat. Childhood stories, legends, and bedtime tales. Had they been real? Had her father all along been planting in his children's minds the information they would one day need to know? Had those tall tales of legendary loyalty been true?

"Oh, *grand-mère*, what did you do?" Jess breathed out.

Mr. Thornbury looked up. "This means something to you?"

Other than the fact that another impertinent, strong, too-brave-for-her-own-good female was lurking somewhere up Jess's family tree? Yes. It meant something. Jess swallowed and allowed her eyes to find his. The stakes had just become too great to ignore. Whatever it took to secure Mr. Thornbury's help, she had to do it.

"Yes," she said, straightening her shoulders. "It means we aren't looking for a painting."

CHAPTER THREE

erek had never been very good at sports, mostly because he couldn't care less whether or not he won, which tended to make his teammates a bit perturbed. In the classroom, though, and particularly in the library, he'd been a whirling bundle of unstoppable energy.

Whatever drove other young men to succeed on the athletic field made Derek rabid for information. History and the way it manifested itself into life and art fascinated him. He couldn't get enough of it. He delved and dug until the minute secrets of the past found light.

The current secret in question, though, didn't appear to have an answer buried in a dusty library tome, protected only by its forgotten presence. Instead, it was held tight by a woman. A woman who, until twenty minutes ago, lived to thwart him.

He still didn't know how he'd angered her, but from almost his first moment in the house, she'd held him in obvious dislike.

Dislike or not, now she needed him, and the opportunity she was offering was going to plague him for the rest of his life if he walked away from it.

The paintings of The Six, a group that wanted only to present the art and not themselves, had always intrigued him. He'd done as much research into them as he could, but there was pitifully little to learn. No names had ever been recorded, though a few had distinguishable habits, such as the one who tended to put a little flick at the end of his short, thin strokes.

But the writer of the diary had known them.

If Derek didn't work with Jess, didn't examine every page of that diary, he'd slowly go insane.

"What does that passage mean to you?" He reread the sentences, trying to make sense of the cryptic statement.

"What else does it say?"

Derek pressed his lips together to keep from muttering to himself. That was how she intended for this to go? He was merely to translate and ask no questions? He hadn't become the foremost expert on antiquities and art history by not asking questions.

She wouldn't be the first to assume his scholarly interests made him weak-willed, though. The question was whether it was more beneficial to go along with it for now or stand his ground from the beginning.

"Mr. Thornbury? What does it say?" Her lips twisted into a smirk. "You can read it, can't you?"

The decision was suddenly much easier—or at least his pride seemed to think it was—but Derek didn't do anything without thinking it through.

He closed the book with a snap, barely avoiding the desire to wince at the rough treatment of the old book, and folded his arms across his chest, casually tucking the book into his jacket beneath his arm. "I'll work on it and get back to you."

The smirk, which had fallen somewhere between teasing and goading, fell into a displeased frown. "What?"

"Unless you care to sit about while I work through the book. Or did you think I would translate on the go, so to speak, and sit here and read it to you?"

"I can't allow this to drag on for months," she grumbled. "This is a matter of some urgency, Mr. Thornbury."

"Yes, yes. Lives at stake and such. I may be a historian, Miss, er, Jess, but I am not unaware of the present and the dangers it possesses. Nor am I ignorant of the fact that association can be just as deadly as intent. You've given me your word but not a bit of proof. Forgive me if our past encounters make me cautious."

Derek bit his lip to keep from grinning at his sanctimonious speech. Everything he'd said was true, but poking at the little cook was also a great deal of fun. He'd never been the type to cause trouble on a lark. Mostly he'd just stumbled into it—usually quite literally—and even then it was no more than a social blunder of some order.

Riling Jess up was a challenge, though, one that required wit and brains and forced him to dodge one step ahead of her mentally. He always had enjoyed challenges of the mind.

"You have one day." Her teeth clicked together. "One day to determine something about the contents of the diary."

One day? He'd never be able to uncover the layers and subtexts and undertones of a significant portion in a single day.

Then again, she wasn't looking for that, was she? She only wanted the instructions, which might be even more difficult, given the pages he'd glanced at.

Still, his mind was engaged, which meant he wasn't likely to do anything else for the rest of the day anyway. He'd have something ready by tomorrow.

She didn't need to know that, though.

"I have a job to do, you know." He took a sip of his tea, trying to look torn and studious.

Jess didn't buy it. She rolled her eyes. "Lord Chemsford is much too enamored with his new wife to care one whit about whether or not you've determined who painted the ridiculous smiling dog portrait you moved to your room. He wouldn't notice if you disappeared for weeks."

"Something I'm likely to have to do if you insist on starting to follow the directions before I have a chance to complete the translation."

One of her delicate golden eyebrows curved upward. "Let me be clear, Mr. Thornbury. I may need your assistance gathering information, but at the end of the day, I work alone."

He arched his own eyebrows and took a slow sip of tea before patting the coat pocket he'd slid the diary into. "Not anymore."

❧❧

Everyone had a point where pushing them would do more to pit them against you than sway them to your view. Jess had dealt with enough people and performed enough negotiations to know that Mr. Thornbury was very near to that point.

If she said anything else right now, her persistence would let him know that her need was so great he could ask her for almost anything in return and she'd have to allow it. At the moment it was best to give the illusion of nonchalance and patience.

Well, not too much patience. She couldn't allow him to take days to contemplate. In her experience, people who sat around contemplating ended up dead.

Curiosity was obviously the carrot to pull him along. She could feed him enough information to keep him involved while leaving him out of the particulars. That was a difficult enough line to walk with someone she knew well. As much as she understood the type of man Mr. Thornbury was, she didn't truly know his temperament.

Jess left him and the diary in the parlor, along with the plate of biscuits, and made her way sedately to the kitchens. There was a large pile of vegetables that she could take out her growing annoyance on. No one would be complaining that the mushrooms in tonight's dinner were too large.

Ten minutes later, the quick, efficient, frustrated slices of the kitchen knife had all the servants giving the worktable a wide berth. That suited Jess. Right now she needed to think.

Most people thought she was a master of manipulation. What they didn't realize was that manipulation required tact and a delicate hand, two qualities Jess absolutely did not possess.

If there was a need for someone to slip in somewhere unseen and gather information? She was that girl. Someone to inflame emotions and cause a riot as a distraction? She'd done it more than once. Watch over someone or something with no one being any the wiser? There were few who could do it better.

Subtly maneuver people into doing what she wanted them to do? Not so much.

She should be good at it. It should be a skill ingrained in her since birth. After all, manipulation made the world go round, and nowhere was it more evident than the politics lining palace hallways. Knowing what to say should have been second nature.

But she'd been too young when her family had fled those gilded hallways, hadn't yet been forced to deal with underhanded maneuverings and unspoken promises. Instead, she'd gotten the necessities of survival sheened over by the remnants of a higher life.

She sliced through a chicken with a skill and precision that would make the royal German chef who'd taught her proud. The memory of her encouraging smiles sliced through Jess as effectively as the knife.

Throwing the chicken pieces into a pan with a few onions, Jess pulled her mind back to her current predicament. There was nothing to be gained by thinking about Ismelde and her cooking lessons, nor the others who had provided Jess's unusual education.

She knew about people, what they did when they were emotional, afraid of betrayal, relying on instinct. The more heightened the emotion around her, the clearer her sense of purpose.

Mr. Thornbury hadn't been emotional, though. She'd expected him to be, given how fervent he was when he pursued a new discovery as far as he could, even if he got in the way of the servants.

That passion hadn't made an appearance upstairs. Instead, he'd been the picture of calculated, knowledgeable logic.

What could she do with that? Nothing, other than wait for him to think it through and try to guess what his questions were going to be so she could formulate answers that would satisfy him without giving anything away.

Patience was another of her less-developed skills.

Her hip banged into the table as she slid the sliced and diced vegetables into a pot of water. The crinkle of paper in her pocket combined with the dull thud of food against metal reminded her that her pride was the least of what was at stake in this situation.

Her mind burned to learn how her brother could possibly be alive, but coded correspondence wasn't the place for such details. Of much more importance was the fact that her brother was attempting to claim governance of Verbonne, restoring its independence and sovereignty.

It wasn't going well.

The letter was by necessity short and vague, but it implied that a great struggle had arisen over the future of Verbonne and much of it hung on an old legend.

The sources didn't know enough about Verbonne's history to know what that meant, but Jess did. It meant she couldn't run out of hiding and see for herself that a member of her family had managed to survive, no matter how much she wanted to. First, she had to follow her father's directive and solve the legend if her brother was to have any hope of succeeding. Depending on how intense the struggle currently was, it might even determine his continued survival.

Jess hung the pot over the fire and began to stir. The raw vegetables swirled in the cold water, crashing into one another and the sides of the pot in a jumbled mess. There was no need to stir it, as the first bubbles hadn't even begun to form on the surface, but stirring made her look normal to anyone walking by. She could think without drawing notice.

And she desperately needed to think.

She needed to come up with a story, one that would satisfy Mr. Thornbury, one that would sound noble and selfless and compel him to help her.

One that was absolutely not the truth, because even if sharing the truth wouldn't put him in possible danger, it was far too incredible to believe. She barely believed it herself and she'd lived through it. Her spencer sleeve, a small-patterned muslin that was neither eye-catching nor remarkably drab, shifted as she stirred the pot, revealing a small scar across the top of her wrist.

She wasn't supposed to have scars. Mama would have been appalled that she'd been in a position to injure herself enough to cause one.

A practiced shrug had the sleeve sliding back into place, covering the jagged line. Mama wouldn't recognize her now. Of course, Jess probably wouldn't recognize her mother either. Or her father or brother or any of the other people who'd run to that little farm in search of refuge.

War had a way of changing people.

Her free hand itched to pull out the letter, to read it again, to dive into the hope that it was somehow true. If she didn't trust the writer so much, she'd have thought it a trap, a trick to pull her out of hiding and into the arms of the people who wanted her dead. People she'd hoped would give up without Napoleon's support.

She'd lived enough, traveled enough, thrown herself into enough ridiculous and dangerous situations to know that peace was fleeting. It didn't last long because contentment didn't sit well with a lot of people. Still waters only meant the path was clear to move forward, to claim what had been too difficult to grasp while conflict raged.

The wooden paddle thudded onto the table as she gave up the pretense of stirring.

In some ways, the restlessness of peace felt more dangerous, left a person more exposed. That was why she'd fled to this hiding place to begin with. Even though peace had been temporary that time, it had made her realize the treacherousness of her previous hiding place.

The past had caught up with her once again.

She jerked a knife from the knife block and began to methodically demolish a loaf of bread. There would be no more hiding. Not only was there nowhere else to go, but the people she left behind would be in danger.

Ten years ago, when she'd thrown herself into the world of shadows and intrigue, it had been a desperate lark. She'd been too lost and too young to know or care about the potential consequences.

When those consequences had made themselves known, she'd gotten out.

She couldn't get out of this. Life wasn't a game. Whatever she did next mattered. Somehow, despite her best intentions, she'd managed to fill her life with people she cared about. She'd lost one family and God had blessed her with another.

No one, not even a hesitant, nosy, too-smart-for-his-own-good scholar was going to keep her from protecting them.

CHAPTER FOUR

*T*he diary was heavy in Derek's pocket as he walked to his little room in the back corner of the house. He'd been in the middle of determining if the painting in the parlor could possibly be a Poussin, but that task had dropped far beneath his attention now. The painting could wait. It wasn't going anywhere.

Of course, the book wasn't going anywhere either, now that he had it in his possession, but setting it aside was impossible. Discovering what motivated Jess's request had immediately become his latest obsession.

Derek knew about obsession. It was a state he lived in often enough. Once his mind decided it needed an answer, concentrating on anything else had to wait until the answer was found.

Fortunately for him, those obsessions frequently aligned with his career.

The room he'd been put in was basic and serviceable, a marked difference from the overwhelming extravagance in the more public rooms of the house. The builder had definitely been creating a showplace.

In the middle of nowhere.

Rather curious, that.

No, only one obsessive question at a time. It was a rule he'd had to create for himself long ago. If he considered too much at once, he'd go mad.

He passed the narrow but comfortable bed and sat himself at the plain writing desk situated along the wall next to the dressing table. Aside from the basic furniture, the room was sparsely decorated. A large blue-veined statue stood in the corner and a pair of nondescript, mediocre paintings—likely from some local artist—hung over the bed.

The smiling dog portrait that he'd brought into the room for a touch of whimsy hung over the desk. The remaining blank expanse of wall was painted a drab color somewhere between white, cream, and grey.

In any other home, the room might have been depressing. Here, it was a blessed retreat where his senses weren't bombarded with color and expression and he could hear himself think.

After placing the book carefully on the desk, he set out a neat stack of writing paper and prepared a quill and ink. Three deep breaths cleared his mind of any notions, guesses, or expectations. Only when he was ready to find anything did he open the cover. Preconceptions had ruined many a historian's perspective.

He went to the beginning and started to read, skipping over words he couldn't easily make out or didn't understand. While the contents were fascinating to him, he couldn't see anything Jess would care about.

In the third entry, the writer confirmed that the paintings were done by students of Fournier. As the only known apprentices of the master painter were The Six, Derek hunched a little deeper over the book. Soon he forgot any notion of Jess's hidden item and lost himself in the intimate look at a group of mysterious people.

Then he came across the same phrase that had given him pause at the beginning of the diary. *Secret passage*. Unlike the last mention, this one was buried among the descriptions of brushstrokes and paint colors. A few lines later, a hidden pathway was mentioned in the middle of a description of a woman watching the sea crash against the rocks.

He'd read many descriptions of Verbonnian paintings over the years, particularly those of Fournier and The Six. It was a near certainty that this passage was describing the painting *The Grace of Oceans Breaking*. While many of the paintings of The Six had been signed by a discreet *F* and a 6, this one had been left blank, leaving open the speculation that there was a seventh member of the group, or it had possibly even been painted by Fournier himself.

All accounts written by those who'd seen the painting in person said it was impossible to look upon it without feeling an incredibly deep sense of loss. The diary, though, made it sound like a depiction of hope. Derek snatched up the quill and began to scribble a translation as fast as he could.

> She watches the hidden pathway, guarding it from those who would do it harm but prepared to guide those who are worthy. It is a preparation that will not see completion in her lifetime, nor in mine. Someday, a worthy one will come, but she will not see it. Her grave lies between her and the future, but she will not despair. She will hope and she will guard until the one with passion and heart comes along to follow where she guides. May the Lord keep her in good hands until the new day arises. May the Lord protect our land until her savior journeys home.

Shaking a cramp from his hand, Derek attempted to ground himself among a swirl of emotions. The anticipation with which he'd opened the diary had turned quickly to fascination and now gave way to great excitement.

This was a clue. It was different from the other descriptions—more emotional, active.

He slid the paper covered in messy scribbles to the side and picked up the quill once more to begin a meticulous and exact translation of the passage. Some phrases he could translate but didn't know the meaning of, so he left a blank section on the paper before moving on.

Every now and then his hair would slip into the edge of his vision, and he shoved it back with an impatient hand. He should have taken the time to go into town and get it trimmed. It was only two miles to Marlborough. The task would have required less than a day, yet he'd not seen the point of doing it.

After writing three pages of notes, he was ready to simply pull out the hair to get it out of the way. Perhaps he should see if his friend's new wife—the recently titled Lady Chemsford—had a few hairpins to spare.

No, much better to take the time to actually go get his hair trimmed. Eccentric was one thing. Cracked was another. Life went better if he maintained at least some sense of social normalcy.

When his hand was too cramped to continue, he sat back and looked over his notes. Fascinating to be sure, but what was he going to do with it? He'd found a clue of some kind, but what did it mean? If he gave this to Jess, would it make any sense?

What would she do if it did?

Derek knew history, knew the way people in power viewed artifacts and treasures, knew how far some were willing to go to possess them. One had to look no further than the museums of London, filled with relics that had never been intended to be on display.

It was why Derek had set himself up as an expert on art and ancient writings, which were pieces that had been designed to be shared and viewed and enjoyed.

Some of the people who poked around old tombs and dead cities were truly interested in learning about the past and documenting a forgotten people. Others simply wanted the treasure.

Which was Jess? What did he really know about her? He doubted even Lady Chemsford, who declared herself and Jess to be close friends, knew much about the little blond cook. Was the book even a family heirloom?

He flipped back to the cover and ran his finger over the royal crest. The woman who had written this diary wasn't plagued by the difficulties of the lower classes, not if her life was consumed by the world of art and paintings.

Had Jess's family declined so far over the generations? Would the type of family that bred a woman as headstrong and intimidating as Jess allow such a decline to occur?

Perhaps the bigger question was, could he live with leaving this mystery unsolved? He'd seen the flash of understanding cross Jess's face earlier. She possessed some additional information that would make the clues he translated make sense. Perhaps a memory or experience passed down through the family, along with the book?

He studied art and history together in order to put the personal with the practical, to give richer meaning to the moment displayed by filling in the surrounding motivations and reactions. Art revealed the people behind the decisions as well as those who dealt with the effects.

This was the ultimate chance to do that.

Was he willing to live with the possible consequences? Was this what had motivated other history-loving adventurers to partner up with the treasure seekers? Could the need for answers overcome the desire for discretion?

His hand still twinged from pinching the quill for so long, but he returned to the translation, lighting a nearby lamp in deference to the waning evening light. Just a few more pages. Perhaps there would be something in here that would tell him what a woman who lived centuries ago would have him do.

Several pages later, he eased the book shut and stared at the faded embossment on the cover.

What had he gotten himself into?

❧❧

The bread was burnt. It was chewable, though, and Jess could even manage to swallow it if she softened it first by filling her mouth with tea.

That was more than could be said for Martha's last attempt at making bread.

Jess hid a grin behind her teacup as Daphne, her friend and the mistress of Haven Manor, made her own attempts at swallowing.

Until recently, Daphne had been the housekeeper of the estate, and before that she'd been the caretaker of hidden illegitimate children.

It was a strange combination of roles that, when combined with Daphne's innate niceness, made her the perfect person to guide women who were attempting to make the best of a rotten turn in life.

It also made her extremely loath to hurt anyone's feelings.

Once Daphne's throat stopped spasming with its attempts to move the charred bread, she smiled. "You're getting much better at this, Martha."

The frown on the brunette's round face indicated she didn't quite believe the praise.

One finger—once soft, elegant, and refined but now work-roughened and callused—flicked at the black bits on the bottom of the roll, creating a tidy pile of burnt bread shavings on the table. "You're only being nice."

"No, she's right." Jess picked up the uneaten portion of her roll and banged it against the table. "See? It dents."

The young girl grinned but still tossed her uneaten bread back onto her plate. She rubbed a hand over her middle, which was just starting to round, revealing the condition that had sent her fleeing into Daphne's care in the first place. In this out-of-the-way refuge, the new marchioness was helping women in the same position she herself had once been, women whose decisions had made the life they'd been raised for impossible.

In a few months, Martha would have a choice. She could allow Daphne to place her child with a new family, to be raised on a farm, happy and healthy and normal. At that point, Martha would return to her old life with a bit more wisdom, a handful of new survival skills, and a load of guilt and questions.

Or she could keep the child, move to Birmingham, and work in the Marquis of Chemsford's new factory, crafting buttons and other trifles to sell to the people she'd once rubbed shoulders with in London ballrooms.

Life was going to be difficult either way, but Jess still envied the girl the clear-cut choice.

Sometimes the fork in the road turned out to be a dead end, and a woman had no choice but to shove her way through the undergrowth and forge her own future. It sounded adventurous and glamorous, but the truth was, it was all too easy to stumble without a path to follow. Tree roots. Animal nests. Cliffs disguised by an abundance of plant growth along the edge. Making a new way was treacherous.

Going backward was not an option life provided, though.

"At least the potatoes look right," the young woman said hopefully, taking her fork and stabbing it into the soft white chunk on her plate.

Jess had to allow the girl was right. The potatoes looked perfectly cooked. She slid a bite into her mouth.

And nearly choked. Her fork clattered to the table as she reached for her cup and drank the contents in three large swallows.

"Don't eat that," she said, gasping for breath and pointing at the offending vegetable. Honestly, how had the thing not shriveled up into dry, dusty crumbs?

Curiosity—and probably a desire to assure the poor girl her potatoes weren't that bad—had Daphne taking a small nibble of the bite she had already loaded onto her fork. She coughed. "I daresay—" more coughing—"how much—" cough, cough—"salt did you use?"

"I used the scoop from the flour." Small white teeth bit into Martha's bottom lip. "Was that bad?"

Jess rose and snagged her cup from the table, intent on refilling it from the bucket of freshly pumped water in the main kitchen. Her tongue, thick and dry and still burning, stuck to the roof of her mouth. Maybe she'd just dunk her head in the bucket. "Yes, that was bad."

"Jess," Daphne admonished.

"Daphne," Jess replied in exasperation. "She's not an idiot. All she needs do is have a lick and she'll know it's salty enough to attract the local wildlife. I believe some of the stew from the servants' dinner is still in the kitchen. I'll bring us some."

While Daphne was willing to sacrifice their mouths to Martha's disastrous attempts at learning to cook, Jess refused to make the rest of the household participate. She cooked the others' food and served them first, leaving the servants' dining room clear for Martha's failures to go unnoticed.

Jess still wasn't sure how Daphne had convinced her to provide the women with cooking lessons. Fortunately Jess had been wise enough to insist that Martha's attempts be limited to times when Lord Chemsford—the marquis, and Daphne's new husband—was away from the house.

With any luck, he'd return from London soon, unable to stay away from the wife he loved more than anything, and they could set these culinary trials aside.

Daphne followed Jess into the kitchen. "Could you possibly be a bit more . . . encouraging?"

"I'll soak the bread in my stew," Jess said as she ladled the remainder from the pot into three bowls. "Show her that what she's made is edible."

Daphne picked up three spoons and fiddled with them. "You're supposed to be teaching her. Didn't you notice her get too much salt?"

No, she hadn't, because while Jess had somehow been coerced into giving cooking lessons, the reality of doing so had been too much for her. Being in the kitchen at all brought up memories that were painful enough. Being the one doing the teaching had sent her mind so far into the past that Jess wasn't sure how she'd managed to return to the present.

She wasn't going to attempt to explain that to Daphne, though. Daphne didn't know where Jess had learned to cook, didn't know that Ismelde's devotion to Jess's family had brought about her demise.

"People learn more from mistakes than instruction," Jess murmured.

"We don't want her to simply learn," Daphne said. "We want her to feel loved."

"*You* want her to feel loved," Jess grumbled. "*I* want her not to burn down my kitchen."

The conversation was brought to a blessed halt by the arrival of Sarah, one of the maids Jess actually liked because she'd once been one of the illegitimate children hiding out in the house alongside Jess and Daphne and their friend Kit.

"I'm not sure he's going to eat it," Sarah said, referring to the tray of food she'd recently delivered to the long-term guest working upstairs.

As tempted as Jess had been to include a helping of Martha's bread, she'd managed to resist.

"Why not?" Daphne asked with a frown.

Sarah shrugged. "He didn't even look up from the book he was reading to acknowledge I was there."

Jess could only hope the book had been her diary.

The stew was a bit cold, but it was flavorful and filling, and soon it had been eaten and the dishes taken to the scullery for cleaning.

Jess was setting her kitchen to rights and preparing for the next morning when Mr. Thornbury entered. He was pale, with slashes of red across his cheekbones, and the bright eyes behind his spectacles were round and wide.

The diary was clutched tightly in his hands.

"Finished already?" Jess asked.

"Where did you get this?"

Jess frowned. They'd been over that. "From my father."

Mr. Thornbury pressed his lips into a thin line. His shoulders hunched a bit and his eyes narrowed. "Where did he get it?"

"From his father." Technically her father had gotten it from his brother, who'd gotten it from their father, but honestly the distinction was irrelevant, at least to Mr. Thornbury. Still, she had to bite her tongue to resist the urge to explain the path the diary had taken through the generations.

"Do you know what is in here?"

"If I did I wouldn't need you." Jess planted her hands on her hips. "You know, for a brilliant man you don't seem very smart."

"What's going on?" Daphne asked as she entered the room from the scullery, the pinkness of her hands indicating she'd washed the dishes herself, instead of getting one of the half-dozen maids she now employed to do it.

They'd have to have another discussion about that soon, but Jess had bigger concerns at the moment.

"Nothing," Jess bit out just as Mr. Thornbury said, "Your cook wants to ensnare me in some wild-goose chase for an artifact that was likely stolen with a book that I have reason to believe was also stolen."

Jess narrowed her eyes as she glared at the man. "Do you even know the meaning of the word *discretion?*"

She abandoned her work and rounded the table to snatch the diary from his hands. At least she tried to. The tight grip he had on the book meant all she ended up doing was yanking herself closer to him.

Close enough to whisper menacingly into his face. Or at least toward his face. He had too many inches on her petite frame for her to get very close.

"Why don't we take a walk, Mr. Thornbury? We can discuss the idea that some things in life are private."

He blinked at her. "It's beginning to grow colder, and I'm fairly certain it's raining. While you and I won't come to much harm, it wouldn't be good for the book."

Daphne cleared her throat as Martha emerged from the scullery as well. "I'm going to take Martha to the upstairs parlor. Perhaps she has some ideas on what I'm doing wrong with the cushion cover I'm embroidering."

"Oh, finally," Martha said, nearly running toward the door. "Something I'm actually accomplished at."

Though it pained her to give the appearance of weakness, Jess let go of the book. She wasn't giving up, simply employing a strategic, temporary retreat.

Did he think his ability to physically look down upon her gave him the advantage? She stepped back around the table and set to sharpening her kitchen knives.

"We've perhaps ten minutes before the servants begin returning to see to their evening duties, Mr. Thornbury. I suggest you make your point quickly."

"I haven't fully translated more than a handful of pages, but I flipped through much of the book to get a sense of its contents."

Jess bit her tongue to keep from rushing him as he settled onto a stool at her worktable and opened the book. As she'd learned earlier, had in fact known from watching him survey the house's contents, this man did nothing quickly. Best to let him meander his way to the point on his own.

"Most of it is about art. I'm even more convinced that the author was intimately acquainted with The Six and Aldric Fournier. Her descriptions of colors and brushstrokes are remarkably detailed and fit the style perfectly." He flipped through a few pages. "Why, here she describes the mixing of paint, how he would—"

"No," Jess broke in, abandoning the idea that she should let him wander his way to the point. "No paint mixing. Ten minutes, remember?"

He cleared his throat and gently turned a few more pages in the book. "Hmmm. Well, here, the book changes. The flowing sentences, almost an art within themselves, are dropped in favor of partial sentences and abrupt descriptions. If the writing weren't in the same hand, I'd think it a different person entirely."

One long finger crossed the page, the clean, trimmed fingernail hovering over the surface. "This woman saw horror. And tragedy." There was a catch to his voice.

Jess slid the knife she'd been sharpening back into the block of wood. Was he going to cry?

Mr. Thornbury took in a shaky breath. "I can't read it all. Some of it is smudged—with tears, I presume. Other parts are written in such a hasty scrawl it would take a great deal of time to study the context and make out the words, but it is very obvious that the

hope she'd had when beginning this journal has been removed."
The finger stopped. "It says that nature managed to destroy what
men had not been able to."

He looked up, those hazel eyes dry despite the emotion he was
so evidently feeling. "This was written by a broken woman."

A suspicious and unfamiliar tightening grabbed Jess by the
throat. Was *she* going to cry? She never cried. Tears were useless
and only delayed a person in coming up with a plan to solve the
issue. She swallowed to remove the sudden discomfort. "What
does she write after that?"

"More art."

Jess was startled into blankness of thought and action for a
moment, but then a small smile curved her lips. Feel the pain and
then get on with it, did she? A sense of kinship Jess had never quite
managed to achieve with her other family members bloomed in
her chest.

Mr. Thornbury wasn't finished, though. "Some of the art descriptions are different—more poetic, if you will." He cleared his
throat. "The more I look at this, the more I believe you're right.
There's something hidden, and you need this book to find it."

Excitement, the kind that had once preceded an assignment or
tricky escape, made Jess's fingers itch. "How long will it take you
to translate the book?"

"I'm afraid it's not that simple."

"What do you mean?"

Derek closed the book and ran a hand over the emblem on the
front. "This book is really more of a directory of clues. It may be
only half of the information."

Jess's brows puckered as the desire to hit something or run
somewhere or maybe just scream at the top her lungs pushed her
the step and a half forward until she was pressed to the worktable
across from Mr. Thornbury. Despite the churn of energy running
through her, perhaps even because of it, Jess forced her tone to
remain slow, even, and perhaps even cordial. "Where is the other
half, then?"

He swallowed hard, his throat jumping and that ridiculous swath of hair that hung over his forehead trembling. "I think it's in the paintings."

"*In* the paintings?" Jess's knees threatened to give way, and she locked them in place to stay upright.

She hated paintings. Well, didn't hate them so much as saw very little point in one over another. If asked before this moment, she'd have said she was ambivalent.

After this moment, she was changing her feelings toward paintings to extreme dislike. If she couldn't think of a plan that didn't involve continued communication with Mr. Thornbury, she would upgrade that to hate.

"In a way. I think one helps to decode the other."

Jess frowned, a suspicious sense of unease crawling through her middle. "How?"

The slash of red on his cheeks had begun to fade, but now it came rushing back. "I . . . I'm not sure. I'd have to see one of the paintings first."

That was what she'd been afraid of.

CHAPTER FIVE

The old woman across from him wasn't knitting.

It had taken him half the trip to London to realize it, but the tiny woman wasn't actually knitting. It was a very good facsimile. The rhythmic click of the needles and the steady looping of yarn would have fooled almost anyone into thinking the bag tucked neatly in the woman's lap was being steadily filled with some sort of shawl or scarf similar to the one wrapped over her head and shoulders.

Only two things marred her ruse.

One, she'd snagged the yarn a bit about half a mile back, nearly sending one of her knitting needles to the floor. The flawed section of yarn had just passed through her fingers for the third time.

Two, Derek knew how to knit. Once he'd given the woman his attention instead of trying to understand the strange scene he'd left behind in Wiltshire, it was soon obvious that she was only going through the motions. Literally.

Derek turned the page on his book, using the excuse of the tightly packed mail coach to pull his arms closer in to his sides and lift the book just a bit higher so he could peer over the top of it at the old woman.

When she'd boarded the coach at the last moment, she'd been nothing more than another faceless passenger headed for London.

Derek's mind certainly hadn't been on picking apart his travel companions.

He'd been too busy trying to understand why, when Jess had been in such an all-fired rush earlier in the day, yesterday evening she'd calmly suggested he travel to London to seek out one of the paintings and find the connection.

Alone.

With a scowl and a shrug, she'd said, *"I do believe one of us might not arrive if we attempted to travel together, Mr. Thornbury. Go to London. Write me what you find."*

Go to London? Write her? When he'd informed her that he couldn't simply up and leave, she'd raised one of those perfect, delicate eyebrows at Lady Chemsford, who had immediately agreed that his cataloguing of the house could wait.

He'd nearly refused on principle, but the combined scrutiny of the women in the house convinced him that leaving was in his best interest. He would go to William, Lord Chemsford, who was currently in London. Perhaps the man would have some insight into why Jess was acting the way she was. He could at least explain his wife's part in the circumstances.

Even if Derek did manage to find one of the paintings and match it up to the diary, what would he do with it? There were numerous paintings described in the diary. Would one painting tell him anything?

No, the more he thought about it, the entire exchange made no sense. He'd been over and over the entire conversation, and all he'd gotten was a sore head.

Perhaps the non-knitting woman was a puzzle he could actually unravel. Learning the secrets of one woman might give him the confidence and insight to solve those of another.

At first glance, she was an older woman. At second glance as well. He narrowed his gaze. The assumption even held on closer inspection.

Her shoulders were rounded and lumpy. Her short, stocky body was covered in several thick layers, despite the warmth of the full carriage. The knitting needles moved continuously, a slight tremor making them click more.

In rare moments of silence when the road was especially smooth and their coach companions especially quiet, the slight rattle of her breath joined the clack of needles.

Hidden treasure, coded diaries, and Jess herself had obviously addled his mind. Why else would he be trying to turn this little old woman into something else? Admittedly, the false knitting was strange, but it was keeping her occupied, so why did he care?

He turned back to his book, but still something about the old woman nagged at him. His gaze wandered her direction just in time to see the snagged yarn slip through her fingers again.

Something was definitely wrong.

This woman obviously wasn't a painting—the movement and rattled breathing clearly indicated that she was among the living—but perhaps he could examine her as if she were.

Starting at the top, he inspected details. Strands of silver hair poked around the edge of the knitted head scarf, which, combined with the down-turned position, blocked the entirety of the woman's face from view.

Assuming it was a woman. If he was going to start thinking that all was not as it appeared, he had to welcome all possibilities. What if it were a man dressed as a woman for some obscure, ridiculous reason?

Before he could stop it, his hand slid along the front of his coat, ensuring that the diary was still tucked neatly inside his pocket.

The suspicion that it might be otherwise left him feeling ridiculous. He wriggled uncomfortably and let his gaze drop to the busily knitting hands. Or rather, the busily not-knitting hands.

Like the head and shoulders, the hands were covered in yarn in the form of knitted gloves that left only the dirty tips of her fingers exposed.

A shudder rolled through him as he looked at the filthiness of the fingertips. Most of the travelers had grabbed a meat pie at the last inn, where they'd stopped to change horses. Had she eaten with such grubby hands?

The satchel in her lap told him nothing. Neither did the drab skirt that could have been either black or dark blue. She wasn't any wider than her bag, though, so it was unlikely to be a man.

Probably she was exactly who she appeared to be. A bit light in the attic, perhaps, but harmless in the way most little old ladies traveling home from taking the medicinal waters in Bath would be.

With a shake of his head, Derek lowered his book and tried once more to read. He spared one last glance at the old woman to complete his perusal.

Only the toes of her worn brown boots peeped out from beneath the dark hem, but it was just enough to see that one of them bore a long, thin, familiar scratch across the top.

✄

Loop, loop, loop. Click, click, click.

Jess acknowledged and then ignored the line of sweat down her back that had turned from a trickle into a steady stream of discomfort. With its thick wig and abundance of wool coverings, her old lady disguise was overly warm at the best of times.

A hot, confined carriage during the heat of a waning summer was far from the best of times.

The monotonous motions of her fake knitting efforts weren't enough to fully occupy her mind, but they were all she had. Her fellow riders didn't require a lot of attention. Even if those threatening her brother had managed to track Jess to Marlborough, they couldn't have known she was going to be on this mail coach or have had time to plant an informant among the people who had climbed aboard ahead of her.

She herself hadn't decided to travel this way until last night, or, really, very early this morning.

Even if they'd been watching and suspected she was the hobbling old woman, the mail coach would arrive in London long before they could follow it. She would be so lost in the bustle of the large city that they would never find her in time.

Jess stifled a yawn and peeked across the carriage at Mr. Thornbury. He was reading a book, pulling his arms in close and holding it high in the confines of the carriage.

He'd looked suspicious at her urging that he travel to London alone in search of the paintings. She couldn't blame him. In the end, she'd insisted and he'd given in, packing his bags to catch the mail the next day.

There had never been any question of Jess going to London as well, even though she had no intention of remaining in that irritating man's company while she did so. She would keep an eye on him while he did his searching, which would likely take him a while. In the meantime, she would do some of her own investigating, learning more about the situation and the direness of interpreting the diary.

The noise outside the coach grew as they approached the outer edges of London. Jess resisted the urge to straighten her back and stretch. Every inch of her ached from holding this hunched position, but it was hardly the first time she'd suffered for a disguise. Aches would fade. Anonymity wouldn't.

If only there'd been more than one mail coach headed to London from Marlborough today, she'd have been able to use one of her more comfortable disguises. The old lady was the best at disguising her face, though.

Finally, with a loud holler and the clatter of wheels, the mail coach pulled into its first London innyard. Jess waited, meticulously tucking her knitting into her satchel with shaky hands while the rest of the occupants disembarked. As she climbed down last, the trembling she'd had to work at earlier in the day was a good deal more authentic than she would like, given the ache in her muscles and the burning desire to stretch them properly.

She collected her second satchel from the baggage pile and hobbled toward the inn head down, dragging her foot slightly the way the old shopkeeper in Marlborough did.

That old lady scared Jess a bit, with her exuberant insistence on nosing her way into Jess's life, never the slightest bit intimidated by scowls or silence. That frail determination made a fabulous inspiration, though.

Just a few more steps. Once she found a secluded spot, she'd switch disguises and be able to walk freely into the city.

"May I help you with your bag, madam?"

Jess nearly groaned. Of course the scholarly Mr. Thornbury wouldn't be so caught up in his own business that he would neglect an old lady struggling a bit with her bag.

Making a point to cough loudly before talking and keeping a great deal of air in her words, she said, "Quite all right, young man. I'm not in any hurry. Either I'll get there eventually or the Good Lord will take me on the way."

Mr. Thornbury snickered. "Delightful. Did Mrs. Lancaster help you with that line? I could see her saying such a thing."

As a matter of fact, that had been a saying Jess had picked up from the shopkeeper. The way she spouted Bible verses as if God was concerned about the condition of her bread was a bit strange but gave evidence to the source of her inner strength.

But how could Mr. Thornbury possibly have recognized the old woman in Jess? He couldn't *know*. Was he assuming she was a resident of Marlborough? Everyone who lived there knew Mrs. Lancaster.

"Afraid I don't know a Lancaster, son," Jess said with a bit of extra rasp. "Run along. Don't let me keep you."

He sighed and moved his own satchel to his left hand before reaching down to grasp her larger bag in his right.

It was either give up the ruse and wrestle him for it or let him take it. Little old women who shuffled across courtyards didn't have very strong grips. If she'd had her knitting needles out, she'd have poked him with one.

She let him take the bag. It wasn't as if he weren't a trustworthy fellow. He was almost annoyingly—and dangerously—honest. "As you wish, then."

He laughed again. She wasn't sure she'd heard him do that much at Haven Manor. Grudgingly, she admitted it was a nice sound. Too many people sounded grating when they laughed. His was mellow, even, warm.

His head lowered until she had to hunch over farther to keep him from seeing her face. "Do you intend to maintain this pace for your entire visit to London? That should make it easy for whoever you're hiding from."

Jess gritted her teeth. No one ever saw through her disguises. This man couldn't possibly be the first. "Can't walk any faster than I'm able. But don't let me keep you. Just set my bag at the door and be on about your business."

Another sigh. "Jess, must we continue this? What are you doing in that mess of wool?"

Apparently sweating herself to death for no reason. Giving up the rasp, she whispered, "Get a private dining room and order a meal. I'll be there presently."

He waited for a moment, keeping pace with her shuffling gait. "Is there actually anything in this bag?"

"Wouldn't bother carrying it if there weren't," Jess grumbled.

He didn't respond, simply strode on toward the inn, presumably to follow Jess's instructions. Nerves and indignation joined the aching in her muscles, making the shaking more pronounced as she plodded on.

Had Daphne told him what to look for? No, she didn't know Jess's ability to disappear in plain sight—hadn't even known Jess intended to go to London.

Jess felt a bit bad about that, actually. The poor woman might not know she didn't have a cook in residence until someone informed her no one was fixing dinner.

There was a note for her to find when she went looking for Jess, telling her not to worry.

Not that it would do any good. Daphne always worried.

Once in the inn, Jess stopped by the retiring room for a moment of privacy, as much to stretch her back properly as anything else. She couldn't shed the disguise, though, not until she'd dealt with Mr. Thornbury.

Was he more than he appeared? She knew some spies who cultivated a single disguise for years, buried so deep it altered who they were. Was he one of those? Had danger been under her nose?

The man wore a self-satisfied smirk as she shuffled into the room he'd secured. That smirk gave her a sense of peace, even as it irritated her. A professional informant wouldn't be crowing over his success at identifying her. He'd be stoic, ready to interrogate her.

The smirk wasn't taunting. It was the look of a child excited that he managed to get the best of his parents.

No, the man wasn't a spy.

Perhaps that meant she'd lost a bit of skill in her years of hiding.

He said nothing as she hobbled into the room, maintaining the ruse in front of the maids delivering the food. As he rose to hold out a chair for her, she prepared to kick or poke him if he said anything in front of the servants.

All he did was thank them for seeing to the comfort of his grandmother as she settled in the chair.

Her foot twitched in a desire to kick him anyway, but he circled the table quickly to return to his own seat. Well, she'd always freely admitted that the man was smart.

Once the door closed behind the servants, she lifted her head to spear him with what she hoped was a withering glare that showed not an inkling of the unbidden respect she felt that he was able to see through her disguise. "How did you know?"

He paused. "Aside from the fact that you weren't really knitting?" He reached for the food with a slight shrug. "Your boots."

Her boots? Jess pushed the chair back and lifted both her feet out in front of her. She saw the telltale sign immediately—a slash across the toe of her left boot. Who knew where it had come from?

That thin white line was a sign that she had gotten much too comfortable in her country seclusion. She knew never to wear anything with identifiable markings, but it hadn't even crossed her mind to check her normal clothing items before using them.

With a grumbling sigh she lowered her feet back to the floor. "Now I'm going to have to buy new boots."

Mr. Thornbury laughed and pushed a bowl of stew and chunk of bread in her direction. "That's all you're going to say? That you need new boots?"

Jess reached for a spoon. What else did he want her to say? "Someone is trying to find me and the diary. If my boots give my identity away, they need to be replaced."

He shook his head. "If someone is trying to find you, as you say, they wouldn't know about a mark on your boots. We're working together, so of course you weren't hiding from me. I'm sure you had every intention of revealing yourself once we were safely in town."

She glanced up to see if he truly believed his words. He didn't. His eyebrows were lifted in exaggerated innocence even as he glared in accusation.

The last thing she could tell him, though, was the truth. If he knew there were parts of this situation she had no intention of sharing with him, he'd refuse to help her.

Already he was far too curious for her own good. If he learned how much of a past she really had, he'd be even more so. "I wasn't sure if you would be able to manage not saying something while in the coach."

Close enough to the truth to be believable. He didn't need to know how deep her lack of trust went.

"You think the other person who wants this diary was on that coach?" he asked with a frown.

Did the man not have any pride? She'd all but accused him of having loose lips and no discretion, and he wanted to focus on her potential danger?

"I don't know who the other person is," she said with a shrug. The memory of the man with a scar caused a spurt of childlike fear. It was almost enough to make her abandon the search for the hidden object, whatever it may be. Her memory of family, though, particularly the memory of her father's conviction that the past could preserve the future, spurred her on.

Even if she, more than anyone, knew the past could never truly be recovered.

They fell into the quiet rhythms of hungry travelers until he broke the silence by saying, "Now that we are both here, does that change the plan moving forward?"

"*We* are not here," Jess said, picking up her bread. "*You* are here. Go on to Chemsford's. Continue on as you intended."

"And what will you be doing?"

Hiding and spying on him probably wasn't the best thing to admit. "I have a few contacts who might know something."

She gave a nonchalant shrug, even though she was anything but blasé about the situation. Mr. Thornbury knowing she was in town made her task a bit more difficult, but nothing overly worrisome. Returning to the people she disappeared from when she went into hiding three years ago, though, was going to be less than pleasant.

It didn't escape her notice that they'd tracked her down when they had a warning to deliver, but not before. Perhaps they were too angry at her to help much more.

She took a bite of crusty bread, ripping her teeth into it more forcefully than necessary before relaxing enough to chew with a bit of delicacy. The bread might as well be savored. It was going to taste a good sight better than the humble pie she would soon be eating.

CHAPTER SIX

Derek gaped at the woman in front of him. She'd always seemed distant, even from the women she called friends, but was she truly so removed that she thought he would simply walk out of this inn and leave her alone in London?

Obviously the answer to that was yes. She'd had no intention of him seeing her. Now that he had, he refused to forget it.

She chewed slowly, her face a picture of contemplation and dismissal that proved her focus was on something outside this small private dining room. The delicate, fine-featured face looked out of place surrounded by an abundance of wiry grey curls and a ragged knit shawl.

The woman was making mush of his normally ordered brain.

Even though he already knew the answer, he asked, "When were you going to tell me you were in London?"

If he expected the question to make her squirm or express guilt, he was doomed to disappointment. She merely frowned and shrugged.

Probably as much of an admission as he was going to get out of her.

"Were you planning to sneak back to Marlborough and wait for me to send word?"

"That was an option," she said coolly. "It would depend on what I found."

What *she* found. This one-sided sharing of information was growing tiresome. Could he even trust her claim that this hunt was a matter of vital importance? He was quickly returning to the idea of removing himself from this entire situation.

"If I am to go to Chemsford's, where are you going?"

She fell still, staring at her bread with an intensity that revealed great internal debate.

If she were a painting—and she was currently still enough to study her as if she were framed and on a wall—he would think her a woman on the edge of a life-changing moment. He would research the history of her life and time to see what great precipices awaited her. He would examine the painter's life to see what agonized and plagued him, for artists frequently buried such turmoil in their work.

He would know where this moment had led her instead of wondering what decision required such effort. It would certainly be nice to know what options she was pondering.

"I suppose," she said, seeming to talk to the bread more than to him, "that I will go visit Chemsford as well. We'll see if your methods yield results before trying mine. Are you assured that you can ask of the paintings without raising suspicions?"

"It wouldn't be the first time I've expressed fascination with Verbonnian art, and more than once I've sought out particular pieces for clients. If Chemsford is comfortable with me using his name, I can ask whatever I like."

If Derek hadn't given up on the idea of being able to understand this woman, he might have been lured into thinking the look in her eyes was something akin to respect.

☒☒

Half an hour later, Derek was positive he'd misread Jess. She'd sent him here, to a street corner just out of sight of the inn, and told him to wait for her.

Like an imbecile, he'd done it. Despite the gentlemanly upbringing that insisted he not leave a lady unaccompanied in a public place, despite the fact that he was beyond certain that she wanted to disappear into the shadows of London's smog and leave him in ignorance, he'd done it.

At least he'd kept her large satchel as an assurance that she would actually show up like she said she would.

Perhaps he wasn't a complete imbecile.

She needed to make that appearance soon. He was starting to get strange looks. How long was she going to make him wait? Did she intend to limp and shuffle her way through the entirety of London? If so, why send him here? Why not simply catch a hack from the inn to take them to Chemsford's?

Five minutes later, a street urchin ran up to him, speaking in a thick accent. "You new in town, guv'nor? For a ha'pence I'll take you wherever you're going. Won't get lost or attacked, guarantee."

Derek tightened his grip on both satchels. He'd heard tales of a grubby child acting as a distraction while someone else performed a robbery. This child was tall enough to cart away one of the bags himself, though. His head nearly came to Derek's shoulder, an event that had likely happened recently given how high the ragged hem of his dirt-smeared trousers rode on the thin leg.

Suddenly, the child's head tipped back and pale amber eyes beneath golden eyebrows laughed up at him.

The satchels nearly hit the ground as Derek's jaw and grip both slackened.

Not limping about London, then. Closer inspection revealed a few similarities to the old woman she'd been at the inn. The knit fingerless gloves remained, though the shawl had been replaced by an overlarge cap capable of covering the entirety of her blond hair and delicate ears.

The homespun skirt was now wrapped around a lump he had to assume was her smaller satchel, making it look like a crudely knotted bag. Her legs were encased in threadbare trousers.

Knowing it was her in the drab items of clothing meant the last thing he should be noticing was the condition and placement of the hem.

Derek tried not to blush even as he averted his gaze, imagining Pieter Bruegel the Elder's *Hunters in the Snow* in an attempt to escape the heat rising up his neck. Jess didn't need anything else to mock him about.

Her ability to transform so completely was both impressive and terrifying. When she decided she no longer wanted him to know her whereabouts, she would disappear. He'd probably end up cluelessly opening the door for her and tipping his hat as she departed.

Despite his growing misgivings about his role in all this, there was nothing for him to do at the moment except play along.

"Yes," he said and cleared his throat before setting a satchel down between his feet and extracting a coin from his pocket. "Can you direct me to, er, Lord Chemsford's townhome?"

He placed the coin in her outstretched hand as she grinned at him.

Really grinned. Not a smirk or a sardonic smile, but a true, amused grin. It was stunning to behold, so stunning he couldn't find it in himself to care that her amusement was at his expense. The embarrassment was worth it to pull such a rare thing from hiding.

She rolled her eyes, still grinning, and pocketed the coin.

In her trousers.

That exposed her legs.

Another lovely rare sighting that had, until this moment, been hidden.

Derek fixed his gaze on her cap, where he intended to keep it as she led him through London. A journey that would hopefully be short. "Should I flag down a hack?"

Her grin faded into an amused smirk as she tossed her sack over her shoulder and started walking. "I know a shortcut."

Snatching up his satchel, he followed her, gaze glued to the huge brown cap.

Even when she turned down a dirty alley, he followed her, though with a bit of trepidation. He couldn't keep his gaze on her cap and watch where he stepped at the same time.

They passed a set of mews that were well past the need of

cleaning and then stepped out onto a street that felt a world away from where they'd been.

Here, neat terrace houses lined the road, well-dressed people walked along the pavement, and the traffic consisted of horse-drawn carriages instead of wagons and carts. It was everything that was polite society.

Not three minutes ago he'd been skirting a dung heap. That was London.

"It won't be long now, guv'nor." She grinned at him over her shoulder before continuing. Just as with the old woman, the disguise was more than a change of clothing. She'd changed the way she walked and the tone and rhythm of her voice. It was a complete transformation.

Two streets later, she stopped in front of a stately terrace house, three windows wide and four windows tall.

"Go up and knock," she whispered in her normal voice. "I'll go around to the back and come in through the kitchens."

Derek wanted to protest. At this point the disguises were a bit ridiculous, weren't they? Did she truly think someone was watching Lord Chemsford's house and would think the grubby lad was really Jess if she went in the front door?

Unless he wanted to bodily haul her up the three stairs and hold her while he waited for someone to answer the door, Derek really didn't have a choice. Her appearance as a poor lad might not draw a great deal of notice, but him seemingly abducting her would.

Besides, at some point one of them was going to have to trust the other. There was no chance she was going to be the first.

He turned to acknowledge her instructions, but she was already gone. With a shake of his head, he climbed the stairs and knocked.

The door was answered immediately.

Even though Derek knocked on the doors of aristocratic homes with regularity and William, Marquis of Chemsford, was someone he counted as a friend, this moment always made his mouth go a bit dry. He'd been raised the son of a gentleman, of decent society, but certainly not the type to rub shoulders with the *ton*.

Yet here he was. Knocking on the door of a marquis and expecting to be allowed entrance. It never ceased to strike a bit of fear and excitement in his belly.

He cleared his throat and extended his card. "Mr. Thornbury, here to see Lord Chemsford. I've a message from his wife."

The butler ushered him into the front parlor and disappeared up the stairs.

Derek hadn't even had time to stow the satchels in the corner before William appeared at the door, chest heaving as he gasped, "Is everything well? Daphne?"

"Yes, yes," Derek rushed to assure him, wishing he'd thought to include that comfort in his initial sentence to the butler. "Your wife is well. She asked me to give you this."

He slid a folded and sealed paper from his pocket, knuckle brushing the increasingly troublesome diary, and passed it over to the marquis. "I haven't read it, of course, but I believe she might have explained my presence here better than I could."

At first, Derek had assumed he was simply the messenger of private words of love and devotion. The way the day had gone, he wasn't so sure anymore.

Lady Chemsford and her cook had worked together, a well-known fact around Haven Manor. It was even more well known that they were still friends. Until now, he hadn't given much thought to the fact that such a relationship meant Lady Chemsford probably knew a great deal more about Jess than Derek did.

Given William's lack of surprise as he read, he was aware of Jess's proclivities as well. Or the letter wasn't about Derek and Jess at all.

"By the by," Derek said, with a nod toward the door, "Jess said she'd be coming around through the kitchens. I have no idea what she'll look like. So far today she's been an old woman and a grubby street child."

William glanced up as if gauging Derek's seriousness. "She really does that?"

Derek nodded. William's lack of surprise meant either Jess had enacted living theater at Haven Manor prior to Derek's arrival or something else in her past or character made the skill make sense.

For the first time in recent memory, Derek wished he possessed the ability to ask people personal questions. Normally, he didn't care to know what someone didn't willingly share.

His life was decidedly not normal at present.

Eyes on the letter, William walked to the bellpull.

A footman appeared before the pull's tassel had settled.

"Have whoever knocks on the kitchen door brought up here immediately," William said.

A slight wrinkle marred the footman's forehead for a moment but soon smoothed back into a stoic, bland expression. He nodded and left.

Derek shook his head. "Does that ever give you airs?"

William looked up from the paper. "What?"

"That." Derek nodded toward the door. "Having everyone take your word as law, never to be questioned, never to be called out as wrong."

"Not here so much as it does at the country houses." William finished reading the letter and gave a small nod before tucking it into his pocket. "I took Daphne to my childhood home, Dawnview Hall, after our wedding. By the time we left, the servants had taken to asking my valet if I was ill, I'd begun explaining my requests so much."

He rubbed his hand across the back of his neck as he looked around the parlor, decorated in dark, sedate colors and simple, elegant furniture. "Daphne hasn't been here yet. I never spent much time here growing up either. It still feels like I'm walking around in my father's home. Most of the servants worked for him."

Having a former housekeeper for a wife would likely call a lifetime of habits into question, even if the woman had been born to the same respectable level of society Derek had been raised in.

Derek had assumed that Jess's background was similar to Lady Chemsford's. Given her antics today, he had to adjust his thinking. In this case, adjust meant throw out everything he thought he knew.

As if his thoughts had conjured her, Jess appeared in the parlor door, looking exactly as he was accustomed to seeing her. A nondescript homespun dress and spencer jacket, plain fabric bonnet, and not a bit of dirt on her porcelain face.

Not caring if it was rude, Derek groped his way to a chair and sat down. This was why he so very much preferred ancient history. History didn't change on a man.

CHAPTER SEVEN

*J*ess knew how to look relaxed. A small smile, shoulders down and slightly rolled forward, elbows slack, and fingers lightly clasped. She'd gone through the mental checklist just before entering the room, ensuring the men would think her at complete ease, even though she was anything but.

"We need you to give Mr. Thornbury permission to seek out a piece of art on your behalf," Jess said. She braced herself for an interruption from Mr. Thornbury, but given his current position inelegantly flopped over a chair, skin looking more than a little pale, she was safe from him claiming control of anything.

"I need *more* art?" Lord Chemsford asked. "I have more than I know what to do with right now." He gestured toward Derek. "I had to hire someone just to determine what all I have."

"You don't have to actually buy it." Jess was equal parts amused and exasperated. Amusement better served her right now, so she let it tilt one side of her mouth upward. "You only need pretend like you might."

"I suppose I could do that." He pulled a piece of paper from his pocket and waved it about. "Daphne says you may have found your family?"

Jess groaned. "Daph has a loose tongue."

It was true what they said: three can keep a secret if two of them were dead. Since Jess was a little too fond of Daphne to kill her and she wasn't entirely sure where Kit was, she might as well accept that at least part of her secret past wasn't secret anymore.

The question was just how much her two friends had told their husbands about Jess. And how much had Lord Chemsford told Mr. Thornbury?

"Your family was lost?" Mr. Thornbury asked, straightening a bit in his chair.

"Her family is dead," Lord Chemsford responded. "At least she thought they were."

"Yes, I thought my family dead." Volunteering a few facts might stem the curiosity. "Most of them are, as far as I know. If even one of them is alive, though, that changes everything." She took a deep breath and looked at Mr. Thornbury. "That's why I need your help."

It was becoming slightly less painful to say those words, even though the more she allowed him to do, the more beholden she became. She didn't like owing people. It left her under their control, at their mercy. Her arms tightened over her chest and her chin lifted the slightest bit as she stared down the men.

The color was back in Mr. Thornbury's face, and that little crease he got on his forehead before asking a question was starting to form.

There was a good possibility his question would go in a direction she didn't prefer, so she gave a bit more. "If my family is alive, there is likely someone out there who wants to change that. I'd rather not lose them again."

She opened her eyes wide, pushing until the strain caused her lashes to tremble a bit. It made her look vulnerable and on the verge of crying. That form of manipulation had always made her feel a bit ill, but it had seemed to work for the children fairly often when they wanted something from Daphne.

Jess blinked, surprised to feel a genuine burn at the edge of her eyes. It had been ages since she'd cried. Lifetimes. But the memories being dredged up in her mind were from a time when crying had been allowed—in private, anyway. "Their only hope is that I uncover the secret of that diary."

Mr. Thornbury's mouth opened and then snapped shut. The line between his brows smoothed. "I'll visit the museum tomorrow."

"I'll go with you," Chemsford offered. "Perhaps my presence will lend credence to your request."

The burn at the edge of her eyes had been bad enough. The strange ache sliding along her breastbone was worse. Jess resisted the urge to rub a hand against the sting, knowing it wouldn't do any good. It wasn't truly there.

She'd felt it before, whenever she encountered someone with the potential to send her life spiraling in another direction. It wasn't any sort of mystic premonition, but something was happening in this room, something she saw but couldn't quite recognize, that her mind considered a threat to her current life.

Since Chemsford had never caused her any distress, that something had to be Mr. Thornbury, the one man she needed if this mission was going to be a success. Keeping him at arm's length was more imperative than ever.

❦❦

The chamber Derek was shown into was vastly different from the one he'd been residing in at Haven Manor. Everything about this room had been designed to impress and give comfort to the occupant. He ignored the cozy chairs and comfortable bedding for the solace of pacing. The busyness and opulence felt unsettling instead of restful.

Or perhaps that was simply the situation.

Tomorrow he was going to seek out an old friend—a professional acquaintance, really. He was going to actively involve himself in this scheme of Jess's. No longer would he be able to claim he'd been a mere bystander. If he did this . . . if he involved himself in the diary's treasure hunt . . . if he accepted the sense of urgency that had propelled Jess to do everything she'd done in the past few days . . .

His thoughts stumbled to a halt as he realized that was the tipping point for him.

Jess.

He'd seen her trembling in the drawing room, seen the emotion in her eyes. Mentioning her family had driven away that irritated, bored anger he was so accustomed to seeing on her face.

This wasn't about the diary anymore. It was about her.

Derek didn't know how to handle a *her*. She was alive and breathing, with life still ahead of her. What direction would that life take if he succeeded?

He swallowed around a suddenly thick throat. What would happen if he failed? If they failed? Because they were a *they* now, whether she realized it or not. She may think he was simply going to hand over the information he learned and let her scamper away, but he was invested now, putting his personal and professional convictions on the line. They were partners.

Derek blinked and stumbled to a halt. He hadn't consciously chosen to entwine his life and immediate fate with Jess's, but the idea was firmly rooted in his mind now and refused to be reconsidered.

All that remained was convincing Jess it had been her idea.

⬥⬥⬥

It took both William's title and Derek's reputation to gain them entrance to the British Institution in Pall Mall. The gallery walls of the prestigious museum were covered in the enormous paintings of foreign masters. Only the resolve from the previous night allowed Derek to walk past them with a mere glance, keeping the objective in the forefront of his mind.

William sighed and shifted his shoulders.

"Try to look a bit impressed," Derek whispered, punctuating it with a nudge from his elbow. "We're supposedly here because of your obsession with art."

"Right," William murmured. He clasped his hands behind his back, tilted his head, and gave a low, thoughtful hum as he gazed at a nearby painting.

Derek resisted the urge to chuckle as he continued the search for his former schoolmate and colleague. They found him in the central exhibition hall, examining the work of one of the resident student painters.

"Mr. Cathers," Derek said, injecting his tone with a note of friendship while maintaining the somberness a room with this much beauty required. "It's been much too long."

The short, portly man turned his head, and a large smile stretched across his face as he extended his hand. "Mr. Thornbury. I had no idea you were in London. What brings you to the Institution?"

Mr. Cathers led Derek and William a step closer to the center of the room as a woman entered with a small easel and a bag of supplies. She set up her easel among the other students lining the room, using the inspiration of the painters they admired to perfect their own work.

Derek had to fight a pang of jealousy as those men and women worked steadily away, the low swish of brush and paint on canvas filling the room with as much gentle ambience as the sunlight pouring through the ceiling glass. There had been a time when he'd aspired to be among their ranks, but his paintings had always been lacking something.

"Ah," Mr. Cathers said, nodding as he looked toward the wall that had captured Derek's attention. The woman was setting up her small workspace beneath an exceptionally large Tintoretto painting. "You couldn't stay away from our Italian masters, could you? They are spectacular. Can I show you around?"

As much as Derek wanted to say yes, the urgency from last night, as well as the fact that William would slaughter him for dragging him about the museum, gave Derek the wherewithal to turn down the offer with a small, sad shake of his head. "Not today, old friend. I'm doing a bit of work on the Marquis of Chemsford's collection."

Mr. Cathers's demeanor shifted in an instant as he straightened his back and smoothed the smile from his face. "My lord." He bowed. "Highest apologies for not recognizing you. Please accept my condolences on your recent loss."

William's eyebrows shot up, and he dipped his head low enough to cover his cough. The death of his father a few months prior hadn't been the blow many assumed it to be. William had considered the relationship lost long ago. Still, he managed a somber, "Thank you."

Derek continued quickly, trying to keep the target in mind. He couldn't afford to forget why he was here. The walls held far too many distractions. "His European collection is quite extensive, and he'd like to purchase a Verbonnian painting to round it out. He's particularly interested in getting one from the Fournier period."

Mr. Cathers smiled. "What luck! We happen to have a Fournier. We hung it just last week. I can't seem to stop coming in here to stare at it."

He gestured toward the wall, and all the men turned to look at the depiction of a grand royal caravan riding along the edge of a cliff. The ocean roared far below them, and the sky stretched wide and glorious above. The characteristic blend of clarity and abstract areas gave it that unique feel of a Fournier painting. At any other moment, Derek would have been overjoyed at this opportunity.

But Fournier had barely been mentioned in the diary and always as the teacher, never as the artist. "Fascinating. We'd much rather locate a work by one of The Six, though. The mystery fascinates his lordship."

William attempted his thoughtful hum and accompanying nod again.

Mr. Cathers sighed as his shoulders slumped a bit, no doubt disappointed at the loss of a potentially hefty commission. "We tried. It was my hope to fill this wall with Verbonnian paintings for our European exhibit. They were once in a single collection, you know. Almost every known work by The Six was in a personal collection in Derbyshire. It was auctioned off about twenty-five years ago."

Auctions. The death knell for any art lover. It became nearly impossible to follow art once auctions were involved. The auctioneers were too protective of their wealthy and noble customers to provide information freely.

Dismay brought a slump to Derek's own shoulders. He was going to fail Jess. Mere hours after declaring himself her partner—albeit only in his mind—he was going to fail to provide the one thing he was supposed to have: knowledge of and access to the paintings.

There had to be something else he could do. He couldn't imagine what it would be like not to know his family was alive and well, living their lives a few miles from Oxford.

No, he couldn't return to that townhome and tell Jess he'd learned nothing.

"Have you any idea who purchased the pieces?" The odds of Mr. Cathers knowing were slim, but God had been known to work miracles before. All Derek needed right then was a small one.

"Not many," the short man said with a shake of his head, already appearing to lose interest in the conversation as his attention wandered to the nearby students. "The auction house sent a letter of inquiry for me. Most of them went unanswered, but one solicitor sent me a polite but firm refusal on behalf of two of his clients, the Earl of Woolsby and the Duke of Marshington. Neither of those men is in dire enough straits to sell."

No, they weren't, but Derek didn't really need for them to sell. He only needed them to let him look. With any luck, William could make a few discreet inquiries and get Derek in front of the paintings. It would be a start.

Part of Derek wanted to flee the room immediately and begin discussing plans, but it would be suspicious for two men who loved art as much as they did—or were pretending to in William's case—to depart the premises without looking about.

They stayed for another half hour, William giving occasional nods and hums while Derek and Mr. Cathers discussed art and mutual acquaintances and occasionally offered guesses as to which of the budding artists paying to work in the presence of their inspirations were going to be successful.

The man standing on a chair to better reach his giant canvas showed a great deal of promise. Certainly more than the girl who had arrived shortly after Derek and William. She'd be asked to leave the Institution within a month, given the bare rudiments of a picture she had managed to produce thus far. The woman on the other side of the girl was moving her brush in short, confident strokes, and the picture coming to life on her canvas was startling. Derek wasn't sure if he liked it or not, but he was certainly going to remember it.

Eventually enough time passed and they could politely depart. Derek nearly ran for the exit, though he made himself drag his feet, taking a few last looks at paintings he'd only ever heard about. For once the idea of what he was going to do—formulate a new plan on the way home so he could return to Jess a conquering hero—held more appeal than looking at what had already been accomplished.

It was a bit sobering to learn on the ride home that William knew neither the Earl of Woolsby nor the Duke of Marshington. At all. That didn't mean he couldn't contact them. He was a marquis, after all, but it did lessen the likelihood of them granting Derek quick and easy access to the paintings. That didn't give him much to offer Jess to convince her he was an equal partner in this adventure.

He was deep in thought as he handed his hat and greatcoat to William's butler. There was no sense in putting off the discussion.

"Do you know the whereabouts of—" he cleared his throat— "Miss Smith?"

"Miss Smith, sir?" the butler asked as William's chuckle echoed in the hall.

"I believe he means Jess, our other guest," William said. "Smart of you, Derek. I should have foisted a surname onto her months ago. It would have made for considerably fewer awkward moments." He grinned. "I can't wait to see what she thinks of it."

The butler looked between the two men but remained stoic in expression. "I haven't seen her since breakfast, my lord. Shall I send a maid to her rooms?"

Derek shook his head. He'd see her eventually. Dinner, at the latest. Perhaps he could have something to share by then. If the earl or duke were currently in residence in London, William could contact them this afternoon. If not, that still gave Derek a few hours to come up with something else to offer as a suggested path forward.

While Jess had been the one to request Derek's help, she likely had a dozen of her own ideas on how to proceed. There was still the diary to translate and the art to inspect and interpret, though. Even if Derek didn't come up with something this afternoon, she still needed him.

It was rather nice to be needed.

His thoughts whirled, bouncing around from idea to idea. Art had always soothed him, so he strolled between the second-floor rooms, taking in the swirls of color, the captured moments in time. Slowly, he wound his way through the remainder of the house, eventually ending up back in the front hall, staring at a statue tucked into the corner, as if someone had slid it over there temporarily and then forgotten about it.

A brisk knock at the door broke his contemplation of the statue. There wasn't a servant in the immediate vicinity, so he stepped over to throw the latch and open the door himself.

Jess strode in. When her glance flickered over his, her mouth went slack for the barest of moments before quickly returning to those smooth, perfect, unrevealing lines.

Derek frowned. The same notion of wrongness that had prompted him to examine the old woman in the carriage compelled him to look Jess over a bit more closely now.

Nothing caught his attention. Her brown bonnet was ordinary, as was the blue pelisse that covered the rest of her. The brown gloves were just as plain. She looked like any other woman in London.

Except she was alone.

"Did you go out?"

She lifted a brow and glanced at the door behind her before smirking at him. "I thought you were supposed to be the smart one."

He fought back the desire to roll his eyes at her like his six-year-old nephew. "Smarter than you, apparently. I took William with me when I left the house this morning."

Even as he said it, he knew the statement was utterly ridiculous. This was why he avoided verbal sparring. He ended up slicing himself more than his foe. He cleared his throat and pressed on. "Where is your chaperon?"

She grinned. "Apparently you needed him more than I did. Relax. I've returned safely, haven't I?"

A maid appeared, poised to accept Jess's bonnet and pelisse. Jess brushed the woman away. "I'll wear them upstairs."

Derek's frown deepened, that sense that he was missing something right in front of him growing stronger. "Why?"

"Because that's the easiest way to carry them."

"You don't need to carry them. The maid can do that."

"I'm going upstairs anyway, so there's no need for her to make the trip as well."

It was suddenly imperative that Derek get her to remove the bonnet and coat. Her insistence on doing something memorably out of the norm must mean that his instincts were correct and she was hiding something.

There would also be the satisfaction of coming out on top in a battle of wills.

He cleared his throat. "I thought we could step into the drawing room and I could tell you what I learned this morning."

Guilt over his lack of anything to actually share nagged at him, but he easily pushed it aside. That fact was irrelevant right then.

"I'll be happy to meet you there after I've had a moment to refresh myself." Jess folded her hands before her. The maid just stood there, looking back and forth between them.

"What are you hiding, Jess?" There was no sense in Derek participating in a verbal game of which she was a master. Blunt and direct had always served him better.

"What makes you think I'm hiding something?"

"Because you won't take off the bonnet."

She turned her back on him and slid the bonnet from her head and over her shoulder before turning back to face him, the fabric hat crushed in her grip. "Happy now?"

He should be. But he wasn't. "May I see it?"

"You want to see my bonnet?" she asked very slowly.

Now the maid wasn't looking back and forth; she was simply staring at him, and Derek couldn't really blame her. Oh well. He was too far gone to stop now. "Yes."

"I don't think it will fit you. My head is a great deal smaller than yours."

"Only in the literal sense."

It was a gamble which of them was more surprised by his quick return. She recovered her shock faster and grinned at him. "Well done, sir."

He licked his lips and forged ahead, wondering if perhaps there was a bit more wit stored in that brain of his. "I deserve a boon."

"It wasn't that well done," she laughed.

"The bonnet, Jess?"

She pinched the loose fabric back of the bonnet and shook it at him. "It's a brown bonnet, Derek. It's nothing special."

"Then you won't mind handing it over." He really hoped something came of this exchange, or he was going to feel like a veritable idiot and never be able to trust his own instincts again.

She rolled her eyes with such perfect technique his nephew would be in awe, then handed the bonnet over. "Here."

He took it. Stared at it. Called himself a total fool.

How was he supposed to know if this was a normal bonnet? He'd never had reason nor opportunity to inspect one before, and he had to assume that women's bonnets were made rather differently than men's hats.

It was one of those loose bonnets that seemed like a floppy bag with a brim on it. He turned it over to see that the hat had been lined with a pale pink fabric. No one but the servants would ever really see the inside of the hat, so why bother? Why put the pretty color on the inside and show the drab brown to the world?

He turned it in his hand once more, and that was when he saw it. A second brim. A second set of ties.

He twisted and flipped and pulled, and the bonnet went from being brown with a pink liner to pink with a brown liner.

The same pink a certain inept painter had been wearing at the Institution that morning. How had Jess managed to gain access to the exclusive, high-priced art hall? No, he didn't care. How she'd done it didn't matter. What hurt was that she'd been there at all.

"'Man looketh on the outward appearance. . . .'" Derek mumbled as he ran a hand along the cleverly constructed headwear.

Jess sighed. "Not you, too."

He didn't know what she meant, but he was coming to expect that was going to be a normal occurrence if he continued to spend time with her.

That was a very big *if*. He refused to be a tool she used when convenient.

"It would seem," he said slowly, "that our meeting to exchange information would be unnecessary."

He handed the bonnet back and strode from the hall without looking back.

CHAPTER EIGHT

*T*he problem with inevitabilities was that no matter how much effort one put into avoiding them, they still happened.

Jess nibbled at the chunk of bread from the dinner tray she'd requested be brought to her room. After this morning's encounter in the front hall, she hadn't wanted to sit across the table from Mr. Thornbury, and she rather thought he didn't want to look at her either.

If only she could avoid other unpleasant encounters with such ease.

From the moment she'd recognized the familiar code in the letter, she'd known that a visit with the author would eventually be necessary.

That didn't mean she wanted to do it. She'd perfected the art of avoiding the past and the truths that came along with it, but none of her skills could save her now.

She had hoped to know more before visiting her old friend, hoped to have a specific need that would allow her to be professional and succinct. Something that would necessitate she keep the visit as short as possible.

Something that would let her pretend she hadn't missed him. Them.

If she'd understood three years ago what family really meant, would she still have run? There was no way to know, no way to turn back time and play it differently. Even if she could, she wasn't sure she would. The people of Haven Manor had taught her what it meant to care for someone no matter the cost. What would have happened to them without her?

Spending precious time contemplating the possibilities was fruitless, as was entertaining the thought that she could possibly repair boats she'd burned. What was done was done and couldn't be changed. That lesson had been fixed firmly in her at the age of sixteen, and she'd held it like a mantra ever since.

Now the path to her future lay in trudging through her past. There were no other options.

Night fell and the house stilled around her. Had Mr. Thornbury told Chemsford what she'd done? Not that she cared. What would the marquis do? He'd hardly toss her from the premises. His wife would call him out for such an act. No, Chemsford was neither help nor deterrent.

Thornbury, on the other hand, needed to be controlled.

Before she could herd him, though, she needed to know which direction to head.

A glance outside revealed she had a few hours before morning. She could take a short nap and still leave the house before anyone else was awake. When she returned, she would, hopefully, know enough to formulate some sort of plan—one that required minimal reliance on the art historian.

The moon was curving down the other side of the sky when she woke. She dressed with the stealth and speed of one who had departed in the middle of the night more than once before stepping quietly toward the door. Fifteen minutes had been invested earlier in learning the precise angle and pressure to put on the latch in order to leave her room without a sound.

In the quiet of the early hours, those fifteen minutes proved well spent.

As the latch cleared its mooring, she prepared to ease the door back only to have it swing abruptly inward.

She didn't yelp, but her breath did surge out of her in a rush as the door was followed by the body of a man rolling backward, head plopping onto her feet.

Dim moonlight played over Mr. Thornbury's face, accenting the sharp angles of his nose, chin, and cheekbones until he looked almost lethal.

His wince and yawn accompanied by a shrug of his dark wool-covered shoulder stilled any idea of him being a threat.

"We're off now, then?" he asked in a rough voice that clung to sleep.

Jess narrowed her eyes as he yawned again. "What are you doing here?" she asked in a low whisper.

He grinned up at her, looking half asleep and entirely too proud of himself. "I didn't trust you to tell me what your next moves were."

She waited for more but grudgingly gave him a bit of credit when he didn't point out that his lack of trust had obviously been justified.

"What disguise are you wearing today?" Still prone on the floor, he craned his head back to look at her shoes before lifting his gaze to take in the rest of her clothing. "I'm certain keeping up with you will be easier when I know whom to look for."

Jess rolled her eyes and offered him a hand up. The observations this man made . . . the War Office should have been hiring artists instead of jaded, hardened spies. "No disguise today."

"Good," he said as he straightened his horribly wrinkled clothing. "Then I don't have to worry about matching. Or calling you the wrong thing when you transform from a grandmother into a street urchin."

"You don't have to worry about calling me anything," Jess bit out. "You aren't coming with me. My, er, the people I'm visiting won't take kindly to my bringing a guest."

"I don't particularly care." His mouth flattened, and he stepped out into the corridor to collect his shoes, pulling the black spectacles from one boot. "As your partner in this endeavor, albeit a fairly clueless one, I refuse to remain in the dark any longer."

"You aren't my partner," Jess said, pushing down the bud of panic the idea created. She'd worked with people in the past—other spies, occasional informants—but she'd always been very careful to establish that any such connection was momentary. She didn't want to become attached to anyone. Not when it was so very easy for the job to take them away.

"One," he said, holding out his hand and pointing to his finger, "you need my expertise. Two"—he pointed to a second finger—"*you* brought *me* into this havoc. And three"—he stabbed at a third finger—"I am putting my professional reputation and possibly more on the line to find whatever this thing is." He gave up counting his reasons and let his hands fall to his side as he gave another shrug. "And if you refuse to take me with you, I'll make such a fuss trying to follow you that whoever is looking for you won't have to try very hard." He grinned, but it didn't soften the determination on his face. "See? Partner."

His threat was an empty one, Jess was certain. Well, mostly certain. Actually, not certain at all. The man had spent the night in the corridor just to make a point.

"Very well," she said quietly, stepping out of the room and closing the door silently behind her. "Let's go. I doubt anyone knows I'm in London, but we'll have plenty of time to wander the streets and see if anyone is following us before we pay a call." Perhaps she could scare him into staying here and making use of the comfortable guest bed for the remainder of the night.

He said nothing, simply followed her down the corridor, footsteps thudding enough to make her wince. London was noisy, even this early in the morning, so his heavy, well, normal footfalls wouldn't be a problem. It was simply the principle of it.

As she passed through the kitchens, where a scullery maid was just starting to stoke the fires, Jess grabbed a small loaf of bread and a chunk of cheese. She didn't look back to see if Mr. Thornbury followed suit as she slipped out the door and into the back alley.

The air was thick with pollution and morning dew. Clouds hung low, skittering across the moon as it slid down the sky and the first rays of sun took its place. Her lungs protested the return to the city after three years of country air, but the rest of her breathed a little easier as she munched on the bread and cheese and disappeared into the anonymity of an awakening London. At this hour, it was all delivery people and workmen. None of them cared who she was unless she got in their way.

"This is probably a different side of London than you're accustomed to seeing, Mr. Thornbury."

"Indeed it is, Miss Smith. Doesn't make it bad."

Jess stumbled to a halt and stared at him. "What did you call me?"

"Miss Smith. If we're going to keep conversing with each other, the proper address issue needed to be resolved. Since you won't provide me with your surname"—he shrugged—"I gave you one. The other option, aside from correcting me, of course, is that you call me Derek."

Why, the conniving . . . she had half a mind to let him continue calling her Miss Smith, but it had been the one part of disguises she'd never managed well. No matter where she was or how she was dressed, she couldn't remember to answer to the wrong name. "Derek it is, then."

"You're a funny duck." He chuckled softly and shook his head before taking a bite of the bread in his hand.

Jess said nothing as she continued meandering about the area, keeping to the lesser-traveled roads as she watched for any suspicious activity. As they walked, Derek chattered, pointing out interesting architecture and where old buildings had once stood. Jess made appropriate noises and, as their safety became apparent, relaxed enough to find the conversation surprisingly enjoyable, or at least tolerable enough that she didn't feel the need to stuff his cravat into his mouth.

Perhaps because it was a far more pleasant conversation than the one she was going to have when she stopped stalling and took them to see the man who had sent the letter that started this adventure.

Did he care if she showed up, or had he simply tracked her down out of a sense of honorable duty?

Fretting about it changed nothing. It was time to act.

As if Derek could sense the change of purpose in her shift of direction, he asked, "Are we returning to the Institution?"

"No." Jess almost wished they were. She'd rather break into a building than face the inquisition that awaited her. "But we are going to Pall Mall."

They moved into the nicest part of Mayfair along with the early coating of sunlight. The gas lanterns were being doused as they passed the gates to Carlton House, the quiet inside indicating the prince regent likely wasn't in residence.

Jess stumbled a bit. She didn't much care about the regent, but what if the man she needed to see wasn't home? What if the family had retreated to Kent or one of the other estates? As much as she wanted to delay this reunion, she really needed to know what he knew.

Finally, she came to a halt in front of a large house. Rows of windows marched across the front, still and silent. There would be servants up, but probably not anyone else. Not that it mattered. Seeing the servants was going to be almost as bad.

Now all she had to do was decide what to tell Derek.

❄❄

The woman was insane. Derek swallowed hard as he looked up at the house. "This is the Duke of Marshington's residence."

"Yes."

He swallowed again, took a deep breath, and counted to five, but she didn't expound upon her answer. Obviously they were here because Mr. Cathers had mentioned the duke owned one of the paintings, but Derek's deductive skills stopped after that. "Do you have a plan?"

"For what?" She didn't glance his way, just stared up at the house.

A wave of dizziness rolled over him and landed in his gut. She didn't have a plan? Every move she'd made over the past few days had pointed to her being a person who always thought five steps ahead, and yet here she stood in front of the house of a man with an exceedingly dangerous reputation that went far beyond the mere political power of an old dukedom, and she didn't have a plan?

He took her hand in his and began walking, hauling her farther down the pavement, away from the house. The warmth of her hand jolted him from his shocked stupor, and he stared stupidly down his arm as if he couldn't quite fathom the idea that they'd both run out without gloves.

He'd never taken a woman's hand without at least one of them wearing gloves.

He dropped her hand as he stumbled to a halt, and she tripped to a stop next to him, looking amused. "What are you doing?"

His thumb rubbed across his palm, though he wasn't sure if he was trying to retain the sensation of her skin against his or remove it. Not that it mattered. What mattered was getting away from the duke's house until they had a plan. He dropped his grip on his own hand and resumed his path. "I'm walking. We can't stand and stare at the duke's house while you formulate a plan."

Jess fell into step beside him. "He has one of the paintings. We need to see it."

The chill of dread that had balled in his stomach traced down his arms and removed any lingering warmth from his palm. "So you were going to do what? Break in? Dress up as a servant?"

"I thought I'd use the ridiculously large and ornate brass knocker and see what happened."

He looked up to find she'd somehow steered him on a path that had brought them right back to the front of Montgomery House, only this time they were at the door instead of across the street.

Before he could stop her, she'd stepped up, wrapped narrow fingers around the metal ring, and slammed it against the brass plate twice. As expected in the home of upper aristocracy, the door opened almost immediately.

Rather less expected was the man on the other side of it.

Derek's knees threatened to run off by themselves.

The duke had seemed more than formidable on the two occasions that Derek had seen him across the room at a large formal function, but standing two feet away in his own doorway, wearing breeches, riding boots, and a hard glare? The man was downright terrifying.

Jess's brain had to be addled with desperation, the same kind that sent hopeless soldiers charging toward the enemy lines with nothing but a sword and a single shot pistol.

Derek stepped a bit in front of her, drawing the duke's slicing grey eyes to him. "Good morning, Your Grace. Deepest apologies for disrupting you, as it appears you are on your way out for a morning ride."

The duke's mouth pressed into a firmer line. "I can delay it."

"Yes. Good." Derek cleared his throat. "Splendid."

The duke's eyebrows lifted, but he said nothing. Derek pressed on, coming up with a story as he went, an action doomed to bring nothing but disaster raining down on their heads.

"I am Mr. Derek Thornbury, an art and antiquities scholar from Oxford. It"—he coughed to try to ease the constriction in his throat—"has come to the attention of my colleague and me that you are in possession of a painting of particular interest to our current, er, work. If it pleases Your Grace, we'd like to, ahem, study it." He paused and attempted to swallow, but his mouth was so dry it simply caused an uncomfortable convulsion in his throat. "At your convenience, of course," he scraped out before falling into terrified silence.

"You and your, ahem, colleague?" the duke asked.

"Yes." Derek glanced over his shoulder to see Jess staring at him. Her face seemed expressionless, but there was some definite emotion lurking underneath that he couldn't identify. He turned his attention back to the duke, who looked quite simply irritated. "Miss, er, Smith."

One eyebrow shot up as the duke settled himself more comfortably against his doorframe. "Miss *Smith*?"

"Yes, Your Grace." Derek was accustomed to talking to members of the aristocracy who had solicited his services. Over the years, some—such as Chemsford—had become friends. He'd never approached one on his own before, though, particularly not one with a reputation such as Marshington's.

The hard face and impression of power gave credence to every rumor he'd ever overheard about the man. No one knew where he'd been for almost ten years, and the speculation ranged from dead to privateering to War Office spy.

At the moment, Derek believed every single one of them.

Except dead, of course. That was more likely to be Derek if his heart didn't stop trying to flee through his boots.

"And you thought eight in the morning would be convenient?"

No, he hadn't, but then again he hadn't thought he'd be knocking on a duke's door this morning either, and if he had, he would never have dreamed the duke would answer it himself. Derek fought the urge to frown in case the duke misconstrued its meaning. Why was the duke answering his own door? "In all honesty, sir, I was expecting to converse with the butler."

A soft snicker drifted over his shoulder, and Derek slid his foot back a bit until it connected with Jess's toe. Now was not the time to show amusement.

Perhaps she was on the verge of hysterics? Had her bravado finally failed her? Should he toss her over his shoulder and make a run for it?

A hint of amusement made an appearance on the duke's features as well as one side of his mouth curled and his arms dropped to his sides. "How fortunate for you that I happened to be the one nearby. We can dispense with the delay my butler's sending you away would have caused."

The duke looked Derek up and down with a brief glance and then aimed his gaze over Derek's shoulder at what little could be seen of Jess before he continued to speak. "Let me make sure I understand this. I am supposedly in possession of a painting that has you and your, er, art colleague excited enough to be up and dressed and about London at an hour reserved for those who actually toil for a living or want a good run on their horses before the parks clog with displays of the latest finery."

"That would be the sum of it, yes," Derek said with a gulp.

"I had no idea my family had procured anything of any value beyond eliciting jealousy among their peers. Do come in." He pushed the door open wider and stepped to the side.

As Derek stepped inside, a sort of calm slid over him. This situation was feeling more like what he was accustomed to. The introduction had been unorthodox, but he could now continue the conversation as he normally would. A deep breath filled his lungs for the first time since he'd rolled through Jess's doorway this morning.

The door shut behind them with a click that echoed through the tall, marble-floored front hall. Derek turned to see the duke leaning against the portal, booted feet crossed at the ankles. "Now, Jess, why don't you tell me why you're really here and why you're letting this man risk an aneurysm of the heart trying to protect you?" He tilted his head, all attention on the little blond woman staring mutinously back at him. "Or should I call you Miss Smith?"

Bright color appeared on Jess's cheekbones, and her body lost a bit of its tension as her shoulders slumped. The fire Derek had grown accustomed to didn't disappear, though. Her teeth were clenched together as she glanced from Derek to the duke.

"You know him?" Derek asked, sidling closer to her, ready to step between them if need be. Although there wasn't much he could do. They were in the house of a powerful duke. He could do whatever he wanted and everyone would believe his tale.

"Oh yes," the duke said, showing no sign of the threatening animosity from moments earlier. In fact, a wide smile slashed through the shadows. "Didn't she tell you? She was once my wife."

CHAPTER NINE

*J*ess narrowed her eyes at the man who had not only saved her life but become one of her only friends in the years after she'd lost her family. She didn't much appreciate his joke, even though she'd made the exact same one the first time she'd met the woman who was now his duchess. This situation was completely different.

Yet, as difficult as that joke was going to be to explain, it lightened a bit of Jess's dread. She'd expected his first words to be scolding or indifference, not teasing.

Seeing Ryland again had overwhelmed her with unexpected emotion so deep it had momentarily frozen her in place. That was the only reason she'd allowed Derek to step in front of her. He deserved a measure of respect for doing that.

She'd rather expected him to run across the street and hide behind a lamppost the moment she'd knocked on the door. That he hadn't was the only reason Jess wasn't doing so herself.

That, and the fact that Ryland was blocking the door.

"We weren't really married," Jess said, hoping the impossible, that she could keep Derek from producing a plethora of new questions about her past. When Jess had made the statement to the future duchess, Ryland had already decided he wanted to marry her and was going to have to tell her everything anyway.

Jess had no romantic notions toward Derek. Yes, it had been

noble of him to try to protect her, and the sensation of his ungloved hand in hers had been far from appalling, but she didn't want his attentions.

One side of Ryland's mouth kicked up. "In some countries, if both parties declare themselves married in the hearing of another person, it's legally binding. I could be committing bigamy right now."

Ryland had always had a bit of a dry sense of humor, but it would seem the quiet life of a retired spy had honed it. Still, it wasn't like him to display it in front of a stranger.

A glance at Derek revealed his avid curiosity had been awakened. She wouldn't be getting out of this without a full explanation. Unless she could distract him with something else.

"It was the middle of a war," she said, directing her gaze back to Ryland. "I doubt anyone is going to knock on your door to enforce an obscure marriage law. Besides, even if we could prove which government jurisdiction we were under at the time, none of the options exist anymore."

Getting out of France all those years ago hadn't been as easy as hauling Jess out of the floor. Afraid of what would happen if anyone knew Jess's true identity, they'd stayed hidden in the countryside for a month, posing as a strange and awkward husband and wife. Then they'd created a story about Ryland finding Jess in a trunk at a French encampment. They'd been a bit better at the ruse a couple of years later when they used it to gather information on one of Napoleon's generals.

As ridiculous as it sounded, it was at least a quick explanation. Her royal lineage and her years spent spying for England might take a bit more time. She spared a look in Derek's direction, only to find him looking far from confused. He understood—or had at least drawn some conclusions—if the look he darted from Jess to Ryland and back again and the paleness of his countenance were anything to go by.

"I think he may need to sit down," Jess murmured. She wrapped her arms around one of Derek's, prepared to guide him gently to the floor if everything became too much for him. She wouldn't blame him. Fainting held a certain appeal right now.

Ryland nodded toward a nearby door. "You're welcome as far as my drawing room until my curiosity is satisfied."

The drawing room was good. The large room was full of antiquities and art that could distract Derek. They might even hold his attention long enough for Jess to keep this conversation with Ryland at least a little bit private.

Derek's eyes didn't wander about the room, though, as she helped him to a sofa. They stayed glued on her.

No private conversation, then. She cleared her throat and turned away from him. "I'm sure Price will let me explore the place." Ryland's enormous ex-smuggler of a butler had always found Jess amusing. He wouldn't throw her out.

"Price is no longer employed here," Ryland said with a smug half-smile.

As much as Jess wanted to ask where Price had gone, she didn't. Ryland was hardly going to offer her information. Unless, of course, it was in trade for something he wanted to know.

"Jeffreys." Jess had been close to Ryland's valet, too. "He likes me."

"He's angrier at you than I am. I believe he's preparing the boiling oil as we speak."

Probably true. "Your wife, then. She'll do anything to be rid of me sooner."

Ryland burst out laughing. It was a sound Jess hadn't heard much, even though she'd known the man for more than ten years. He'd become her mentor, teacher, brother, at times even something resembling a father, and eventually a friend, yet she'd rarely heard him laugh like that. There wasn't much to laugh about when trying to survive while finding the thing that just might save your country from annihilation. When his laughter subsided to a chuckle, he said, "You might be surprised. Motherhood has made her a rather protective hen."

Motherhood? She'd known it was possible, even likely, given the amount of time she'd been away, but the confirmation of such an event hit her with a painful stab. Such a significant moment in her friend's life and she hadn't even known. For the last three years, she'd helped care for the children of Haven Manor and learned a lot about the significance of tiny young humans. The idea of a miniature Ryland running around brought a small smile to her face. "Congratulations."

Ryland nodded toward Derek, who was silent but very noticeably observant. "Is he really an Oxford man?"

She nodded. "Yes. He's helping me interpret a diary."

His eyes narrowed. "There really is a diary? And you've had it this entire time?"

After news of the royal family's capture had spread, the countryside had erupted in people searching for Verbonnian treasures that had supposedly been smuggled from the palace, but the diary had not been among those rumors. As far as she knew, the book had been a family secret. "How did you know about the diary?"

Ryland's answer was more silent accusation.

"Yes, I have the diary." She sighed and gestured helplessly toward Derek. "Well, he has it right now."

"I see." Ryland shifted his weight and crossed his arms over his chest. "Am I truly in possession of a painting that is somehow connected to it?"

Jess nodded. "It would seem the diary was written while a group of Verbonnian artists, who had recently sought asylum in England, generated a significant amount of art. Queen Marguerite had clues hidden among them."

"Clever."

"Annoying."

"I've brought tea. Should I lace it with arsenic?"

Jess turned her head to see a wiry man with a large, heavily laden tea tray and an even larger frown.

"Definitely friends of yours," Derek mumbled, so low she barely heard him and knew no one else in the room had.

She fought back the urge to smirk at his observation and turned to Jeffreys. "I didn't know valets were bringing tea these days."

"I didn't want to miss the chance to dump it on your head." Jeffreys's frown softened a bit. "Three years, Jess. We thought you were dead."

"I didn't." A feminine voice joined the group in the drawing room. "I knew you were too stubborn to die."

Miranda, Duchess of Marshington, strode into the room with a young child on her hip and a quiet woman in a light grey dress trailing behind.

Jess swallowed and gave a curtsy. "Your Grace."

The duchess paused, and two pale eyebrows shot up as her green eyes widened. "Really? We're doing that?"

Jess blushed. "I think, perhaps, I owe you an apology." More likely several. Jess had rather relished making this woman's life difficult for several months. She wasn't even sure why she'd been determined to be such a pest. It wasn't jealousy. As friendly as she and Ryland were, Jess had never entertained such notions, even when they'd been pretending to be married.

Instead of taking her due, the duchess rushed to her husband's side. "Quick, Ryland, send for a physician. There's something terribly wrong with Jess."

The duke chuckled and scooped the little girl from her mother's arms. "This one's up early."

"Yes," Miranda said, reaching out to tweak the child's toes peeping out from under a muslin gown. "She hasn't yet had her breakfast, but I wanted Henrietta to have a chance to meet Jess." The duchess grinned. "It could be another three years before she gets the opportunity again."

How was Jess supposed to answer such a statement? This woman had never liked Jess before, grumbling often that Ryland needed to fire her or send her to work somewhere else, and now she wanted Jess to meet her daughter?

Apparently so, as Miranda claimed her daughter back from her husband and crossed the room to stand in front of Jess.

Dark brown curls framed bright green eyes that looked at Jess with the confident directness of a child.

Three years ago that would have sent Jess scampering beneath a sofa, but she'd had a lot of time to learn about young people and how they worked. Seeing this child was different, though. She was the daughter of the man who'd saved Jess's life—twice in a very literal sense, but in countless other ways as well. He'd helped her find purpose and strength when she'd barely known how to breathe.

"Henrietta, this is, er, Jess." Miranda sighed and glared at her husband over their child's head. "With all the unconventional relationships you have, it will be a miracle if we manage to teach her proper manners. She's going to be laughed out of court when she gets presented."

Ryland leaned against the wall and gave a half shrug. "What is life without a little unpredictability?"

"Jesh," the little girl said while sticking one finger in her mouth and twirling her other hand into her hair. "F'oorboards."

Jess choked in surprise and sudden laughter while Miranda cast her eyes to the ceiling in exasperation. Her frustrated groan was belied by the grin on her face.

"Yes," she said, pulling her daughter in closer. "This is the girl in the floorboards."

Jess crossed her arms over her chest and cocked her head as she considered Ryland. Not only was he sharing stories, he was sharing the truth. "Did you decide your exploits made for good bedtime stories?"

He gave another nonchalant shrug. "Some of them."

"Good thing the war is over, then," Jess muttered.

"Off you go now." Miranda passed the girl to the waiting nanny and then set about serving tea. "I hope you've a fascinating story yourself, Jess. That might be the only thing to appease Ryland. He's rather miffed at you for running away."

Jess had expected as much, though she hadn't three years ago. Back then, she'd assumed their connection was one of loyalty or shared experience. She'd thought Ryland and Jeffreys and everyone else could be left behind the same way she'd walked away from other people she'd encountered over the years. It was a lie she'd clung to even as she'd learned that the gaping hole in her heart wasn't fear or even boredom. Years of refusing to look back, refusing to remember, had helped her continue the pretense.

Here, now, with Ryland and Jeffreys and even Miranda staring at her without any attempt to mask their hurt, she couldn't pretend anymore.

Miranda held up a cup of tea. "Would you like to sit for this or simply gulp it down where you stand?"

Jess dropped into a chair before her legs could give out and send her to the floor. How strange to be treated as a guest. When she'd lived here before, she'd been welcomed, treated as an equal, but she'd still held a position. As head parlormaid, she'd never been idle, but now . . . Now there was no reason for her to be here other than Ryland and Miranda's generosity and Derek's guess that the paintings were required to interpret the diary.

With wide eyes, Jess glanced over to Derek. What was he making of this?

At some point he'd propped himself on the arm of the sofa, likely when the duchess had entered and manners dictated that he stand. Now he was sliding back down to the seat, appearing a bit shaky, but only in the physical sense. His mind must have recovered as the look he returned was steady and full of emotion she couldn't read. Anger? Confusion?

She turned away, trying to act as if his presence was completely ignorable. So what if he was confused? She spent most of her time in his presence feeling senseless. All his thoughts and logic and knowledge, the way he'd seen through her disguises. It would do him good to feel a bit lost.

"Why don't we start from the present and work our way backward?" Ryland eased into his own chair and took a sip of tea. "You can start by introducing your friend properly. He's caught an earful already, so I'm trusting that you wouldn't bring a man of loose lips into my house."

Derek was a lot of things, not the least of which was a thorn in Jess's side, but he was not prone to gossip. Sometimes he wasn't even prone to finishing sentences. If he had thoughts unrelated to art and history, he'd always chosen to keep them to himself.

Until now, Jess hadn't cared what he thought about her, or at least she thought she hadn't. Faced with the vulnerability created by Ryland and the others, she had to admit it was one more lie she'd told herself.

CHAPTER TEN

*D*erek was having tea with the Duke and Duchess of Marshington, the duke's valet, and a reclusive country house cook who had most certainly been withholding significant information.

Jess could have—should have—prepared him for this. Obviously she wasn't the simple country lass she'd wanted him to think her, though he'd never completely believed that idea anyway. He'd known the gulf between him and her trust was wide, but he'd never imagined it so large as to provoke her keeping a secret of this magnitude.

This morning, their conversation had been almost friendly as they walked through London in the early dawn. He'd thought it was the beginning of a new direction in their partnership.

It would seem she thought otherwise. He didn't know her at all.

The people in this room, however, did, and unlike William's new wife, they had no problem talking in front of him. Derek would sit quietly and see how much he could learn.

Then he would corner Jess and demand answers for his growing list of questions. If the explanations were not forthcoming, he would walk away. He would. Art and history had frequently stolen his attention to the detriment of his awareness of place and time, but the mix of past and present he was currently walking in was an emotional torture rack.

Before he walked away, though, he'd need at least a few more details to satisfy his curiosity. Such as how Jess had come to be known as the girl in the floorboards.

The tea and biscuits made their rounds, but no one returned to the conversation. They just sipped, looking contemplatively at one another and occasionally glaring at Jess, who in turn stared into the depths of her cup.

The valet, Jeffreys, snapped a biscuit in half, breaking the tense silence with a cracking noise that only seemed to make everything heavier.

Then the duke smiled and turned to Derek.

Derek almost dropped his tea. They were supposed to be interrogating Jess so that he could learn more about her.

"Where are you from, Mr. Thornbury?"

Jess slumped lower in her chair with a heavy sigh before glaring at the duke. "Unfair."

The duchess didn't bother smothering her grin. "You brought him here."

The trepidation he'd felt on the front stoop returned as Derek took in the duke's easy posture. The eyes gave away the lack of true relaxation. They held a sharp perception that indicated he saw far more than he acknowledged.

"I'm originally from Cowley in Oxfordshire, Your Grace."

The large man waved a hand in the air as he set his teacup on a nearby table. "No need to bother with the 'Your Grace.' You may call me Marshington."

The offer was probably made to make Derek feel more at ease. It didn't.

Was he supposed to offer that the man be allowed to call him Derek? Or Thornbury? He'd rubbed shoulders with many a high-ranking man, but always in the capacity of education or work. And while this didn't quite feel social, it was hardly Derek's normal element.

"Yes." Derek swallowed, simply resolving to not call the man anything. "Thank you."

"And what do you do?" The duke picked up a biscuit and contemplated the pattern baked into the top before taking a bite.

"I teach some, but mostly I work with antiquities and art. I appraise them, catalogue them."

The duke looked around the drawing room. "Interesting. I've never had the contents appraised. Is there anything of value in here?"

Derek had been aching to look around the room but for once thought it might behoove him to give more attention to the occupants than the furnishings. This was obviously some sort of test, but one Derek had complete confidence he could pass as he gave in to the urge to look around. Statues and paintings were ever so much easier to understand than people.

Whoever had decorated the room had a keen sense of style and an eye for creating a beautiful room instead of a gallery of wealth. A Rembrandt hung on one wall beside a piece that he didn't recognize but guessed had come from a modern painter who'd studied the work of Rembrandt. The works looked good together, but one was clearly of superior quality.

Well, the quality difference was clear to Derek. Probably not so much to the rest of the people in the room.

"I would need to inspect them more closely to give you a full report, but from here I can see at least two pieces of significance."

One dark brow lifted and the man inclined his head, asking without words for Derek to elaborate.

At least in this Derek knew he could excel without bumbling. "The Rembrandt on the wall there is of great value. It's one of his few mythological pieces and quite desirable among many collectors of his work." With a hard swallow, Derek pointed toward a bronze statue on a table near the window. Even knowing that he knew what he was talking about, the unbroken attention of the duke made him nervous. "If I'm not mistaken, you've a Giambologna piece over there, possibly one of the ones he made for the Medici family. If it's genuine, you could get a great sum for it."

"It's genuine," the duke said softly. "A gift of appreciation."

With that single statement, Derek was pulled back into the mystery around him, and his heart started thundering once more. Fortunately, he'd already set his teacup on a nearby table. What sort of deed could the duke have done to merit such an expensive show of gratitude? "You must have been very helpful."

"Hmmm."

A movement in the corner of his eye caught his attention, and he turned to see Jess poised to throw a biscuit at the duke. That she would even contemplate tossing food at a man in his own house was quite the indication of their close relationship. That she would consider tossing food at a duke anywhere was quite the indication of her audacity. Just what had Derek gotten himself into?

"Where did you meet Jess?" the duke asked.

Jess groaned and bit into the biscuit instead of throwing it. "Where do you think?" she mumbled as she chewed.

"How would I know?" The duke turned narrowed eyes in her direction. "You didn't see fit to tell anyone where you were going."

"It's hardly hiding if you tell people where you are."

"And you didn't trust me to keep your secret? Try again, Jess."

As much as Derek was grateful to be freed from the direct and uncomfortable gaze of the duke, he didn't delight in the fact that it had been turned on Jess without the benefit of the veneer of charm.

He'd seen moments of vulnerability—fleeting, yes, but enough to know that she could be hurt. Something about this situation had put her at risk.

"I met her in Wiltshire," Derek said, clenching his hands in his lap to keep from fidgeting with them. He never brought attention on himself. On his knowledge and expertise, yes, but never himself. "I was working on cataloguing an estate for the Marquis of Chemsford."

The duke's attention swung back around to Derek, looking a bit more relaxed around the eyes. "The new one or the old one?"

"Wouldn't the old one have to be dead for there to be a new one?" his wife asked with a tilt of her head.

"Yes," the duke sighed, "but he could have hired Thornbury here before popping off."

It would seem dukes didn't need permission to address a person informally.

"But then he would be working for the new one, wouldn't he? He would hardly be doing a job he wasn't getting paid for."

The duke frowned at the duchess. Jess coughed and looked down into her tea, a smirk on her face. Jeffreys, who until now had been sitting silently and glaring in Jess's direction, gave a soft chuckle.

"Very well," Marshington said with an inclination of his head. "He works for the new one. Chemsford's a good man. A bit reclusive, but good."

As William hadn't volunteered to approach the duke on Derek's behalf after learning he had a painting, Derek could only assume the duke knew William by reputation or chance meeting or a habit of observing every man who came into his title.

"This estate," the duke said. "What is it called?"

"Er, um." Derek scooped up his tea and took a great swallow of it to buy a moment of time. It wasn't that he didn't know the estate's name, but it had held a great secret for the past dozen years or so, one that Jess had been a part of. It was all in the past now, but Derek didn't want to be the one to bring the old news into light if it hadn't come out already. Would naming the estate tell the duke anything about what Jess had involved herself in?

"You know where I was," Jess said. "You sent the message."

It was now Derek's turn to glare at the little woman. She really should have prepared him for this.

"Yes," the duke said, his voice even icier than his stare. "I did send the message, and you received it nearly six months later than you should have. If you had seen fit to tell me where you were going, we could have notified you as soon as we had news about your brother." He shrugged. "And as soon as he made you the target."

Jess's eyes narrowed. "Whose target?"

"Possibly everyone's. The details are murky on who truly wants what, but there's quite a bit of disagreement over what should happen with your former home."

"The palace?" Jess asked before cutting a short look Derek's way. He'd already considered she was somehow tied to the royal family based on the diary, so that wasn't news.

"The country," the duke corrected. "Nicolas emerged after the war and declared himself the rightful king and stated that Verbonne should be its own sovereign nation again. Others disagree. Some say the land is unstable and should be part of one of the adjoining countries. Others say it should be sovereign but that your brother shouldn't rule it. There is a great deal of closed-door political wrangling, and we aren't even sure who all the players are."

"What does that have to do with Jess?" Derek couldn't stop himself from asking, then wished he hadn't, because the question drew not only the duke's attention but everyone else's.

"Because Nicolas told everyone that she was in possession of the proof of his lineage. He said the queen had written a diary about her escape and where she'd hidden the heart of Verbonne, and it proved Nicolas is the heir of the last ruling monarch." The duke slid his narrowed gaze from Derek back to Jess. "A diary I wasn't aware existed."

"Hardly the point at the moment," Jess murmured.

"Debatable," the duke answered. "He's implied that you are holding the proof, which is supposedly some artifact of great value, but you won't come out of hiding until he is safely on the throne and able to offer you stability. He's talked this up so much that the other powers in this matter have told him to produce something of substance or step aside. The time limit they've given him is only a month away.

"If someone else manages to produce the diary or some other convincing artifact other than the ones Napoleon stole, they'll have a strong claim that they should control Verbonne and its port."

That certainly would make Jess a target. Derek swallowed and slid a hand over his side, where the weight of the diary in his jacket pocket suddenly felt much more significant.

Everyone was silent for a moment, then the duke said, "You have questions."

"Yes," Jess said in a near whisper. "Many."

"So do I."

Jess flattened her mouth into a grim line. "At the moment, the most important one is whether or not they know where I am."

"No. Even if someone knows who you are and that I didn't actually find you in a French general's trunk, you'd be difficult to trace. The War Office wasn't told you came to work for me. The official record has you moving to the border of Scotland after you healed. The fact that someone is searching up there now is why I don't have more information. I've been discreet in whom I've chosen to talk to. The man who saw you in Marlborough, though, wasn't one of mine. He's never been known to have qualms about selling to the highest bidder."

Jess nodded and straightened her spine before setting her cup on the table and staring down the duke with a coolness that matched his own. "Perhaps we should forgo the interrogation, then, and set about finding the painting."

One dark eyebrow lifted. "You don't think the diary is the artifact in question?"

"No." Jess took a deep breath and let it out in a long rush. "I think it tells us where it's hidden."

Derek wanted to grab Jess and shake her, to scream at the room in general that he had questions as well, and the main one consisted of what in the world was going on here. He wanted to toss the diary in Jess's lap and walk out the door. He wanted to have never learned what little he had, because the seriousness before him indicated that the danger was very real.

She'd said the fate of a country rested on it. She hadn't been exaggerating.

The duke's gaze narrowed. "No more disappearing, Jess. You're a woman of honor, and I'll be having your word before we go another step. You will never disappear again. I didn't save your life only for you to throw it away by being stubborn."

"You have my word," Jess bit out. "But I'll have a promise from you as well."

The duke, who looked far more comfortable with his threatening coldness than Jess did, took a sip of tea and lifted his eyebrows. "You may request one, of course, but you'll not force a promise from me." He set the cup aside. "And should your life or person be in danger, that promise becomes void."

Jess knotted the fingers of one hand together but otherwise remained still. "You have a daughter. A wife. A title. I want you to promise me that you will protect them before protecting me."

He gave a small, sharp nod.

"I don't mean mere physical protection," Jess added.

"I know," the duke said quietly. "You don't want me to participate in this little search of yours."

"If they manage to find my path, my association with you will be old and cold, just as I intended it to be. You will be watched but safe. *They* will be safe. Don't jeopardize that."

Derek was very glad he was sitting down as his legs went numb. Jess had put a contingency plan in place three years ago? Clearly her past was a great deal larger than she was, and this task was a great deal more important than he'd considered.

The duke watched Jess silently for another moment, then turned to his wife and held out his hand to her. She took it and squeezed before giving a small smile in return.

Derek looked away from the intimate moment. There'd been nothing untoward about it, but it seemed like he'd just witnessed an entire private conversation. What would it be like to know someone that well? To be known that well? He'd always been something of an enigma, even among his friends and colleagues and especially his family. It hadn't made him lonely, but it was rare that he was truly understood.

"I'll agree to stay out of it to a point," the duke said.

"Ryland," Jess growled, adding one more brick to the crushing weight of questions in Derek's mind. She was referring to the duke by his Christian name. How? Why?

"I'll stay here." The duke held up both hands in a motion of surrender, even though it seemed very much like he was determining his own conditions. "But I want to help you. If I am in possession of one of these paintings you need to see, it stands to reason that the rest of them are in places as impossible to reach. I can open doors for you."

"They. Come. First," Jess said, mouth flattened into a firm line and arms crossed over her chest. She was half the width of the duke and could maybe poke him in the shoulder if she reached high and stood on her toes, but she met him glare for glare.

He gave a sharp nod. "They come first."

Jeffreys, who had been silent while steadily working his way through a plate of biscuits, said, "That's it? A few glares and a promise and we're going to forgive her for slipping away like a thief in the night?"

"You have a better idea?" the duchess asked.

"We should get an apology dinner or at least a tea," the wiry man grumbled.

"Make her pay her penance in the kitchen?" the duchess asked. "I do like the sound of that."

"Her *coq au vin* is fabulous," Derek said, before remembering he intended to stay as silent as possible.

Three shocked faces swung his direction while Jess stared up at the ceiling. "I thought you hated that dish," she said.

"It wasn't hard to see that you stopped cooking anything I complimented." It had been embarrassingly obvious, actually. He'd then begun grumbling about his favorite dishes so they appeared more often.

"She's cooked for you?" Jeffreys asked in clear astonishment.

Derek rubbed one hand over his leg in discomfort as he looked around the room. The grim, serious expressions had all been replaced with curiosity. Hadn't Jess been the cook here? Hadn't it been the same friendly connection between master and servant that she had at Haven Manor?

It would seem not. Then again, if he'd learned anything this morning it was that assuming he knew anything about Jess was dangerous. He cleared his throat. "She's the cook for Chemsford's estate."

The duke laughed. A deep, full laugh that had him bending forward to brace against his knees. "You've spent the past three years in a kitchen?"

"Yes. No." Jess sighed. "It's complicated. Can we look for the painting now?"

The duke was still grinning as he nodded. "Of course. Hopefully it's here and not down at Marshington Abbey. What painting is it?"

"We don't know," Jess grumbled, inspiring another chuckle from the duke.

"Makes it harder," he said.

As the conversation was shifting back to the actual art, Derek felt a bit more confident in speaking up. "We're looking for a painting by a Verbonnian painter, one who was part of a group called The Six."

"So you're looking for a painting, but you don't know what it's called, what it looks like, or even who painted it?" The duke looked from Jess to Derek and back again. "How in the world are we supposed to find that?"

Jess beamed at Derek, nearly sending him into shock all over again. She'd never given him a smile like that before. He'd never seen her give anyone a smile like that. "We use him."

CHAPTER ELEVEN

I can't quite decide if I'm fascinated, bored, or questioning everything I ever thought about myself," Ryland whispered to Jess as they strolled through yet another room in Montgomery House, watching Derek examine the paintings.

Jess wanted to admonish him but she couldn't, as she had been battling the same thing. Yes, she still found Derek's wealth of knowledge and ability to know absolutely everything an incredible annoyance, but if she looked past that, his obsessive enthusiasm became just a bit . . . endearing. The fact that he hadn't run screaming from the house after everything he'd heard in the drawing room probably had a little to do with her softening attitude.

Several paces ahead of them, Derek motioned to yet another painting, telling Miranda about the artist and the circumstances being depicted. He hadn't known every painting they'd passed, of course, but he'd known enough. Miranda made admiring, polite noises of interest as any well-trained lady would.

That type of polite diplomacy was something Jess had never learned. Mama's attempts to teach deportment and etiquette had been difficult to take seriously with thirteen people squeezed into a four-room cottage and a barn.

"Do you think she's actually listening?" Jess asked.

Ryland winced. "Enough to subject me to a torturous discussion about it later tonight."

"Does that mean you should be listening so you can partici-pate?" Jess really hoped not. If Ryland felt the need to close the gap growing between him and the art discussion, Jess would have to follow.

"No. She'll find it much more enjoyable if I have to pull answers from my imagination."

Jess laughed. "She'll find it ten times more irritating, you mean."

He shrugged. "Then I'll find it more enjoyable."

They walked along in silence until the group climbed the stairs to the first floor. Halfway up, Jess paused, staring at the wood grain of the polished banister railing. "How did my brother survive, Ryland? I saw that man's face that night. I felt his anger. He had no intention of leaving anyone in my family alive."

"No, he didn't." Ryland guided Jess the rest of the way up the stairs but paused in the gallery at the top. "Somehow in the course of that evening, one of the servants was mistaken for Nicolas. We don't know if he lived long enough to proclaim his innocence, but if he did, his captors didn't believe him."

"So Nic became the servant?" Jess knew the hard work that came along with such a deception. At least she'd had the benefit of close relationships with those who'd employed her. How had her proud brother survived it?

"Yes," Ryland said. "A few of the servants were interrogated and then put to work—without pay or consideration, of course, but at least they had their lives. Nicolas had the presence of mind to continue the charade after his identity was misconstrued."

The words formed on Jess's tongue to ask if Ryland knew if Ismelde had been one of those who lived, but she didn't voice the question. It was better to assume the kind German cook had somehow survived than to have it confirmed that Jess was the only one still making the woman's secret rye bread recipe.

"War and time make people forgetful," Ryland continued. "Eventually Nicolas found work at another estate. Real work. He disappeared until the war ended."

Jess frowned. It was a lovely story, one that inspired hope in the middle of the chaos war left behind, but it seemed almost too lovely. "How do they know it's really him?"

Ryland rubbed a hand along the back of his neck. "He has a documented birthmark and was questioned thoroughly when he came forward to claim the palace. I think in the end it was his ability to open the secret treasure vaults that convinced everyone."

"Not much of a secret anymore, then," Jess muttered. She knew of the vault, hidden away beneath the floor somewhere in the throne room, but she'd never been shown it. She tried to tell herself it was because she'd been so young when they departed the palace, but she didn't quite believe it. Her value had never been that great to the country.

Until now, of course. Now she was the only person who could secure the throne her father, uncle, and grandfather had dreamed of redeeming.

"Has he been looking for me?" Jess asked.

"We've fallen a bit far behind," Ryland said, taking her arm and continuing their walk down the corridor.

"Ryland," Jess said, irritation flaring. "I am not a child who needs coddling, nor an innocent who thinks the world is full of daisies and sunshine. What aren't you telling me?"

Ryland frowned. "We—that is, my contact—doesn't think Nicolas actually believes you're alive. There is no record of you from that night. It was assumed you'd died, and since we never told anyone who you really are, that assumption held. Your unconfirmed fate allowed him to make claims about you and buy some time. He's been making gestures toward setting up a government but has also spent time scouring the palace."

"He's looking for the diary," she murmured, trying to keep her thoughts practical. Nicolas would have mourned her death long ago just as she had mourned his, assuming a single survival was an utter miracle. If she'd had an inkling that her brother might be alive, though, Jess would have done everything she could to find him.

"He's more likely looking for something that would pass for

the artifact itself," Ryland said. "He has a month left to produce what he claims is the key Verbonnian tradition and legend. He's put such effort into convincing everyone of the importance of the land's legends that if someone else can produce something related to them, they'll probably be able to claim the throne."

Jess's skin itched at the implications. Her entire life, there'd been someone else who wanted the throne and wanted it badly, claiming they were the true inheriting bloodline. If they were still alive, they would certainly attempt to claim it now.

What if there was another guide, one that was less cryptic than the diary? Queen Marguerite hadn't laid her clues in isolation. If those other persons were traveling the same path, searching the same areas, Jess's anonymity and years of remaining unseen might not be enough to protect her.

For that matter, someone else might actually know what was at the end of this hunt. The heart of Verbonne could be any number of things.

Every answer she found just made this situation more complicated.

Ryland stumbled to a halt as they turned a corner and found Derek studying the corner of a painting.

"Is that it?" Ryland asked.

Derek glanced at them and then back to the painting. Miranda's look was longer and a great deal more accusatory.

"No," Derek said, "but it's fascinating. I've never seen this signature before. I want to look it up later."

"Shouldn't he be in a hurry to find this painting?" Ryland asked Jess in a rough whisper.

"Trust me," Jess answered on a sigh. "For him this is quick."

A low chuckle shook Ryland's shoulders. "Given all the times you foiled my plans by barreling in and doing it your own way, it's rather lovely to see it happen to you."

Jess coughed. "Since when do you use the word *lovely*?"

"Since I became a stodgy old duke, settled in his business and homes, and, apparently, incapable of handling matters of secrecy and danger. I had no idea a man could fall so far in such a short amount of time."

Jess fought the urge to groan, knowing any reaction from her would just encourage him to air his soreness over her betrayal—or what he saw as her betrayal. She had meant it as a gift and still considered it as such, particularly given recent events. Her danger and risk had been removed from his family. It had also been removed from Ryland's control, which was, of course, the thing he couldn't quite stomach.

Still, it wouldn't hurt him to appreciate her intentions.

Finally, Derek moved on, gazing longingly at a few other paintings before moving to the next room.

"Why do you have so much art?" Jess grumbled, hoping to move on from the discussion of the past.

"You think I chose any of this?" Ryland scoffed. "I couldn't care less what the walls of my houses look like." His silver-grey eyes shot Jess an assessing look. "What have you told him?"

"Less than you did." Jess wasn't looking forward to explaining away everything that had been said in the drawing room. The visit wasn't over yet either.

"Ah well." Ryland gave an exaggerated sigh. "I suppose it's easy to forget a person's preferences if you don't see them for three years."

"It's done, Ryland," Jess said flatly. She refused to consider how it could have been different. If she opened the door to guilt and shame and what could have been, the ensuing avalanche would bury her alive. She needed a subject enticing enough to distract Ryland. "How did you find me?"

"Billings saw you at Chemsford's wedding."

Jess thought she'd caught sight of him in the back of the church, but she'd hoped he wouldn't recognize her, since the last time they'd seen each other she'd been spouting German and working in a tavern. To say Billings was willing to sell information to the highest bidder, though, was an understatement. "I can't believe you trusted Billings enough to tell him you were looking for me."

"I didn't. He mentioned it in passing. Didn't even realize he was in possession of valuable information."

Well, there was that at least.

"I must confess," Ryland continued, "I was surprised you stayed that close to London."

She was, too. Her original intention had been to go to Ireland, but then she'd stumbled across Kit in a London back alley, holding off a group of drunken gentlemen with nothing but her wits. Jess, with a bit more than wits at her disposal, had stepped in to even the odds. When Jess had offered to teach the other woman a few defensive tactics, Kit had offered a new destination, a refuge from everyone she'd ever known.

What was supposed to have been a few months' stay in order to teach another woman how to walk safely in the shadows had turned into three years.

It would have been longer if Ryland's letter hadn't arrived. It was possible Jess would never have left.

After this was over, there'd be no reason for her to hide anymore, though. Her life would be wide open.

How terrifying.

There was always the chance she might not survive, of course. The fact that such a consideration made her less afraid, instead of more afraid, proved just how scrambled her head was.

"Years ago," Ryland said, breaking Jess from her memories, "you refused to let me handle a situation alone when someone threatened the new life I was trying to build." He stopped and curled his hands over her shoulders, dipping his head to look her in the eye. It was the position he took when he was moving from friend to mentor. "I told you to let me go alone and you didn't listen. If you had, Miranda and I might both be dead. You were right then."

Jess released the breath she'd been holding as she braced for the censure that usually came with his shift in attitude. Confirmation of her actions was a surprise.

"This time, you're wrong."

Ah, there it was.

Ryland squeezed her shoulders until Jess was forced to look up at him or challenge him to put enough pressure to cause a bruise. "This time *I* am right, and I refuse to let you go alone."

"I'm not alone," Jess said, forcing a jaunty smile. "I've got the brains of Derek Thornbury."

They both paused and looked across the room, listening to Derek's speculation on the origin of one of Ryland's tapestries.

"If nothing else," Ryland said wryly, "you'll be able to pull out your knives while he talks your adversary into a stupor."

"They use silk to create the depth against the wool," Derek said, pointing to an area of the tapestry.

"Is he always like this?" Ryland asked in a toneless whisper as they approached the wall hanging.

Jess gave him a wide-eyed look. "You have no idea."

Derek shot them a look that proved he wasn't as ignorant of their conversation as Jess had thought. "That's why I'm here." He ran a hand along the side of the tapestry. "If you knew everything I knew, you wouldn't need me."

"You only have a month," Ryland said.

"I know," Derek returned, looking at Jess instead of the duke. "But at the moment I'm still deciding if lending you the use of my brain is worth the danger that comes along for my person."

He didn't wait for an answer before moving back into the corridor to continue his search.

Ryland chuckled as he fell into step behind the art historian.

"Why are you laughing?" Jess huffed.

"He's a good fit for you."

"What?"

Ryland shrugged, his attention seeming divided as they were now standing in closer proximity to his wife. The large man always looked a bit like a puppy when he watched his wife.

Jess shook her head. "You think because you found a normal person who could handle your crazy past, the rest of us will be able to as well." She grinned at his lovesick expression. "I never thought you a romantic."

He folded his hands at his back and gave another shrug. "I don't think it's about romance so much as living life. I've learned a lot about doing that the past few years. Have you?"

As much as Jess wanted to dismiss his statement as the ramblings of a man suddenly luxuriating in a life of leisure, she couldn't. Haven Manor, Daphne, Kit, and even the children and Martha's burnt bread had shown Jess what it meant to care about people who had nothing to offer in return except their own regard. There was no hiding behind practicalities, no lies to tell herself.

That was why she'd stayed, even when the house was no longer a hidden refuge.

Was that what living was? Putting yourself and others at risk because you couldn't bear to lose them? Did Ryland consider that love?

If so, love was foolish and selfish, and Jess had been smart to leave Ryland and Jeffreys and the rest of them three years ago. The war was over—or at least everyone had thought it was—and the people who had hunted her and her family down would have been free to return to England. As the visible maid of a powerful man, her position had held too much risk of exposure. Remaining in London would have been tempting fate.

Just like staying at Haven Manor had been. She hadn't been willing to put herself through the turmoil again, though, couldn't rip herself away from her friends. They'd needed her at Haven Manor in a way Ryland, Jeffreys, and the others never had.

That was selfish thinking, though, wasn't it? Staying because being needed felt good, even if it meant she spent all day every day in the kitchen.

Did that mean she'd cared more for the people she'd left in London than the people she'd stayed with in Marlborough?

It was a conundrum that made her head spin.

"'Look not every man on his own things, but every man also on the things of others,'" Ryland said.

Jess dropped her gaze to her toes to avoid the urge to glare and sigh. She'd understood and even encouraged Ryland's frequent

Bible quotations and prayers during the war. All she'd had to do was look around her to know they desperately needed God to intervene. The matter before them now was certainly serious, but it wasn't anything they couldn't handle yet.

She was saved from having to come up with a response when Derek stopped at the door to the duke and duchess's private parlor, a look of awe and reverence on his face as he swiped his hair back from his forehead.

"We've found it," he said quietly before his mouth curved into a large grin.

CHAPTER TWELVE

*D*erek had seen a great deal of art in his lifetime. Paintings, sculptures, tapestries, anything people made to commemorate moments both significant and mundane had filled his life.

Never had he seen anything like this.

The paintings of Fournier and his students had always given him pause, though he'd had few occasions to see them in person. The first time he'd seen a painting by one of The Six, he'd stared for a full twenty minutes in awed silence. There was such depth and life to their work.

Before him now was a prime example of the masterful wielding of an art brush that had marveled many an art scholar. Beyond the skill, though, beyond the technique, there was something *more*.

His hip bumped the doorframe as he stumbled into the room, not even looking around to see what room he was entering. All he could see was the painting. Even blinking was an irritation.

A young woman stood on a cluster of rocks, flat and wide with grooves worn from the trails of the tide, a thick wall that had been built in an attempt to tame the sea and only partially succeeded. Water sprayed around her as the waves crashed against the wall. Beyond the wall, a single rock formation jutted out into an ocean roiling with turmoil and chaos. Dark clouds stretched to the horizon, a storm powerful enough to stir the sea into a cauldron of fury.

The image was so real, so alive, that Derek had to resist the urge to wipe his brow and clear it of salt spray.

Whether it was moments or hours before someone cleared their throat and broke his reverie, he didn't know. He blinked and pulled his gaze from the painting to look around at the rest of the party.

Beside him stood the duchess, the epitome of quiet ladylike grace she'd been throughout the tour of the house. The duke stood on her other side, looking a bit softer than he had in the drawing room but no doubt still as lethal. He possessed a leashed power one would have to be an idiot to miss.

Derek wasn't an idiot. He swallowed and shifted his head in the other direction, seeking out Jess, expecting her to be looking at him with that same hint of condescension she'd frequently worn at Haven Manor, or perhaps the quiet curiosity of her aristocratic friends.

He found neither.

She was, without question, deeply affected by what she was viewing. Awe filled her features along with a sign of sadness. There was something incredibly despondent about the woman on the rock wall as she looked out across the tumultuous water. Perhaps Jess was beginning to see the power of art, the way a picture could transport a person in the way a history book never could.

"Is this the painting, then?" The duke's quiet voice startled Derek, and he turned to find the duke had moved to a spot just beyond Derek's shoulder, forcing him to look up to see the other man's profile.

"Er, yes, Your Grace, this is it." Derek resisted the urge to wipe his palms on his trousers. Some of the powerful men he'd worked with in the past had been terrifying and unbalanced. They never made him as nervous as the combination of intimidating duke, tenuous situation, and mysterious woman.

"Good," the duke said with a nod. "This has always been one of my favorites."

"You have exquisite taste," Derek murmured, cringing a bit at the inanity of such a phrase.

What should he do now? He'd brought the diary, afraid something would happen to it if he left it at Chemsford's, including Jess sneaking into his room to take it back and leave him out of everything. A small sketchbook remained in his other pocket, part of the reason he always had his coats cut a shy too large. What should he do with them, though? Pull out the diary and find the appropriate passage for a comparison? Sketch the essence of the painting so he and Jess could discuss it later? Both?

He glanced to Jess for direction. Until that moment, his knowledge and abilities had given him the upper hand in this adventure, but he hadn't the first idea how to move forward in the actual hunt.

Jess was still staring at the painting, but her face had changed. Gone was the raw emotion of earlier. Now her features were smooth and blank, as if she herself had become polished marble.

Derek moved to her side, close enough that their sleeves brushed as they breathed. He tilted his head a bit closer and pitched his voice low. "Are you all right?"

His voice broke her trance, and she blinked rapidly before turning in his direction. In a raspy, thick voice, she asked, "Why aren't you telling us about it?"

Why wasn't he . . . was she serious? Did she not understand the importance of this moment? This wasn't just Derek telling someone about the art they owned. This painting had been created with some greater purpose in mind, giving the viewing of it a very weighty significance. Here was the first step toward the hidden treasure indicated in the diary.

Until now it had all been hypothetical.

He'd accepted that the danger was real, but until he'd seen this painting he hadn't been sure that the treasure hunt was. Walking away from everything was no longer an option he could even pretend to entertain. History was speaking directly to them. There would never be another chance to experience something like this.

Going into it blind wasn't an option, though. He wanted to continue experiencing mundane moments that might pale in significance to this one but would signify that he was still among the living.

"We're going to have a conversation later, you and I," Derek said quietly, "about what we will and will not share. So you can be prepared, the only answer I intend to accept is sharing everything. I'll not be walking into another situation already back on my heels."

Jess lifted a haughty eyebrow in his direction. "I'm sure I don't know what you mean."

Derek shrugged. "I assumed you wouldn't want to have this conversation here, as you obviously have a relationship with the duke—one you chose not to disclose, by the way—but if you'd rather discuss it now, I'll defer to your wishes. We're among *your* friends, after all."

A low chuckle came from behind them. Derek glanced over his shoulder to find the duke grinning.

The wide, tooth-baring grin was nearly as frightening as his earlier scowl.

Derek pulled the diary from his jacket. A few translation notes jutted from between the pages and caught on the rough wool. After a bit of shifting, he opened to the passage he thought matched the painting. "I believe this is one of the earliest paintings described. She never calls them by name, but she's incredibly descriptive in the subject matter, methods, and materials."

There were a few ocean paintings described in the first part of the book, discussing the mix of colors and angle of strokes needed to create proper water. The seventh passage, though, was different. It discussed how to create the depth and turmoil of a stormy sea, but there was more than just the details. "There's a shift in her manner when she describes this one as opposed to the ones before it."

He turned another page and pulled out the translation notes he'd tucked inside. "I believe this goes along with the opening passage, the one we read at the house. 'She looks toward the secret passage that will one day be opened; hope is her beacon in the storm that surrounds her. Where she leads, the worthy will follow until they have all they need to right the wrongs of the past.'"

"It's a map." The duke's voice held an element of surprise as he looked from the diary to the painting to Jess to Derek.

"What?" Derek looked up from his notes and at the painting. Was there an image within it that he hadn't seen? Something that would help them finish the clue in the diary?

"It says she's looking toward the secret passage, so it must be in that direction, right?" The duke pointed to the wall beyond the frame.

It was the most literal consideration for the meaning of the words, which was never a bad place to start when interpreting old texts. "Possibly," Derek said quietly, "but if it is a map I haven't any idea how to read it. She's looking toward hope. Perhaps if we knew where she was, we would know where she looked. Could the paintings indicate an actual path we are supposed to take?"

"It's the ocean," the duke muttered. "That could be anywhere."

"I know where it is," said a small voice that Derek could only attribute to Jess by process of elimination and direction.

He looked up from the diary, surprised to see her looking as small as she'd sounded. The woman had always been short in stature, her head just barely grazing Derek's shoulder. Despite her size, she'd never looked like she believed herself to be tiny.

"I can't do this." She whispered so quietly he could barely make out the words.

"I don't think I've ever heard that word come out of your mouth," the duke said, moving around to stand on her other side.

She glanced in his direction, and a ghost of a smile curved her lips. "Yes, you have. Mostly when I'm telling you that you can't stop me."

"True," he said with a nod. "And if I can't stop you, this hundred-year-old painting shouldn't either."

Derek coughed. "One hundred fifty-six."

"What?" the duke and Jess asked at the same time.

"The painting." Derek nodded toward the wall. "It's one

hundred fifty-six years old." He held up the diary. "According to this, at least."

"Right," Jess said.

Derek cleared his throat. "You know this setting?"

She nodded. "It's the coast of Verbonne."

"The Verbonne coastline is made up almost entirely of the port of Mermaison. The rest is pure white sand." Derek frowned. "A rock formation such as that one would wreak havoc with a port area."

"It's behind the Royal Palace," Jess said. "There were more rocks in the area, but they dug them out and used them to build the palace." She nodded at the painting. "And the wall. You have to go through the private gardens and take a short trail down to sea level."

Derek closed the diary and ran a hand over the royal crest on the front. Hearing Jess casually mention her connection to royalty still knocked him a bit sideways.

Jess took a deep, shaky breath, but her words didn't waver when she spoke again. "I was standing in that same place the first time I heard the story. She's looking toward England."

⁂

"Finally ready to admit that you are a member of the royal family?" Derek asked in his matter-of-fact, I-know-everything-and-will-find-out-what-I-don't voice.

Jess really hated that voice.

Not quite as much as she hated how much of herself she was going to have to reveal, though. It would seem the stories had been true. The queens had taken an essential piece of Verbonne's sovereignty with them and didn't want anyone not connected with the royal family or at least the old government to find it. That was what was meant by *worthy*.

It didn't seem the most apt definition of the word.

"I am not royal." That was true, so far as it went. She hadn't really been considered royal, even though she lived in the family

127

wing of the royal palace. Her uncle was the king, but he'd moved his extended family into the palace after the French revolution, for fear that similar sentiments would leak over the border of his beloved little country.

Jess had been born within those walls, and they were all she knew until even that safe haven was threatened.

"I'm not royal," Jess repeated, "but she is."

She pointed to the woman in the painting. Jess had never seen this painting before, never even heard of it, but she'd seen the woman. That same woman, dressed in that same dress and with the same ring of flowers in her hair, hung in the portrait gallery of the palace.

"That's Queen Jessamine. I was named after her." And she'd grown up with stories of her namesake uttered in reverent tones normally reserved for saints and war heroes. "It was when Leopold the First was the Holy Roman Emperor. His power was lessening by then, but he still had enough to take over Verbonne. She ran away with the heart of Verbonne, or so the stories go. He might take over the land, but he wouldn't take over the soul."

"That's when Fournier and his students fled the country," Derek said. "In Fournier's painting, their departure is in the dead of night, and they're wrapped in fishing nets."

Jess nodded. "It wasn't only one fishing boat, though. There were four that left Verbonne that morning, all to convene at the larger ship anchored near that rock outcrop, away from all the normal water traffic."

"Four boats?" Derek frowned. "But his painting shows him and what is assumed to be The Six huddled in one boat."

"I suppose art isn't always an accurate representation, then. Or perhaps the stories designed to ignite the passion from one generation to the next aren't accurate." She shrugged. "Maybe both."

Jess took a deep breath. She could do this. She could separate her family's ancient history from the father who'd told it to her. These were the stories of people long dead and a country she didn't really know. It should be easy to disconnect them from the man who'd told her bedtime stories, showed her the stars, and used his last breath of freedom to shove her to safety.

She would keep to the facts, or what she'd been told were facts, and stay far away from anything she'd actually experienced.

"Queen Jessamine fled and took much of the royal family with her, including the king's mother and the young prince." It was so similar to her own story, with all of the family retreating to the farm, leaving King Gerard behind to govern the country alone. Unlike her uncle, though, King Nicolas, whom Jess's brother had been named after, hadn't been able to rejoin his family, even for a while.

There were those who believed that the queen had been with child when she left that night, but no one knew for certain. Jess glanced at the diary. Did the book say? Would she find that the people who had hunted her family down, stating they had the true right to the throne, had a valid claim after all?

She kept that part of the story to herself. It wasn't relevant to the hunt.

"She sent word back to her husband with instructions on how to send for her once it was safe to return. It took years, but King Nicolas finally came to an agreement with the emperor. The king was left as little more than the caretaker of Verbonne. He sent word for his wife to return, but it was too late.

"His mother wrote back with the news that Queen Jessamine and their young son had died. Later, she sent him the diary, saying she still believed that Verbonne would return to glory and that one day someone would come retrieve the heart of Verbonne. At least we think that's what she said. The king burned the letter before hiding the diary."

Jess could almost hear her father saying the words, embellishing the tale with colorful descriptions of life before he'd been born to see it. "The king married again, determined to continue the line in hopes that one day Verbonne would be restored as an independent nation. He told no one of the diary save his eldest son, but he spread tales of his wife's heroism everywhere.

"That line continued until my uncle. His sons were very young as war knocked on Verbonne's borders once more in the form of Napoleon. So he told his brother of the diary, and he, in turn, told all of his children, since they had no idea who would manage to survive the war they knew was coming."

Jess stopped talking there, allowing her companions to draw the conclusion that she was one of the children raised on the story of the brave queen and the diary and a legacy passed down through the blood of generations. Raised on the idea of a country she could barely remember, let alone feel connected to.

Even though Jess hadn't shared anything personal about herself, she felt raw and exposed. Ryland knew some of it, of course, as he'd been sent to rescue them before Napoleon's men could find them. The dissolution of even the semblance of the Holy Roman Empire had left all of Europe vulnerable. England had been hoping to maintain access to the port of Verbonne through the king.

Derek held up the diary. "What is this a map to, then?"

"If I had to guess," Jess said, "it shows where Queen Jessamine hid the coronation bowl. Evrart the Wanderer had the bowl made soon after establishing his kingdom. In the center is the waterstone."

"That must be what Nicolas claims will prove he's the true king," Ryland said. "He's been ripping apart the palace, hoping to find something that hasn't been there in a hundred years." He glanced in Derek's direction. "Sorry. One hundred fifty-six."

Jess shook her head. "We'd always assumed the heart of Verbonne was the young prince. We had no idea it was the coronation bowl. I always thought that was tucked away in the secret vault."

"What is the waterstone?" Derek asked.

"A large opal said to have been pulled from the mouth of the spring that Evrart stood by when he claimed the land."

Derek frowned. "That's not where people find opals."

Jess shrugged. "I don't think legends much care about that. The old law stated that the king must be anointed by water that has rolled over the waterstone, and any party of royal lineage that is in possession of the bowl at the time of coronation becomes the rightful king."

CHAPTER THIRTEEN

*P*art of the reason Fournier's and his student's work was so mesmerizing to Derek, beyond their incredible skill, was the mystery surrounding them. Much of what Jess was now telling him had never made it into a history book, and he had to resist the instinct to write it all down and press her for more details.

Had the queen mother been one of the painters? He glanced at the roiling ocean on the wall. Had she painted that? Were other royal family members part of The Six?

He could spend weeks, months, possibly even years digging into all the nuances of what had happened, taking what Jess knew of her family history and matching it to fragments of other known events, but right now, moving forward was possibly more important than understanding the past. Except understanding the past was the only way to move forward. It was rather a conundrum.

"When did your father give you the diary?" Derek wanted—needed—to understand more fully how Jess herself fit into this picture. Not for the sake of the hunt, obviously, since the long-dead diary writer would have no way of knowing which ancestor would be charged with interpreting her clues, but for his own peace of mind.

"Before he died."

Derek gritted his teeth and counted to ten.

"If you're going to dole out information at that rate," the duke said with a shake of his head, "I'll have rooms made up for you."

"We have rooms," Jess said, crossing her arms over her chest and glaring up at the duke. "At Chemsford's."

The duke grinned again, making Derek squirm at the way the man's happiness seemed tinged with threat, as if knowing that he was about to win a battle was the only thing that made him giddy. "Chemsford doesn't have your trunk."

"He will once you send it to him," Jess returned.

"You know me better than that."

The duchess appeared next to her husband, looping her arm into his. Derek glanced to where she'd been earlier. How had she moved so quickly and silently?

The duke gave a small grunt and then turned to his wife, his face softening instantly. "Did you pinch me?"

"Why didn't you tell me she was a princess?" the duchess hissed.

"Because she's not," the duke returned in a whisper that was anything but quiet. "She's a duchess."

"I wasn't even that," Jess said with a roll of her eyes. "My mother was a duchess. I was a lady, though I doubt I'm even that anymore." She shrugged. "Whatever state the country is in now, it's not the same one I left. I think, for now, I'll stay the farm girl from France who spent a bit of time as your parlormaid."

Normally, Derek did quite well with silence, retreating into his brain to think, but the quiet that filled the private parlor now was the sort that demanded one pay attention, even though it seemed nothing was happening.

With this group, something was probably always happening.

Even now as Jess and the duke did nothing but breathe in each other's general direction, Derek suspected a silent war was raging between them. Jess broke eye contact first, so he had to assume she'd lost whatever argument they were having.

She turned to him, that golden gaze looking shuttered. "I understand if you want out. If you could leave whatever translation notes you've completed, I would appreciate it."

"This bowl," Derek said, ignoring her offer, "whoever has it becomes the king of Verbonne? A true king, ruling over a free nation? Everyone has agreed to that?"

"If Nicolas has convinced them to uphold the old laws from the country's prior freedom, yes. Possession of the bowl and the stone would be strong argument in that person's favor, particularly if they could prove a royal blood connection."

"That could lure a lot of people," Derek muttered.

Jess looked to the duke. "How many claims have been made?"

"Only two that carry any weight. Both are claiming they can produce proof, but Nicolas is the only one with known lineage."

The nod Jess gave indicated she wasn't surprised by such a thing. "For the past hundred years there have been grumblings of another heir, the rightful king. Proof was never given, but the line has been a continual problem for Verbonne's royal family."

There was more to what she was saying, Derek knew, because her mouth tightened at the corners just a bit. She didn't volunteer it, though, and Derek didn't know what question to ask to get her to share.

"No one has seen the bowl since the night of the Great Flight. If someone possesses it, they will be able to say it's passed through their line—a claim that would be difficult to refute." Jess's face was grim.

This mattered. This hunt, the results, deciphering the clues, the pictures, all of it mattered. One day, there would be paintings made of the coronation of the new king of Verbonne. Assuming there was a new king, of course, and another country didn't swallow the land at the end of a month's time.

Derek could be a part of that. How often did a man get to do something that would have lasting, true historical significance?

And if it came to light that Jess and her brother were, in fact, the imposters and the other line was the rightful one? Having an uninvolved third party along to verify the validity of the clues would ensure everything turned out as it should, right?

In two hundred years, someone might be reading about him or seeing him in a painting. That was a seductive idea indeed.

That was also a great risk. History was filled with people who had been caught up in the idea of power and legacy only to have it go horribly wrong.

As long as he remained aware and alert, he could make sure any painting depicting him down the road wouldn't tell a cautionary tale but a heroic one.

He took out his sketchbook and began to draw. "We don't know yet how these paintings fit together or if there's some sort of symbolism, so I'll make a sketch for future reference."

"What about the rest of the paintings?" the duchess asked.

"The earliest accounts of paintings by The Six had them, for the most part, in a single collection. They were meant to be looked at together." Derek sighed and brushed the hair from his forehead with an impatient swipe before he resumed drawing. "That collection was auctioned off twenty-five years ago. Unfortunately, auction houses don't give up their lists of clients easily."

"Well then," the duke said with another of those wily grins, "it's a good thing people like doing favors for dukes."

⚔⚔

With most of the world's precious art residing in the homes of the rich and powerful, Derek had been in many aristocratic homes. Certainly he'd been in enough to know that when said aristocrat wanted something done, it happened as quickly as possible.

The Duke of Marshington's servants, however, were miracle workers. How else could they have retrieved Jess and Derek's belongings from Lord Chemsford's townhome before the duke and his unexpected company were able to finish their late breakfast? Derek didn't even want to think about how the servants had managed to convince William to let them take everything.

After the meal, which was a combination of idle chatter that seemed to veil more serious statements and awkward silence, Derek was shown to a room, told to be dressed in his nicest day clothes and ready to go to the auction house at two, and then left to his own devices.

Any remaining wavering thoughts were silenced by the time he pulled on the only coat he'd had cut to truly fit his frame and left the room. The risk was worth it. If he didn't take it, he'd always wonder. The chances of Jess succeeding in finding the bowl within a month without his assistance were slim. Derek couldn't risk being the reason a country, a culture, ceased to exist. Jess didn't have to know that he intended to discover who the rightful heir should be as they went along. She wasn't the only one capable of keeping secrets.

She might have agreed to tell him everything, but Derek wasn't foolish enough to believe she actually intended to do so.

The duke was waiting in the front hall, the classic, utilitarian lines of his earlier riding clothes exchanged for the fine tailoring and dashing impressiveness of a perfectly made suit of clothing. A diamond pin sparkled from the center of his cravat, and a jewel-encrusted cane rested against his leg as he pulled on a pair of pristine white gloves. Jeffreys draped a many-caped greatcoat across the duke's shoulders, completing the transformation.

Beside him stood a young servant lad, dressed in neat, simple clothing very similar to the valet's, if a bit loose. Likely, the clothing had been inherited from another servant and the boy hadn't yet grown into it completely.

Derek narrowed his eyes as the servant handed the duke his hat. "Good afternoon, Jess."

Her head tilted up immediately, revealing a face that was neither masculine nor adolescent but was heavily shaded by the brim of a cap set over some sort of dark-haired wig. Pale eyes narrowed at him, but she didn't say anything.

The duke chuckled. "Perfect fit," he said as he situated his hat upon his head before gesturing toward the door with his glittering cane. "Shall we?"

The three piled into a waiting carriage, Jess taking the seat facing backward, the way an actual servant would do if riding within the carriage. It was a wonder she hadn't climbed atop the roof or held on to the back to extend the ruse.

At the auctioneer's office, the duke breezed right past the servant attempting to welcome them and take their coats.

"I never trust my coat to a servant I don't know," the duke said in a snotty tone, followed by a short, sharp sniff of disapproval. "I brought my own coatrack." With that, he plopped his hat onto Jess's head, further obscuring anyone's attempt at seeing her face, and draped his coat over her outstretched arms. "You may take my companion's coat, though. He is less fastidious than I am."

Derek shrugged out of his coat and gave it to the waiting servant, pretending he didn't notice the fine trembling in the man's hand and the furtive looks in the duke's direction.

Mr. Ashley, the auctioneer, was more than happy to have a duke of wealth, power, and reputation in his office. "What a pleasant surprise, Your Grace," he said, bowing a bit too low and smiling a bit too wide. "What can I do for you?"

The duke sniffed again and tilted his nose in the air. "I have decided I need a theme—I say, boy, you're to stand within my sight at all times, but not at such proximity that I can smell the stench of your breath. Go over there." He frowned and gestured for Jess to move deeper into the room, tucking herself into a corner beside a short plant.

With a dismissive sneer, the duke turned back to the auctioneer. "As I was saying, I require a theme to my private parlor. I like consistency in my life. I have one piece of art already that I wish to use. I want to find more paintings by the artist, and this man"—he gestured in Derek's direction—"assures me that you know where they are."

Derek was going to strangle both Jess and Marshington. He didn't care if one of them was a duke. Once again he'd been plopped into a situation with no explanation, no warning, no clue of what part he was to play.

Derek smiled—not too big a smile, of course—and nodded at the auctioneer, whose returning smile looked considerably more genuine than Derek's felt.

"Tell him what I require," the duke said.

Derek blinked and maintained his fake smile until he realized Marshington had been talking to him.

Yes, Derek was definitely going to harm a duke. Hopefully there were a few nice paintings to look at in Australia.

He cleared his throat. "The painting currently in the space is by one of Fournier's students. It was bought at an auction from this house twenty-five years ago. The duke wants more of the paintings that were auctioned then."

"We don't make it a practice to hand out our auction results," Mr. Ashley said hesitantly. "I could perhaps contact them on your behalf."

The duke sneered. "If that is what we must do. Retrieve the list. I will wait."

The auctioneer's mouth dropped open a bit, but he recovered quickly. In his line of work he'd probably seen many a demanding and selfish man and learned how much he needed to give in order to keep them placated. "I can hardly contact them while you're here, Your Gra—"

"If you don't get the list," the duke bit out, revealing some of the hardness Derek had sensed in him that morning, "I won't know which paintings I desire." His lip curled into a sneer once more. "Unless you can list the items in question from memory."

"Yes, of course, Your Grace," Mr. Ashley mumbled, because really, what else was he going to do? "One moment."

The auctioneer riffled through a file cabinet, triumphantly coming up with a list nearly ten minutes later. In all that time, Jess didn't move from her position as a human coatrack. The duke moved only his head, looking about the room in disdain as he waited. It appeared to be only Derek who wanted the entire ordeal to just be over.

With the list produced, the auctioneer began to share the names of the paintings from the auction. Occasionally the duke would hold up a hand to stop the man and turn to Derek. "What do you think?"

What did he think? He thought Marshington and Jess needed

to tell him his lines if they were going to shove him into the middle of their little play. They didn't have time for the auctioneer to do the contacting for them. Besides, given the value of the paintings, one or two might be willing to sell, but the whole lot of them certainly wouldn't.

He stumbled through, keeping his answers simple: "Yes, that one would go nicely" and "While every painting by The Six is incredible, that particular one wouldn't go with the theme we're creating." It was utter nonsense, but Mr. Ashley didn't seem to notice.

"That one," the duke said suddenly, looking over Derek's shoulder.

"What?" Derek said dumbly.

"That painting," the duke said with a note of awe in his voice. "That is the look I want in my parlor. Tell me about this one." He rose and walked across the room to get closer to the painting that seemed to have fascinated him.

Derek turned in complete bafflement. The auctioneer couldn't possibly have a Verbonnian painting hanging in his office. Derek would have noticed immediately.

Looking at the painting in question didn't reduce Derek's confusion. If anything, it grew. On the wall was a painting that was not historic, important, or even all that good. Derek had to look at the corner to distinguish the artist because it was so similar to other works of the same nature. Still, he started saying things about painting in general that would apply to the work, hoping it sounded impressive.

"Not you," the duke growled. "Him." He pointed to the auctioneer and waved the man over. "Tell me about this painting."

The relief was easy to read on Mr. Ashley's face as he left his desk and approached the painting. Most of what he said made Derek want to make choking noises the way his brother had done when they were children. Obviously the auctioneer was excited about the possibility of selling off an essentially worthless painting and avoiding having to contact important men about decades-old purchases.

"This," the duke said with growling emphasis. "This is perfect. I'll take it." He reached up and began to remove it from the wall.

"Your Grace, I—" The auctioneer stumbled to a halt as the duke glared at him.

"Your job is to sell art, no?" The duke smirked at the smaller man. At least Derek could now see where Jess had picked up the habit.

Mr. Ashley adjusted his cravat. "Well, yes."

"I want to buy this art." The duke frowned. "What is the problem?"

"Er, uh, there isn't a problem, Your Grace."

"Good." The duke shoved the painting into Derek's hands. "My solicitor will send you a bank draft for whatever Mr. Thornbury tells me is a fair price."

Derek looked at the auctioneer and, trying to set the man's mind at ease, gave him a smile and a wink. He had no idea what Marshington intended to send, but Derek was going to make sure it was enough to make the auctioneer feel like a bit of a bandit. It was a small revenge, but contemplating it made Derek feel better.

The duke wasn't finished, though. "You will find me other paintings by this artist. I want to see if any of the others speak to me the way this one has."

"I . . . Of course, Your Grace." Mr. Ashley looked a bit dazed.

The duke gave a sharp nod and snapped his fingers. Jess scrambled from her corner, almost knocking the plant to the ground in the process. She fell in behind the duke's heels and followed him out the door. "Good day, Mr. Ashley," Marshington said over his shoulder. "It's been a pleasure doing business with you."

"And to you, Your Grace," Mr. Ashley called to the duke's retreating back.

Derek struggled out to the front hall with the painting they'd sort of purchased. He accepted his coat from the servant, while the duke took his outer garments from Jess. Then Marshington strode out the door, nose so high he couldn't possibly see his own feet.

Picking up the painting again, Derek followed the duke out to the carriage, a little awed, a little angry, and more than a little dumbfounded. What in the world had just happened?

CHAPTER FOURTEEN

*J*ess bounded out of the carriage behind Ryland and rushed ahead of him to open the door, desperately trying to maintain appearances. Ryland always did well enough disguising himself, but he sometimes forgot the team aspect. She shot him a glare as she bowed him through his own front door. He just pulled one side of his mouth up in a grin.

A footman appeared to relieve her of her position at the door, and Jess followed Ryland through the house to his study, listening for footsteps to make sure Derek had fallen in line as well. Her mind churned with the possible next steps. There was so little time in which to answer so many questions.

A problem for which she could only blame herself. She didn't even have time to relish the idea that her brother had survived, not if she wanted to find the one thing he needed to fulfill his destiny.

In the study, she dropped the semblance of servitude and crossed to the chairs situated in front of the dormant fireplace. She didn't sit, though. Instead she propped one booted foot on the hearth and put a hand on the mantel to lay her head against as she stared unseeing at the cold, charred stones.

A grunt and a bang pulled her from the potential future in time to see Derek almost fall through the study door in his attempts to maneuver the painting through it.

"What are you doing?" she asked with a small grin.

He leaned the painting against a table and kicked the door shut before propping his hands on his hips and attempting to frown through his slightly quickened breathing. "I'm carrying a painting that we technically just stole."

Her grin widened. "Why didn't you leave it in the carriage?"

He blinked at her, mouth opening and closing once before settling into a firm scowl.

"Come away from the door," she said, pushing away from the mantel. "Jeffreys will be bringing tea any minute. He can't stand to be left out of the planning."

Derek stepped away from the door and took off his hat and coat, frown fading into confusion as he tried to decide what to do with them without a servant to hand them to or a rack to hang them on.

It was enough to turn her grin into a smile. "You can leave them on that table."

Derek looked over at her, eyes wide in his round spectacles. "What?"

"Your coat and hat. Put them on the table over there. One of the servants will take them to your room later." She gestured to the table where he'd leaned the painting. It was empty for just this reason. Ryland had made a habit of always wearing his hat and coat into the study when he returned from somewhere. It made it much less obvious when those articles had been part of a particular subterfuge.

Such as today.

Jess grinned once more at their success.

Derek laid his coat across the table, his hat gently resting atop it. "What do we do now? Wait?"

Ryland set his hat on Derek's coat and took his own coat over to the desk. "I didn't just buy an atrociously ugly painting in order to sit around twirling my thumbs."

"Yet that's what you'll be doing," Jess said, cutting over to the desk and sliding the stack of papers from the coat's hidden inner pocket before Ryland could decide to hold them hostage. "Your assistance is appreciated but no longer necessary."

Ryland frowned. "We talked about this already."

"You talked. I disagreed."

Ryland grunted and turned back to Derek. "How much is that painting worth, anyway?"

Derek stated an amount that probably wouldn't have even paid for the coat Ryland had just thrown across his desk. "Mr. Ashley likely thinks you a bit light in the head at the moment."

"Good," Ryland said. "That way he won't suspect me later."

"I'd love to know who he suspects instead," Jess murmured, wishing for the first time that she had the network of spies and informants at her fingertips that she once had.

"Hmm, yes, I'll have Jeffreys send someone to watch the office, find out who Ashley contacts or who else comes visiting."

As much as Jess wanted to turn him down, to keep him and all his people uninvolved, to walk away today and not look back, she couldn't. She couldn't be in two places at once. "I'd love to say no, but you have my permission."

"Thank you," Ryland said dryly, "but I didn't ask for it."

"You think someone else knows about the paintings?" Derek asked.

Jess sighed and ran a hand through her hair, dislodging the wig of short, brown hair. "Assuming the people doing the painting knew they were creating some sort of map, you have a minimum of eight people involved in the hiding of the bowl. The chances are great that at least one of them passed down some form of story about the importance of the paintings, and it is most likely whichever family decided to make a claim for the throne. So, yes, I expect someone else has been or will be looking for the paintings."

"I've someone watching the Institution as well, so we'll know if someone takes the same path you did," Ryland said.

"*I* will know," Jess said in as hard a voice as she could muster. "I may have to accept help, but I will be in charge of this, Ryland."

"How?" he asked, bracing himself on the desk and leaning forward. "You've a great deal of travel ahead of you if you're taking him to see the paintings. Communicating with you will be nearly impossible. It makes sense for me to be the person coordinating everything."

Jess leaned in as well, rising on her tiptoes in order to reach farther. "And when the problem shows up on your doorstep and endangers your wife and baby girl?"

He shrugged. "I'll send them to Kent."

"If something happens to you . . ." She shook her head. "I won't have that on my head, Ryland."

"I'm a duke, Jess, living out in the open. I'm eccentric, yes, but I'm seen. Someone would have to be very daring to do anything to me."

"Some people would risk a lot to gain a country."

"Excuse me," Derek said, leaning in and wrapping an arm around Jess's shoulders to pull her back and physically separate the argument. "May I remind you that despite these great plans you seem to be making, we don't know who bought the paintings."

"Yes, we do," Jess and Ryland said at the same time.

Triumph filled her as she held the sheaf of papers up. In this, at least, she was the capable and knowledgeable one. "Here's the whole lot."

A look of marvel flitted across Derek's face, spiking her sense of triumph into something resembling pride. It was nice to be able to surprise Derek with her accomplishments for once.

And just that quickly, her pride faded to sadness. If ever she needed proof of where she truly belonged in the world, that was it. The only place she shined was in the shadows. Perhaps, when this was all over, she should return to the War Office. Yes, Napoleon had been defeated and whatever had been happening with the former colonies seemed to have simmered down, but surely it was only a matter of time before England got into another skirmish somewhere in the world.

Before she could consider that, though, she had to settle the issue at hand and safely haul a scholar around to look at paintings without anyone noticing.

Take therefore no thought for the morrow. . . . Sufficient unto the day is the evil thereof.

Jess shook her head. Now they had her thinking in Bible verses. Obviously living with Daphne for three years had influenced her more than she'd thought. Of course, Jess had no idea where to find that verse, what the context was, or even if she was quoting it correctly, so its usefulness at the moment was debatable.

"Do you have a copy of *Debrett's*?" Jess asked as she ran a finger down the paper, looking at names and trying to remember anything she knew about any of them. Who were the heirs of the ones that had died? Which ones were heavy gamblers or in other financial trouble and likely to have sold or traded the painting? Who had homes in town or estates in the country?

Ryland turned toward the bookcase, but Derek was still staring down at the paper. "How . . . when . . ."

The door opened, and Jeffreys brought in a tea tray, frowning when he noted they had already circled around the desk. Miranda entered behind him and shut the door with a gentle click.

She stopped short when she saw the newly purchased painting. "What is that hideous thing doing in here?" Her head lifted to look at Jess. "If you brought this as some sort of apology gift, know it's going in the same place as the tea set you gave us as a wedding present. This is almost as ugly as that teapot."

Ryland chuckled.

"His Grace saw it in the auctioneer's office," Derek explained. "He said it spoke to him."

"Did it, now?" Miranda murmured. "Was it saying, 'Burn me, please!'?"

"No," Ryland said with a chuckle. "It said, 'I'm on the other side of the room and will provide a nice distraction while Jess borrows a few papers.'"

Derek looked at Jess. "But you never moved. You were in the corner the entire time."

"Was I?" Jess hummed. "Interesting." She'd had to be careful not to snag Ryland's coat on the plant like she'd done when they were leaving, but sliding the papers from the desk had been simple.

Mr. Ashley had been more than happy to abandon them in favor of a simpler sale.

Derek took the papers from Jess and flipped through them. "That's stealing."

Jess looked up with a blink. "I'm going to give them back. Not right away, of course, but once this is all over and it won't matter if someone else sees them. I'll sneak in and slide them between the desk and the wall. He'll think they fell back there. If he seeks them here in the meantime, Ryland can pretend to be excessively offended by the accusation."

"This is war, Thornbury," Ryland said. "The rules are a bit different."

"We're not at war," Derek said, his voice losing the confusion and wonder it had held. "And even if we were, that shouldn't change the rules of human decency."

"It does if you don't want to end up dead," Jess said, but inside she squirmed a bit. Hadn't that been her biggest struggle? Having to decide where the line was that she wasn't willing to cross? Others had thrown every compulsion in the river and done whatever necessary to get the job done. She hadn't been willing to do that, but she'd had to pick and choose what she kept.

What if she'd chosen incorrectly? What if doing more things the right and polite way would have brought about a better outcome? What if her family—

No. Jess shut out those thoughts with an iron gate. She could not start second-guessing the choices she'd made. They couldn't be changed. No amount of remorse would alter the past. She could only move forward from where she was now.

Was she going to have to move forward without Derek? She could. Would. If every painting were like the one upstairs, she should be able to translate the diary quickly enough to know what direction she was supposed to look.

That was a rather large *if*.

Derek was silent for a few moments—long moments, moments in which Jess's heart pounded harder than she would let anyone see.

She forced her breathing to remain steady and slow, even though it made her lungs burn and her throat ache to gasp. As annoying as she found him and his brain full of knowledge that made her feel ridiculously inadequate, she wanted him to stay.

She needed him to stay.

He shook the too-long shock of hair away from his eyes and sighed. "Auctions are usually attended by a small set of serious art collectors." He held out a hand. "Let me see if I recognize any of the names."

Jess was very glad that her hip was still braced against the desk as she handed the papers to him. All her relief settled in her knees, making them more than a little bit shaky.

As Derek's eyes roamed the paper, he said, "We can also try to determine what paintings go with what title. The queen's descriptions in the diary are detailed. I don't think every painting is a clue, but I haven't quite determined how to know which ones matter."

Ryland, who along with Jeffreys and Miranda had been watching the exchange in silence, cleared his throat. "This is going to require a good bit of travel."

Jess took a deep breath and nodded. "You said Nicolas had a month?" That wasn't very long. Not when some of these paintings could be at country estates. "Travel takes a lot of time."

"And money," Derek added.

"We'll let His Grace here help with that, since he's determined to be involved." Jess smirked. "I've some money, but I wouldn't say no to more, since we'll need to hire horses to stay on the move. We'll borrow your shabbiest unmarked carriage."

Miranda crossed her arms. "And a chaperon?"

Jess bit her lip to hide her smile as Ryland chuckled. "My dear, chaperons are the last thing someone wants when they're sneaking about."

"And that's the first thing someone will notice when they're seen."

Jess's smile faded. Miranda was right. Hoping she was managing to look casual and unworried, Jess shrugged one shoulder. "We'll travel as a married couple, then." A choked noise came from her left, but she ignored it. "It won't be the first time I've pretended to have a husband in order to travel without notice."

No, it wouldn't be the first time, but as Jess glanced at Derek from beneath her lashes, she had to admit that it might be the most difficult.

Married? She wanted them to pretend to be married? What exactly did a charade of that nature entail?

Derek looked at Jess, prepared to argue the idea, but quickly diverted his gaze back to the list he'd been studying when she made her pronouncement. She was still in her servant costume, consisting of boots, trousers, shirt, and close-fitting vest. The trousers were the part he couldn't quite get over. Clothing that had seemed too large when he'd seen her standing beside the duke now looked much too fitted as she leaned over the desk. Whoever had decided the female form should wear layers of draped fabric had the right idea for certain.

He didn't dare suggest Jess go put on a dress, though, not if he didn't want her deciding they should travel as brothers instead of a couple.

Not that the couple idea was going to work either.

"We can't be married," he said, reading through the titles on the paper over again, even though he couldn't find enough spare thinking capacity to remember the diary's details and guess what description matched what name. The paper was the only way he could reasonably keep his eyes away from Jess.

"It's not real, Derek, just a story to keep anyone we encounter from being too curious about me."

"What about their curiosity over me?" His frustration allowed him to look up from the paper and keep his gaze on her face. Didn't she see the problem? "I will see some of these people again. What do I tell them when I am no longer married?"

She shrugged that annoying, indifferent shrug that made him

want to shake her until she decided to care. "You would hardly be the first widower in existence."

He choked. "How, pray tell, are you to have died? Should I have suffered a tragic and immediate loss, or the slow, painful agony of watching you waste away with illness?"

"I don't much care."

"Jess," Miranda said softly, but Jess ignored her.

"Pick your favorite tragic painting and pretend that happened to me." She turned away from Derek and moved to the shelves. "You must have a lineage book in here somewhere. Where do you keep it, Ryland?"

That was it? Discussion over? "What if they see you again? England is large, granted, but seeing someone you know has been known to happen."

"I doubt they'll see me again. If we're successful, well, I'm not sure what that will mean. More than likely I'll return to Haven Manor. It's as good a place to live out my life as anywhere."

Live out her life? He wasn't sure how old she was, but he would be surprised if she were anywhere close to seeing thirty yet. Living out her life could take a while.

"I was led to believe earlier that you didn't particularly care for your position as cook." Everyone's reaction to learning what she was doing proved she'd chosen isolation above comfort. She would be able to choose differently after this.

She spun from the bookshelves and flattened her hands on the desk so she could lean toward him. Her hard face should have been glaring at him, but her eyes were flat. Emotionless. "It doesn't matter. You need to understand that this is dangerous. I will shield you however I can, make sure no harm comes to you because of your assistance, but the fact is I may not have a future beyond this. My brother has, possibly unknowingly, painted a target on my back. Even if we are successful, my future could quite possibly be something completely out of the realm of current contemplation. Planning is an exercise in futility, and I refuse to participate in fruitless endeavors."

Derek didn't know what to say to that. Nor did it appear that the room's other occupants knew what to say. For several moments, no one moved, at least not in a way that made any sound. Derek couldn't see them, his gaze trapped by Jess's. It was the calm coldness that convinced him she truly believed what she was saying. She would not look beyond her next objective.

"I'll chaperone," Jeffreys said. "You're going to need a driver anyway, and it might as well be someone who knows how to pick a lock almost as well as you do."

"We're going to pick locks?" Derek asked.

Another shrug from Jess. He was going to tie a plank to her shoulders before they were finished with this. "We have to get in the houses somehow."

"That's true," Ryland said, returning to the desk and pulling out a sheet of paper on which he started listing routine household occurrences. "Most houses run on a rather basic schedule. It shouldn't take much observation to know where and when your best entry point would be."

"Why don't we simply knock?" Derek asked.

Jess, the duke, and Jeffreys all looked at him blankly. The clink of cups as Miranda poured tea was the only thing that kept the room from falling into uncomfortable silence once more.

Derek resisted the urge to squirm. "It won't work in Town, obviously, but in the country, most housekeepers are happy to give a tour in return for a coin or two."

Ryland chuckled and threw his pen down on the paper. "I think we've been doing this too long, Jess."

"Or we've taken too long a break from it," she returned.

"That only leaves determining which houses to visit," Jeffreys said. "There's only so many you can visit in a month, even with continually renting fresh horses."

"Are you going to be able to match the names to the descriptions?" Jess asked.

Derek shook his head. "Not with this alone. I'll need another source, something that puts the titles with a description of the painting."

"Do you know where we could find one?"

He took a deep breath and was thankful Miranda began handing out tea, as it gave him an excuse to sit down. After taking a small sip, he set his cup aside and finally answered. "Yes. I know where such a book is."

"Excellent. We'll go there first. Where is it?"

"In my room," Derek said quietly. "At my parents' home in Oxfordshire."

CHAPTER FIFTEEN

*T*he carriage ride away from London was decidedly different from the one they'd taken there. For one, the carriage
was small and private.

Two, Jess was dressed as, well, herself in a simple muslin dress
covered in pale purple flowers and a purple spencer jacket.

Three, as the only occupants in the carriage, Jess and Derek
each had their own comfortable seat with enough space to give
their legs an occasional stretch.

Four, Jess had nothing to occupy her mind beyond listing all
the ways in which this ride was different from her last.

She couldn't plan because she knew nothing beyond their next
destination. There was no imminent danger within the carriage,
and it was impossible to convince herself that there was a necessity
to pay attention to the possible implications of every rut, bump,
and jostle.

Across from her, Derek was working away on the diary, a travel
desk on his lap and papers spread out across the seat. A few had
fallen to the floor. Jess had picked them up the first time they'd
fallen, but two more had fluttered down as soon as she placed
them back on the seat, so she'd left them alone.

It wasn't as if they were going anywhere. They were stuck in
this carriage just like she was. The only difference was they had a
purpose. She was currently useless. And bored.

Derek slid the short steel-nibbed pen into its holder on the travel desk and rolled his shoulders with a groan. He stretched his head from side to side as he waited for the messy scribbles to dry on the page so he could add it to the stack around him.

"Is there any way I can help?" Jess asked.

He looked at her, eyebrows raised until they edged over the top of his spectacles. "I thought I was here because it would take you too long to translate the diary."

That was true, but she was going crazy with nothing to do. She hadn't had nothing to do in ten years. "How much longer, do you think?"

Derek leaned toward the window and took in the passing scenery. "Not too much, I think. Another couple of hours." He glanced upward. "Maybe an hour the way Jeffreys drives."

An hour. She could do an hour. Compared to the last day and a half, an hour was nothing. They'd departed London with the first rays of yesterday's sun, but even with Ryland sending servants ahead to arrange for fresh horses, they couldn't make the journey in a single day.

The night they'd spent at the inn had been uneventful. Jess had lain in her room, sliding in and out of a restless sleep, until it was finally a decent hour to rise and start their journey again.

Derek yawned and let his head fall back against the cushioned seat. "Pardon me," he mumbled.

Jess glanced at the number of papers strewn about the carriage, a far greater number than there had been the day before. "How many candles did you burn through working on the diary last night?"

"Four." Derek scrubbed a hand across his face, dislodging his spectacles so they hung off one ear. He slid them back into place and blinked at the view again. "We can't tell them we're married."

Jess hadn't given much thought to what they would say to his family. She wasn't accustomed to going into situations where the people involved already knew her, or, in this case, knew who she was with. "What do you suppose we should tell them?"

"Certainly not the truth," he said with a shake of his head. "Not that they would believe it."

"I'll take care of it." Jess stood up into a crouch and banged her hand on the roof of the carriage. "I just need to get something from my trunk."

"You will not be a tiger," he growled, referring to the young boys who frequently rode on the backs of carriages and acted as footmen. "In fact, for this entire journey, I insist you remain a woman. I'm having a difficult enough time with my part of this charade. I can't slip up and call you my wife when you're dressed in trousers."

Jess blinked at his disgruntled pout and had to bite her lips to refrain from smiling. "Very well. I'll remain a woman."

"You could let me go alone," Derek grumbled. "I don't see why you have to accompany me in the first place."

"May I be frank?" Jess asked with a sigh, already regretting the offer.

"That would be a delightful change, yes."

"Aside from the fact that we're much too close to Marlborough for me to be comfortable showing my face anywhere, I don't trust you."

"Well." He cleared his throat and shifted in his seat. "That was honest."

"What if your family asks questions you don't know how to answer? What if you get frightened and don't meet us in the morning? What if we aren't as safe as we think we are and need to flee in the middle of the night? You don't know how to handle those things."

"That . . . seems a rather different idea of trust."

Jess shrugged and began digging around in the small satchel she'd brought into the carriage with her, not wanting to delve into the meaning of a word she'd had little acquaintance with for several years.

The carriage rolled to a stop, and the trapdoor in the roof flipped open, revealing Jeffreys leaning back from the driver's seat. He was covered in road dust but didn't look the least bit tired yet. "Why did we stop?"

Jess wriggled out of her middle-class spencer and donned the plain brown pelisse she'd pulled from her bag. "I'm going to be married to you while we visit Derek's parents. We'll say Chemsford allowed me to come along because we'll be going near to my own family's home."

"Bit of a strange story," Jeffreys said.

"It will hold if we state it plainly."

Jeffreys gave a nod, blew her a kiss with a cheeky grin, and then shut the trapdoor before getting the carriage rolling again.

Jess buttoned the pelisse and then looked up to find Derek studying her, the lenses of his spectacles distorting the squint of his narrowed eyes. "What?"

"How many false husbands have you had?"

She shrugged. "Ten, maybe? Eleven? I know it seems like I suggest it a lot, but most of the time I don't need it. I don't often travel in a capacity that would make someone question my connection to my companions, nor stay in one place long enough to need such a disguise."

"Does it mean anything to you?"

What did he mean? Did he think she got caught up in the sentimentality of her own lies? "It's merely a disguise, Derek. Like changing my coat. It simply keeps people from taking a closer look."

"Do you think it will mean less to you when you truly marry?"

He was scraping a rusty knife across her soul. It was on the tip of her tongue to make a cryptic comment that jabbed at his wit, but she couldn't. She remembered the way he'd stumbled over asking for rooms for him and his wife at the inn last night. Derek was an innately honest person. Only the fact that he appeared genuinely curious and not the least judgmental allowed her to answer him truthfully. A small bit of honesty in private was the least she could give him.

"I doubt I'll ever marry," she said.

He tilted his head to look at her through narrowed eyes. "Why not?"

"Given the fact that I am not made of paint and canvas, I suppose it's possible you haven't noticed that I am not the usual sort of female." Jess looked out the window on the pretense of determining how much farther they had to go.

Not that she knew. This part of the country was as foreign to her as the Americas would be. Looking out the window was better than watching him scrutinize her. Most of the time, being strange didn't bother her. She'd much rather have the abilities and wit to take care of herself in any situation than the life of luxury that left one scrambling for purchase when things didn't go as planned.

It made her different, though, in a way that not all people would see as good. Those she allowed into her life on a prolonged basis saw no problem with her strangeness, but her life didn't lend itself to the sort of closeness marriage would require. Marriage would gain her nothing materially, so companionship was its only lure.

"Not every man wishes for a conventional wife," Derek said. "Lady Chemsford is hardly a typical marchioness."

"Nor was she the kind Lord Chemsford was looking for."

Jess leaned a bit closer to the window. Daphne might not have all the typical feminine graces of an aristocratic wife, but if trouble came knocking, she'd tuck herself behind her husband's coattails. Jess would climb out the window in order to circle around and stab it in the back. No man wanted that in a wife, not really.

Derek murmured a sound somewhere between a grunt and an actual word. Jess took that to mean he saw her point and agreed.

Irritation at his agreement had her gritting her teeth. Irritation at herself for finding his acceptance of the truth irritating had her flopping back into the carriage seat and tossing him into the uncomfortable position.

"What about you?" she asked. "When do you intend to marry?"

He blinked at her as if the idea had never occurred to him. "When I meet someone who suits me, I suppose. I'm quite comfortable, but I'm not amassing a great deal of wealth and I'm not the eldest son, so my marrying isn't all that imperative."

"But mine is?" Jess raised an eyebrow, hoping he could feel the daggers she was throwing at him in her mind.

He shifted in his seat and looked out the window. "We're nearly there. I should probably try to gather these papers into some semblance of order."

Jess sighed and leaned her head back on the seat. Maybe that was what she could give him in return for his assistance on the diary. By the time this trip was complete, Derek Thornbury would know how to stand his ground.

❧❧

Awkward moments were nothing new to Derek's family. With Derek prone to spouting off distantly relevant pieces of history; his older brother, Lewis, trying to turn everything into a competition of athleticism; Mary, the elder of his sisters, missing the meaning behind every single one of their father's sardonic jokes; and his youngest sister, Jacqueline, placing flower fairy crowns on everyone's head, family interactions were tumultuous to say the least.

The presence of a couple no one could quite explain sent the entire raucous family into a stunned silence. It didn't help matters that Derek had forgotten Jess was supposed to be married to Jeffreys and had first introduced her to his mother as Miss Smith. Jess had smoothly corrected him by saying, "It's Mrs. Smith, actually. May I say what a lovely garden you have?"

Derek blamed the fact that he still didn't know the infernal woman's name, but in truth the moment had scared him a bit. If he didn't come up with a way to keep their supposed story straight, he was going to get them killed or something equally as horrid.

That was assuming, of course, that he managed to make it through this one single evening at home with his sanity intact.

"You all work for Lord Chemsford?" Derek's father asked as Mother passed tea around the gathering. It was just Derek's luck that the entire family had been home when the unknown carriage had pulled up to the door. He'd been hoping that his elder sister, at least, would have been at her own home on the other side of the village, but no, she, her vicar husband, and both of their children had come for dinner.

Nothing could make them go home until they'd heard everything.

"We don't want to be an imposition," Jess said as she accepted a cup of tea. "Mr. Smith and I can find an inn for the night and return for Mr. Thornbury tomorrow."

Derek narrowed his eyes at Jess. Given their discussion in the carriage, he knew the offer was as fake as her marriage. She was depending upon his family's curiosity to turn down her offer.

And drat it all, Derek knew the ploy was going to work.

"Nonsense," his father said, because that man wasn't about to let an evening like this one pass. He would have fodder for jokes for years the way this evening was going. "We've plenty of room here. Can't you stay more than the one night? We only saw Derek for a week or two before he went off to work for Lord Chemsford."

Jeffreys did an admirable job of looking regretful. "I'm afraid we can't linger. We've other items to procure before we return home and a very strict schedule to keep if Mrs. Smith here wants to catch her family at a good time."

Derek had to admire the fact that, aside from the marriage bit, Jess and Jeffreys had managed to participate in much of the conversation without saying anything that was actually a lie. Misleading, yes, but not a lie. That made it even more difficult for Derek to keep up. What was he supposed to share? What did he hide? What truths had Jess told him that were crafted in a way to deliberately mislead him into thinking she meant something else?

Maybe it was a good thing Jess hadn't let him come here alone.

"I thought you were cataloguing Lord Chemsford's collection. Why do you need your books?" Lewis asked Derek. His brother had never quite understood what Derek did for a living. None of his family did.

Derek swallowed. It was his turn to attempt an honest prevarication. "I need my books to, um, fully comprehend the meaning of an, er, item I came across in the, um, parlor. Its connection to, um"—he shifted in his seat and had to make a conscious effort not to look in Jess's direction—"a particular class of art could have significant impact on its importance."

Complete silence met his statement. No one even moved a teacup.

"No one understood that, did they?" Mary asked. "It wasn't only me?"

Her husband gave her hand a pat but said nothing.

"Not only you," Lewis muttered.

Yes, if they died on this adventure, it was fairly certain Derek would be at fault.

"Why don't I show you to your rooms?" Mother asked. "You can freshen up for a bit."

"That would be lovely, thank you," Jess said, the sweet tone of her voice sounding oddly natural. When had she started using the word *lovely*? If he didn't know better, he'd believe she always behaved this way.

Did he know better? What if this *was* her natural state and the prickly woman who'd refused to cook him Naples biscuits was a false persona?

As she passed where Derek was seated, she stepped hard on his toe and threw him a warning glance before following his mother from the room. He sighed in relief as he wiggled his sore toe.

It would seem he wasn't entirely wrong about her.

Jeffreys trailed behind her, shaking his head and chuckling softly.

Once the soft sounds of their footsteps and chatter had faded up the stairs, the drawing room rumbled with his family's questions.

"What is really going on here, Derek? You'd let us know if you were in trouble, wouldn't you?"

"What do they do for Lord Chemsford? Are they servants? Should Mother be putting them in the guest room?"

"Do you think the fact that one of his fingers is missing makes driving the horses more difficult?"

"I've always wondered what it would be like to be driven into the woods and left to fend for myself."

"Father," Derek groaned. "They aren't going to leave me in the woods."

His father shrugged. "Woods, middle of a village, seaside cliff . . . you'd best make sure you're keeping some funds on your person."

Mary clutched her husband's hand. "Father, do you truly think they mean Derek harm?"

Derek held up both his hands to silence his family. "No one means me any harm." Any harm he might encounter on this trip would be intended for Jess, a possibility that choked him up a bit. "I asked for the detour by here to pick up the books because I wanted to satisfy my own curiosity. William"—his father's eyebrows lowered and Derek quickly corrected himself—"Lord Chemsford doesn't have a particular interest in these details, so my visit will be short as it's, uh, not for him."

This was tiresome. Derek's father was a land-owning gentleman with an estate that kept the family comfortable and allowed them to circulate in the society of the village and, occasionally, nearby Oxford. He'd rubbed many a shoulder with a titled man, and of course he'd sent his sons to university with them, but he'd never approved of nor understood Derek's familiarity with a few of the upper-class people he'd met over the years.

Derek had never understood why a man's title mattered more than his character when it came to choosing whom he associated with. Over time, he'd learned to simply not talk about it. That hadn't been a difficult decision, really, as Derek preferred to talk about the art he worked with anyway.

Fifteen minutes later, Derek had finally reassured his family, but then his mother returned to the drawing room and he had to start over again. By the time he escaped to his own room, he was exhausted. He took a spare taper up with him, though, because he knew he wouldn't be able to sleep until he'd located the books.

Since he was alone in the upstairs corridor, he knocked lightly on the guest room door as he passed.

It swung open to reveal Jess. She was still in her traveling dress, but her hair had been brushed out and braided, giving her a softer appearance. "Is something wrong?"

"No," Derek said. "I was . . . I'm not sure why I knocked. I suppose I'm making sure we didn't need to do anything tonight."

"You've finished with your family already?"

The surprise on her face sent a wave of guilt through Derek. He hadn't seen them in months, though they'd exchanged many letters in that time. Despite their vast differences, his family was close. Perhaps that was the problem. "I find I'm not very good at lying to them. When this is over, I'll return and have a proper visit."

Her gaze cut briefly to the right before she looked back at him, chin raised a bit. "We'll have you back here as soon as possible."

Even if they failed, he'd be back in a month, barring some incredible danger. He didn't mention it, though. He'd noticed that for all of Jess's practicality, she didn't entertain the notion that she might fail.

"We'll leave at the earliest polite moment tomorrow," Jess continued. "As soon as we decide where to go."

Derek nodded toward the lit candle and extra taper he held. "I'm working on that now. The sooner we decode the diary, the better."

"I'll help." Jess stepped through the door, crowding slightly into his space, and pulled it shut behind her.

"Help?" Derek choked out.

"I do know how to read, Derek." Jess glared at him. "I'm assuming your books are in English?"

"Well, yes, but . . ." He cleared his throat. "They're in my room."

She rolled her eyes. "I'll try not to muss your bedcovers. Lead on."

"Should we get Jeffreys?" While Jess might see the other man only as another member of their party, Derek considered him the chaperon keeping them from total impropriety. If he were to join them, having Jess in his room would feel less awkward. Hopefully.

"No." Jess jerked her head toward the door. "He's already asleep. Stripped the covers from the bed and made himself a pallet before I'd even had a chance to say I'd take the floor. If his snores are any indication, the floor isn't bothering him any. I won't wake him now. He can't afford to nod off while driving the horses. You and I can always nap in the carriage."

There was no refuting that logic. Derek cast a glance at the closed door, forced to consider an unforeseen aspect of this charade. Would he be sharing a room with Jess? He couldn't even handle the idea of looking at books in such a private space, much less bedding down, even if it wasn't in the same bed. Perhaps he'd simply have to sneak out and join Jeffreys wherever he slept.

That was a problem for the future, though. Not far in the future, but not tonight. "We can look at the books in the morning."

Jess's shoulders tensed and her gaze narrowed. "Give me the candles, then."

"What?"

"The candles." She held out her hands. "If you aren't going to be looking at the books tonight, you won't need them."

"I'm not giving you the candles," Derek sputtered, even as part of him acknowledged that he could easily hand them over and go down and get more. It was the principle of the matter. Jess was not going to take away his candles like his mother had done when he was a little boy and tried to sneak them into his room and read late into the night.

"I'll not allow you to keep information from me," Jess said, looking ready to skewer him with his unlit taper. Or perhaps even the lit one.

"I never intended to," Derek ground out. He'd never felt the urge to argue with anyone, at least not over something other than art and its historic implications. Jess riled him up, though, in a way he didn't completely understand. She frustrated him and, unlike a mysterious painting or an unknown sculpture, no amount of research was going to clear up the confusion she stirred.

"Why won't you let me see the books, then?"

"They. Are. In. My. Bedchamber." Derek leaned a little closer with each word he whispered. "Have you no sense of propriety? We are in my father's house, he assumes you are married to another man, and you want to spend the evening in my bedroom. My apologies, but I don't quite have the same disregard for normality that you seem to."

Something about his words meant something to her, because she jerked back and all of the aggression fell from her body and face. "You're right," she said softly. "I'll see you in the morning."

Before he could adjust to her new attitude, she'd slipped back into the room and shut the door.

Derek stared at it until a drop of wax from the candle he was holding splashed onto his thumb and jerked him from his reverie. Books. He would go bury his head in books. At least there, things made sense.

CHAPTER SIXTEEN

*J*ess was taking delicate bites of egg and smiling at everything Mrs. Thornbury said when Derek stumbled into the breakfast room the next morning. In addition to the flop of hair across his forehead, there was now a spray of it sticking up from the back of his head. His spectacles only emphasized the tiredness of his eyes. The clothes he wore yesterday still hung on his body, though a bit more wrinkled, and the faint odor of burned tallow clung to him.

Jeffreys, who'd already eaten and was now seeing to the horses, should have gone to Derek's room and used his bed. Obviously it had been empty all night.

Mrs. Thornbury simply clicked her tongue and shook her head before asking the maid to bring coffee. "How many candles?"

"Only two," he answered, running his hands over his face.

"I'll make sure the maid goes up today to clean the scorch marks from the wall and desk."

Derek frowned. "I've learned how to trim a candlewick, Mother. The smoke left a streak on the wall, of course, but that couldn't be helped."

"Unless you'd gone to bed like a sensible person," Jess said, so low that no one would hear her except possibly Derek, who had taken the seat beside her at the breakfast table.

Derek frowned at her, indicating he had, indeed, heard her little comment. His only answer, though, was to take a bite of toast.

Lewis joined them a few minutes later, making a few teasing comments about Derek's appearance. When the younger brother didn't respond, the elder soon fell into conversation with their mother.

Eventually Jess couldn't stay at the table any longer without drawing suspicion. She'd hoped Mrs. Thornbury and her eldest son would go about their day and leave Jess to talk to Derek while he ate. If she were a believer in luck, she'd think hers had long run out.

"I believe I'd like to take a turn in your lovely garden before cooping myself up in a carriage all day," Jess said with a sweet smile, trying to look and act like her friend Daphne. Even before the woman had become a marchioness she'd been . . . nice. It was a simple word, but the reality was far more difficult.

Jess had only been attempting it for a few hours and found the business wearying. Disguises that required her to be a bit harder than she was were much easier. That, or complete and total mutton brains. She rather enjoyed those as well. A simple, graceful, *nice* girl, however, the kind who was welcomed in most of the genteel world, was the most trying of all identities.

As she escaped to the garden, she subtly lifted a hand to massage cheeks that were sore from all the soft smiling she'd done over breakfast. The door opened behind her, and Jess sighed silently before putting the mask back in place. She turned to see Derek shuffling out toward her and relaxed. "What did you learn last night?"

He rolled his shoulders and rubbed his neck.

Jess laughed. "Aside from the fact that sleeping in a chair at a desk is never going to end well."

"I learned that lesson a long time ago," Derek answered. "I just choose to ignore it on a regular basis."

"Do you know where we're going?"

He nodded. "Not far, to start. We're going to Oxford. There's a book in their collection."

"More books?" Jess shook her head. "Derek, we need paintings, not books."

"It's a book of paintings, or at least the engravings of paintings. When I was reading back through the descriptions of the collection of paintings by The Six, I remembered seeing one in this book. Another of their paintings also hangs in the Ashmolean."

That she could work with. The possibility of finding not just one but two paintings before the day was out gave Jess a bit of hope she'd been loath to admit was lacking. "What do we need to do to get into the Ashmolean?"

Derek's eyebrows lifted. "Walk up the stairs? It's open to the public. Always has been. My grandmother would take me there when I was a boy. What I saw there made me realize how much more to the world there was. Most people never get to see such wonders. Once seen, some of them still don't make complete sense."

"For example?"

"There's a stuffed bird there, very strange looking. Huge long beak, squat legs. A dodo bird, it's called. Seeing it on display, it's impossible to tell what it would live like, but then you see the sketches of life on Mauritius, and it makes more sense."

"To Oxford and the Ashmolean, then," she said with a sharp nod. His statements made sense to Jess, at least on a certain level, though she didn't know that she agreed with him. Art was nothing but frustrating. She always wanted to know what wasn't there, what was about to happen next. Apparently The Six and the queen had felt differently, which was why Jess needed Derek—if only she could keep him focused. "Let's say our farewells."

He nodded and turned back to the house. "There aren't any dodo birds left, you know. They all died when the Dutch settled there. Pictures are all that remain."

Jess shook her head, but instead of wanting to shove a wad of linen in his mouth as he continued on about birds, she discovered she was amused. At least he was moving toward the carriage, even if he couldn't stop himself from reciting every obscure fact about the smallest thing that no one in his vicinity even knew about, much less cared for.

They said farewell to his family, all of whom were still watching Jess and Jeffreys as if their descriptions might be needed by the magistrate later, and climbed into the carriage, Derek still discussing the wonders to be seen at the Ashmolean.

❦

Derek loved the scent of books. Paper, ink, leather, and dust created an aroma that always made him feel at home. He could spend hours in this library, wandering the shelves, perusing the books, and learning new information.

He could, but the two people creeping silently behind him would probably threaten to burn the place down.

"Here it is," Derek said, pulling a large book from the bottom shelf and laying it gently on the table running between the sets of dark wood shelves.

"How do we find it?" Jeffreys asked, reaching for the book.

Derek slid it out of reach and leaned over the tome, turning the pages gently. The picture was in here, he knew, but as page after page of attempts to recreate masterful pieces of art flipped by he could feel the tense anticipation of his companions.

"You could be looking for the painting in the Ashmolean," he said, hoping to get them to stop looking over his shoulder.

"What good would that do?" Jess asked. "I wouldn't know it if I saw it, and even if I did, I wouldn't know what to look for."

Derek could tell them where to go, but he didn't know what to look for either, and the reminder that his single purpose on this trip was to provide that direction only added to his apprehension. His heart pounded and his hand trembled as he turned one more page and then stopped, breath halting in his lungs. "I found it."

Immediately, the other two crowded in next to him. Jeffreys leaned over from the right while Jess pressed in on the left. Her small hand curved over his shoulder, and Derek felt a small pang of excitement that normally only came from viewing a rare painting he'd been dreaming of seeing in person. He cleared his throat and pointed to the book. "I found *The Day That Never Was*."

"Is it in the diary?"

Derek pulled his satchel up to the table, careful not to dislodge Jess's hand while doing so. He liked it there, liked the idea that she was leaning on him, depending on him, even though she could easily have stood on her own. "Yes. Though nothing is listed by name, it's described well." He opened the satchel and thumbed through his notes before extracting the page in question. "This isn't a true rendition, obviously, as it lacks the detail and magic of the real one."

As fascinated as he was with the works of Fournier and The Six, this was one painting he rather hoped he never saw in person. The block print in the book almost brought him to his knees. The real one would probably rip his heart out. This was the first time his companions were seeing it. How were they remaining unaffected?

Maybe Jess needed him more than he'd thought.

"The diary talks of traveling forward to find the past. I'd have to check on a map, but from the orientation I'm guessing this road goes northeast out of Brookland in Kent."

Jess glanced at him and then leaned closer to the book. "How can you possibly know this depicts Brookland? It's just a village."

"The church." Derek pointed to the picture, trying to focus on the unique angled structure of the St. Augustine's Church bell tower and not look at the people. A bridal party walked away from a group of funeral mourners. Rosemary branches lay across a fresh grave, and wheat and flower blossoms trailed behind the bride as she walked down the road, head bowed.

Derek pulled out his sketchbook and began drawing the scene.

The details were difficult to see and nearly impossible to capture in a quick sketch, but he was almost certain that what was important was the church. There wasn't another one like it in the world. The bell tower consisted of three angled tiers, like cones stacked atop one another. The distinct porch and the rough rock walls extended out from there.

Silence pressed in on him as the others looked over his shoulder at the book. He spoke as he drew. "Did you know the sheep that graze on Romney Marsh are bred for meat and wool? Some of the best long-staple wool comes from there."

Two heads turned slowly in his direction.

"It's also a known smuggler's landing," Jess said. "What has that to do with anything?"

"The church. Brookland is in the Romney Marsh." Derek pointed at the picture, where a few sheep straggled along in the retreating wedding party. "There's sheep in the picture."

"Does that tell us what it means?" Jeffreys asked.

Derek looked up at their faces, but they only stared blankly at the book. Couldn't they see the story in front of them? The bride burying her groom instead of marrying him? Walking away because she was still alive? It fit the story Jess had told of a queen fighting for the revival of a lost country so well that Derek could only stare in awe at the skill and imagery.

They didn't appear to share his fascination.

"I don't think so." Derek cleared his throat. "I think the sheep are just part of the painting. My guess would be they're there to help establish the location. The painting is a point and a direction like *The Grace of Oceans Breaking*." He paused. "I think."

It was the best guess he had. The theory worked so far, anyway.

Jess stood up and looked around the library. "Is there a book of maps in this place?"

"I brought Ryland's map of England along. It's in the carriage. We can use that copy to keep track along the way if this theory proves correct," Jeffreys said.

"We might as well look at the other painting on our way back to the carriage, then." Jess moved toward the door, her skirts not even making a swishing sound as she walked.

Derek quickly replaced the book on the shelf before rushing to move ahead of her. They'd seen no one when he'd slipped them in the back of the library, but that didn't mean the passages had remained empty. He wasn't going to breathe easy until he knew he wasn't going to have to explain the presence of unauthorized visitors.

The freedom of sunshine put a bit more spring in his step as they walked the short distance to the Ashmoleon. Clearly he was not meant for a life of whatever it was Jess had done on a regular basis.

"Which one is this?" Jess asked as they stood before the painting a short time later.

"*A Work Completed.*" Derek had been viewing this painting since he was a little boy, would have said he could sketch it from memory except that he could recall nothing about it that seemed to match the significance of the other two. Even as he pulled out his sketchbook to record the scene, he didn't see how they all fit together.

There was nothing identifiable in the field of piled-up hay. A farmer sat on one of the piles, while a woman poured water into his cup.

Other than the sensation that one could reach into the painting and feel the water, there was nothing particularly striking about the picture. Still, he sketched.

Back at the carriage, Jeffreys pulled the book of maps from his trunk and joined them inside. Using their knees as a table, they opened the book.

Jess pulled ribbons from her leather satchel. She laid a yellow one across the bottom of England. "That would essentially be the direction Queen Jessamine was looking in Ryland's painting."

Derek took a blue ribbon from her and placed it where he'd thought the painting from the book indicated.

"They don't meet," Jess said with a frown. "How are we supposed to know where those haystacks are?"

"I don't think the haystacks matter," Derek said, pulling out his notes. "Not all of the paintings are written about the same way. There are four others, perhaps more, that mention traveling or departure in addition to *The Grace of Oceans Breaking* and *The Day That Never Was*. There are a few more that talk about the past and the future, which makes sense given the story."

"You're saying some of the paintings are a false lead?"

"I think so." He pulled more notes out and spread them across the map. "I noticed last night that some of the writings were more, well, poetic, for lack of a better term. I think those are the important ones."

"So we don't need to find them all?" Jeffreys asked.

"No."

The papers trembled a bit as Jess's legs shifted and shook the book. "What you're saying is that we can actually do this. There may actually be time to connect the diary to the paintings and find the coronation bowl."

Until that moment, with the vulnerability he'd glimpsed in William's drawing room making another appearance, Derek hadn't realized she'd had doubts. He'd thought she never considered failure. "Yes," he said, firming his voice with a confidence he wasn't sure he felt. "If we can see the paintings, we can solve the map."

"They aren't all going to be this easy," Jeffreys said.

"Then we'd better get started." Jess nodded to Derek's scattered notes. "Who has the paintings we need to see?"

CHAPTER SEVENTEEN

As it so happened, finding the next painting turned out to be far easier than pretending to be married to Derek. Several inns, a couple of house visits, and one Verbonnian painting later, she was back to wondering how in the world this entire charade was supposed to work.

Jess looked out the window at the ivy-covered estate they were pulling up to, bracing herself for the dread and uselessness that was about to bombard her.

The dread was familiar. A similar feeling preceded every entry into a kitchen, where memories she'd spent half her life avoiding were going to be stirred up as surely as the ingredients in her mixing bowl. The uselessness, however, was new and very unwelcome.

There was no denying it, though. Derek didn't need her to get him into the houses. His suggestion that they pose as travelers and simply walk up and request entry was working far better than she'd thought it would.

"This is Westmore, one of the estates belonging to the Earl of Bristford, right?" Jess asked. "Which painting does he own?"

"*The Lifting of the Skies.*" Derek tugged on his ill-fitting coat. "It's one of the few I wasn't able to confidently identify. This might be a waste of a visit."

"They all might be, given the fact that most of these men have multiple homes in which they could be storing the paintings. We won't know until we look." The second house they'd toured had been just such a disappointment. Right owner, wrong location.

As they moved into their second week of searching, what had started as a niggling worry grew stronger, and she was becoming desperate to push it away. Worry was pointless and fruitless, as she reminded herself whenever she considered what her brother might be doing. Such ponderings could do nothing but paralyze her, and right now, she needed to focus on moving forward.

The memory of Mrs. Lancaster spouting off a verse about each day having enough concern of its own and letting the Lord handle the rest nudged at the other side of her mind, but Jess pushed that away as well.

The old woman from Marlborough terrified Jess with her determination to act as a mother figure, doling out hugs and wisdom and eyeing her as if she knew Jess wasn't always as confident as she appeared to be.

Jess rolled her shoulders and repeated her mission over and over in her mind to bring herself into the present. All that mattered was getting into this house and seeing if the painting was here without raising suspicion.

Derek jumped out first and held his hand up to help Jess down. She let him, but only because it was possible someone was watching from the house.

He tucked her hand into his elbow, pulling her close to his side.

Instinct had her pulling away until he looked at her with slightly raised eyebrows.

Right. She was supposed to be his loving wife, enjoying a rare holiday through the countryside.

Ryland was the only man she'd ever pretended to be married to for a significant length of time. As neither of them had particularly fond and loving parents upon which to model their false marriage, it had been decidedly businesslike.

Derek's family, as she'd seen with her own eyes, wasn't like that. At every house and in the public rooms of every inn, he'd been *there*. Constantly offering her his arm, seeing to her comfort, being so nice and accommodating that it made her uneasy. To her recollection, no one had ever asked her if she was comfortable with the pace at which they were walking or shifted the chairs around at a table so that she could sit closer to the fire on a day chilled by low grey clouds and then made sure the choicest morsels of food ended up on her plate when dinner arrived.

Her pretend husband had done all that and more.

She allowed him to pull her into his side once more as they approached the door and knocked.

The housekeeper appeared, and Derek began his story about wishing to see a bit of the glamorous estate they'd heard so much about on their travels. Subtly he extended a coin. The housekeeper took it with a smile and opened the door wider.

Jess tried not to frown as they entered the house. What sort of foolish people allowed strangers to tramp through their home simply because they knocked on the door, smiled, and held out a coin? The coin wasn't even going to the owner.

This was the third house that had granted them entrance, and if Jess were the thieving sort, she'd be far richer now, having seen multiple ways in which she could have absconded with small, valuable trinkets or returned later for larger thefts.

No one was likely to find their way out to Haven Manor and ask for a tour, but Jess made a mental note to make sure Chemsford wasn't allowing any such nonsense at his other homes.

"The morning room is furnished completely from the Chippendale catalogue," the housekeeper said, ushering them through a room.

Beneath her hand, Derek's arm tensed, provoking Jess's desire to laugh and making her smile a bit more natural. Obviously the man knew some burning fact about furniture, saw a particularly fine piece of art that she couldn't even begin to recognize, or something in the room wasn't actually Chippendale.

Whichever of the three it was, Derek was greatly disturbed by it, because his arm didn't slowly relax the way it usually did. As the housekeeper moved them along, Jess couldn't help leaning in and teasing Derek a bit. "It was the table, wasn't it?"

He jerked his head in her direction. "What?"

"In the morning room. Was it the table?"

His eyes widened, the hazel flecks sparkling through his spectacles. He tipped his head closer and whispered, "How did you know?"

Her amusement bubbled up into a small, breathy laugh. "I didn't. It was a complete guess."

"Oh." He pouted and straightened as they continued after the housekeeper. After a few steps, he mumbled, "The legs were wrong."

"Of course they were." She took her free hand and patted his arm.

As her hand fell back to her side, she curled the fingers into her palm. How strange that she found it so easy to play this charade in the mode he'd created. Her pace now adjusted to his without thought, making walking arm-in-arm an easy feat. The first inn they'd entered as his version of husband and wife, she'd nearly taken out a chair trying to walk at his side. Even his small touches and glances were becoming easier to return.

The housekeeper smiled at them as she led them through a long gallery. "Where did you say you were from?"

Jess pinched his arm to keep him silent, one benefit his close proximity provided. "Derbyshire," she said, naming the next county over, a reasonable distance for a holiday but not so far that one would wonder at their ability to make the trip.

"Beautiful country there," the housekeeper said. "It's nice to see a love match." She looked around as if someone would overhear them, even though they had yet to see another soul for the entire tour. "The master and missus don't have much to do with each other these days, as I'm sure you heard when they told you about the house. This room is rather well known."

With that, the housekeeper opened the door to a salon, and Jess had to work to keep her mouth from gaping.

The room was split in half. Two walls were green, two were cream, and the furniture made distinct groupings in the two corners. On what Jess assumed was the wife's side, though she probably shouldn't make assumptions about anyone who would create a room such as this, the furniture was pale blue, with curved delicate lines. Sheer white drapes covered the window.

Smooth, pale brown wooden furniture filled the other corner. Both had writing desks and a small conversation grouping, though a person sitting in one area could never easily converse with a person sitting in the other.

"There was a great argument over who should use this room, as it gets the best light in the evenings." The housekeeper stepped to the center of the room and stood demurely, obviously expecting that this was the room they'd come to see and that they would need to take some time looking at it.

Derek's arm tensed again, and Jess immediately went on the alert. She tuned her ears to listen for signs that someone else had entered the room, but there was nothing.

Then Derek was guiding her over toward the master's side of the room. "There," he whispered.

She looked up and saw a painting of angels tripping through clouds. It was much better suited to the other corner, with its delicate, frothy wisps of cloud and sky. The husband had likely hung it here out of spite so his wife couldn't see it.

"Is this what you thought it was?" Jess whispered back.

Derek shook his head and moved her on so that it wasn't obvious they were staring at the painting instead of the room. "No. I think it might be another one of the false leads."

Jess's hope plummeted. They couldn't afford to chase after false leads. Not that she blamed Derek. They were having to piece together so many broken pieces of information, there was bound to be a misstep or two. The queen had intended the collection to stay together, after all, for someone with diary in hand to be able to pick out the important pieces and put the picture together.

Guilt joined worry at the edge of her mind. Their brief time allotment was entirely her own fault. If she'd only told Ryland—no. Jess didn't contemplate *if*.

Without the painting to look for, Jess wasn't sure what to concentrate on for the remainder of the tour. They could hardly just turn and leave, so Jess dutifully followed Derek's cues, taking in the views of the grounds and the apparently exquisite crown molding.

This was not enough to distract her mind from the detrimental emotions waiting to eat her alive. Her only available choices for diversion were the house or Derek. As the house wasn't going to tell her anything of interest, much less importance, she turned her thoughts to Derek.

She looked up at his profile, the spectacles perched on a long straight nose over a pointed chin, all of which was topped with that hair that never quite seemed to stay where he put it. Why didn't he cut it or purchase a pomade? Did he like it constantly dropping into his eyes? It made him look like a little boy who had forgotten he'd grown into a man, as if at one point his brain had matured so quickly that the rest of him forgot to keep pace.

"We could," Derek said with a laugh, jarring her from her thoughts. "But that would make it difficult for us to return to our inn before nightfall." He dropped his gaze toward Jess, obviously intending for her to be in on whatever conversation he'd been having with the housekeeper. Instead his eyes met hers as he caught her staring at him.

Jess jerked her face away, stunned to feel heat crawling over her ears. Was she blushing? She couldn't remember the last time she'd blushed.

This house tour needed to end. Now.

She made it back to the front door without looking at Derek, then all but ran from the house as soon as they crossed the threshold. Only the firm grip of Derek's hand holding hers against his arm kept her at his side. His long, thin fingers completely covered her smaller ones, meaning that if she wanted to retreat she was going to have to make a scene first.

He said his final pleasantries and guided her back to the carriage at an agonizingly moderate pace.

Jeffreys was waiting there, awkwardly angled to hold the door open for them while holding the reins in his good hand. Ryland's watchdog couldn't quite hide his grin as he watched Jess trail alongside Derek like a demure little wife.

As far as Jess was concerned, they could both go dunk their heads in a bucket.

She clambered into the carriage, both to get them on their way and to remove herself from public viewing. If no one could see them, there would be no reason for Derek to keep her close or be overly attentive. In private, she could tell him to let her be.

Derek climbed into the carriage after her and paused, hunched over in the doorway, staring at her silently.

She frowned and stared back at him. Why wasn't he getting in? She gave a pointed look at the seat across from her. He merely tilted his head.

More heat spread up Jess's face as she shifted to the front-facing seat—the one a gentleman would always offer to a lady. Even without the prying eyes, he insisted on treating her as such. She'd never been a lady, not really. Farm girls, spies, and servants received a different sort of treatment.

"Thank you," Derek murmured as he sat in the backward-facing seat and pulled his sketchbook from his bag. As the carriage rolled forward, he put down the lines of the painting they'd just seen.

Jess waited until he was finished to speak. "You don't have to do that, you know."

"What? Draw it out? I think it wise. Even though that painting wasn't the one I thought it was, there might be a detail in it we need later."

Jess didn't even want to think about how they would fit a group of frolicking angels onto a map of England. "You don't have to bother with the seats." She gestured between them. "It's only you and me in this carriage. No one is going to know where we sit."

"I'll know," Derek said in a matter-of-fact voice.

"As will I, but I'm saying it doesn't matter. Riding backward doesn't bother me."

Not like he did.

Jess sat back with her arms crossed and watched the countryside roll by, just as it had for the past week. Half the time they rode in silence, half the time he droned about what he'd learned in his studies that she could never hope to understand or cram into her brain, and half the time she poked and prodded at him in an effort to make him as miserable as she was, only to have him sidestep her jab with the grace of a skilled pugilist.

And yes, she was well aware that three halves were greater than a whole. She hadn't completely missed being taught her maths. That was just how long this interminable trip felt to her.

Perhaps if she used these carriage rides to learn about the diary and what Derek thought he was looking for in the art, she'd be able to cut Derek free.

All she had to do was convince herself that it didn't mean anything that he was smarter than her. Her entire life had been spent surrounded by people who knew more than she did, and until now she'd seen that as an advantage. She would gather what she needed from them and then move on. It was how she'd learned languages, fighting, and a host of other skills.

If doing such now had the added benefit of removing the disturbance he brought to her emotions, so be it.

"Did you know," Derek said as he glanced up, "that some of the more detailed paintings of the seventeenth century were done on thin copper plates rubbed with garlic?"

No, she didn't know that. Why did *he* know that? Why did *anyone* need to know that? The interminable "did you know" questions were absolutely the worst part of being trapped in a small carriage with him. She never knew. Ever. She didn't know useless facts about history or architecture or whatever else he'd spent his life studying.

While she was aware that two halves made one whole, that was the extent of her mathematical skills, with the exception of a rather good ability to estimate how far away she was from a target and therefore how many revolutions her knife would need to make before it reached them.

That was a good talent. She would bet Derek didn't know that. She could play her own game of "did you know" and see if he knew at what angle to pull a man's thumb so that it caused an excruciating amount of pain, thereby allowing his opponent to get away, even if she was half his size.

Only the fact that he might have seen some obscure painting that allowed him to cite a better technique than hers kept her silent.

She cleared her throat and gave him a short smile, just as she'd been doing every time he asked her "did you know?" for the past eight days. "No, I didn't know that."

He nodded and went into more detail about it.

When he started winding down, she brought the conversation back to the diary. "Have you learned any more from the translations?"

Derek had been methodically working back through every line. Given the cryptic nature of the writing, they couldn't afford to have only a general idea. They needed to know exactly what was said.

He reached into the bag and pulled out the book, frowning at it but not opening it.

"Your family . . . legend, for lack of a better word. Does it say how Queen Jessamine died?"

Jess shook her head. "If it does I never knew it. That probably wasn't considered a vital piece of the puzzle to pass along. How she died didn't matter. She wasn't even part of the royal lineage anymore."

He cleared his throat and shifted in his seat, looking uncomfortable, a rare occurrence for him. He always seemed perfectly happy to be his odd self. And why shouldn't he be? The man had friends, family, and a career he loved. He had no reason to be unhappy.

He ran a finger along the spine of the diary. "These other people claiming the throne, who might be after you, do you know anything about them?"

"Only a guess," she said softly. She didn't want to think back, not when she was alone and certainly not with him in the close confines of a rolling box where mere inches separated their knees. If she wanted to solve this, though, she needed her memories. How could she trust anything she remembered with the mindset of a child? Revisiting the stories as an adult, trying to see her father as he truly was, called everything into question.

"Several years after Verbonne joined the Holy Roman Empire, when the kingdom had passed to King Nicolas's eldest son by his second wife and then on to the second son, Johannes, after the first died with only daughters, another man arrived, claiming that he had the true claim to the throne. He claimed that Queen Jessamine had been with child when she left Verbonne, and he was the son of that son.

"The emperor liked King Johannes better than the interloper and thus declared his claim void and without grounds. Every few years, the man tried again until the emperor had him executed. Five years later, his son made a claim to the throne."

Derek winced. "You think those descendants are trying to claim it again, now that it's once more a free country?"

"It's possible. The fact that we're scrambling across the country on the trail of clues in an old diary is proof enough that family legacy can be a powerful thing. Pass enough passion along to the next generation and it doesn't die." Jess jabbed one fingernail into her palm and watched the skin change color. "They still cared ten years ago. The rise of Napoleon renewed their hope, I suppose. They joined forces with him, which was why, even though Verbonne was ready to peacefully change empires for the sake of survival, my family had to go into hiding. Napoleon declared my family traitors and acknowledged the other claim. He vowed to hunt my family down and end any future problems they might cause."

Jess swallowed hard, fighting back thoughts she hadn't allowed herself to entertain. In her mind, Verbonne had been lost. She'd assumed that if it survived the war intact, the other line would gain control and rewrite history before moving the country into the future. Now, it seemed that even though the war was over, there was still a battle to be fought. Was it possible for this to end without one of the lines being eradicated?

"Why do you ask?" Jess brought her thoughts back to where they needed to be, the here and now.

Derek ran a hand over the cover of the book. "Because I finished another passage last night. If one were to read that entry in the right way, it's possible the queen died in childbirth."

Jess didn't know what to say to that, so she said nothing.

Neither did he.

The silence continued for a time that could have been five minutes but felt closer to an hour.

"Did you know that—"

"No," Jess cut Derek off. "No, I didn't know, likely no one knows besides you, and at this moment I don't particularly care."

Was it possible everything her father had worked his entire life for, what he had died for, was a lie? Had the queen borne the true heir while in England? Was the other claim to the throne legitimate?

If there had been a child, who had raised him? Had King Nicolas known? Was it in the letter he burned?

Given Derek's hesitation at mentioning the passage, Jess had to assume that the diary answered none of those questions. Her gaze dropped to the book sitting on the seat beside Derek. She wanted to know what it said, but what if . . .

What if her loss had been worthless? What if everything she'd known had been wrong? Worse than wrong. Stolen.

Then again, what meant more? Blood or birth? None of the other line had ever lived in Verbonne. Could they love it enough to lead it properly?

Did any of that matter now? The country was practically having to start over.

"What does it say?" she asked quietly.

Derek looked at her, the brown hair swooping gently across his forehead and dipping into his eyes so that he had to brush it back with an impatient hand. He smoothed the diary open in his lap. "With the symbolism of the rest of the book, it's hard to say. She does write that nature managed what man could not when she mentions the queen's death. But then it says that even in death she ushered forth a bright and glorious future."

Derek set the book aside and slid his spectacles off in order to wipe them with a handkerchief. "It could be a child, or it could simply be because she is the starting point of this journey. Much of the book is written as if she is the one taking the various paths. It's quite clear that the queen mother adored her daughter-in-law."

The one Jess was named after but not actually related to.

Queen Marguerite had never gotten to meet her son's second wife nor any of the children that union produced. She had lived out her days in England, possibly more of an actual hero than Jessamine had been. The notice of her passing was the only other message sent back to Verbonne after the diary. The queen mother had left Verbonne behind, giving it a final gift and a hug farewell. As far as anyone knew, she'd never looked back.

Perhaps Jess should have been named after her instead.

"Do you think there was a baby?"

"The diary isn't clear, so I don't know. I would have to think that the fact that the diary was sent back to Verbonne would seem to indicate she thought that the rightful heir was there."

This was why Jess hated history and scholastic thinking. It was so grey, so shilly-shally. There were no definitive answers. In Jess's life, it was usually yes or no. It was about survival and making choices in the moment and living with them.

"I don't know what to do," Jess admitted through a tight throat.

Derek gestured toward the window. "I suggest we get a bite to eat, then bed down at this inn for the evening."

"Food and sleep aren't going to fix this, Derek."

He winked at her. "They won't hurt either."

CHAPTER EIGHTEEN

Derek kept what he knew of the history of cooking to himself as they ate bowls of stew and crusty bread. It was only him and Jess tonight. Most nights the three of them could eat together without drawing too much attention, but this inn was nicer than the others, and dining with their driver would have drawn notice. Jeffreys ate with a group of other grooms and drivers, leaving Jess and Derek to dine alone.

After five minutes of silence, in which Jess looked at everyone and everything besides him, Derek started voicing his observations. It was a bit more difficult than pulling facts from his head, but it was also enjoyable to observe the people around them and point out details as if they were a painting come to life.

Twenty minutes later, Jess joined him.

Her observations were nothing like his. Where he noticed what people wore or carried, if their hair had been recently cut or their bag patched a few too many times, Jess saw movement. That person limped, but only when she thought someone could see her. One man was seated in such a way that he could see all the possible entrances to the room. Another was slumped over his cup, but his eyes kept jerking to whatever table the serving lass was visiting.

"We look at the world differently, you and I," he said.

She stiffened. "Yes, I suppose we do."

He took a bite of stew and studied her. Why hadn't he learned before that people were a form of art? If there was so much to be learned from someone else's interpretation of a moment, wasn't there even more to be learned from his own?

The mediocrity of his art skills meant he'd never been able to get the image in his head onto canvas in a satisfactory manner. Had he walked away from observing the life around him when he'd walked away from his brushes? How much had he missed because of that?

If he were to paint this scene, this moment, what would it look like? Jess would certainly be harshly drawn, with sharp angles and deep shadows. He'd make the seat of the chair higher and a bit wider, giving her a place to hunch behind and hide. Her focus would be outside the frame somewhere, perhaps behind the viewer, making that itch appear between their shoulders until they turned their head to see if someone was lingering behind them, watching them.

She would be defensive. Distant. Shielded.

He picked up his bread and looked at it as he carefully tore off a piece, giving her as much privacy as he could while sitting at the same table. "Do you think that's a bad thing, our seeing the world differently?"

"Isn't it?"

With a shrug of his shoulders, he popped the bread in his mouth and turned to look about the public room as he chewed and swallowed. Then he turned his gaze back on her. "I don't think so."

"There are others who do not share your opinion," she said, giving him a haughty look and a smirk that tried to convey that she knew more about people than he did.

Perhaps she did know more about people, at least modern people, but he didn't think so. People were people, even when the clothing changed. Despite the change of styles and mediums, it was easy to see the thread of humanity over the centuries of art. Love, grief, anger, ambition. None of it was new; it just manifested itself in different ways.

"Interesting thing about opinions," he said, folding his arms on the table and forcing himself to hold her gaze, even though it made his gut quake a bit. "They tend to vary from person to person. If they didn't, they would be facts."

Her smirk drifted into a frown, and Derek fought the desire to grin. It was difficult to argue with the statement of a word's definition. But if anyone could come up with a way to do it, it would be Jess.

Surprisingly, she seemed inclined to continue the conversation instead of turn it into an argument. "Whose opinion should influence me, then?"

Derek stopped holding back his grin. "That's a matter of opinion."

She cast her eyes toward the ceiling and gave her head a small shake before sitting back in her chair, lips curved into a smile instead of a smirk. "Where do you stand on the topic?"

"My own opinion I suppose comes first. God's, of course, though whether His thoughts are opinions or facts can be debated. Did you know that—"

She held up a hand. "Stay with the subject, Derek."

He cleared his throat. "Right. At the end of the day, it's only my opinion that guides my decisions. That opinion is influenced I suppose by God, my family and friends, my colleagues."

"More than that." Jess tilted her chin toward the young girl who'd served them their stew. "Her. What was your opinion about her? Not one you form now, but one you already had."

He paused for a moment, trying to follow her instructions and quiet the thoughts that immediately came to mind. "I didn't have one."

"Precisely. She is a servant girl—unseen, unnoticed. I know. I've been a servant girl in many a country. It's the best way to gather information. No one sees you or notices you. You're like furniture."

She pushed her bowl away and dropped her gaze to a scattering of crumbs on the table before continuing. "I don't think or behave in a way that is normal. That limits where I belong. Opinions may not be facts, but they are not solely your creation. They're conditioned."

Had Derek never seen this part of Jess because he'd never looked, or was this the first time her defenses had lowered enough to allow it to emerge? "I never knew you were a philosopher, Jess."

She stiffened, her face falling back into its blank mask. "I'm not."

"Why not?" he asked.

"Philosophy is all of that complicated nonsense found in books and papers. It's what you do with a painting, drawing all the information together to see the story and the intent of the artist." Jess shook her head. "That's not me."

The shadows on the painting in Derek's mind shifted. No longer were they all around Jess, creating dagger-like angles and edges. Instead, he deepened the darkness between her and the rest of the room, almost as if the shadow weren't created by her, but by some sort of invisible shield she'd erected between herself and the rest of the world.

At the moment, he was being allowed to peek around the edges of that shield, and it was changing everything about how he saw her.

"You're a thinker, Jess."

One eyebrow lifted and the smirk returned. "Anyone I've ever worked with would dispute that. I'm rather known for charging in on a gut decision rather than developing a plan." She gestured between them and then out to the room. "This is more of a plan than I've ever executed. Normally I act first and see what happens next."

"How is that working out for you?"

"I'm still alive." She shrugged. "My instincts haven't failed me yet."

He pointed a finger at her. "Because you're a thinker. A quick one, I'm sure. What's your opinion of the serving girl?"

"She likes working here." Jess tilted her head. "There's a difference between forced happiness and real happiness. You see it in the way people walk and hold themselves. Real happiness extends everywhere, while the false kind tends to be limited to the face and the feet."

Derek chuckled and stopped the hand that was reaching for his ale. "The feet?"

She nodded. "They tend to bounce and smile. But the hands are still limp, the chest is still low." Her gaze followed the girl about the room. "She's not like that. She's practically dancing between the tables, waving to people, chatting to those she isn't serving. She's happy."

"Where did you grow up?" Derek asked.

"Why do you ask?"

"If opinions are conditioned, I'm curious where yours were formed."

"A bit of everywhere, I suppose." She looked away. "I left Verbonne when I was eight. Until then I'd known only privilege and comfort. Hiding and the tense situation was a shock, but children are adaptable. Ryland rescued me at fifteen. Since then, I've been all over. I've seen people do horrible things in the name of ambition and even more terrible things in pursuit of peace. Sometimes I helped those things happen."

She wrapped her hands around her mug. "I've also seen people smile at a funeral. I've seen joy in the middle of war. I've experienced grace from people who should have condemned me."

"So seeing the world differently is not a bad thing." Derek wound his fingers tightly together to keep from reaching across the table and taking her hand. He'd never felt such a compulsion before her, but somewhere between the second inn and the second house, reaching for her had become less about projecting the idea that they were married and more about finding a way to reach over the seemingly impossible barrier between them.

Attacking that division required he take the time to really see her, to try to understand her. Was one a natural extension of the other? Did his attempts to connect with her on a mental level somehow manifest themselves in the urge to reach out physically as well?

That was something to think about later, but for now she was sharing details about herself she never had before. He wouldn't risk stopping that by taking her hand. He pushed on. "What would you choose for the world, then? Should everyone be as happy as the serving lass or as glum as the man drowning his sorrows in ale over there? If everyone were the same, how would we know happiness from sadness?"

She shook her head, but the frown she'd been wearing began to curve upward a bit at the edges. "I think you, Mr. Thornbury, are the philosopher now."

"Then you admit you were one earlier."

Her hand gripped her remaining hunk of bread as if she were considering throwing it at his head.

He grinned as the image in his mind changed a bit more, the shadows shifting to allow a small, hidden glimmer of light. She was a painting come to life, with every angle revealing something new. Every secret he managed to uncover brought up three more. "Tell me more about the people you experienced. The good and the bad. Show me what conditioned your opinions."

"I went to Spain once." She rolled the crumbs around the table with her palm. "Helped incite a riot." Her amber eyes glanced up at him through her lashes. "I'm rather good at that, though this one didn't really need me." Her attention dropped back to the crumbs. "A lot of people died, but it changed the war. In the end, it freed a lot of people."

"The second of May, 1808," Derek said.

One of Jess's eyebrows lifted. "That's hardly had time to make it into one of your history books."

"Two years ago, Goya, a Spanish painter, depicted that night and the next day. I've never seen the paintings, of course. Few have. A colleague in Spain sent me a letter, telling me about wrapping them and putting them into storage on the king's orders. His descriptions of the paintings were memorable, though. You were there?"

Jess nodded. "At the beginning. Once tempers were running high, I left."

Her voice was flat as she went on to tell of her limited involvement in short, stark facts. "I didn't do that type of thing often. My main skills were in getting in and out of places unseen. There were many English sympathizers and informants willing to share their information. I went and got it from them. Most of the time I wasn't anywhere near the fighting."

"And when you were?"

"I got out as soon as I could. I can defend myself against an attacker, but I can't take down an army single-handed." She picked up a crumb and ground it into dust between her thumb and forefinger. "There was a girl, once. I took her with me until we made it out of the battle. We got to a creek bed barely running with a trickle of water but cut deep into the ground. I told her to get low and run. I never knew if she survived."

Jess dusted off her hands and lifted her gaze to meet his, some of the tightness around her eyes fleeing as she blinked. "I learned Italian and spent a great deal of time in that area. Napoleon's control kept it from being an easy place to stay." A wry grin touched her lips. "It was the British gaining a bit of a foothold that got me wounded badly enough to cause a problem, though. Ryland managed to get me home in the hold of a British warship. Healing took a while."

Wanting to keep the companionable moment, Derek shared his own memories, not of facts and world history, but of his favorite paintings and the people he'd encountered in his studies. As he spoke, details about those people he'd never realized he'd collected emerged.

Perhaps he'd been paying more attention than he thought. Perhaps their taste in art had influenced the way he viewed them. The question of why he saw people certain ways was going to drive him mad now.

One thing began to become clear as Jess told him about getting caught in the wrong place during the British invasion of the Adriatic coast, her hand sliding to her arm almost without conscious thought. Through all her stories there was a glimmer of hope. Hope that what she was doing would come out well in the end, hope that she could save someone, hope that her walking through darkness would mean someone else, perhaps that girl in the creek bed, wouldn't have to.

It changed the way Derek saw her. He glanced at the serving girl when her laugh grew loud enough to drift over the chaotic noise of the tavern crowd. It was changing the way he saw everyone. Perhaps the madness that came along with paying attention to people wasn't so bad after all.

Eventually, the public room grew emptier, and they made their way upstairs. For the first time this trip, they'd been forced to take a single room.

Inside, Jess began gathering some of the bedclothes and making a pallet on the floor.

"I'll sleep there," Derek said, shrugging out of his jacket and telling himself the action held no great significance due to the abnormal location.

It felt different, though. He felt exposed. It made him rethink removing his boots.

Jess laughed and threw a pillow onto the pallet. "Have you ever slept on a floor, Derek?"

"No," he said, moving forward to stop her from removing the blanket, "but I have slept at many a desk. The floor has to be better."

"There's no need," Jess said, her voice a bit more strained. "I've done it plenty of times before."

"That doesn't mean you have to do it tonight."

Why were they whispering? It wasn't as if anyone was going to overhear them, despite the thin walls. They'd hardly been yelling before.

The single candle they'd brought up with them sat on the table beside the bed, barely giving off enough light for him to see the sheen of her pale hair and the shape of her face. There was no detail, no sign that this moment meant anything to her beyond the debate over who would sleep where, but it felt momentous to him.

They'd changed in the tavern below, changed their relationship into something more than grudging partners. She wasn't who he'd thought she was, and now, with his earlier resentment replaced with understanding of her prior behavior, he didn't know what to make of her.

The compulsion to reach out and touch her rose in him again, but he didn't give in. There was no audience here, no performance. Here he had to remember that they weren't truly married. Hopefully, after tonight, they could at least be friends.

"I'll sleep on the floor," he said and dropped onto the pallet.

A few minutes later, he heard her climb into the bed and the pale light of the candle disappeared.

Her breathing evened out soon after, but it was a while before Derek found sleep. The floor was seriously uncomfortable.

CHAPTER NINETEEN

Morning light had a way of picking out the cracks caused by mistakes of the night before, and the next morning's early dawn was no different. Jess rushed through her morning preparations, which didn't take long, as she'd slept in her dress and had to do little more than slip on her shoes. She cast a glance to the huddle on the floor where Derek was curled onto his side, his shoulder rising and falling with his steady breathing.

How could she have allowed him to convince her to enter that conversation last night? Never had she talked that much. If he'd been working for the enemy, her side would have been as good as dead. The fact that she wasn't sure who actually comprised her side and whether or not they were in the right was irrelevant.

Verbonne was a fairy tale to her. A distant memory and a bedtime story. England had taken Jess in, given her purpose. Somewhere in the middle of that was the family that had raised her, instilled an idea within her that could, quite possibly, have been built on a lie.

While she waited to find out for certain, she would maintain her current plan. One thing she couldn't wait to do, though, was shore up the vulnerabilities created by her late-night confessions.

Refusing to face Derek within the walls of the inn, she fled to the carriage. Everything that had happened in that inn could remain there.

Jeffreys was just beginning to harness the horses when she arrived at the stables.

"You're early. Grab that strap there, will you?"

She quickly took over the smaller buckles needed to hitch the rented horses to the carriage. He'd never admit it, but his missing finger had to make those more difficult. "Will we reach the next house today?"

Jeffreys nodded. "A nice drive north. It's a lucky thing that owning one of these Six paintings is a coup worthy of putting on display in the public rooms."

Jess gave a short laugh. "Unless you're the Duke of Marshington."

"I think we can safely assume that no one else is the Duke of Marshington." Jeffreys shook his head while he tightened the final strap.

"Good morning," Derek said as he approached the carriage.

The smile immediately fell from Jess's lips as she turned halfway toward him in greeting. Enough to acknowledge him, but not enough to meet his gaze. When she turned back, Jeffreys gave her an odd look.

The valet turned coachman pressed his lips together. "Perhaps we should take a look at what we have so we can better know what we're looking for today."

Jess gave him a narrow glare. They'd reviewed what they knew before yesterday's stop. It wasn't as if suddenly they had more information than before.

"Of course." Derek strapped his valise to the back of the carriage and then climbed inside.

Since not climbing in would only delay the inevitable, Jess joined Derek. Jeffreys leaned in the doorway to keep an ear out for the horses.

Derek pulled out his sketchbook and diary notes while Jess retrieved the map of England from beneath her carriage seat. They'd pinned three ribbons to the map, none of which told them anything.

"The last painting doesn't add another ribbon, does it?" Jeffreys asked.

Jess shook her head. "Even if there was something significant about the way the hem of one angel's robe fluttered to the right, we have no way of knowing where a bunch of clouds are supposed to be."

Derek and Jeffreys both looked at her. Jeffreys with concern, Derek with accusing resignation.

She squirmed in her seat.

Jeffreys's hand came out and pointed to the green ribbon they'd added at the first house. "Are we sure about that location?"

"Not in the least," Derek murmured. "It was a manor house. It could be anywhere. That was our best guess based on what could be seen on the hills behind it. Even if we knew for certain that the house hadn't been remodeled to remove that distinctive fountain from the front, we couldn't hope to simply stumble across it."

"Know anyone who frequents country house parties?" Jeffreys asked with a laugh.

Jess winced. She did know someone who went to a lot of house parties, but she was more than hesitant to say so. Endangering more people was out of the question. It was bad enough that she'd pulled Derek, with his slow, methodical ways, into this situation. She couldn't watch over everyone, even if her friend Kit's new husband had attended a house party at every grand estate south of Scotland.

Jess slapped the book of maps closed, shoved it beneath the cushion, and sat over it. With a lifted brow in Jeffreys's direction, she dared him to challenge her.

Challenge her to what she hadn't the faintest idea, but she'd welcome anything to ease the restlessness rushing through her veins.

Jeffreys looked from her to Derek. "Something I should know about?"

"We already established we know nothing new," Jess said, arms folded across her chest in an attempt to look big and imposing. "Unless you can identify the house better than we did, we're right where we were three days ago."

He clicked his tongue. "Not exactly. Three days ago, you two were what one might call friendly strangers." He gestured from Jess to Derek and back again. "This morning you won't look at him and he won't look anywhere but at you."

Jess jerked her head around to find that Derek was, indeed, studying her from behind his wire spectacles. He blinked but didn't drop his gaze. What was he seeing? What was he remembering?

Probably every word she'd said. She'd practically been a living history book.

"I would like to think we're friends," Derek said.

Jess shrugged one shoulder. "That's a matter of opinion."

He flinched as if she'd punched him.

She forced a smile to cover the churning in her gut that made her want to shove Jeffreys aside and run for the nearest retiring room. "I'm simply frustrated this is taking so long. We have no idea what's happening in Verbonne."

Finally, Derek looked away. Away from her, away from Jeffreys, and out the opposite window where there was nothing to be seen but the side of the stable. "Of course. We should be going."

"Right," Jeffreys said, his voice low, slow, and full of speculation.

As the horses left the innyard, Jess tried to put herself into one of her personas. She was someone cheerful and optimistic. Exuberant, even. They were making progress, even if it was slow, and despite her lapse in judgment last night, Derek wasn't going to use his new knowledge to harm her.

After a while, Derek's posture shifted, and he settled deeper into the seat, a small smile on his face. When she remarked on the trees bordering the lane they were traveling, he chuckled.

She told herself not to ask. Nothing would be gained by turning the conversation personal again, even at an innocent and superficial level. As he kept watching her and grinning, though, the urge to confront him overwhelmed her.

"Your spirits seem higher," she said, keeping her tone to one of icy politeness that people used at parties when they had to talk to someone they'd rather avoid.

"Yes," Derek said. "I find my disposition greatly improved."

"Why?"

"Because"—he leaned forward and braced his elbows on his knees, watching her intently as his smile broadened into a grin—"your hands are sad."

Then he sat back, looked out the window, and remarked upon the trees.

❧❦

There was something wrong at Greenwood Park. Derek sensed it the moment the housekeeper granted them entrance, but it took touring three full rooms for him to grasp why. It was so obvious that he had to blame the distraction that was Jess in order to keep from feeling like an idiot.

All the art was French.

All of it.

It wasn't that it was bad art, but the distinction was an oddity in an English home, particularly after the lengthy war the country had just gone through. Charles Le Brun, Antoine Watteau, and Georges de La Tour adorned the walls, while sculptures by Antoine Coysevox, Claude Michel, and Jean-Baptiste Lemoyne stood in corners and on bookshelves and tables. This was not a random coincidence. It was a carefully curated collection.

A collection that, given the overall feel of neglect to the house itself, should have been parted with in order to enrich the family coffers a bit.

"Something's wrong," he whispered to Jess, who had slipped her hand from his arm after they'd passed through the first room.

She simply nodded and asked the housekeeper about the rug.

Derek tensed even more. She never asked about the rugs, never asked about anything, but from the moment they'd crossed the threshold, Jess's touring persona had been different.

She simpered.

There wasn't another word for it. If he'd encountered her this way at their first meeting, he'd have been thoroughly convinced that she hadn't a single coherent thought in her head. She chose ridiculous things to admire and asked questions a child who had grown up in any sort of quality home could answer.

If someone were looking for a crafty, intelligent spy, the housekeeper would swear there hadn't been one at her house. It wasn't a bad disguise, but Jess was taking the idea to an extreme. She was a walking caricature.

In the portrait gallery, the art began to look more standard. Portraits by renowned sixteenth-century English artists began the line, followed by a succession of other recognizable styles.

As they approached the modern paintings, though, the detailed realism of the British Rococo gave way to the softer lines of the style's French originators. Yet another sign that the home's decor was certainly not an accident and that the owner had likely not been pleased with the recent defeat of Napoleon.

The last portrait in the line was of a man with a high forehead, a thin scar, and a thick, curly black beard.

Jess's incessant prattle stumbled into silence for a moment, and he could feel the tension emanating from her across the small space she was maintaining between them. He reached out a hand to . . . to . . . what? Comfort her? Calm her? Assure her that he was with her?

When his hand landed on the back of her spencer jacket, he didn't feel the warmth of her body through the fabric. He felt four hard ridges. What were those? He shifted his hand a bit. They were long and smooth, one end rounded more than the other. They almost felt like . . . knives?

She stepped away from him to cross to the window, and his hand dropped back to his side. Nearly pressing her face to the window, she gasped and said, "Is that a lake? Every grand room should have a view of a lake."

Before the housekeeper could answer, Jess flipped the latch and pushed open the window in order to stick her head outside. The wind whipped at the ribbons of her bonnet, and she untied it and took it from her head before leaning a bit more out the window.

The housekeeper rushed over and pulled the window in, forcing Jess back into the house. She pouted for a moment, then gave a shrug and a smile and glided back to the family portraits. "Is this the current owner, then? Lord Bradford?"

"Yes, madam," the housekeeper said stiffly. She was probably debating whether an afternoon spent with this nitwit was worth the coin they'd given her.

"Is he home? Will we see him?" Jess bounced on her toes like an excited child. What was going on? Jess had suddenly gone from empty-headed to downright annoying. What part was he to play? What would he do if he were her husband?

He hadn't a clue. Not in his wildest imaginations would he marry someone with whom he couldn't hold an intelligent conversation. He could pretend she was his sister, though. Derek's youngest sister, Jacqueline, was nearly this excitable, silly, and exasperating.

Of course, she was also twelve.

"Dear," he said, crossing the floor and trying to look like he loved her inanity. "We talked about this. We came to see the house, not the people."

She gave another pout. "It doesn't hurt to ask."

The housekeeper stepped closer and inclined her head. "As it happens, his lordship is in the area, though not expected home until this evening." She flattened her lips in what might have been an attempt at a smile but fell horribly short. "Perhaps it would be best if we cut this tour a bit short. Maybe the drawing room before you depart?"

Derek opened his mouth to protest. They needed to see as much of the house as possible. Before he could speak, though, Jess said, "Oh, that sounds lovely. Is the dining room near that? I'd love to see where he eats. And then we would have time to walk the grounds, wouldn't we?"

"Yes, the dining room is at the bottom of those stairs," the housekeeper said quickly. "And the grounds are absolutely where you want to spend your time. The distant views of the house from the parkland are splendid."

Jess grinned and nodded before looping her arm into Derek's and pinching him hard above his wrist, sending him from confused to worried.

What he'd seen was concerning, but whatever Jess had noticed clearly implied the problem was more pressing than Derek knew. She felt the need to get them out of this house sooner rather than later, even if it meant not seeing the painting.

They'd talked about the danger and he'd believed them, but this was the first time he'd felt it. Thus far it had been all silly disguises and sneaky subterfuge. Trickery, but not danger.

Blood crackled in his ears as the housekeeper led them down the stairs and into a large dining room that could more aptly be termed a sort of banquet hall. High ceilings and a large chandelier over a broad, long table gave the room a dominating presence.

On the wall at the head of the table was the painting.

The Feast of Future Fortune.

The assembly of people in the painting wore crowns, and jewelry dripped over their velvet robes and shiny slippers. A banquet table ran along one wall of their assembly room, but all the silver and gold dishes were empty. Each person held cups of gold aloft as they danced. Upon closer inspection, Derek saw their crowns and belts were without jewels, though the spaces for mounting gems remained.

Derek moved toward the painting, his eyes eating up every detail. There was nothing distinguishing about the room, but on the wall behind the party was a painting. Or perhaps it was a window? He stepped around the table to get a better look.

Jess didn't follow him to the painting. Instead, she moved to the glass doors and looked out. "We really must look at this garden, my love."

Derek blinked. *My love?* After her distance in the carriage, the words jarred against his ears and sent a choking stab from his middle to his throat.

"Mmm-hmmm," he managed to get out. He didn't trust his voice. Jess definitely wanted them out of this house.

"Would we be able to go out these doors?" She gave the housekeeper a bright, happy smile. "We could work our way through the gardens and back to our carriage." She pouted. "Since we don't get to see the bedchambers, we might as well look up at the windows of the private salons."

"Whatever makes your tour more pleasant," the housekeeper said as she rushed to open the door for them.

Jess stepped immediately through the door and lifted her head to the sunshine. Derek's confusion grew as he followed. They were on the back side of the house now. Wouldn't it have made more sense to continue to the drawing room and the front door to get to the carriage faster?

She took her sneaking about to extremes sometimes, but until now she'd always seemed rational.

The door closed behind him so swiftly it almost hit the heel of his boot. He jumped out of the way and followed Jess across the stone terrace and down the steps into the garden.

She took an immediate right, keeping them close to the foundations of the house instead of strolling farther into the garden. Her childish persona was gone as she folded the edges of her bonnet back and tucked her gloves inside the bodice of her gown.

"What are we doing?" he whispered.

She looked over her shoulder at him. "Leaving."

They crept along the back of the house, staying close to shadows and shrubbery. At the corner, she peered around the house and stiffened again. One hand pushed against his chest, flattening him to the wall, while the other slid up her back and underneath her short spencer jacket. A moment later, it emerged with a knife clutched between the slim, delicate fingers.

Had Derek seen it in a painting, he'd have admonished the artist for not making something more believable. There it was before his eyes, though. A woodland nymph with a knife, ready to defend him against their foe.

Whoever their foe was.

Then, suddenly, the knife was gone, slid up her sleeve with her hand curved slightly to keep it in place.

After a moment, she whispered, "Those trees over there. We'll cut through them to the lane. Jeffreys will meet us there."

"How will he know?"

Jess didn't answer him, just continued with her instructions. "If something happens, go on without me. Tell Jeffreys. Whatever you do, don't try to be a hero. I can't rescue you and myself."

They were going to need rescuing? Did they already need rescuing?

Derek's heart started to pound as if he'd already taken off running. A chill permeated his skin, despite the sun shining down from the cloudless sky.

Part of him wanted to protest, to insist that he would step between Jess and the apparent imminent danger. The ease with which she'd pulled that knife—the fact that she even *had* that knife—was proof that her competence outweighed his gentlemanly honor in this particular instance.

He nodded his agreement, unable to get his tongue to unstick from the roof of his mouth. She nodded in return and adjusted her bonnet once more, leaving two fingers curled around the knife while she retied the ribbons.

Obviously, she'd done this before.

She nudged his side with her elbow and gave him a wink. "Let's go."

Then she started to skip.

He walked after her, staying close but trying to look like the weak husband he'd portrayed inside the house—not through intent but by confusion. She didn't look anywhere besides the wood, but he couldn't manage to do the same. He snuck glances to his right, where she'd peered before leading them across the section of open lawn.

Part of the front drive was visible, as was an older carriage with a faded crest on the door. At one point, it would have been considered an extremely nice carriage. Like the house, it spoke of money long past but now gone.

Did it belong to Lord Bradford?

A groom stood at the head of the horses, staring their way and shaking his head before saying something to a nearby footman.

The footman started toward them.

Derek did a quick guess on whether they would reach the wood before the servant reached them. It was going to be close.

Jess simply skipped on. She lifted her head to the sun and spread her arms out, looking carefree and in love with life. What would it be like to see her truly that happy?

The immediate concern of the approaching footman kept him from contemplating that possibility for long.

"Ho there," the footman called. "What's your business here?"

Derek waited a beat to see if Jess would say anything. She stumbled to a halt but stayed silent. Derek took a deep breath and tried to match her apparent lack of concern. "We, er, petitioned the housekeeper to see the house and the grounds."

The man gave a cold smile and glanced at the house. "And she let you?"

"Only a few rooms," Derek said, not wanting to get the house-keeper in trouble, though he wasn't sure why. If she'd let people in when she wasn't supposed to, she should be let go.

Jess snugged up against him, her face carefully tilted so the brim of the bonnet obscured her face, the hand with the knife tucked up her sleeve hanging loose at her side. "I want to see the trees." She held the last word for a long time and with a slight whine.

The footman winced. "How did you get here?"

Jess stuck out a foot and wiggled her boot. "We walked. Now we're walking home."

"You live near here?" His eyes narrowed.

"Oh no," Jess said with a giggle.

"The, er, inn in the village," Derek said, and Jess pinched his arm.

"I suppose you'll have to carry on, then." He looked like he wanted to tell them they couldn't leave, but he also didn't want them there.

The woods was five steps away. In another ten, they could be out of sight.

Derek would very much like to be out of this man's sight.

"What's going on here?" another voice called from the drive.

Jess began pushing at Derek as the groom turned. "Visitors, my lord. They were just leaving."

Derek walked just fast enough that he barely felt the pressure from Jess's hand, assuming she would know how quickly they could walk without someone chasing them. At the edge of the woods, she pushed harder and he stepped faster.

There were voices behind him, but he couldn't make them out. All he could hear was his harsh breathing and his heart pounding.

Another few steps and Jess shoved him into a run. Soon she took the lead and led them to a turn in a country lane where their carriage waited, Jeffreys perched on top with a blunderbuss aimed at the woods.

"No one to shoot," Jess said as she threw open the door and clambered in, Derek diving in after her. She reached out to close the door. "Get us out of here."

The carriage lurched, throwing Derek onto the floor, since he hadn't quite gotten himself situated on one of the benches.

The trapdoor in the roof of the carriage banged open.

"What happened?" Jeffreys called down.

"I know Lord Bradford, though not by name," Jess said, her face pressed against the window to look back at the woods they had just emerged from. "He worked with Napoleon."

Jess flopped back onto the seat and twisted to replace the knife in the holder beneath her jacket. "He took my father."

CHAPTER TWENTY

There weren't enough words in any language to describe Jess's emotions upon seeing that portrait and realizing just whose house she was in. Darkness had crept along the edges of her vision until looking up at that portrait had been like looking up through the floorboards.

Childlike terror competed with the resilience of the woman who had learned to fight. She'd wanted to run, wanted to grab her knife and slash through the painting until the image was gone, wanted to cry, wanted to . . . wanted to . . . There were so many warring desires she didn't even know what she wanted to do.

Fortunately, she'd known what she needed to do. Before anything else, she'd needed to get Derek away from that house.

He sat across from her now, thoroughly shaken by the entire experience, if the fact that he was allowing her to ride backward was any indication. He shoved his hair off his forehead and re-settled his spectacles.

The rattle and noise of the carriage clipping along the lane filled the space, thanks to the open hatch in the roof.

"I'm not seeing anyone," Jeffreys called down. "No one followed me when I left either, though I got some strange looks. More than one gardener will remember it."

"How did you know to go to the lane?" Derek asked, shifting

so he was perched on the edge of the seat and yelling to be heard over the horses.

"Jess gave me the signal," Jeffreys called back.

Jess sighed, peeking over at Derek to find the accusatory look she'd expected. If he wanted to know all the safety measures she and Jeffreys had put into place for this trip, it was going to be a very long conversation. Even now, they weren't headed to the original next destination but to a nearby village, where an old associate of Jeffreys would likely grant them a place to stay without asking too many questions. It might be a barn or an empty crofter's cottage or even an attic. Jess had utilized all sorts of places in moments like this, and she and Jeffreys had determined several options when they'd set out the path.

She'd hoped Derek would never find out about it.

"There's a signal?" Derek said, lowering his voice enough that Jess knew he was talking to her and not Jeffreys.

"Yes, there is a signal. I would never walk into an unknown situation without some established form of communication with my partner."

His eyes narrowed and his mouth flattened. "I thought I was your partner."

Jess resisted the urge to squirm. Thankfully, the noise outside prevented Jeffreys from hearing anything beyond yelling, or he'd be chiming in, making this discussion even more of a mess. "You were with me."

"And apparently in some danger I had no idea about." He crossed his arms and glared at her, saying nothing but obviously thinking.

He was always thinking. He'd claimed she was, too, but she didn't think like he did.

The more he stared, the more the desire to squirm built in her and the more she pushed herself to remain still and appear nonchalant. Never give the enemy a sign of weakness.

Not that she considered Derek her enemy, of course. She thought of him more as a . . . as a . . . Heat speared across her cheekbones, and she turned to look out the window, even pressing one cheek against the cool glass in an attempt to battle the threatening blush.

"The window," Derek said, tilting his head to consider her new position. "The whole business with the bonnet at the window. That was when you knew we needed to leave."

Her skin once more feeling normal, she turned back to face him. "Yes. Fortunately, the portrait gallery faced the front of the house."

"And you simply took for granted that I would follow your lead? That I wouldn't insist upon seeing more of the house or ask about your odd behavior?" He planted his feet wide and leaned toward her, hands planted on his knees, elbows jutting outward. "That's quite a risk. Am I your docile pet, then, trotted around at your whim?"

"Your job is to look at art. Mine is to keep us safe," she said stiffly. The man had no right to be angry. "Just because I haven't had to do anything until today doesn't lessen the importance of that. I could have handled any normal reaction from you, whether exasperated or docile. Neither would make the housekeeper blink. Nervous fear, however, would. We'd have found ourselves searched for stolen trinkets."

"Are you saying you believe I'd be foolish enough to put us in even more danger?"

"I'm saying you're a liability." As soon as she said the words she wished she could take them back. She didn't mean them. Not really. He wasn't a liability. If anything she was impressed with the way he'd handled himself thus far—the heavy travel, Jess's various characters chosen the moment she got an impression of the housekeeper, and even the way he'd remained calm and followed directions as they fled the house.

She could probably have sent him on this journey with only Jeffreys and he'd have been fine. Her presence was the only reason they'd been in significant danger today.

No matter what she told herself, though, she couldn't form the words to take the sentence back, to apologize or claim it was said in the heat of the moment. She wanted—no, needed—to be necessary. If Derek saved Verbonne, where did that leave her? She would still be the child in the floorboards, useless and helpless and unable to save her family.

"I see." The tension drained from his body as he slumped back in the seat, but the anger remained on his face. "What a shame I can't simply loan you my brain, then, so you could do this without me."

"That would make it easier," she agreed, hating herself just a bit more. She had a reputation of easily telling people they were wrong or acting a fool, but this was a level of nastiness she didn't recognize in herself.

He took three deep breaths through his nose, arms crossed over his chest. "And the dining room?" he asked, his voice surprisingly even, if a bit lower than normal. "How did you know the painting was there?"

"The title had the word *feast* in it, so it seemed a reasonable gamble," Jess mumbled. She knew that was ridiculous, that artistic-minded people didn't think that way or make those sorts of connections, but she hadn't been willing to allow a further search of the house. Once more, she could thank her instincts, or what Ryland claimed was the prodding of the Holy Spirit, or whatever it was that had guided her over the past years.

"*Feast?* The title had—" Derek snapped his mouth shut and shook his head.

His face was tilted toward the window, but she didn't think he was seeing anything. Only the noise of the rolling vehicle kept the interior of the carriage from being tensely silent.

Instead it was simply tense.

He didn't rant or rave or do anything Jess was accustomed to normal people doing when they felt hurt or angry. Either or both of those feelings would explain his current behavior, so she'd expected some form of attack.

But he just stared out the window, face stern, arms crossed over his chest.

Because she was watching him so intently, she saw the moment he came out of his mind and returned to the carriage. Those hazel eyes blinked and the stern, grim line of his mouth turned down into a frown.

"Where are we going? This isn't the road to Lincolnshire." He turned his gaze on her, pinning her to her seat. "Another part of your contingency plan, I assume?"

Jess swallowed. On this, at least, she felt confident, even if her decision not to tell him could, possibly, deserve questioning. "Yes. We'll hide for the evening somewhere safe and assess whether or not we need to change the rest of our plan or continue on."

"Hmmm." He gave a pointed look at his seat and then hers before dropping his gaze to the floor.

Jess sighed and gathered her skirts, preparing to make the slightly awkward change of seats in a moving carriage, but he didn't move. His gaze caught hers briefly before he laid his head on the back of the seat, closed his eyes, and went to sleep.

❧ ❦

"Based on his prior involvement, we have to assume he is a part of the other claim to the throne. They have to have some connection to those who fled, so we also have to assume he knows the paintings are somehow important."

Derek listened to Jess with a growing sense of awe. Her voice was even, calm, matter-of-fact. There was no tension, no worry, no haste in her tone as she spoke.

"If he has given up," Jess continued, "making a change in our plans won't matter. If he hasn't, he'll start moving to put whatever paintings he can out of our reach. We need to prioritize those he's most likely connected to and hope we can fill in the holes."

As Jess and Jeffreys bent over a table in the hayloft of a barn, Derek reclined on a pile of hay covered in a rough blanket. He'd been listening intently, but so far he had no assistance to offer. It had all been about strategy and potential problems.

Derek shifted to adjust a bit of hay that was jabbing into his back. He'd never been in a hayloft before, but he imagined most of them weren't like this. Blankets, a table, four chairs, three methods of departure, two guns, and a map of England marked with the fastest routes to the nearest known smugglers' ports didn't seem like the average hayloft inventory.

That last item didn't make sense, even after Jeffreys had explained that sometimes the safest place for a spy wasn't their home country.

Jess hadn't been willing to explain anything. She'd simply spread their map on the table, along with his diary translations, and gotten to work.

"Is it time to enlist some help?" Jeffreys asked. "We could send other people out to these paintings."

Derek leaned a bit closer in order not to miss Jess's response. It was true. They had some semblance of an idea what they were looking for. A sudden discomfort in his gut had him pressing a hand to his middle. Was he disappointed at the prospect of not continuing to be a part of this? After the way his heart had nearly exploded on that short walk across the lawn this afternoon, he should be delighted at the idea of going home.

If it was all about placing the setting and establishing a direction, that didn't require any deeper understanding of art or symbolism or anything else. He could return to his normal existence and not worry about whether the side that eventually won this quietly fought battle was the one that actually should.

No, they didn't need him now that they knew what they were looking for.

Except that today's painting hadn't been the same. In the other paintings, it had been obvious—a place, a path, a journey. *The Feast of Future Fortune* had been set inside a building. No one was going anywhere.

Yet he knew this one was part of the map. It had been the clearest of all the diary entries. Obviously, he'd missed something when it came to what they were looking for in the paintings.

He closed his eyes and pictured the painting: the crowns without jewels, the bare platters, toasting cups tilted at various angles and as empty as the serving bowls.

He needed to sketch it while the details were still fresh in his mind and before they lost the light of the setting sun. It was unlikely that Jess and Jeffreys intended to light the lantern sitting on the corner of the table. Even Derek knew that a light in a barn at night could draw notice.

As his pencil moved over the paper, he searched for lines, some indication that this painting, like the others, was sending them somewhere.

There was nothing.

With his new knowledge of where The Six had come from and why, he had to assume that this painting was one of hope. They were celebrating the future freedom of their homeland. Were the people in the painting The Six? Had Derek ever seen a portrait of Fournier?

Perhaps Jess had recognized one of the people.

He looked back toward the table in time to see them packing away everything and planning the path they'd take toward London tomorrow.

"I'll take first watch," Jeffreys said, stretching his arms over his head. "That way I can sleep before I have to drive."

Jess shook her head. "Better to split it into three. I'll take the first and third. I can sleep in the carriage tomorrow."

The last edges of sunlight slid over the windowsill on the far side of the hayloft as Jess lowered the main ladder and climbed down, supposedly to keep an eye on the surrounding area.

"I didn't think anyone followed us," Derek said.

Jeffreys shrugged and gathered two blankets before moving to the haystack beside Derek's. "Not that we saw. The chances of them finding us are small, but it's often a slight crack in your guard that sends it tumbling down."

Derek nodded, but before he could think of something else to say, the other man had thrown one blanket onto the hay, lain down, and covered himself with the second. In moments, his breathing steadied into the smooth flow of sleep.

Derek hadn't even had time to pack away his pencil and sketchbook.

He got up from his pile of hay and moved to the window to look down. Of course he couldn't see Jess. She knew what she was doing too well for her to allow that to happen. Then again, she could be on the other side of the barn.

Pulling back from the window, he looked at the shadowy lump that was Jeffreys. He and Jess worked well together, as if they shared a single mind. Jeffreys, though he looked a good bit older than Jess, would make a much better partner for her than Derek.

Not that he should care. He didn't care. Jess's not needing him was hardly a surprise. All she needed was a walking history book who could translate Italian. He just happened to be the conveniently available one.

As quietly as he could, he packed away his sketchbook and resettled onto the hay, biting his lip to hold in his body's groan of protest. Eventually, he wriggled his way into a somewhat comfortable position and dozed off, but not so deeply that he didn't hear Jess return up the ladder and gently wake Jeffreys. Whispers of sound accompanied the vague shadows as the driver made his way to the ladder and Jess settled into his abandoned bed of hay.

"I could take a turn," Derek offered before she could drift off to sleep. There were three shifts and three people. It wasn't right that Jess should take two while he took none.

She chuckled. "What would you do if you found someone?"

That was a very good question. "Scream, I suppose."

Hay crinkled as she shifted. "That would allow Jeffreys and me to get away. You would be dead or captured by the time we could get to you, of course, so we would just grab the papers and run."

"That doesn't sound like good team camaraderie."

"We don't help anyone if we all die."

Her pragmatic view of death drew Derek's curiosity enough to have him shifting in his hay pile, turning toward her even if there was nothing to see but varying shades of darkness. "I'm not sure I'm helping now."

She didn't immediately reassure him he was wrong.

A piece of hay tickled his nose, and he grabbed it and twirled it about his finger. As Jess had mentioned in the carriage, his job was to interpret the paintings. He couldn't find the direction in today's painting for the life of him.

That was an expression that suddenly carried a bit more meaning than it had a month ago.

"You are."

Her voice came as such a surprise that he jerked, nearly falling off his hay. Did she truly believe that? "Jeffreys was right. You could send others."

"No," she said quickly. After a moment of silence, she spoke again. "There's something we're missing. The writing is too poetic to be that simple."

The pounding of Derek's heart eased a bit. That was solid reassurance, coming from Jess. He could rest on that for a while, couldn't he? He let the silence return, knowing she needed to grab her sleep while she could.

"There's something I've been wanting to ask you."

"Of course," Derek said automatically. Jess was too practical to start a fight instead of sleep, so whatever she was going to ask him must have been weighing on her mind for a while, brought out by the safety of the night and the unique circumstances.

"How did you know it was me? In all my disguises, how did you know? Even Ryland doesn't see me."

The duke was her benchmark for who knew her well? Someone she hadn't seen in three years? "I looked at you like a painting. Meaning is in the smallest details in art."

"What do you mean?"

"Art isn't a slice of life—not real life, anyway. It's an interpretation of it. You see what happened but also the effects of it, or perhaps it's the representation of a feeling, like a dream or desire or fear."

He shifted onto his back and stared at the dark ceiling. "Before you, I never thought of looking at people that way. In that carriage to London, though, something kept nagging at me. I didn't understand it until you pointed out the serving girl at the inn. It's changed people for me."

Her laughter was light. "Is that a good thing?"

"I suppose." He grinned. "It's certainly not convenient, though."

The hayloft fell quiet again. This time Derek prolonged the conversation. "You could do it, too, you know. You could look at paintings the way you look at people."

"Paintings don't move," she muttered. "I can't see where the people are going."

"Have you tried?"

There was a long pause before she took a deep breath and admitted, "No."

A surge of triumph went through Derek, similar to the kind he felt after identifying a particularly quarrelsome painting. "I could teach you."

"I'm not a very good student."

There was more to that statement than an excuse. Derek wished he could see her, that he could study the details, look for the little nuances that told him what she wasn't saying. In the dark he could only guess at what was behind her words, and it frustrated him.

"I doubt that," he said. "I'm sure someone taught you how to handle that knife you were holding earlier."

"That's different," she whispered.

"Not really. The mind is a tool, just like a knife. Imagine me flipping that thing about like you did this afternoon."

Her chuckle made him smile. "You would probably cut your own finger off."

"I have a feeling you will make a better art student than I would make a knife student."

"Care to see?" she asked.

"What?"

"You and me. We'll trade lessons. You tell me about art, and I'll teach you how to sneak about. Knife lessons might be a bit difficult in a carriage."

Did he want to learn more of Jess's world? The affirmative yearning that answered that question surprised him.

"Yes," he said, "but on one condition."

"What?"

"We're partners. We do this together. You teach me, I teach you, and we find this coronation bowl together."

He had to wait for fifteen heartbeats for her to answer. He counted each tense one, wondering if it would be the last one he made as part of this endeavor.

"You have a deal. We're going to London tomorrow. If any of the painting owners is a cohort of Lord Bradford, it will be Count Rashido. He's an ambassador from Russia. He's not completely trusted, even though he's never been caught doing anything nefarious. He's watched."

"I don't suppose Russian is one of the languages in your repertoire, is it?"

"*Ya robaryu tolka shtobyi ostatsa v jhivyix.*"

He really hoped that meant she knew enough to keep them from getting killed.

CHAPTER TWENTY-ONE

*T*rue to her word, Jess spent the ride to London sharing her plans, though nothing was certain except their return to London and her intention to take the bowl back to Verbonne once it was found.

Admittedly, there had been times when Derek had felt a bit superior mentally, but that notion died as she discussed the many angles and contingencies that depended on what she found around the next bend. By the time she paused long enough for him to ask a question, he was overcome by a bit of awe.

"Do you intend to take the bowl to Verbonne alone?"

She nodded. "It's difficult enough to sneak one person onto a ship and then into a country."

Somehow Derek had thought the danger to Jess would be over once they found the bowl, because then his part could—would—be completed. For her, though, the danger would just be beginning. She'd be in possession of the treasure itself, not just the map.

She couldn't be allowed to face that alone. He'd purchase his own passenger ticket before he'd let that happen.

Jess continued, unaware of his newfound resolve. "How quickly do you think you could teach me about art examination?"

Derek frowned, dragging his mind back to the present. "Why?"

She sighed. "Because this is dangerous, Derek."

"More so than I ever imagined," he agreed, "but you aren't getting rid of me."

The fact that she was trying to do so stung. What about the something more they were missing? What about needing him? Had everything she'd said last night just been to placate him while they were still close enough that he could have made his way back to Lord Bradford's?

"I know how to handle it."

"How many people do you know who have gone up against a danger they knew how to handle and lost despite their skills and abilities? I don't think one can go to war and not lose friends."

She swallowed and dropped her gaze to the floor. "No, you can't."

"I'll do whatever you tell me to. I'm not an idiot. I won't stand between you and your adversary in some misbegotten idea that I can be a hero, but I will have your back." He wanted so very much to be there for her. The more he learned of her, the more he pictured her as that woman on the rocks from *The Grace of Oceans Breaking*, watching the storm throw the ocean into turmoil. Lonely, desperate, but somehow still hopeful.

He didn't want her to be alone anymore, but even if she didn't want him, he needed her to stay safe. "If not me, take Jeffreys."

She snorted. "And leave you alone? I don't think so."

"I'm not a threat to anyone."

"Bradford, or anyone else looking for me, doesn't know that. Anyone helping me is in danger. Physically you are the weakest link, and that is always the easiest to pull." The sadness on her face left him wondering how many weak links she'd pulled in her days. Her gaze moved to the window. "I'll not watch them take away anyone else I care about."

Derek smiled at Jess's confession of caring and then pushed his lips up into a grin because the maudlin emotion filling the carriage wasn't one he was accustomed to getting from her, nor one with which he wanted to become overly familiar.

"Aw, Jess," he said, hoping his teasing tone would pull her away from the heavy, dark feeling. "I didn't know I meant that much to you."

She groaned, but that look, the one that reminded him that a lost child still lurked inside her, fell away. In its place was an expression he thought might be a hope she was afraid to admit she held. He wanted to feed that hope.

"When this is all over and you don't have to look over your shoulder anymore, what will you do?"

Her face went blank, invalidating his idea that picturing a worry-free, normal life would lighten her mood further. Instead, she looked like she was experiencing some sort of shock. Hadn't she dreamt of such a day at some time? Wasn't that the point of what she was doing?

"I don't know."

He searched her face for a sign that she was lying. If it was there, it was too well hidden for him to see. The very real possibility that Jess had always assumed her future didn't extend much past the current moment stayed with him until they reached the inn, both lost in their own thoughts.

❦

Jess was trying to be honest with Derek—really she was—but a lifetime of keeping secrets made it more than a little difficult.

Opening up to him had left her more vulnerable than she'd thought. No one in her world asked about the future. They all knew it wasn't guaranteed. The only thing she had was the task ahead of her, so that was where she would direct her attention.

Her current task was to determine a way into the ambassador's house. During the war, it had been watched constantly, along with the residences of a few other suspicious people. Nothing untoward had ever happened at the ambassador's house. Nothing much happened there at all.

No one was ever allowed in.

The little inn where they'd stopped just outside of London wasn't one of the better establishments, but it suited her purposes.

In the common room, shabbily dressed animal herders shared stories and ale. Not a single one of them would have even thought to care about who was taking the upstairs rooms.

At least half of those rooms were empty, but Jess and Derek had only taken one of them, so as not to draw suspicion. Sharing a room still made Derek look a bit queasy, though, and after delivering her small trunk, he'd gone down to help Jeffreys with the horses.

Jess rummaged through the trunk, her frown growing. She'd put together a plan for tonight, but it appeared she hadn't packed the necessary disguise. She was going to have to get it from Ryland's.

The thought of her good friend made pain throb at the base of her skull. She hated to admit it, but he had been right. Jess needed help.

Despite her claims to Derek that she could do it all herself, with the potential pressure of Lord Bradford and the quickly encroaching deadline, it just wasn't possible. It was time to see who was really willing to bestow those favors they'd assured her were hers for the asking over the years.

She remembered the codes she needed to write the messages, but she wasn't sure exactly what she was asking for or how to send them. If she gave them to Ryland to deliver, he would consider himself fully involved and try to take over everything. She didn't want that. Nor did she want someone helping her out of fear of the duke or the reputation he'd gained as a spy.

The table in the room was rickety, and the single chair was less than comfortable, but it was functional and, honestly, more than she'd expected to find at such a simple inn. She prepared a quill, smoothed out a piece of paper, and waited for the right words to come.

A knock sounded at the door, and Jess gave it a quick glance before picking up the quill, determined to write something. "Enter."

The latch lifted and the door swung open to reveal Derek, wearing a dark frown. "Doesn't it make sense to lock a door when one is expecting imminent danger?"

She shrugged, not about to tell him she'd left it unlocked in case he ran into trouble downstairs and needed to make a hasty retreat. "Danger doesn't often bother to knock."

"No, I don't suppose it does." He eased the door closed until a very proper three-inch gap remained.

Jess grinned. "Danger does, however, like to eavesdrop."

His frown hardened, but he closed the door and reset the latch. The way he fidgeted and shifted his weight from foot to foot made it obvious he didn't quite know what to do when closed in a room with her and not sleeping.

"Relax," Jess murmured before blowing on the note she'd written. She'd settled for a basic request and a meeting time. That gave her a day or so to determine the details of what she needed to ask. "Imagine it's a really large carriage."

He glanced about the room. "I suppose one could fathom the idea of a bedchamber on wheels. I rather wonder that no one has thought of it. Not this large, of course, but doable." He paused. "I suppose that's really what the Romani wagons are, aren't they?"

Jess shook her head, but she couldn't help smiling as he paced the room, rambling about the possible contents of a tiny home on wheels.

"I've seen the exterior in paintings, of course, but never the interior. Very private people." He frowned. "I wonder if they allow unmarried men and women to ride in them alone."

"Derek," Jess interrupted, trying not to laugh. "We've taken the room as a married couple. No one is going to think anything."

He stumbled about the room as if looking for somewhere to sit. His options were limited to the bed and the floor, but she'd let him make that choice on his own.

The reminder of their pretend marriage had sent her thoughts skittering back to Derek's question of what she intended to do after she was restored to her brother.

Would he expect her to marry? To live alongside him and create a new idea of normal? Marriage was something she'd never planned to experience, but what if it became a possibility? What would her future husband think of all the men she'd pretended to be married to for the sake of safety and disguise?

She snorted at herself as she laid out a second sheet of paper. Pretend marriages would probably be the easiest part of her past to explain.

Derek finally elected to perch himself on the edge of the bed, sitting with his back straight and feet flat on the floor. She opened her mouth to ask his opinion on what a man would think of her past but snapped it shut just as quickly.

The lines of communication were more open between them, but there was no need to bleed her thoughts all over him. Particularly when she wasn't sure what to even call them. She was feeling emotions she hadn't experienced in years—if ever. Derek had been more of an asset than she'd anticipated. He didn't deserve her pulling him into another awkward moment that was unessential for survival or the success of their goal.

"What are you doing?" Derek asked, saving her from the mawkish road her mind had been crawling down.

Jess held up a folded message. "Calling in a few favors. It's time to admit that I—we—need a bit of help." She took a deep breath. "What sort of assistance would be most useful?" she asked Derek, surprising him into gaping a bit.

He took a deep breath and straightened his shoulders. "I suppose that depends on what abilities your friends have."

Friends probably wasn't the right term for some of the people she was contacting, but she didn't correct him. He offered logical and useful thoughts that would never have occurred to her. If those ideas were delivered with a few extraneous words and a miniature history lesson, well, that was what came from talking to Derek.

Finally, she threw her quill down and stretched her cramped hand as she finished her final words.

"Three requests," she said, holding up the missives. "Now I just have to hope no one sees me traipsing about London to deliver them."

Derek shoved his hair off his forehead. "Why don't you use the

Penny Post? Even if someone sees you drop a letter there, they won't know where it goes. The letters will be delivered by evening."

Jess started to protest and then stopped. What could possibly be more reasonable and hidden than using a system already in place to do exactly what she needed? Even if someone had followed her to London, they would have no time to finagle a way to intercept the post.

"That's . . . a good idea," she said slowly.

Derek grinned and rubbed his hands together. "Truly?"

"Yes," she said with an answering grin. His enthusiasm was infectious, and she grabbed onto the rare moment of giddy discovery.

They ate a light meal, and then Jess took the letters to the Penny Post before strolling around aimlessly enough to make sure no one was following her.

Then she had Jeffreys drive her to Ryland's house to retrieve what she needed for that night's plan. Even though she'd slipped away and left Derek back at the inn, he stayed in her mind the entire time.

She could protect him, could go about her evening plans without returning to the inn to collect him. He would be angry, but he would also be safe. Was she willing to hurt him with yet another betrayal to save his life?

CHAPTER TWENTY-TWO

*D*erek was well accustomed to being the most awkward person in the room. He wore his jackets unconventionally large, was often socially inept, and could never quite seem to remember to get his hair cut. It didn't matter much to him, though, if he was the worst-dressed man at an event, since he was probably going to stare at the walls the entire time.

Being the best-dressed man in the room—even if he was the only man in the room—sent him beyond awkwardness into a form of maladroitness. In his normal clothes he at least knew who he was, but in a complete set of finely tailored, elegant evening wear? He hadn't a clue.

The clothing had arrived an hour ago, and ever since he'd put it on, he'd been pacing the small room, checking his reflection in the mottled glass above the derelict table that acted as a sort of washstand, rereading the note that had accompanied the clothing, and sitting to adjust the unfamiliar silk stockings.

He stepped to the window to peek across the innyard at the clock by the stable. Fifteen more minutes.

The circuit began again.

If you want to come, wear this. Down back stairs at 7. Be quiet.

Derek didn't need to go by the table and read Jess's note again. It was rather easy to memorize. Though irritated that she'd slipped out and left him to stare at the unadorned walls all afternoon, he was pleased that she'd brought him in on whatever she was doing tonight to get into the ambassador's house.

What he wanted to know, though, was where she'd gotten the clothes and how she'd known his size, even though the possible answers left him slightly terrified.

Was there a dandy lying trussed up in a ditch somewhere? Had she measured Derek in his sleep and pressured a local tailor into altering someone else's order for him?

Derek moved back into view of the small mirror and checked his cravat once more. It was a bit crooked, but he couldn't risk redoing it and having it grow limp or show too many creases. Tilted was better than disheveled.

At least he assumed it was. Unless he was going to pretend to be a man who'd imbibed a bit too much and was looking all the worse for it. Seven was rather early in the evening for that, but since his experience with society was limited mostly to academic parlor gatherings, he'd bow to Jess's judgment.

The first chime of the hour sent him nearly running for the door. Once there he took a deep breath and then eased the door open before stepping through.

If anyone was behind him as he made his way to the back stairs, he didn't know it. Jess had once said that half the art of being ignored was looking like you knew what you were doing, so Derek didn't glance around. At the stairs, he kept close to the wall—another of Jess's tips. Apparently steps were less likely to creak from there.

A few weeks ago, he couldn't have imagined needing to know such a detail.

The door he assumed was the exit was at the bottom of the stairs. All he had to do was cross the corridor leading to the kitchens. Praying that the corridor stayed clear, Derek braced himself for the putrid smells of waste and animals and slipped outside. The smell hit him as soon as he crossed the threshold, but its impact was nothing compared to the view of a resplendent carriage sitting alongside the filth of the back of the property.

Jeffreys was perched atop it, wearing clothing almost as fine as Derek's. The door to the carriage stood open, allowing him to see the velvet covering the inside of the door and the fringe that topped the window.

"Get in," a low voice said from inside the carriage.

Derek, still more than a little shocked, stumbled his way into the carriage, pulling the door closed behind him. Though the carriage they'd borrowed to travel in hadn't been shabby, it didn't have seats as plush as these. In the dark, shadowy confines, he ran his hands along the bench and wall. There was enough velvet and draped brocade to have made Marie Antoinette a happy woman.

Despite the dimness of the interior, his companion on the seat across from him sparkled, the glinting jewels proving she was as elegantly dressed as he was.

"Where are we going?" Derek asked.

"To see the painting. The ambassador bought *The Inspired Change of Desire*."

"Yes, and the entry is rather vague." Derek shifted in his seat. "If it weren't for the part that says 'all desires point to the true king on his throne,' I'd think it was one of the false leads."

Jess shifted as the carriage turned a corner. One bright shaft of moonlight fell across her face. "He's been living here for nearly thirty years, only rarely going to his home country. Hopefully the painting has stayed in the building."

"We know he owns it, or owned it at one time, but we don't know if he ever hung it," Derek said thoughtfully. "It could be wrapped in storage. How do you expect us to get in and find out?"

Jess turned from the window and blinked at him. He could almost swear that a hint of a smile tugged at one side of her mouth, but he couldn't be sure with this lack of lighting.

"We're going to a party."

Derek swallowed. "At the ambassador's house? Won't that many people make sneaking about difficult?"

"Parties are actually ideal for looking through places, but the ambassador doesn't hold parties. He's not very interested in entertaining of any variety." She picked up a small square of parchment from the seat beside her. "His neighbor, however, is a different story."

The carriage slowed to the creeping pace that indicated it had entered a sea of traffic. More light filtered through the heavily curtained windows, flickering and jerking as the carriages and their lanterns moved along.

Finally, the carriage came to a stop, and the door was opened.

"Stay quiet and follow my lead," Jess said quietly.

As if he would do anything else.

Jess ducked her head and extended an arm for the footman to assist her from the carriage. As she stepped into the light, he saw she wore a dark grey cloak over a dress of yellow silk, scattered with tiny jewels. Her hood draped down her back, revealing pale blond curls wrapped in pearls and yellow silk ribbons.

Derek tried not to gape at the transformation as he exited the vehicle with as much grace as he owned. With his feet on the ground, he did a momentary check of his clothing, ensuring that the unaccustomed outfit was as it should be.

Then he glanced at Jess's face to gather an indication of his next steps.

Or rather, he glanced at where her face normally was.

Instead of the angles of her pointed chin and sharp cheekbones, he saw the delicate curve of her bejeweled bodice, a bodice that he was fairly certain was a bit more well-endowed than it should have been.

Not that he'd ever looked. Or noticed. Beyond pure academic observation, anyway.

His gaze drifted upward until it found her face, her eyes at least six inches above where they normally resided.

The slight smirk beneath the amber eyes was the only thing that assured him he was, indeed, standing next to Jess and not some sort of adult changeling. Even if the mystical beings were real, they wouldn't be able to copy the arrogance of that expression.

She glided forward in tiny, elegant steps that were entirely different from the way she normally moved. Derek fell in beside her, offering his arm as if he were leading, even though his best guess was to follow the stream of people up the steps. From there, he had no idea where they were going.

He was learning she didn't necessarily know either. Her idea of a plan was often little more than a starting point. Everything else she made up as she went along.

The house they entered was brightly lit, candles and lanterns everywhere. In contrast, the ambassador's house to the left was dark, looking almost abandoned. There was no doubt about the proper location for the night's frivolity.

Jess presented the card to a footman and moved them into the receiving line.

Curiosity faded as Derek's panic built. Where was he? Whom was he about to see? Who did they think he was? What should he say if someone talked to him? As glad as he was that Jess had voluntarily included him tonight, he didn't know how to make anything up. He was equipped to dole out facts and history, not fluff and nonsense.

They eased forward, Jess slow, graceful, and incomprehensibly tall at his side, until a woman dressed in a blue gown was looking at them, her smile fading as she gazed from Jess to Derek and back again.

"*Mia cara*, Charlotte," Jess chirped in a lilting Italian accent as far removed from her normal voice as Derek was from a penguin. "I was so pleased to get your invitation. It has been too long! You must find me later and tell me everything. I must know how your George is doing at Harrow. You were so concerned about him last year."

Derek watched in awe as the hostess's concerned frown became a confused smile. He gave the woman a half bow and trailed behind Jess as she worked her way boisterously down the line, gripping hands and declaring her joy like a long-lost friend finally returning home after years abroad.

Despite marveling at yet one more strange incarnation of Jess,

Derek was tense until they'd left the receiving line and melded into a growing crowd of people at the edge of the ballroom. Later he'd convince her to tell him how she'd known about George and everything else she'd said, but right now he was simply glad to be away from the conversations.

They drifted among the other couples until they found themselves at the other side of the ballroom, where Jess led them out the side door and into an unlit portion of the garden. Flattening against the wall of the house, Jess's fake, simpering smile fell away, and she worked her jaw back and forth, one hand lifting to massage her cheeks as if the force of her wide smile had hurt them.

Derek tried not to laugh. For the most part, he was successful.

She frowned at him and reached behind her to tug at something on the back of her dress. Though he gave a great effort not to look down at the bodice of her dress again, it became impossible as the entire thing shifted and drooped forward, the upper portion retaining its shape, proving it had indeed been padded. A shrug and a few more tugs and the entire glittering gown fell away, revealing a grey dress that would have been much better suited for a maid, except for the daringly low neckline.

The yellow gown pooled into an impossibly small ring, aside from the narrow shaped bodice. Jess stepped from the circle, revealing the secret to her additional inches.

Giant fabric-covered platforms were tied onto her feet. Derek dropped into a squat to inspect them.

"Untie those while you're down there, would you?" Jess asked.

His fingers were already moving toward the shoes in curiosity, so it was easy enough to snag the bow at her heel and give it a tug. She'd worn her normal boot but shoved it into the fabric wraps of an old chopine. With one of the platforms freed from her foot and safely in his hands, Derek stood to inspect it.

"Amazing. Where did you find it? I don't think anyone has used anything like it in a hundred years."

Jess knelt to extract her other foot. "Unutilized but not forgotten," she said as she stood with the other shoe and the dress in her arms. "Should anyone remember me later, they'll never be able to recognize me."

Derek glanced down at his undisguised self. He'd even worn his normal spectacles. "What about me?"

"Unless the man is an arbiter of fashion or a man of political prowess, no one tends to notice."

More shifting and tugging drew Derek's gaze to a wide leather strap that circled her waist. Jess wriggled until the satchel that had been hanging across the back of her legs, providing additional shape to the dress, swung free.

Derek could only stare as she bundled the dress into a small folded rectangle and shoved it and the shoes into the bag.

After flipping the flap closed and securing the satchel so that the strap crossed her chest, she rose and started walking. "Come along."

Without a word, Derek fell in behind her as she cut through the dark garden to a tall fence. She shoved one boot into a small shrub, turning it until it looked secure. Then Jess grabbed the top of the fence before pulling herself up. She glanced down at him, a white grin glinting in the moonlight. "Think you can follow?"

Given the fact that his fingers could graze the top of the fence while still standing flat-footed, he was fairly certain, with the aid of the same sturdy bush, he could make it to the top.

Still, he waited until she'd gone all the way over in case his attempt was less than graceful.

CHAPTER TWENTY-THREE

The chopines had been useful on more than one occasion as they lifted Jess to an average and unmemorable height, but walking with six-inch blocks strapped to her feet was no easy task, and she was more than happy to have her feet back on solid ground.

Surprising Derek with her new height had been fun, though.

It was a good thing Jess didn't ever give precious space in her mind to regretting her decisions, because if the struggle she'd had when debating whether to send Derek the clothes was any indication, the second thoughts she'd be having now would have been debilitating.

Especially as he hoisted himself inelegantly over the top of the fence and rolled over to fall to the ground at her side.

Even though it resembled a fish flopping out of a boat, the man managed to land somewhat on his feet and without calling out, so Jess would consider it well done. Not that she'd have said anything either way. Derek was keeping up with her despite everything, and, while she'd never admit it aloud, she was rather glad to have him with her tonight.

The house and the garden were both dark, and the uproar from the party covered any slight noise they made as they moved to the house. So far, everything had gone according to plan, if not better.

The receiving line had been short but not empty, allowing them to move through quickly but with an excuse not to linger.

If they found an unlocked door on the back side of the house, Jess would have to admit that maybe, just maybe, God wanted Jess's forced journey into facing her past to be as painless as possible. Ryland had said as much when Jess went to his house to collect the dress. At the time she hadn't given the statement much merit.

Though the servants' doors were likely unlocked, Jess avoided approaching that portion of the house. Her sources said the ambassador spent every evening at the club, particularly if his neighbors were entertaining. When the master was away, the mice tended to sleep or head out to their own enjoyments, so the main floors should be clear of people.

Heading up the stairs to the back terrace, she peered into every visible nook and cranny. If any staff were there, they were masterful at remaining still. Derek remained close behind her, a steady, solid presence she could sense, even though he seemed to be giving her space to maneuver.

Starting in the darkest terrace corner, she checked doors and windows, looking for easy access. When one of the windows gave way beneath her questing fingers, that familiar combination of excitement, trepidation, and wonder slid through her. Even as she'd grown to hate everything about the war and her part in it, the success of this sort of challenge had still given her a thrill.

She pulled the window the rest of the way open. It wasn't as good as a door, but it saved the time required to pick a lock.

With one hand she braced herself on the window frame while the other hauled up her skirt in preparation for stepping through. A choked cough sounded behind her. It was the first noise Derek had made since climbing the fence, and Jess was immediately at attention. Had he heard someone? Seen something?

Spinning around, one hand went to the knife tucked into a sheath near her waist, but her companion wasn't staring down some surprise adversary. No, he was staring at the exposed portion of her legs.

Jess rolled her eyes and said in a toneless whisper, "You've seen them before."

"In trousers," he hissed back, not quite as low as she had been. "And I tried not to look."

"Then don't look now."

He cast his gaze skyward as she turned back to the window with a shake of her head, unsure why her chest suddenly felt a bit tighter and breathing was a bit more difficult. Surely she wasn't bothered by her exposed legs. It wasn't the first time she'd had to be a little bit less than ladylike in order to get through a tight space. Still, she draped the skirt a bit more over her outside leg as she climbed through the window.

"Come along."

The window had dumped them into a music room, ornate and gaudy, but not holding anything she thought was a Verbonnian painting, though she didn't completely trust herself to know one when she saw it.

Grunting from behind her indicated her companion, despite his lack of inhibiting skirts, was finding the climb through the window a bit difficult. She allowed another grin to fade into the darkness around her as his muttered *oof* preceded the dull thud of his knee landing on the carpet-covered floor.

She peeked over her shoulder. "If you'd like we could just go around front and use the knocker."

He pushed to his feet and straightened his spectacles. The lapels of his evening jacket were still askew, but he didn't seem to notice. "That won't be necessary."

No running footsteps or inquisitive calls sounded through the house, so the soft thud had likely not been heard. "I don't suppose you've a notion of where he keeps the painting?"

"Auction houses don't exactly ask for an intention of display." He kept his voice quiet, but there was no question that the tone had grown hard and biting. She was starting to influence him. Was that good or bad? "We'll just have to go room by room like we've done everywhere else."

She grunted, acknowledging that her question had been a bit ridiculous. The petty urge to strike back at him refused to be doused. "No stopping to look at anything else. If it isn't our painting, we move on."

After exiting the music room, Jess felt the weight of the responsibility of keeping Derek safe.

He crowded close behind her, and the smell of soap that she'd been able to ignore in the carriage and garden enveloped her. The fact that he'd taken time to clean up before dressing in his disguise twisted something inside her. Had he done it for her? Eventually, she knew she would stop smelling it, but until she reached that point, it was distracting indeed.

Room by room, she tested for weak floors and paused at doorways to listen and look before moving slowly along. The ground floor was filled with large public rooms that could be quickly searched. While treasures abounded, some of which Jess had a suspicion might have been obtained through less-than-honorable means, the painting they sought wasn't among them.

That meant they were going to need to go up the stairs. Their imminent danger increased, while their options for escape decreased. Jess's heart steadied into a slow thump. Her breathing settled into a silent rhythm.

And a male hand wrapped around her elbow and clung tightly.

Even as she cast her eyes to the ceiling in exasperation, she felt pleasure that he trusted her enough to keep going. There was no hesitation in his grip, just a desire to keep them close. Hoping he remembered what she'd taught him about stairs, she headed up.

Three rooms later, in a private parlor considerably less ostentatious than the drawing room below, they found it.

Jess didn't need Derek's sudden squeeze to know, but she was glad she hadn't thought to slip in by herself and abscond with it. The painting was enormous, almost as wide as she was tall. None of the other paintings had been this large. One of The Six must have been more ambitious than the others.

Leaving Derek in front of the painting, Jess crossed the room to open the drapes. They'd been walking through the dark house without a candle, but now simply seeing shadows and shapes wasn't going to be enough.

Moonlight brightened the room into a silvery haze.

Derek examined the painting closely, but Jess didn't join him. From where she stood she couldn't make out any details but could see the basic scene, see the enormous number of people in it—children, mothers, fathers.

"Do you recognize anything?" Derek asked in a hushed, awed tone. "I think we've been missing something in the other paintings, something that relates back to Verbonne."

It made sense. Which meant Jess was the only chance they had of seeing beyond what was mentioned in the diary. She should cross the room and look at the painting, try to remember her childhood.

She didn't want to remember, didn't want to make this mission any more personal than it already was. When things were personal, people tended to make very costly mistakes.

But not looking would be the height of cowardice. That would not—could not—be part of who Jess was. Her bravery and resiliency were all she had, so she stepped across the room and let her eyes roam over the canvas. The figures were the place she wanted to look the least, so that was where she forced her gaze to go.

A group of finely dressed people huddled beneath a tree as rain pummeled the makings of a pleasant picnic outing. Other figures ran about in the background, presumably the servants trying to gather the items. There was nothing remarkably notable about the setting. Trees and a field. Faded objects in the distance that looked like possibly a lake and a house might have told her more, but it was too dim to really see them.

That was going to be a problem. Hadn't they determined that part of the secret to the paintings was knowing where they were set?

"I think—"

Jess clamped a hand over Derek's mouth as something else pricked at her senses. She held her breath and then heard it again.

Movement. People coming up the stairs, unconcerned by whether they were heard or not and therefore likely to be there by invitation.

She glanced about the room, looking for a means of escape. The door they'd entered wasn't an option. It opened directly onto the landing, near the top of the stairs. There were two other doors in the room, though, both of which headed to rooms away from the landing and therefore away from the people. Hopefully they could find the servants' stairs from there.

She grabbed Derek's arm and jerked him toward the closest of the two doors, watching behind her as she opened the door and pushed him through before following him and pulling it shut.

Her nose smashed into Derek's back, and he gave a quiet grunt.

"Unless you've an axe for me to use, I can't go any farther," Derek whispered. "And I feel I should warn you, before you produce an axe from some random corner of your person, I haven't the ability to chop wood silently."

Jess winced. Short sentences. Didn't the man know anything? In times of danger, distribute necessary information in as few words as possible. Although in this case, she didn't even need words to know what the problem was.

He shifted around until he faced her, and even though she craned her neck, she couldn't see a thing. Deep, dark blackness pressed in on them.

She'd hauled them both into a closet.

They were quite effectively trapped.

CHAPTER TWENTY-FOUR

A spike of anxiousness shot through her but was immediately quelled by the deep breath she took. The mind-numbing scent of Derek's soap rushed in with her calming breath. She huffed it out in frustration. That was not what she needed right now.

Focus. Assess. Plan. She'd been in worse situations and managed to get out. She was the girl who didn't get caught. Ever.

The best scenario at the moment would be that the approaching person was a footman or butler, taking a trip about the house. After a few minutes of hiding, they'd be able to slip out of the closet, examine the painting, and leave as planned.

On the other side of the possibility scale was the chance that Lord Bradford had sent word to London—or worse, come himself—to ensure she didn't get her eyes on any more paintings. All it would take was one noise, one opening of a door, and Jess and Derek could find themselves wrapped in ropes and enduring torture by morning.

Jess never liked to risk the worst possibility.

She pushed farther into Derek's half-turned body and slid her hand along the doorframe to ensure it had latched behind her. It had; the door was as secure as it could possibly be. The only problem was that there was no latch on the inside. Getting out of this closet was going to be an interesting endeavor.

Almost as interesting as pondering why in the world a parlor had a closet in the first place.

But nowhere near as interesting as what she would need to do if the door were opened from the outside. If they survived the next few minutes, she'd find a way to open the door. That was the least of her problems.

She forced her breathing to remain slow, steady, and silent to combat the pounding of her heart and the burn that tightened her muscles. Hiding wasn't nearly as enjoyable a part of spying as breaking in was. As long as they stayed quiet, there was no reason for anyone to look for them in this closet.

Unless, of course, they already suspected she and Derek were in the house.

Pushing her shoulder closer to Derek's chest, she slipped a hand up to cover his mouth, just in case he was tempted to do more long-winded whispering.

A sharp nip on her palm had her jerking her hand back to her side in silent outrage. She tilted her head up, trying to squint through the dark.

It was useless. She couldn't see a thing, but somehow she felt his irritation at her, could almost picture him glaring at her. The man had bitten her, and he had the audacity to glare as if she'd done something wrong?

Her breath huffed out of her in a muted growl, causing Derek to shift and press his hand against her mouth. Long fingers pressed lightly into her chin and cheek. She turned more fully toward him, difficult in the confined space and dangerous because one wrong move could send whatever was stacked in here toppling to the floor.

A sound beyond the closet door made her still her movements and remember her priorities. Get out alive. Then blister the art scholar's ears until they fell off.

There was too much noise beyond the door for a single person. So much for it being the butler making his rounds.

Light slid around the edges of the door, making Jess feel

vulnerable, even though the closet would look no different to the room beyond than it had a moment earlier.

The group spoke in rapid French, with multiple conversations making it difficult for Jess to listen effectively. If this were a social call, she and Derek were going to be in this closet for a very long time.

If it weren't a social call, there might be much to be learned if she could simply distinguish the voices from one another and follow the most important conversation.

Jess's muscles loosened a bit as laughter covered some of the conversation. The group was at ease, relaxed, and unconcerned, not looking for suspected interlopers.

All she had to do was wait it out.

With a male hand slapped over her mouth.

The fact that she couldn't afford to fight with him about it was irritating. Not quite as irritating, though, as the fact that her minute relaxation about the events going on outside the closet heightened her awareness of what was going on inside the closet.

It wasn't the first time she'd been pressed up against a male body in the name of self-preservation, though shoving herself into confined spaces was something she usually did on her own. Being little had its advantages. She'd hidden beneath desks, under beds, on top of wardrobes, and even inside walls.

This was different. She'd done her best to pretend their relationship was the same as it had always been, but the conversation in that inn and the night in the hayloft had changed everything.

Now, despite the fact that keeping them safe was her responsibility, she had the ridiculous urge to snuggle into him, embed herself beneath his arm, curl up against his warmth, and indulge in whispered conversations about everything and nothing.

It was nonsense.

As much as she wanted to call it mere relief at knowing she wasn't about to die, since the conversation outside revolved around possibly attending the party next door and whether a particular lady would be in attendance, she knew better.

She'd felt attraction before, but until now it had always occurred at the initial meeting. Even Ryland had inspired a few jittery insides until she'd gotten to know him. It hadn't taken long for the idea of anything other than friendship to make her shudder. Attraction had been the last thing she'd felt upon meeting Derek, though.

So why would it show up now, months later?

Derek shifted slightly and brought his mouth to her ear to whisper in low, toneless words, "What are they saying?"

Her answer was stopped by the fact that his hand was still pressed over her mouth. She considered biting his palm, but he'd done that to her, and she didn't want to mimic him. He was probably expecting such an assault.

She could lick him, she supposed. That would be gross enough to momentarily get his hand off her face.

"It almost sounds like a party," the low whisper continued. "I'm afraid my French isn't skilled enough to make out such a jumbled conversation."

The realization that she, too, had lost track of the conversation made her want to kick something. Preferably her own backside.

How could she have been so foolish as to allow herself to be distracted, especially by something as unhelpful as *feelings*? Their lives could very well depend on her knowing what was being said on the other side of that door.

She reached up to peel his hand off her face and eased her shoulders away from the warmth of his chest. Even as she felt the loss, her brain slid back into doing what she expected of it at a time like this.

They weren't talking about the party anymore. They were most definitely interested in the artwork now, admiring the shading and the strokes, the subtle depths.

Was there something broken in her that she didn't share the fascination of staring at something someone else created and seeking the meaning behind it? A painting of an apple was a painting of an apple.

Unless, of course, you were one of her great-great-great-grandmother's Verbonnian painter friends, in which case your painting of an apple was actually an indication of the way the surface of the sun glinted on the dome of St. Paul's and told you that what you truly sought was somewhere on the east side of London.

Or some other similar ridiculousness.

Derek's arm slid across her and landed on her shoulder, effectively surrounding her with his presence.

She should hate it, but she didn't. The normal instincts that jealously protected her personal space rolled over and succumbed to that attraction she'd finally acknowledged, along with some other emotion she couldn't quite identify. Whatever it was made her skin feel tight and her breath determined to flee from her lungs.

There suddenly seemed as much danger inside this closet as outside it.

Did he feel the pull as well? Was that why he was holding her? Or was it some misbegotten notion of being her protector? Was he trying to save her? As if there was anything they could do if that closet door swung open. There was nowhere to hide.

He eased closer to her until they were pressed so tightly together that they had to breathe in unison or risk throwing the other off balance.

She fought for focus, listening as another voice joined the group, still speaking in French but with a touch of a foreign accent. The ambassador, if she had to guess. A loud scraping noise, followed by a thump that could be felt through the floorboards, made her wonder if they were as safe from discovery as she'd thought.

Gritting her teeth, she turned her face away from Derek, closed her eyes, and concentrated. Between the door and the way the men talked over one another she could hear only bits of the conversation.

". . . not sure what it is for . . ."

". . . if she wants it . . ."

". . . waste of time . . ."

". . . can have the art . . ."

". . . once we have the crown . . ."

Jess stiffened. So much for hoping the voices in the room were unrelated to the interlopers in the closet.

Lord Bradford's voice had not been among the ones in the room. Despite the spread of years, she'd have recognized it. What if he wasn't part of whatever had brought the men to this painting? It was true that other people wanted Verbonne, even the English government. Was it possible someone she trusted had turned on her?

The effort required to keep her breathing slow and shallow grew until she was reconsidering how quietly she could pant.

She couldn't stop whatever they were doing to or with the painting, so she abandoned all thoughts of it, instead planning what she would do if they opened the closet. Such an event could mean the end of Jess and Derek's lives.

Hers they might spare, as they believed she held the secrets and possibly even the bowl itself, but they would consider Derek the larger threat and expendable.

Could she bargain for his freedom? Probably not in any permanent fashion. No matter what she did, they would consider his only value was getting her to do what they wished. They would torture him, maim him, whatever they thought would convince her to capitulate.

But once she did, they'd kill him.

Panic clawed up her spine at the very idea. For a moment, she couldn't breathe at all. Every last bit of air had left the closet, and she was going to have to open the door before they somehow drowned in nothing.

The arm around her shoulder tightened, pulling her back into him. His chin rested atop her head and one of his legs even shifted until his foot was in front of hers. She was engulfed in him, wrapped in warmth and the scent of his soap.

She would be finding that soap and tossing it out as soon as they returned to the inn.

The panic was seeping from her brain, though, sending a fine tremor rolling through her body. Her mind was once again her own and she could do what she did best. Assess. Plan. Survive.

They weren't looking for her and Derek. Had no idea they were here.

That scrape had probably been them taking the enormous frame from the wall. Hopefully Derek had seen whatever he needed to see. It was a frustrating loss, to be certain, but an unavoidable one, so Jess disregarded it.

Their closet was safe, at least relatively so. All they had to do was wait.

If the ambassador or anyone else opened the closet, Jess and Derek would be blinded by the light from the lantern. What little light seeped around the door wasn't enough for their vision to adjust. They'd be captured before they even saw their attackers' faces.

As soon as the scenario played out in her mind, she knew what she would do.

She would save Derek. The diary and painting were important, as were her country and her family, but they were nebulous. A concept she barely understood.

Derek would not be sacrificed for those.

Did that mean she was willing to sacrifice them for Derek? That was an uncomfortable thought she was going to have to ponder another time. For now, she would simply accept her decision and worry about the motivation later.

It was a bit disturbing, though, knowing that she, a woman who had risked life, limb, identity, and occasionally even sanity for the sake of her adopted country, would throw the country of her birth to the wolves in order to save the man beside her.

She took a deep breath, and her shoulder pressed deeper into Derek's chest.

He wrapped her tighter, angling his shoulders so that, should that door open, he would be vulnerable and exposed.

She was the experienced one, the brave one, the one who'd hidden for her life more times than she could count, and yet this art scholar was trying to protect her.

Something inside her melted. Yes, she would sacrifice Verbonne to save him, and there wouldn't be a bit of guilt about it later.

CHAPTER TWENTY-FIVE

*I*f Derek had needed proof that he wasn't ready for a life filled with danger and tension, the way his shirt was clinging to his body and his sweaty hair was matted against his head would have been enough. A drop of sweat slid across his spectacles and dropped into his eye. It stung, but he didn't dare do anything about it.

Beneath his arm, Jess shifted, tensing and then relaxing again. Of the two of them, she had far more experience hiding in closets so he wasn't sure if the moments of tension were born from worry, fear, or excitement that it was all about to be over. No matter what emotion coursed through her, Derek wasn't moving until she told him it was safe.

Assuming they were able to emerge on their own timing.

When she'd trembled earlier, he'd thought that was it, that there had been an indication that they knew there were intruders in the house. He'd instinctively moved to protect the woman at his side, though he'd known it was foolish the moment he'd shifted his weight. They were in a closet. The best he could hope to do was push himself in front of her when the door was flung open and maybe provide enough distraction that she could get away.

Not that Jess would run. He was pressed against her enough to know that she wasn't wearing more knives on her back. Likely they were in the bag that hung at her side, but how long would it take her to get to them?

Derek was under no illusion that he would be any sort of effective fighter, but perhaps he could buy her some time to execute whatever plan she'd formed. Not that there was much he could do beyond bodily throwing himself onto another person and hoping their combined weight would send them to the ground. Possibly effective but rather limited in usage.

The voices drifted away and darkness returned to their little hideaway, but still they waited. For a while Derek tried to determine how much time had passed by counting seconds, but his overwhelmed brain kept falling back to forty after forty-nine.

A soft chuckle filled the tiny space as a small, strong hand covered his and pulled it from the shoulder it had been holding so long that his fingers were a bit cramped.

"You can let go now," Jess said, her voice gentler than he could ever remember hearing it.

"What? Oh yes. Of course." It was only as he straightened and pulled his arms and legs back into his own space that he realized just how entwined around her he'd managed to become.

Fortunately, the complete darkness of the closet meant she wouldn't be able to see the heat flooding his face. "What do we do now?"

"Get out of here as quietly and quickly as possible." She shifted forward, and soon the scrape of skin on wood indicated her search for the latch.

Did closets have latches on the inside? Obviously not, since she kept moving and the door remained shut.

"Why is there a closet in the parlor?" Derek asked, running his hand along the back wall. He wasn't sure what he was hoping to find, but as the danger passed, his curiosity spiked. He encountered a set of hooks, some empty and others draped with a garment of some kind.

"I thought the same thing, but I'm more concerned about how they knew the paintings were important."

Derek paused his search. "Why do you say that?"

She lowered herself down toward the floor, and her arm brushed his leg. "They said they wanted to get to the paintings before I could. We've already assumed the other line knows something, though not everything, about the paintings, but no one mentioned Lord Bradford. If the importance of the paintings has become known by the other interested parties, finding the bowl becomes nearly impossible."

"Let's say those men were in league with Bradford, then." Derek rubbed a hand over his neck. "Do you think finding this bowl will end the feud?"

She froze for a moment and said in a small voice, "I hope so."

She stood, the wood of the door groaning slowly until the outer latch released and the door swung open.

He blinked in the pale moonlight until her face came into focus enough that he could see her grinning at him. One of her hands lifted and brushed hair off his forehead. Then she shook her hand and wiped it on her skirt as she chuckled. "Nervous, were you?"

"It was simply hot in this closet." And it was, but not enough to make him look like he'd taken a dunk in the Serpentine. He dropped his gaze to the flat metal bar in her other hand. "Where did you get that?"

She patted the leather satchel resting against her hip before sliding the metal inside. "There are a few tools I never break into a house without."

"You break into homes regularly?"

"That's where the best secrets are." She pushed the door open wider and took half a step into the room before turning and looking back into the closet. "Speaking of secrets, I don't think those men were concerned that someone was in the house. We have a bit of time. Let's find out what we've stumbled across."

With a little trepidation but a lot more curiosity, Derek turned to examine their hiding place. Most of it was empty. The garments he'd encountered earlier were coats, hung tightly together across the last four hooks along the back wall. On the other side of the closet, a trunk stood on its end, a strange collection of items haphazardly stacked on top of it. Among them was a large black cube with a round extension on one side.

"Well, well, what do we have here?" Jess said.

She'd never seen one of those? Had the war affected her childhood that much? "It's a magic lantern," Derek explained. "You put a candle in it and then place a slide against this tube here and it projects the picture onto the wall." He shrugged. "It's a common parlor game."

"I know what it is," she said, smirking up at him, the pale moonlight cutting across her features and making them appear sharper. "But why is it stored here like this?"

Her face turned away as she rummaged through the other items on the upturned chest. Then she stuck her hand into her bag and pulled out a candle with a flint and striker tied to it with a piece of twine. In moments she had the candle in the box and lit. "The interesting thing about magic lanterns," she said as she closed the lid and the candlelight shone from the round opening, "is that light only comes out in one direction. It's a great way to discreetly light a small area."

She beckoned him, and he stepped over to join her in the closet doorway. "Who brings coats up to a parlor?" Jess murmured.

"Marshington takes his to his study," Derek said.

"Exactly," Jess answered, moving toward the coats. "That's because it's the easiest way to hide something."

As she started patting down the coats, they parted to reveal another, smaller door in the wall, the kind that usually provided access to the rafter area in an attic or a section of roof.

They weren't anywhere near the roof.

The door opened, and the light from the magic lantern shone on the inside of the door, which had been covered with a sheet of smooth white paper. The area behind the door was small, holding a cup of pencils and two baskets of magic lantern slides.

Jess took one and slid it into the magic lantern. The slide was long, holding three pictures.

A weak image appeared on the paper: a nondescript picture of a lady. The painting had been scratched and marred but didn't appear to have been anything special to begin with.

Jess slid the slide to the next picture.

It was similar. A scratched and damaged painting of a woman in a garden.

"Ingenious," Jess whispered before passing the lantern to Derek, kneeling by the door, and grabbing a pencil. She quickly marked every nick and scrape. "Go back to the first one."

Derek adjusted the picture, and she marked the paper again. He shifted the slide to the third picture, and now the markings began to form crude letters.

The short sentence that was revealed wasn't all that exciting, at least not to Derek. Romney Marsh followed by a date, a time, and a name.

"Smugglers," Jess murmured as she sat back on her heels and stared at the paper. Derek pulled a basket of other magic lantern slides toward him. Were all of them scratched up? Even if they'd been painted with the purpose of relaying a secret code, it hurt his heart to see the marred art. Near the bottom of the basket, the slides had only one image on them and had been painted with far more care than the other crude images.

One looked vaguely familiar, but given its miniature state, he couldn't quite tell why.

Without asking, he replaced the slide on the lantern.

"Derek," Jess admonished, "what are you doing?"

Derek couldn't answer, could barely breathe as he pointed at the picture now on the paper.

It was a basic representation of the painting they'd just seen. The details such as the servants in the background and the depth of the pouring rain were obviously lost, but the essence of the picture was there.

"Do you think there are more?" he asked, digging into the basket.

"If there are, we want to look with better light than this." Jess ripped the paper from the door and grabbed the second small basket of slides before closing and securing the small door, moving the coats so they once again disguised its presence.

Her movements were so rapid that he couldn't tell what she was doing until it was done, but within minutes, her gown had been tied about her waist, the chopines tied at the straps and looped through the makeshift belt to hang by her leg, and the baskets of slides tucked into the leather satchel. She blew out the candle, shook the pool of wax onto the ground, and rewrapped the striker to it before placing it back in the bag as well. With everything secured, she stepped out of the closet and beckoned him to follow.

He almost tripped trying to chase after her, but soon they were moving back down the stairs. She didn't bother returning to the music room, instead taking him to the first room with a door in it and strolling through it as if she hadn't a care in the world.

They were on the other end of the back terrace from where they'd entered the house. The party next door had quieted some. Did they need to go back there? He ran a hand through his disheveled hair and winced. Anyone would certainly notice his less than polished appearance, and Jess looked like some sort of traveling vagabond. She wouldn't draw much attention on the streets were it not for the bright yellow of her dress sash standing out so starkly against her dark grey dress.

She stayed close to the shrubs and led him toward the back of the property. "I hope those shoes are comfortable."

He looked down at the evening slippers, which were nothing like the boots he was accustomed to wearing. Normally, he only had to wear shoes such as these to stroll down to dinner and then to the drawing room. "Not particularly."

"Hmmm." She started walking down an alley.

He followed. "Where's Jeffreys?"

She lifted that brow he was coming to think of as a prelude to her condescension, but this time it came with a bit of a smile, which lessened his dread. "I would imagine he's gone to bed. Or perhaps he's reading a book."

He wasn't waiting at some prearranged meeting place? Hadn't traded the gaudy, fancy carriage for a much less noticeable one?

At his look of confusion, she shrugged. "I couldn't possibly know what the best exit point from that house would be or when we'd need to leave." She untied the dress and bundled it around the shoes before tucking the lump beneath her arm. "Besides, this is London. Walk far enough and you'll find a hack to hire."

"We can risk hiring a hack?"

Her laugh rolled over him. There was something suddenly freer about her. She even nudged him good-naturedly with her shoulder. "You think Lord Bradford has had time to replace every hack in London with his own drivers? That takes considerably more time than two days and is nearly impossible." Jess shook her head, the artful blond curls looking more than a little wilted after the evening's adventures.

He liked it. As beautiful as the curls and pearls had been, they hadn't looked like Jess. Then again, he had trouble remembering her in that severe bun she'd worn back at Haven Manor as well. This relaxed yet somehow confined style suited her better.

"So I should hail a hack?" He'd been following her through a network of alleyways until he was thoroughly lost—not that he knew his way around London much to begin with.

"No." She laughed again. "Chemsford's house is only three streets away. It's late, but I think he'll let us in."

"If not, you can simply claim to be the chimney sweep, pull a brush out of that bag of yours, sneak down the chimney, and let me in the back door," Derek grumbled with a shake of his head.

Her head drooped a bit. She looked . . . defeated? Surely not.

"They bother you, then? The disguises?"

His gut said yes, that he couldn't stand not knowing what was going to happen next, but he paused before answering. Was he truly that bothered by the changing appearances? The old lady had been amusing, and his anger over the art student had been more about her deceit than her ability to sneak in. No, it wasn't the disguises themselves that bothered him.

248

"Which one is you?" he asked.

Her head jerked up, and she stumbled as she looked at him. "What do you mean?"

He continued, his voice a bit stronger as realization set in. "The disguises are simply window dressing—a new look to fit in. I'm starting to wonder, though, if I've ever actually met you. Has every moment been a part you've played?"

Her reply was a low whisper, barely discernible over London's night noises. "Does it matter?"

"Yes," he said, "it matters. I like you—at least I think I do— but I'm wondering if I merely like one of your personas. Are you truly that prickly, argumentative woman who threatened to spear me to the wall of the kitchen if I came down to look through the ceramics one more time, or are you the woman who talked to me in the hayloft?"

"Why can't I be both?"

"I don't know. Perhaps you can." The idea disheartened him, but he didn't want to tell her why.

The woman at Haven Manor hadn't liked him at all, had wanted him gone, and would have been happy to lace his breakfast with arsenic if she thought she'd get away with it. The woman in the hayloft had seemed like she wanted him around.

Was it only because she'd needed his help? Could he trust that he was getting to know the real Jess? Or did she still hate him?

"I like you, too," she said quietly as they emerged from the alley onto a street he vaguely recognized. "I didn't expect to, but I do." She stopped and looked up at him. "You're a good man, Derek Thornbury."

Before he could respond, she went up the steps to knock on the heavy front door.

He followed slowly, wondering why her admission had sounded more than a little bit sad.

CHAPTER TWENTY-SIX

*Y*ou will explain to me right now why there is a duke in my drawing room"—Daphne paused to look at the tall clock in the corner of the front hall—"at three in the morning." She crossed her arms and tried to look stern but ruined the effect by adding, "Please."

Jess tried not to laugh in the face of her clearly distraught friend as the front door shut behind her. She didn't quite contain the hint of a smile, though.

"This isn't funny," Daphne said through gritted teeth. "He's a *duke*."

"You're a marchioness."

"Not a real one. Not like this. He's scary. He got here an hour ago and has been visiting with William. Mrs. Hopkins is beside herself wanting to take in a tea tray, but I haven't let her because we don't know what he likes or if he's hungry. I think she might quit if I don't stop fretting about it."

Jess bit her lip. She could only assume the duke was Ryland. He'd known she was back in London, obviously, since she'd gone to his house to collect the dress and get his assistance procuring Derek's evening clothes. She hadn't told him she was coming here afterward. Obviously Jeffreys had, the snitch.

"What are *you* doing here?" Jess asked Daphne.

"William wrote me that you and Mr. Thornbury were here but

then a servant had come to collect your trunks and he'd heard nothing since." Daphne sniffed. "I was worried."

"Have you been in London for two weeks?" The smile dropped from Jess's face as she searched Daphne's for any sign that her friend was unwell. Daphne hated crowds. The attention of groups of people had been known to make her faint in panic. For her to voluntarily spend more than a handful of days in London because she was worried about Jess was a humbling thought indeed.

"Daph, I don't care if there's nothing but water in that pot, get the tea tray in here now or I'll—oh. Finally decided to show up, did you?"

Jess jerked her head around as she recognized Kit's voice. Seeing her was even more surprising than seeing Daphne. This was Daphne's husband's house, after all.

"What are *you* doing here?" Jess asked, a thread of worry creeping into her thoughts. Kit had been so busy gallivanting about England with her new husband that Jess had thought her safe from whatever might happen. Even Daphne had been distant enough at Haven Manor for Jess not to worry.

Now both of them were here in London. The last thing Jess needed was more people she had to convince to stay out of danger's way. Daphne would have been easy enough to handle. Kit was a different matter.

"Me?" Kit pressed a hand to her chest. "I'm visiting with a friend, as I often do when passing through London. Graham and I always check to see if Daphne is in Town." Her gaze narrowed and her hands propped on her hips. "And you are avoiding Daphne's question."

"I'm not, actually," Jess said, shifting her bundle to balance against her other hip. "She hasn't asked me a question, only demanded an explanation. But in the interest of expediting this rather annoying middle-of-the-night gathering, Ryland will eat anything and will drink any form of black tea. Whatever you have on hand. He won't complain."

Daphne paled. "You call the Duke of Marshington *Ryland*?"

"Most of the time, yes, though at the moment I'm considering using something more along the lines of Meddling Mamie."

Her friends looked at her in stunned silence. "I'm finally realizing," Kit whispered, "just how much we don't know about you."

"Yes, well, you're better off. He's in the drawing room, you said?"

"Er, yes," Daphne said with a nod. "I'll send up that tea."

Jess turned to follow Kit to the drawing room and found Derek standing off to the side of the hall watching her, his head cocked to the side as he slowly cleaned his spectacles with a handkerchief. His forehead was slightly wrinkled from his lifted eyebrows as he glanced at Daphne's retreating back.

This was getting out of hand. How was she supposed to protect all these people if they simply refused to stay away from her?

Emotion, something that normally dallied about the fringes of her consciousness, moved through her in an unrecognizable, uncontrollable wave. Apparently she'd decided to make up for a decade of tepid feelings in a single night. She could do without that, thank you very much. The entire mess made her want to lash out at something, to attack something, to make the problem about something, someone other than herself.

Perhaps there was something convenient about Ryland's presence.

Jess pushed past Kit and stomped toward the drawing room. Ryland would hear her coming and, if he knew what was good for him, tremble at the thought.

Both men watched her silently as she strode into the drawing room and dropped her satchel and clothing bundle onto a chair. Slowly, they stood, but Jess had a feeling that courtesy had been for Kit, who'd followed a few steps behind Jess.

She shouldn't care, but Derek's treatment the past two weeks along with the many roles she'd had to take on had left her a bit mixed up. The irritation put her in the perfect mood to take on a duke who'd forgotten he'd retired from the spy life.

"You are determined to put yourself in the line of danger, aren't you?"

Ryland cocked an eyebrow and glanced around the drawing room. "Are you telling me you just willingly put Chemsford and his wife in danger by coming here?"

"Of course not," Jess bit out. She hated when he used logic to refute her. No matter that she had learned a great deal about logical thinking from him over the years, he still managed to be just a little bit ahead of her.

"Jeffreys told me the game has changed," he continued. "They may not know where you are, but they know where you've been and where you're likely to go."

"We have to see the rest of the paintings," she said. "We don't know enough to determine the map."

"You don't have to see anything," Ryland said quietly before pointing at Derek. "*He* does."

"You are not asking me to sit here and eat biscuits while he puts himself in harm's way. I know you aren't suggesting such a thing."

Her tone was cold, icy enough that even she was a little taken aback by the implied threat under her words. There weren't many people she considered true friends, but most were currently in this house. The last time everyone she loved had been in one place, the door had been broken in, and every last one of them had been carted off to potential death.

"No," Ryland said gently, using the voice he reserved for animals and scared bystanders. "I'm not suggesting that. I'm simply saying you are the one they're looking for. You are the one who can't be seen."

"I'm never seen."

"Are you willing to bank his life on that?"

The question was a rock that threw the room into stillness. She wasn't, of course she wasn't. But if she didn't go, who would? She would still be asking someone else to risk themselves for her. She couldn't do that either. She wasn't worth it. At this moment, she wasn't even certain Verbonne was worth it.

"We may not have to," Derek said, stepping up to her side. He stood, his arm pressed to hers, a solid wall of support.

She glanced at him from the corner of her eye, expecting to see sweat or to feel him tremble, to find some sign that he was nervous about the confrontation. There was none. He was disheveled from their earlier adventure, but that honestly made him look more like himself. He looked like he had at Haven Manor when he talked about art and the potential findings. He looked confident.

"Explain," Ryland demanded.

The housekeeper entered with a tea tray then, looking flustered and exasperated. Daphne trailed behind her with a second tray.

Jess smiled. She couldn't help it. There were probably maids giving in to fits of the vapors in the kitchens right now, just as aghast as the housekeeper was that a marchioness would consider carrying her own tea tray.

Ryland shifted in his seat and Derek waited patiently as Daphne bustled about, handing out cups of tea. Then Derek turned to his friend. "William, have you a magic lantern by any chance?"

<hr/>

Derek owed everyone he'd ever met the largest of apologies if this was how they felt when he started talking about how fascinating a piece of art was.

As it turned out, William did indeed possess a magic lantern, though no one had used it in years. The Argand lamp inside provided a significantly brighter beam of light than the candle had in the closet.

Instead of looking at the slides of the paintings as Derek had assumed they would do, Jess and the duke were obsessively working their way through the coded slides, marveling at the ingenuity but also the fragility of such a method. With every code revealed, they fell into a discussion of the possible significance.

"Most of them are clearly meeting times," Jess said as she took down another paper holding a decoded message. "Why not destroy the slides after reading them?"

"He might not have trusted the person sending them and wanted to hold on to them in case something went poorly." The duke flipped through another few panes of painted glass, as if he could tell just by looking what ones might hold an interesting message.

"Perhaps," Derek said slowly, "it might be a good idea to look at the slides that might be the paintings? Surely most of these meeting times are in the past, whereas the mystery of the paintings is a bit more pressing." He swallowed as the duke's grey eyes landed heavily on him. "Marshington."

Despite the fact that he'd been told to call the duke Marshington last time they'd met, it still felt strange, even wrong to do something so socially inappropriate.

Not that anything about this evening could be considered normal.

Perhaps he was dreaming. That would explain it.

Actually, no it wouldn't. His mind could never come up with this night's sequence of events.

He could just return to his resolve not to call the man anything. It should be simple enough to do since the other men in the room were asleep.

The wives had left long ago to seek their beds while William and Lord Wharton had stayed, only to succumb to the natural order of things anyway. Their heads lolled back against the chairs. One of them let out a soft snore.

The duke didn't seem to think a thing of Derek's use of his name as he abandoned the basket of coded slides and pulled the second basket closer to him. "Are the paintings in here?"

Derek pulled a slide from the basket and slid it into the magic lantern. "I'm not sure if they're the paintings we're seeking."

A simplified representation of the ambassador's painting appeared on the wall. Considering the size of the slide, it held a great bit of detail. Whoever had painted it had been as careful as possible.

Jess came nearer, rubbing one hand up and down her arm. "I should have remembered what was important."

Her voice was quiet, guilty. Derek tried to make his shrug as unconcerned as possible, even though he quite agreed with her. "I think it's rather like me getting distracted by a painting. It happens. Fortunately, we aren't distracted by the same things."

"No, we aren't." Her voice was pitched low, almost to a whisper. "I suppose that makes us a decent team."

Before he could react, she moved past him to approach the wall and look at the painting. "They know the paintings hold some significance. It would seem they've been trying to collect the images over the years as well."

Derek joined her to look at the image on the wall. "This seems a strange way to document them. Why not simply keep sketches? They allow for considerably more detail."

"There was already a system in place for hiding slides and presumably for obtaining them. Continuing those methods is less suspicious."

The duke pulled the slide and inserted another one. "What about this?"

"That's the painting from Lord Bradford's house," Derek said. "I'll have to get my sketchbook to compare them, but I think the painting in the background is significant. Nothing else could be specific to a location."

The painting disappeared, replaced for a moment by a harsh, bright circle of light. It flooded over the angles of Jess's cheeks and revealed deep shadows beneath her eyes that were not solely the product of a direct light source.

They all needed to sleep. Besides, it was likely the servants would be rising soon, destroying any hope of privacy.

The next picture slid across the wall. It wasn't a painting Derek had seen before, and without being able to see the styling and the details, he couldn't say for certain that the work had been done by one of The Six. It did, however, fit the method of the paintings they'd seen for the most part.

An archer, with a just-released arrow flying toward an animal that was little more than an indistinct blob near the woods, took up the foreground of the picture. That was certainly a directional indicator. In the back was a castle that was probably distinctive, but on the slide it was simply a series of towers.

"Could be a number of tower keeps," the duke said. "They all sit on a hill and possess a similar shape."

Derek frowned. That didn't seem to fit the other paintings. While there were certainly details missing, he couldn't see any indication of where that identifying detail would be. Perhaps this was one of the decoys.

They looked at two more paintings, one of which was most certainly a decoy painting and the other a carriage with high mountains on either side and a flock of birds crossing overhead.

"Either Cheddar Gorge or the Peaks," Jess said. "Hard to say."

"Those are both large areas," Derek said. "It will be hard to determine where it is exactly and find the direction."

The last painting slid onto the wall.

"That's not one of them," Derek said. "That's by John Michael Wright. I've seen it. It's signed. Same time period but definitely not one by The Six."

"So it's not one of the ones we're looking for?" Jess asked.

"No," Derek said with a shake of his head. "But it also means they don't really know what they're looking for either."

"Well," the duke said, "that's one small favor."

"That's one more painting," Jess said as she began packing up the slides. "Maybe two. How badly do we need the rest of them?"

"Seeing as I have no idea if what I've determined thus far is correct, I'd say we need them fairly badly." Derek ran a hand through his hair and almost got his fingers stuck in the knotted mess.

He really needed a trim.

"They'll be looking for a touring couple," the duke said, rubbing his chin. "Who else can get in to see privately held paintings?"

Jess laughed, though the mirth sounded sluggish and thick. "Anyone with enough nerve and a bit of coin can knock on the door. As it happens, though, I've already taken care of it."

Derek snapped his head in Jess's direction. What did she mean? She cleared her throat and busily straightened the already-neat stack of slides. "I sent a few messages today—well, yesterday—to men who can draw." Her gaze flicked up to meet Derek's. "You said you looked at a lot of paintings as a student, didn't you?"

Derek nodded. When he'd thought he could be an artist himself, he'd petitioned for entry into a home or two to study particular paintings. Even then he'd been more interested in the works of the masters instead of his own. That should have been a clue as to what he really wanted to do with his life.

"You're calling in your favors?" Marshington asked, clearly in a bit of awe.

Derek looked back and forth between Jess and the duke. "What are we talking about?"

"I look rather like my mother. I can't risk them recognizing me." She swallowed. "I'm also running out of time."

"*We* are running out of time," Marshington corrected.

"*You* have all the time in the world," Jess grumbled, "because *you* are not getting personally involved, remember?"

Derek cleared his throat. "What are we talking about?"

Jess's eyebrow rose, but only a little bit, an indication that she was surprised by his question but didn't yet consider him a complete fool. "Sending other people to look at the paintings."

"An individual can ride a horse faster than a carriage, especially if he changes horses repeatedly," the duke added.

"We still need—" Jess stopped in the middle of her sentence to yawn and give her head a small shake. "We still need to meet with them to make sure they know the most important details to capture, and I need to know where to send them. I have three, if all of them answer."

"They'll answer," Marshington said with hard assurance. "But you aren't sending anyone out tonight. Get some sleep." The duke looked at the two men flopped back in uncomfortable chairs. "I suppose we should wake them."

Jess snorted. "We should have woken them two hours ago."

Derek shook his head. "They wouldn't have gone to bed then."

The duke gave him an assessing look. "True. Well, we're all off to find some sleep now. You two find a couple of beds that don't have bodies in them."

"How kind of you to offer up someone else's home," Jess murmured.

"As if he wouldn't offer were he awake." Marshington waved a hand in William's direction.

"A convenient assumption."

"You know the rules of war, Jess. You take what you need."

Jess didn't disagree with his assessment, but she didn't look exactly comfortable with it.

To tell the truth, Derek wasn't either.

CHAPTER TWENTY-SEVEN

ecause Daphne's housekeeper appeared on the verge of quitting and because Ryland had nothing to do besides follow Jess around and try to steal her sanity before breakfast, she insisted they move the proceedings to Montgomery House.

If she'd thought that would put some distance between her and the disapproving glares of Kit and Daphne, she was mistaken. They packed up and came along with everyone else.

The sudden influx of visitors, even ones with their own home a few streets away, didn't make Miranda or her housekeeper blink. Of course, the housekeeper had once dressed as a man to join her husband in the army, routinely forging ahead to remove ammunition from fallen soldiers of both sides to distribute to her comrades until her husband became one of the fallen, so her composure was difficult to rattle.

As for Miranda, she was the perfect lady when she chose to be.

Of course, she could also be a renegade when she chose. She and Jess had never gotten on well, but Jess had to admit most of that was her own fault. It was probably too little too late, but she was doing her best to make up for it now.

"Thank you for making room for us. We won't be here long," Jess said as Miranda showed her to one of the guest rooms. They'd be here longer than Jess liked. She had nowhere to go while they waited for her contacts to go get their sketches.

"Stay as long as you need," the duchess said gracefully. She gave Jess a nod and then turned and glided for the door.

"I'm sorry," Jess blurted, wincing at the harsh way she'd thrown that into the conversation. She took a deep breath and tried again. "I'm sorry for being, well, difficult. At first I was just trying to protect Ryland from making a mistake. I didn't think you'd be able to accept him as he was."

One side of Miranda's mouth tilted up. "And then it simply became a habit?"

"Yes." No. Then it had become about jealousy. That wasn't something Jess wanted to admit—not to herself and certainly not to Miranda. She wouldn't understand.

It wasn't that Jess wanted to be married, and it especially wasn't that Jess wanted to be married to Ryland, but she envied Miranda having such a sense of who she was that she could truly be a lady but know when those rules weren't necessary.

"I'm starting to wonder, though, if I've ever actually met you."

Maybe Derek was right. Maybe Jess was nothing but a series of masks covering up the nothingness she'd embraced when it looked like there was nothing else.

Needing to get out of there, just for a little while to get herself back under control, Jess followed Miranda out of the room and went to find Derek and Jeffreys. They needed to get their belongings cleared out of the inn if they were going to live at Montgomery House for the time being, and they needed to meet with the men she was sending off. She'd given them times and places to rendezvous. Hopefully they would show up.

Climbing into the carriage with Derek felt familiar, and she let out a heavy sigh as she leaned back into the worn seat.

"What's wrong?" Derek asked.

"The idea of staying still agitates me," Jess lied. "I hate waiting."

At least that second part was true.

There was going to be a confrontation, that much was certain.

At some point, she and the people working with Lord Bradford were going to come face-to-face. It was inevitable. The question was, who would have the upper hand when it happened? In order to make sure it was Jess, she was going to have to lie low for a while and wait.

That didn't mean she had to like it.

"I have to admit I'm looking forward to not covering miles a day in this vehicle." Derek patted the cushion next to him with a wince. "Did you know that before the invention of elliptical springs such as this carriage has—which, by the way, has made the ride ever so much better than it could have been—carriages were suspended with leather? Imagine all that weight on four measly strips of leather."

Jess grinned. She knew how to remove an axle pin and dislodge a tire from its wheel, but she'd never thought to look at the body of a carriage. "Why do you know that?"

"I was curious as to why the shape of carriages suddenly started changing in the paintings. Style didn't seem to be a reasonable explanation. The older ones were significantly more ornate, probably to disguise the necessary suspension. Then, of course—" He stopped and shook his head. "I'm doing it again, aren't I?"

"Yes," Jess said with a laugh, "but I don't mind."

It was surprising, but true. She no longer minded that he knew facts she didn't, as long as he didn't share them while they were hiding from people who might want them dead. He wasn't telling her because he thought she was stupid, but because he thought it was interesting. Information excited him, and the facts just sort of spilled out.

He was sharing something of himself with her, and she couldn't find it in her to complain about that. He was letting her see how he worked, offering for her to get to know him.

"Did you know," she said, her tongue feeling a bit thick, "that willow bark can be used to make the hair brown?"

He stared at her for a moment, and then a slow smile spread across his face, drawing dimples into his narrow cheeks. "Have you used it?"

"Yes, but I find wigs are better most of the time. Faster and easier to change." She grinned. "I save the willow bark for the aches and pains that come from hiding in cramped positions for hours."

"Good," he said and then winced. "Not good that you were in pain, of course, but good that you don't change your hair. Or, well, I like it blond."

How was she supposed to respond to that statement, or the warmth that spread through her chest as a result of it? This was different from attraction, different from friendship, different from anything she'd ever known.

This made her feel vulnerable.

This was terrifying.

Thankfully, the carriage pulled up to the inn. One good thing about moving to Montgomery House was that she and Derek would be in separate rooms again. Obviously their prolonged private exposure was starting to affect her.

The prospect of crossing the Channel for the first time in five years to approach a brother she didn't know anymore was inspiring a plethora of feelings to rattle about inside her. She didn't need whatever Derek was stirring up as well. If emotion overtook her, she'd be a danger to herself and others.

She needed to clear her head and focus, even if that meant leaving him behind.

⚜

The first meeting went well. Langley didn't ask any questions beyond what he needed to know, didn't ask who Derek was or what Jess needed the sketch for. That amount of trust being placed in her was humbling. She and Langley hadn't worked together in years, and he still took her at her word implicitly.

It took a mere half hour for Derek to explain what Langley was looking for and for Jess to give him warnings of what to watch out for—then the man was off.

The second meeting went much the same, though Mathis asked a few more questions. He and Jess had been injured in the same skirmish, but it had taken him a bit longer to get home and he now walked with a limp. Jess had wanted to express concern about the length of riding she was asking him to do but bit her tongue. He knew his abilities, and as the best artist of the three men she'd contacted, she couldn't afford for him to walk away.

It was the third meeting that jarred Jess's growing confidence.

Leonard Merkins, the only man she'd contacted who still worked for the War Office, sat on the ground, back to a tree in the park where they were meeting, and threw a crust of bread to a nearby bird. "How is this painting going to fit in with the others?"

Jess stopped nudging a rock with her toe and narrowed her gaze. "What do you mean?"

"There was a man named Richard Bucanan who contacted us a few months ago, trying to tell us something about some paintings." Merkins shrugged. "Thought it was crazy ramblings until now, but if you're looking for these paintings, too, there must be something to it."

"What did he say?" Jess asked, gut twisting. Had Lord Bradford appealed to the English government when his bid with Napoleon had failed?

"He said that he feared what would happen if the feud continued, and he wanted to end it. If we helped him find the paintings, he could put the rightful man on the throne of Verbonne." Merkins's gaze met Jess's. "Seeing as England isn't all that interested in Verbonne having a throne at all, the man was sent away. He talked as if he thought we knew a lot more than we did."

"Did you know him?" Likely if it had been Lord Bradford, someone would have been able to identify him. The man was a peer, after all.

"No. He owns a small farm up north. Not the kind of man I'd have thought would care much about a bunch of paintings."

No, not the description Jess would have expected either.

Merkins popped the last of his bread into his mouth and gave Jess a long look. "What's it matter to you what happens to Verbonne? You're loyal to the Crown, aren't you?"

"Let's say I'm repaying an old promise," Jess settled on saying. Feelings and memories she'd thought dead and gone made her question everything these days. "Are you going to help me or not?"

"I'll help you," Merkins said, "but this makes us even."

As if she would ask him for anything else. Just asking for this made her want to lurch for the nearest bushes and revisit her breakfast. "Agreed."

"If I find something that threatens England, I'll not keep quiet for your sake, but I will keep your name out of it." He stood and looked Derek up and down. "Strange one you got with you there. All he's talked about is the painting."

Jess stepped between Merkins and Derek, arms crossed over her chest. "That's all you needed to know from him."

Merkins stared down at her. "You always were a strange one. This painting isn't far. I should be back in three or four days."

"Thank you," Jess said, though without much warmth.

With a final nod, Merkins strolled away, looking like a man with nothing on his mind and nowhere pressing to be. Jess and Derek moved in the opposite direction.

"I wonder if Ryland's contacts can learn more about Richard Bucanan," Jess mused. Just how many people knew the secret of the paintings?

"Your friend isn't exactly cheerful," Derek answered.

"Nor is he my friend." Jess sighed. "That was a transaction, nothing else. Credit and payment."

"Why did he owe you?"

"He was tasked with transporting some papers, but he got sloppy and they were confiscated and locked in a trunk by one of Napoleon's men."

Derek grinned at her. "You retrieved them."

"Yes. I had to hide under a bed for the better part of a day until the key was left where I could get it. More importantly, though, I never told anyone."

Even then she hadn't done it for him. She and Merkins had never been friends. She'd done it because it was the best way to move forward. Merkins hadn't lost the papers through betrayal; he was still loyal to England, and most of the time he was good at what he did. It didn't make sense to report him.

Where had that logical part of her gone? Maybe once she found the bowl, she'd be able to find herself, too. She couldn't afford to get lost in contemplation until everything else was settled. In the meantime, she'd have to stay away from everything that encouraged her to give in and let it overtake her, including Derek Thornbury.

⬥⬥

Three days later, Jess was ready to strangle everyone in Ryland's household, including the guests.

Especially the guests.

Every last disgustingly happily married one of them.

Had Ryland gathered them all for a late-night chat to share his theory that Derek was a "good fit" for Jess, or was it simply because they'd all managed to settle into blissful marriages that they wanted her to be in one as well?

Whatever it was, Jess felt like she was back in the war, ducking beneath tables and into alcoves when people approached, taking different routes every time she went somewhere, and retreating to the attic eaves so she could relax. Dodging conversations and ruining their schemes to make Jess and Derek share the same space was exhausting, but at least it gave her something to do.

Jess stretched her neck and shoulders as she finished dressing for the day. It wasn't that Jess didn't like Derek—it was, in fact, the opposite. Jess liked Derek rather a lot and enjoyed his company, but she didn't want it ruined by flowers and sonnets and pointless rides that did nothing but bring you right back where you started. Even if she'd had time for courtship, what was the point of all that drivel that had nothing to do with what life with that person would actually be like?

What they were all refusing to realize was that Derek didn't seem inclined to utilize their efforts on his behalf. She'd tried explaining that to Jeffreys, because even that cantankerous unmarried clod was conspiring against her, but he'd simply shrugged and said, "It isn't good for man—or woman—to be alone. Says it in the Good Book."

The last tug of her brush through her hair was a bit stronger than the previous ones. Why did they keep quoting scripture? It had been good and helpful during the war, of course. Ryland had shared quite a bit of it during their time together.

The stories of Jesus and the idea of peace in the middle of such chaos had drawn her in. She'd needed that peace and was more than happy to latch on to Someone no one could bust through the door and take away. It wasn't possible to count the number of her prayers as she traveled the continent to wherever she was needed or the number of times she'd asked Ryland to tell her a story from the Bible.

But now, or at least until recently, everything was good. Shouldn't God be focusing His efforts on the people who were as desperate as she'd once been? She still believed—knew—God would be there when this entire ordeal became too much for her to handle—but she wasn't to that point. That meant she didn't need Him yet. Didn't it?

The brush cracked against the dressing table as Jess threw it down and secured her bun with two more pins.

Pondering questions she had no hope of answering was a useless endeavor. There were better uses for her time and brain. She had a job to do, a secret code to unravel, and it was time for her to take what she knew of the history of Verbonne and the legend of Queen Jessamine and apply it to the search.

Anyone who insisted on foisting their romantic notions on her could find themselves with ipecac in their tea.

Derek's notes and sketches were spread out in Ryland's study, along with the map and ribbons they'd already determined. Well, the ones they had already guessed. It was still possible they were interpreting the diary completely wrong, there was no secret treasure, the map wasn't going to come together, and the old queen had simply been a frivolous poet.

After circling through the garret rooms and startling three

maids, Jess came down the servants' stairs to avoid the private parlor where Kit and Daphne occasionally liked to sit. Then she darted through Miranda's dressing room, knowing the woman would have been long since dressed and meeting with the housekeeper. From there, it was easy enough to make it to the main stairs and down to the front hall.

Although almost everyone started the day in the study pretending to be able to find something new in their search, it was possible they were still breakfasting at the back of the house. Jess had requested a tray be sent up to her room, and Miranda wasn't quite to the manipulative point of refusing that request, particularly since some of the maids were still rather loyal to the girl who had once worked alongside them.

After two turns and a brief pause that involved balancing in a window and tucking her legs up behind the drape, she made it to the study.

Derek was already in there when she arrived, but he wasn't hunched over the desk the way he had been the past two days—something that reaffirmed for Jess that Derek was either oblivious of the machinations around them or as determined to avert them as she was. Now, though, he sat in one of the chairs that flanked the fireplace. Low flames flickered in the hearth in deference to the encroaching chill and dampness. Soon travel would become more difficult.

A glance around the room revealed the materials they'd labored over had been neatly stacked and set aside.

Jess approached the fire slowly. What was he doing? What was he thinking? Should she leave before he noticed her arrival? Hide until someone else came in as well?

Given everyone's obsession with leaving Jess alone with Derek, she could only imagine what they'd think if she started the day that way by her own choice.

"Good, you're here." Derek jumped out of the seat, startling Jess enough to pull a small gasp and jump from her. He rubbed his hands together, a look of giddy anticipation on his face.

"Yes, I am. Where is everyone?"

Confusion fell briefly over his features as he looked around. Had he truly not noticed he was alone? "I don't know. They were here earlier. I told them I was taking a break this morning because you and I had been thinking about nothing but this for weeks, and we were obviously missing something."

"Obviously," Jess said quietly, trying not to groan. No wonder none of them were here. They'd have grasped on to the possible implications of such a statement with the grip of a child with a sweet.

"That's why I move around so much when I'm working at a house," Derek continued. "Fresh looks are the most telling. You only see something new when you stop seeing what you saw before."

It made sense, but Jess could think of many ways to step away from this fiasco that likely didn't involve whatever he had planned. She opened her mouth to tell him they could take a break separately, but his grin stopped her. She hadn't seen him this excited since, well, since he thought her roasted beef had been served on a piece of rare pottery and he'd attempted to ransack her kitchen in an attempt to find more.

She'd quashed his smile quickly then. She didn't have the heart to do it now. He'd suffered through some horrible experiences on her behalf. She could suffer through one morning. "What are we doing?"

With a flourish he stepped aside and indicated a basket that had been sitting at his feet. "This!"

Oh please, no, not a picnic.

He knelt down and opened the basket to reveal . . . Jess coughed. "Is that yarn?"

"Yes." He rose with a grin of triumph. "I'm going to teach you to knit."

"To . . . knit?" Jess pinched herself. She was dreaming, wasn't she? There wasn't possibly a man standing in Ryland's study, excited about teaching her to knit.

The sting in her arm said otherwise.

Well, she'd just decided she could suffer through a morning with him. What did the activity matter as long as he enjoyed it?

"Yes, knit." Needles and yarn spilled from the basket as Derek sat and began emptying the contents onto a table between the chairs. "That was what told me something was wrong in the mail coach. You weren't really knitting. If you actually know how to knit, your old lady disguise will become much stronger."

Jess froze, one hand on the back of the second chair. He'd chosen this activity for her. What a bizarre, unexpected, and considerate thing for him to do.

"All right," she said, slowly lowering herself into the second chair. "Teach me to knit."

"For what you're doing you don't need to learn anything particularly difficult. A basic stitch will do." He grabbed a set of needles and a length of yarn. "You hold the needles well, of course, or the ruse would have been more obvious, but the yarn is held this way."

He demonstrated the proper position and Jess tried to copy it.

"No, the yarn threads through like this." He knelt in front of her chair and adjusted her hold.

The feelings of attraction that had rushed over her in the ambassador's closet returned. Without the imminent danger to subdue them, they were harder to push aside. Did he feel it, too? The urge to extend the contact? To form whatever excuse was necessary to maintain it?

His hands were steadily correcting her hold and motions, so it was likely he didn't feel the same. That was good. If he didn't, then she could find a way to ignore it, could convince herself it didn't matter.

She lifted her gaze to his for confirmation.

He wasn't looking at the yarn.

Instead he was looking at her, a small smile on his face. Fine lines creased the area around his eyes, as if the smile was larger than it appeared at first glance. A sense of wonder glazed his expression, as if he felt the same way she did, only without the ensuing terror.

She swallowed hard. If he wasn't afraid, she wouldn't be either. She'd faced death, imprisonment, and war without flinching. Knitting and attraction wouldn't be the thing that sent her fleeing, even if they felt far more dangerous than any fight she'd ever entered.

CHAPTER TWENTY-EIGHT

*D*erek had studied romantic interludes in the context of art and the multiple ways it had impacted people throughout history, but now, faced with a real-life example, he had many questions.

Could attraction come from other emotions? Could the body manifest the feeling in order to mask or distract from fear and anxiety? Was it possible for his lungs to actually stop breathing? His chest felt solid, as if it no longer possessed the ability to expand and contract.

It had seemed so logical to teach her knitting this morning, to see if this attraction still existed when the moment wasn't fraught with tension or weighed down by impending doom. Now he wasn't so sure. What was better? Not knowing if he was truly feeling something for this woman, or not knowing if there would ever be something he could do about it?

"You have to hold it gently," he said, talking to himself as much as to her. As much as he wanted to drop the yarn and simply hold her hand, he'd never been a man given to impulse. "Allow the yarn to move as it needs to."

He adjusted her hands once more, running one finger along the edge of the yarn to show her the proper looseness. Her hands were small but strong, roughened in a way that confirmed she'd done a great deal more than kitchen work in her life.

For now she was holding the yarn correctly, so he had no excuse to remain at her feet, leaning into her space. He shifted back to his seat and picked up his needles. Knitting was fairly simple once one got the pattern down, but it was awkward at first. Likely he would have to adjust her hold again, but he refused to artificially create a reason to feel her small hands in his. It wasn't the time.

It may never be the time.

Keeping his movements slow, he demonstrated the basic stitch. It took her a few more minutes and a handful of corrections by him, but soon—rather faster than he would have liked, in all honesty—she had the hang of it.

"Unraveling it is a bit more difficult." He shifted his hold on the yarn to pull his stitches out. "You may need to have two sets of stitches going so you knit one and unravel the other as you go."

They sat there, knitting and unraveling, as the morning drifted by. Her movements got smoother, and eventually he was showing her more advanced stitches.

"How did you learn to knit?" she asked as she whipped out another row of simple stitches.

"My grandmother. She lived with us, but her eyesight and her health were failing. There was little she could do besides sit in her rocking chair and knit. She couldn't see the yarn well anymore, but she could feel the stitches."

"Why you?"

"Why not me?" It didn't seem very polite to say that the rest of his family hadn't had the patience to sit around with a cantankerous old woman who had spent half her time grumbling about what she could no longer do and the other half barking at people to do it for her. "She didn't handle her immobility well, and my family couldn't block it out, I suppose. I started watching her knit as a form of distraction. It was easy enough to ignore her ramblings if I had something to study."

Jess lowered her block of knitted yarn to her lap and stared at him.

Derek shifted in his seat but kept working, though he wasn't paying attention to what stitches he was making. "One day she realized what I was doing and handed me a set of needles and a ball of yarn. She became a bit less difficult after that. Teaching me gave her a purpose, I suppose."

His father hadn't loved the idea, but he enjoyed the yelling of his mother even less, so he'd allowed Derek to continue. Neither his father nor his brother—nor even Derek, truth be told—would have guessed that one day, that would be the skill he would use to test his bond with a woman.

"Do you still knit?" Jess yanked on the end of her yarn with enthusiasm, grin widening as the entire business unraveled. As the last stitch gave way, she let out a soft laugh.

Would she laugh in truth if he admitted that he did, in fact, still knit? It had been a source of mockery in his own home until his mother had scowled everyone into silence. What would Jess think?

"Yes," he said, after taking a deep breath. "I do. At first it was to finish the blanket my grandmother had been working on. It seemed wrong to leave her last work incomplete. I found the project relaxing."

It was more than that, of course. Knitting followed a set of rules. Unlike painting or drawing, which needed that extra little flourish to become art instead of simply lines, knitting was all about the tension of the yarn and the consistency of stitches. The talents that made him a connoisseur of art instead of an artist made him good at knitting.

"I learned cooking as a distraction."

His fingers paused as he looked up. Jess's needles clicked on, her entire attention focused on them. Should he say something? "From your mother?"

A burst of wry laughter shook her body. "Goodness, no. Mother never gave up hope that we would all one day return to the palace, so she did everything she could to maintain that lifestyle. She tried to make that four-room cottage a twenty-room palace."

She fell into knitting again, but this time Derek remained quiet. Like paintings that revealed themselves over time, she required patience. Grasping for more might yield results, but he would lose the nuance, the little details that told him more than her words did.

"It wasn't only my family in that cottage. Some of my uncle's advisors and our personal servants came, too, aware they'd be the first targeted after we disappeared. Everyone was tense and solemn, except for Ismelde, the palace cook."

"Your cook knew enough state secrets to be in danger?" Derek couldn't hold back the question. Advisors and secretaries made sense, of course, but cooks? Had the maids come, too?

"No," Jess said with a shake of her head. She stopped knitting and twined the yarn through her fingers. "She was from a village on the Rhine. She was afraid what the French would do to her. As a child, I found her happiness far more enjoyable than everyone else's gloom. Cooking was more fun than trying to learn how to take tea and behave at court, especially since I had to pretend the crops were the other people."

"Ismelde taught you to cook, then?"

Jess nodded. "She was amazing. Even with our limited resources and rudimentary kitchen she managed to produce the most splendid meals. Desserts and puddings were rare, but they were her favorite."

"No wonder you enjoy cooking."

She was silent and still for a moment before she pulled the yarn from between her fingers and began knitting again. "Actually, I hate it."

Derek placed his knitting aside and leaned forward, bracing his elbows on his knees so that his face was level with hers. "But you're a cook."

"The end of the war made me vulnerable, so I had to leave London. I knew that should Verbonne ever become its own country again, someone was going to want what I had, even though I wasn't even sure what it was. That's dangerous, you know, having a secret you can't even bargain with because it's a secret even from you.

"Ryland did a good job convincing everyone I was someone else, that he'd found me somewhere else, but it was a story that couldn't hold if someone really started looking." Jess shrugged. "Becoming a cook was the best way to hide."

"How did you end up at Haven Manor?" Derek didn't know everything about the history of the ladies working at the secluded country estate, but he knew they'd been hiding children who would ruin important reputations.

"Kit was in London on . . ." Jess flashed a grin. "We'll say she was here on business. She ran into a bit of trouble. I helped her out of it. In return she gave me a place to go."

Derek knew there had to be more to it than that, but that wasn't what he was most concerned about at the moment. "Why a cook, though?"

"Cooks stay in the kitchens."

"You felt a need to hide among a group of people who were already hiding?" Derek asked with lifted eyebrows.

She sighed and let her work fall into her lap. The pale eyes she lifted to him were flatter than any he'd ever seen. The spark of life and determination he always saw in her was nowhere to be found. "I know Ismelde probably didn't survive that night. She wasn't valuable enough to imprison, and her thick accent was one no Frenchman would want in his household. Cooking reminds me of what I lost. It reminds me how quickly everything changes." She poked at the yarn. "It reminds me not to become too attached."

Her face tilted toward him, her normal smirk back in place though the spirit wasn't yet visible in her eyes. "Besides, the only cooking Daphne does is boiling the mess out of something before smashing it into submission. Kit can make stew. Eating their cooking for years on end wasn't an option."

Derek laughed with her, though it took a bit of effort, given the pain slicing through his heart for Jess's loss. "Tell me about living with them."

To his surprise, she did. Her yarn and needles were forgotten as she shared about the way they'd forced her to interact, their friendship non-optional. She talked of the children they'd cared for with a bit of awe and fear but also affection.

He shared his favorite travels and paintings.

She spoke to him in seven languages.

By the time the clock in the main hall chimed noon, Derek knew a great deal about her that he hadn't at the beginning of the day. Most of all, he knew he'd never again meet a woman like Jess. Even the greatest goddess ever painted couldn't impress him more.

The thing was, despite her confidence, he didn't think she saw herself as someone impressive.

He reached one hand across the space between their chairs and placed it on top of hers. She looked up at him through her lashes but didn't move her hand. "Jess, I—"

A throat cleared from the doorway, causing Derek to jerk back hard enough that the chair rocked on two legs for a moment before crashing back down.

"Jess, you've a visitor," Miranda said, not even bothering to hide her fascination at the scene she'd walked in on. "Ryland refuses to let him past the front hall."

Jess stood, the knitted lump falling to the ground as she adjusted her skirts. Derek stared at her, but she never gave him so much as a glance. "I'll be right there."

⁂

Not looking at Derek required every last bit of Jess's effort. She wanted to look his way, offer him some sort of reassurance, but any attention she bestowed on him would only make the situation worse.

Miranda grinned as she stepped aside to let Jess through the door. Despite the discomfort, part of Jess was thankful for the interruption.

She was less thankful for the fact that as soon as this apparently unwelcome visitor was taken care of, Miranda would be in Ryland's ear, as well as everyone else's, about what she'd seen.

Jess didn't care what they did with that information as long as they didn't say anything to Derek. If Ryland even thought to make life difficult for the scholar, Jess would cut him down with a plethora of embarrassing stories about him. They wouldn't make Miranda love him any less, of course, but what wife would be able to resist teasing her husband about the time he had to go a week in trousers that were five inches too short and an entire person too big in the waist because they were the only ones Jess could procure?

Jess entered the front hall to see Ryland standing, feet braced, arms crossed, and icy glare directed at a very docile Leonard Merkins.

Ryland's gaze shifted as Jess approached, turning on her with the same hardness. It was almost enough to make her flinch. No wonder Merkins wasn't being his normal obnoxious self. "You enlisted his assistance?"

Jess kept her expression blank, refusing to let him see how his glare affected her. "He can ride fast and draw well. Besides, he owed me a favor."

Those grey eyes narrowed further. "You've helped him before? Why didn't you tell me?"

"Because you didn't need to know," Jess said. This was the worst part of working with Ryland. He always assumed he was right and that he should know everything. Honestly, Jess didn't know how Miranda put up with it. Turning her back on Ryland, Jess reached a hand out to Merkins. "Do you have the drawings?"

"Yes." His teeth snapped together as he talked. "But if you're working with him on this, I don't think I want to give them to you."

"I'm not working with him," Jess said, giving Merkins a hard glare. "I'm simply using his house." It was only a partial lie. Ryland's assistance thus far had definitely been on the side.

"If you don't want to find yourself staying here indefinitely as well," Ryland said in that low, gravelly voice that had made more than one grown man sweat, "you'll hand over what you came to deliver."

Merkins held out a leather portfolio. "There's several sketches in there. It would have been suspicious if I'd only done one of the paintings, so I did a few more. I've no use for them, so you might as well keep them."

He sneered at Jess but avoided looking at Ryland again. "Whoever told you those paintings had significance lied. The only reason the previous earl bought that painting was that it matched the view from his front porch."

With a cocky smile, he spun toward the door.

"You don't mention this," Ryland said to Merkins's retreating back.

"Of course he won't. If he does, I'll happen to mention why he owed this to me."

Jess had her own version of intimidation.

With a huff and a few muttered words that were likely not complimentary, Merkins left.

"What a brilliant show," Miranda said as the door shut behind Merkins. "Do you think you could use that on the gardener at Marshington Abbey? I don't think he's doing everything he could be for the roses."

A laugh gurgled in Jess's throat as Ryland's hard exterior immediately dissolved. He ran a hand over his face before giving his wife a look so soft Jess felt like she shouldn't be witnessing it. "I'll see what I can do."

"Good." Miranda grinned at him and then cut a glance in Jess's direction. "While you're at it, you should remind Jess to make sure she sets up some sort of early warning system to notify her when someone approaches if she intends to have more private moments with Mr. Thornbury."

Ryland's face, which moments before had been honed granite, broke into a grin.

"I'm going to look through these pictures." Jess held up the portfolio and then turned on her heel. "Perhaps this will be the one that breaks the code for us."

Heat scorched her cheeks as she walked back to the study. They needed to find the location of the bowl soon. Not only because her brother's fate required it, but because if the past three days in this house had been difficult, the next were going to be impossible.

CHAPTER TWENTY-NINE

*D*erek flipped through the sketches quickly. "He's very talented."

Ryland grunted and scattered the papers across the desk. "Which one is the one you need?"

"This one." Derek slid one to the middle of the desk. "It fits the description and the concept. There's the direction."

His long thin finger followed the line of a horse race. It wasn't a track but an overland race with a string of horses heading over a hill toward a cluster of trees. "This one is called *The End of the Beginning.*" Derek sighed. "I've no idea where it is. There's a village and a set of crumbling ruins. That strange-shaped rock outcropping is probably distinctive, but where is it?"

"Merkins said the view was from the front of the house. I'm sure he'd have kept the information to himself if he'd known how badly we needed it," Jess said with a rather satisfied smile.

Jeffreys pulled out the map. "They'd be riding east, then."

Derek pinned a length of ribbon into place. The newly laid ribbon overlapped the blue one at a spot very near to Haven Manor.

It was a little too coincidental for Jess's comfort.

"How long until your other recruits return?" Ryland lifted his gaze from the map and looked at Jess. "Am I going to want to throw them out of my house as well?"

Jess couldn't quite read the expression in Ryland's face. It wasn't anything she'd seen from him before. Had he expected her to never act on her own or do something differently than he did?

"The second could be back this afternoon." She squared her shoulders and lifted her chin in his direction. Given the quality of the sketches, she'd been right to choose Merkins. "The earliest the third could arrive is tomorrow."

Derek braced his hands and leaned over the map of England, shoulders hunched almost to his ears as his head hung down. "I'm missing something."

Without conscious thought, Jess took his arm, once more hit by the warmth she felt whenever she touched him now. "We're taking a break today, remember?"

"What?" Derek shook his head before tilting it up to look at her. "Yes. Right. What should we do, then?"

Jess grinned. He'd taught her to knit. Perhaps she could return the favor. "Have you ever thrown knives in a ballroom?"

⚔⚔

The problem with throwing knives in Ryland's ballroom was that he wanted to join them. Today, he brought Miranda with him. Everyone else followed.

"Are you teaching her to throw?" Jess asked with a nod toward the duchess.

"Me? No," Ryland scoffed. "She might get frustrated and try to stab me like you did."

"I didn't stab you," Jess grumbled.

"No, but you tried."

That was true. She had. Frustration hadn't been her motivation, though. Anger had.

He'd been trying to teach her how to defend herself, and she'd been a horrible student, cringing at the idea of doing anyone harm. He'd said if she didn't want to end up in the same place as her family and make her father's sacrifice pointless, she needed to act differently.

Jess had attacked, Ryland had fended her off, and she'd landed in a heap on the floor, where she'd cried for the first and last time since losing her family. Then she'd taken Ryland's words to heart and chosen to act differently.

"I'm sure I could do better now if I tried," Jess said, trying to move away from the emotional trip down memory lane and back toward the lighthearted jest it was supposed to be.

Daphne, Kit, and their husbands had been watching in silent fascination, but the exchange drew timid snickers from their little huddle.

Ryland grinned. "I've learned a few tricks myself in the past ten years." He grinned at his wife. "I won't teach her, but I thought you could."

Miranda frowned. "A lady does not throw the cutlery. My mother says so."

Jess tried to turn her laugh into a cough. Miranda's mother was the most ladylike woman Jess had ever met, so there was no question that she had an extensive rule book on what should and should not be done. Still, this seemed extreme. "Your mother actually told you not to throw knives?"

"Hmmm, yes. When I was nine and Georgina was complaining about the size of the tarts." Miranda gave a graceful shrug and an innocent smile. "Tarts are one of my favorite treats, and I didn't want the cook to stop making them just because Georgina complained."

"I say," Kit broke in with a frown, "does that mean I should give up throwing knives?"

"You were never any good at it," Jess said, wishing her friend had remained too intimidated to participate in the barbed discussion.

"Oh, I'm not complaining," Kit said. "I'm just thankful for the excuse to remain awful at it."

Jess looked away. It was nothing but a humorous anecdote when Miranda said it. Kit viewing the idea of knife throwing as inappropriate solidified that Jess wasn't meant for the polite world anymore.

Ryland stepped up next to her and nodded to where Derek was inspecting Ryland's knife-throwing targets. "Good fit."

Ryland was wrong. Derek's interest had nothing to do with knives. He probably thought the straw figures were some type of statue. "I'll bet he's never thrown a knife in his life," Jess whispered. "You name the stakes."

The duke's snort of laughter tickled Jess's ear and made her jerk. "Of course he hasn't. But he knits."

Jess frowned. Ryland had made the statement as if it made complete and utter sense, but it didn't. What did knitting have to do with throwing knives? If anything, it showed how completely opposite they were from each other.

He didn't mean anything derogatory by his statement, did he? Jess jerked a glance to Ryland's face, but his expression was completely blank. Then his eyes widened.

Jess turned to see Derek had abandoned the straw dummies and was now in the center of the room on his hands and knees, examining the intricate inlaid woodwork on the ballroom floor.

Of course he was.

Jess shook her head and left him to it, taking the time to lay out her knives on the table. She honestly didn't care if he learned to throw knives or not; it was just the first idea that had come to mind when she'd needed to get him out of the study.

She should have known he'd care more about the ballroom floor than knife skills.

"Are you sure you don't want to learn?" Jess asked Miranda. "It would hardly be the first time you defied your mother." Hopefully Miranda saw the invitation as the peace offering Jess meant it to be.

"No," the duchess said with a shake of her head. "If I learned how to handle a knife, there might be times I would truly want to throw it at him."

"Another reason for me not to learn," Kit said.

Her husband, Graham, laughed. "You never get mad at me."

"You make me angry all the time," she muttered.

"Only when I point out things that make you angry at yourself."

Jess stepped away from the happy couples. After checking to make sure Derek was well out of harm's way, she threw three knives in quick succession. It felt good. She'd thrown knives in the woods at Haven Manor on occasion, but there was always this sense of the forbidden about it.

As the thwack of knives in straw echoed through the ballroom, Derek yelped. When she turned to face him, he strode across the room, mouth slightly agape. "You're really going to throw knives in here?"

She'd told him that's what they were doing, hadn't she? "Yes, are you ready to try?"

He looked positively appalled. "What if I miss?"

Ryland coughed. "Oh, you will."

"I am not risking putting a gouge in this floor. Have you seen it?"

"Derek, people walk on this floor."

He crossed his arms over his chest. "Not on knives, they don't."

"Clearly you've never been to a London society ball," Miranda murmured.

Jess couldn't hide her grin.

"If you want to throw knives about, do it over there." He pointed to one end of the ballroom, where strips of wood formed a wide border around the large central mosaic. Without waiting for an answer, he grabbed one of the dummies and began moving it.

Shoulders shaking in silent laughter, Ryland grabbed another and joined him.

Miranda stepped up next to Jess and sighed.

"What was that for?" Jess asked.

"Ryland gets to reject any social activity for the next month."

"Why would you agree to that?" Jess asked. "It means you won't go anywhere except dinner at the Duke of Riverton's house."

"I know, but I didn't believe him when he said Mr. Thornbury was the perfect man for you."

Jess stiffened. "I hope you also made a bet on nothing coming of this supposed perfect match."

"Maybe I did, maybe I didn't. If I tell you, it might affect the outcome." Miranda grinned and followed the men over to the far side of the ballroom.

Kit and Daphne stepped up on either side of Jess.

"Daphne," Kit said musingly, "do you think it's too late for us to get in on that wager?"

Jess sighed. As much as she hated everyone trying to get her married and settled when there were far more important things to worry about, it wasn't escaping her notice that no one was telling her she was a perfect fit for him.

⊷⊶

If life were a series of paintings, Derek was currently living in one by Giuseppe Arcimboldo. From a distance, all might look normal, but upon closer examination nothing was quite as it seemed.

They were at dinner. Everyone was nicely dressed and the food was exquisite. That was where any similarity to his previous dinners ended.

The duke was telling William, a marquis, the best ways to sneak his wife in and out of social events in order to achieve maximum appearances with minimum interactions. The future earl was assuring the marchioness that all of her illegitimate children—Derek had to assume he was referring to the ones who had been under her care at Haven Manor—were faring excellently well with their new families, and the duchess and viscountess were trying to convince Jess that a more fashionably cut spencer would still sufficiently cover the leather harness she used to carry her throwing knives.

As if that weren't strange enough, every now and then the servants bringing the food to the table would add in their thoughts and opinions on whatever subject.

The only confirmation Derek had that he wasn't completely losing his mind was that William and Lord Wharton were also a bit startled every time one of the servants said their piece.

Jess was seated to his left, and she never gave a second thought to the servants talking. She simply answered them as if they had a spot at the table.

Derek leaned toward her and pitched his voice low. "Are all of the servants here former spies and soldiers?"

"No," she whispered back. "Some of them are reformed criminals."

And he spiraled a little further into a world where Arcimboldo's portraits of people made of vegetables actually made sense.

Mr. John Langley arrived at the house while the men were drinking port after dinner. Obviously Ryland liked Langley, as he invited the man, coated in travel dust and wearing clothes that would never grace another duke's parlor, to join them for a drink.

Langley took him up on that offer, looking like he felt more at ease with the concept than Derek did. Without Jess at his side, Derek didn't have the same sense of belonging. Despite the fact that he and William were friends and had spent many a pleasant evening discussing history and current events, adding His Grace and Lord Wharton to the mix left Derek feeling like an apprentice painter hung among the masters.

He left them to their discussions and took Langley's sketch to the study. As the lantern light flickered across the drawing room, frustration welled inside him.

This was another odd sketch, though he knew it mattered to the puzzle. Like Lord Bradford's *The Feast of Future Fortune* and *The Inspired Change of Desire* at the ambassador's, this was a single setting with no movement and no direction.

The scene was the kitchen of a manor house. By modern standards the kitchen would be poor, but during the time of The Six it would have been the height of luxury. Two well-dressed women with aprons over their elaborate gowns were packing food into baskets. At the door of the kitchen, a third woman was handing a basket to a shabbily dressed family. A line of people in rags stretched behind.

On the other side of the kitchen, the door was open to the larder, its shelves completely bare. Every cabinet and table beyond the packaged food was also empty.

What did it mean, though?

Derek pulled the sketches of the three similar paintings together on top of all the other papers. The circle of lantern light spilled over them but didn't bring any additional enlightenment.

"Couldn't stay away?"

He was almost accustomed to Jess's silent movements, if the

fact that he barely flinched was any indication. "Another drawing arrived."

She stood next to him, her shoulder pressed against his arm, and looked down. A frown puckered between her brows.

He watched her for several moments, an endeavor that was far from difficult. It was easy to watch her when she didn't know he was watching. "Do you see something?"

"I . . . maybe?" She tilted her head to the side and sighed in frustration. "What am I supposed to be seeing?"

Maybe that was the problem. He was looking at these the way he usually did, bringing himself into the picture, finding the meaning to him now. While these paintings still elicited emotion even when reduced to a sketch, that wasn't the point. Right now, they were something other than spectacular art.

He scooped the three papers up and moved toward the bookcase. "Bring the lantern."

The light around him grew as he propped the sketches up against a set of books. These three paintings unlocked the puzzle. They had to. The others were creating some sort of framework, but these mattered more. Their entries had been more poetic, more obviously important.

Excitement buzzed through him until he was nearly shaking. They were close. He could feel it.

One quick shove had a small table positioned in front of the shelf, and he set the lantern on it before stepping back and pulling Jess to his side. Light flickered across the three drawings, but they stood on the edge of the bright circle, shadows creeping into their space.

"We've been doing this wrong," Derek said.

"We have?" Jess asked quietly.

Her tone broke his concentration for a moment as he glanced down at her, the pale color of her hair seeming to glow in the limited light. He swallowed hard and faced the drawings again.

"As difficult as it is to say, yes. I've always thought there wasn't a wrong way to look at art; there was simply what you experienced with it. With this, though, we need to look at the more concrete elements. These were intended to be a hidden source of clues."

Realizing he still had her arm in his grip, he dropped it and nodded to the bookshelf. "Look at these and tell me what you see."

She gave him that smirk that said she thought he'd left the lantern lit in an empty attic, but then she dutifully looked at the paintings. "The subjects are rich."

Derek nodded. Gold, jewels, and expensive gowns abounded. As much to move away from her as to make some sense of what they were seeing, he grabbed a candle and lit it from the lantern before moving to the desk to make notes. "Rich. What else?"

Jess sighed. "Those two are inside." She pointed at two of them. "That one isn't, though, so I guess that's not important."

The people at the picnic weren't inside, but they were under the shelter of trees. From an art perspective, that could be a building of sorts. Derek didn't say anything, not wanting to distract her, but he made the note.

"Those two are sad." Once again she pointed to two of them before waving a hand at the third one dismissively. "That one's most decidedly not sad, despite the fact that they don't have any food."

He jotted more notes down, but something about the last statement niggled at him. "Food." He licked his lips. "Food is always important in art. Well, not always, but often."

"There's nothing the same there, though." Jess started at one end and poked at each picture in turn. "They don't have any food, they're giving all of it away, and their food is getting ruined."

Derek sighed. He'd thought they'd been on to something, but what she said was true. Without a commonality, they couldn't learn anything. "What else do you see?"

Her eyes flitted between the pictures, the line between her brows getting deeper and deeper. Finally she rubbed a hand across her face and sighed. "I don't know what you want from me, Derek."

Derek looked at her, the light playing across her face like a Caravaggio painting, the shadows behind her growing darker as the night filled the house.

He wasn't sure what he wanted from her either.

CHAPTER THIRTY

*F*eeling that the something they were missing was somehow locked in her own mind was almost as frustrating to Jess as the waiting had been.

Queen Marguerite had sent the diary back to Verbonne. That had to mean she thought the paintings would mean something to someone from there. Of course, more than one hundred years had passed between the diary and Jess's life. Had the country been similar enough for her to experience the necessary elements in her childhood?

The diary was the connection between the paintings the refugee group had created and the home they'd left behind. Even if Queen Jessamine had a surviving child, the obvious intention had been for the royal line to remain with the existing king. It had been about Verbonne.

Jess slept fitfully all night, using every technique she knew to ease her body back into a restful state every time she awoke. Sleep was a commodity that sometimes had to be skipped, so it was only smart to gather it when she could.

Still, at the first sign of a new day, she was up, dressed, and headed toward the study. She passed a servant in the hall, a young girl she didn't recognize—a true sign that life here in London had moved on without her. The girl nodded as she passed, but Jess called her back and asked her to see if breakfast could be sent to the study.

She was going back in there and she wasn't leaving until she'd found whatever it was Derek had needed from her last night. Was there something she'd already seen that was important?

Derek had been excited about the food at first, but the only thing Jess saw was that the people who didn't have any food seemed a great deal happier to not be eating than the people watching their food float away in the rain.

Jess stumbled to a halt on the stairs. The people were happy not to be eating.

There wasn't much she remembered about her life before the cottage and what she did remember was painful to think about, so she avoided doing so with remarkable dedication. However, that was the Verbonne the painters had known. That was the Verbonne she needed to connect the paintings to.

Heart pounding, she ran down the stairs and into the study. The translation papers were strewn about the desk, but she didn't know where to look.

Kit and Daphne found her in there a few minutes later.

"I told you this was where we'd find her," Kit said, folding her arms. "You've been avoiding us."

"You can't really blame her," Daphne said in her gentle voice. "It can't be pleasant to know we might be as blunt with her as she was with us."

Kit snorted a laugh. "I'd like to see you lose tact."

Jess shook her head. She did not have time for these two this morning. She waved a hand through the air to cut them off. "I need Derek."

Daphne blinked. "Well, that was easier than I expected."

Jess growled. Why did she consider these women friends again? Not even mere friends, but family she'd been unable to leave even when her conscience prodded her to. Right now she would have no problem telling both of them farewell.

In fact, she needed to do just that. Something was lurking in her mind, something important, and she wouldn't lose it because some people were so in love they refused to see that others were simply too scarred to be comfortable in it.

The maid she'd stopped in the corridor entered with a breakfast tray in hand, Derek trailing behind her. "Getting an early start this morning?" he asked. "Did the last sketch come in?"

Jess rounded the desk and took the tray from the maid, placing it on the table by the fireplace, then shooed the other women from the room. "Out, out."

The maid gave Jess a quizzical expression but turned and strode away without a word.

Daphne and Kit were not quite so accommodating.

"Should we leave them alone?" Daphne asked. "It's not proper, is it?"

"This room is ten times the size of that carriage," Jess said. "Out."

Daphne bit her lip but edged toward the door. "It seems different."

"Unlike you two," Jess said through gritted teeth, "I'm trying to accomplish something worthwhile."

"I think our goal rather noble," Kit said with a smile, but she took Daphne's arm. Before stepping through the door, she looked back over her shoulder with a grin. "I'll just close this for you, shall I? Wouldn't want the duchess walking in without a warning again."

Jess's hand itched to snag a knife and bury it into the doorframe Kit was leaning against. She resisted by grabbing a piece of toast from the tray and tearing it in half before taking a large bite.

Kit's laughter could be heard through the closed door.

"Jess?" Derek asked softly. "What's going on?"

She took another bite of bread and then left both halves on the tray before moving back to the desk. Taking the diary from the corner of the desk, she held it out to Derek. "Read it to me."

He watched her as if she were some sort of violent animal as he took the diary from her hand and eyed the scattered pages of notes. "It will be easier if I read the translated pages. Give me a minute to put them back in order. What part did you want?"

"No, read it in Italian." She placed herself back in front of the three drawings exactly where Derek had put her the night before. "If I hear it, I'll understand it."

"What are we looking for?"

Jess ignored the little jump her heart gave when he said *we*. She needed to focus. "I don't know. At least, I don't know how it connects, but all I could think about was how you said food is important."

"Not always," Derek said. "There aren't any hard rules when it comes to art."

"There was a holiday in Verbonne," she said, hating that her voice and her knees trembled as she forced herself to remember, forced herself to go back. "The Feast of the Forgotten. After she left, though, it was called The Feast of Queen Jessamine. On that day, the royal family wouldn't eat. All the food in the palace larder that normally would have been used to feed the people who lived there was given to the poor and needy, but the palace still held a large party. Helping was a reason to celebrate, not mourn. The queen and the rest of her party fled the day before the feast. Instead of giving the food to the poor, it was bundled up and sent with the fleeing group as provisions."

Her eyes darted from sketch to sketch, trying to determine how it connected, why it mattered. "That's why they changed the name. The entire capital city went without eating that day, in despair for the country that was hoping they could survive whatever came."

"What are you saying, Jess?" Derek asked.

Jess swung her arm at the three drawings. "I'm saying no one is eating. The last thing the group knew of Verbonne was the Feast of the Forgotten, and no one in these paintings is eating." Her breathing was harsh, her chest heaving with the idea that she might just be right. "You said art was about emotion?"

"Yes, well, sometimes, in a way." Derek set the diary back on the desk and shoved his hair out of his eyes. "It's about holding a moment in its entirety. Often it's meant to draw something out of the person looking at it, but—"

"Then we look at it that way," Jess interrupted. "The painters loved Verbonne; they loved it enough to leave it, in the hope that they could one day save it. We have to look at the paintings with that in mind." She swallowed hard, hating the fact that understanding someone else's emotions meant having to open up her own.

It took only moments for her to add all the sketches they had to the bookshelf, and then she stepped back to look at all of them in turn. "Read me the diary."

"'*Cavalcano e perseverano nella speranza che il vero re un giorno regni di nuovo, unto e potente e in cima alla collina,*'" Derek read in a low voice. His verbal Italian wasn't the best, but it was enough. She could hear the nuance, the shades of meaning, everything the original writer had put in.

"They ride on and persevere in hope that the true king will one day rule again, anointed and powerful and atop the hill," Jess whispered, looking to the drawing of horses racing over the hill and toward the trees. Toward hope? Was the hope in the trees? What other pictures had trees?

The rained-out picnic. The country lane. If there was some sort of hidden picture in the leaves, they'd never know it from these sketches.

Derek read on. When his voice got scratchy, Jess poured him a cup of cold tea from the forgotten breakfast tray, and he continued. Entry after entry went by. Every now and then a phrase would get Jess thinking one way, but nothing ever seemed to match up. Other times a phrase would be written and placed in such a way that it was clearly important.

She just didn't know why.

"You're right," Jess said, gathering up everything but the three pictures they'd been looking at last night. "It's these. The others are right there. If you have the diary and the painting it's clear. There's something more to these."

Derek didn't respond. He hadn't responded to any of her mumbles or rambles, letting her try to find something she wasn't sure she had.

"'Ungi il re con disperazione, speranza e amore . . .'"
Anoint the king with despair, hope, and love.
*"'. . . poiché dove questi si incontrano, sulla sua testa sarà la
capacità di governare con grazia, dignità e umiltà.'"*
For where these meet, on his head will be the ability to rule
with grace, dignity, and humility.

Derek's words stumbled to a halt. Jess looked over to find him
staring at the drawings for the first time since he'd started reading.

"Despair, hope, and love," he whispered.

"What?"

He set the diary aside, grabbed the drawings, and went to the
map of ribbons.

"These ribbons are crossing near Stonehenge," Derek murmured. "And there was a painting of Stonehenge in the background
of the party." He pulled out the drawing of *The Feast of Future
Fortune* and one of the sewing pins they'd stuck in the map to
hold the ribbons, then fixed the paper to the map where the two
ribbons crossed in Wiltshire. "There's hope."

Jess looked at where two more ribbons crossed in Norfolk.
"Which one goes here?"

Derek looked between the other two. "I have no idea."

No. Jess knelt before the map. They were not going to have
unlocked this piece just to have it taken from them. There was only
one ribbon for the third placement. She picked up the rained-out
picnic. "Are there any great houses on this line? One that could
be this shape in the background?"

"I don't know." Derek grabbed up the third drawing of the
kitchen with the empty larder. "That would put love here, somewhere."

Jess looked at the drawing and then at Derek. "You think that
one's love?"

"The other choice is despair."

A little girl in the drawing had a hand on the empty shelves as
the women passed out baskets of food. Jess had hated The Feast
of Queen Jessamine as a child, certainly feeling something akin

to despair as she had watched roasts, puddings, and bread leave the palace in wagons while her belly grumbled and her father told her to smile.

"Yes," Derek said, "this is love. Whether these women are going to be able to fill their larder again or not doesn't matter. They have to love these people to be giving them everything they have. It's not just about helping them survive. They're taking care with the baskets. This is a gift that the giver has to sacrifice for. That's love."

If that was love, then Jess wasn't sure she'd ever experienced it. She certainly didn't think she'd ever given it. She'd helped others, yes, but had it ever been at her own peril?

With difficulty, she pushed the thought aside. They were too close to solving the map for her to ponder philosophical riddles. "How do we know exactly where it is?"

"We don't." Derek pinned the paper where the ribbons met in Norfolk. "Let's see if that's close enough. Now we just need to find ourselves a castle."

After a moment's silence, Jess looked up to see him staring at her, an expression that could have been concern, pity, or a mixture of the two on his face. He cleared his throat. "We're going to need help on this one."

As much as she hated to admit it, he was right. Her knowledge of England was limited, as was his. There were others in this house, though, who had traveled the land extensively. Jess sighed. "I'll go get them."

The sentence was easier to say than Jess would have expected. Either the business of asking for help was getting easier, or Jess was simply too numb from the continuous onslaught of emotions to feel the pain anymore.

In the end, it took the combined efforts and memories of everyone in the house, along with details from three travel books, but they finally determined that the picnic was in front of Lyme Park.

"Despair," Derek said as he pinned it to the map.

"Anoint the king where these meet," Jess murmured. Assuming

they'd placed the pins in the correct place, the bowl should be at the center of the triangle they created.

Holding her breath, Jess leaned in at the same time as Derek. Their shoulders pressed together, their breaths mingled, they traced imaginary lines from each of the points until they landed on Kettering.

"Kettering?" Jess sat back on her heels, feeling every bit of the despair the flooded picnic painting implied. "How are we supposed to find it in Kettering? We can't possibly pinpoint the places of these paintings well enough to determine where in Kettering the bowl is."

Derek placed a hand on her shoulder. "We're closer than we were. I'll keep reading the diary. There will be something there. She wanted this to be found, remember?"

He was right. Jess had strolled into many a town knowing nothing beyond her end objective. It may have taken her a while, but she'd never failed yet.

CHAPTER THIRTY-ONE

Once the destination of Kettering was announced, Derek had assumed he and Jess and Jeffreys would head out like they had before. The others did not make the same assumption. In fact, the debate over who was going to Kettering was long and loud.

"A whole carriageload of us trooping off to the middle of the country is going to be rather conspicuous," Jess growled.

Derek searched her face. Obviously Jess had been of a mind to keep it the three of them as well. Was it because she thought it less conspicuous, because she wanted her friends safe, or because she wanted a bit more time with him before all of this ended? He never would have thought it, but Derek was going to miss Jess painfully when he no longer saw her every day.

"The best thing," Jess continued, "would be for me to go on my own."

That answered Derek's unspoken question and crushed his flickering hopes. Jess was protecting the people she cared about at the risk of her own safety. How had she not understood which painting was love?

"I think—" Derek began, refusing to be left behind. He might have to say good-bye to her soon, but not yet, and he wanted every memory of Jess that he could collect before they parted ways. She was the nuance and vibrancy of art come to life. He might never get to experience that again.

His sentence was cut off by the duke, though. "You think it's easiest to do everything on your own, but who watches your back when you do that?"

"My back is a very tiny target," she yelled back.

"You're being ridiculous," Jeffreys joined in, not acting at all like a servant in this moment. "You can't waltz into a situation like this without assistance." He gestured one hand between him and Jess before pointing at the duke. "You didn't let him do it before, and we're not letting you do it now."

Jess jabbed an angry finger toward Ryland. "*He* knew there was someone waiting for him with a gun and a loose mooring. No one knows I'm going to Kettering."

"Actually," Derek butted in quickly, "we don't know what they know."

Three gazes turned toward him, eyebrows lowered and faces frowning.

"Now you've done it," William muttered. Until now, the rest of their group had been standing in a silent circle, most looking on in some form of fascinated horror. Lady Wharton frowned, her eyes narrowed, while the duchess exhibited the calm, exasperated patience of one who had seen this play out before.

Or perhaps Derek should call them Kit and Miranda. Despite the abundant titles, this group seemed rather bent on informality.

"That's true," the duke said with a shrug.

Derek cleared his throat and continued. "They had two of the key paintings. All of the other paintings were simply to help establish the locations of the key paintings, but if they knew where the settings were, they might know about Kettering."

"But only two of the paintings were on the slides," Jess said stubbornly, "hope and despair."

"How do we know they haven't seen the third one at some point? Perhaps there were more slides somewhere. What if they have their own diary or some less abstract code that passed down through their family?" Jeffreys crossed his thin arms and stuck his crooked nose in the air.

"You're going," Ryland said, pointing at Jess, "because you'll be taking the bowl to Verbonne once we find it." The finger swung in Derek's direction, and he tried not to flinch. "He's going because we have no idea what we'll run into in Kettering, and if there's more art and diary clues there, we'll need him."

"I'm driving the carriage," Jeffreys said, looking ready to fight anyone who said anything different.

The duke nodded before pointing a thumb at himself. "I am also going because someone needs to watch your back, scrawny though it may be. Besides, you might need a distraction as you run for the hills—or the water, in this case."

"England is at peace," Jess said dryly. "You can't just blow up a building in the name of distraction."

"You aren't the only one who can cause a riot. If I buy enough rounds at the local taverns I can unleash an entire squad of drunk men on the town." The duke grinned as if he was considering doing just that, regardless of the outcome of their search.

"That leaves one open seat in the carriage," Kit said. "I think I'll take it."

Never had such silence filled a room so quickly. Derek rather imagined this was what it was like when Thomas Gainsborough's portraits had first been presented at the royal art shows. No one had known quite what to do with them.

Then the silence exploded as everyone started talking at once. Derek became dizzy trying to identify the speakers and pull their sentences from one another. Life had no compulsion to stand still and allow a person to examine it the way art did.

Kit glared them all down as her husband chuckled. Why wasn't he concerned? Yes, Lord Wharton had struck Derek as a rather happy fellow, quick to make a joke, but surely he couldn't laugh off his wife walking into danger.

Unless she was also more than she appeared to be. Derek narrowed his gaze in her direction. He didn't know her well, having only seen her a time or two while working at Haven Manor and then these few days here at Montgomery House. The grit she'd had to possess to care for all those children in the middle of nowhere was admirable, but was it enough to prepare her for something such as this?

Jess didn't protest, though the duke and Jeffreys were vehemently campaigning against it. Even Miranda was looking nervous about the idea.

Then William and his wife spoke up, adding their support for Kit. Lord Wharton had stopped chuckling, though a wide grin remained, and he set a hand on his wife's shoulder in solidarity.

"Are you sure, Kit?" Jess's voice cut through the yelling mob.

Ryland frowned. "*She* can go but I can't?"

Jess lifted a brow in the duke's direction. "I thought you'd declared you were going. If you're there, she can be, too."

The duke crossed his arms and glared. Even though the glare wasn't aimed his direction, Derek took a step back. Jess crossed her arms over her chest and glared back.

"I'm not taking a future countess into danger," he said.

"It's hardly my first time." Kit stepped into the circle, keeping Jess between her and Ryland.

With the ladies a united front, the duke turned to Lord Wharton. "You are ready to allow this?"

"I can't say I'm thrilled with the idea, but Kit isn't going to be stupid. She knows how to get in and get out and how not to be seen. I've lost her enough times to give testament to that fact."

Jess leaned back into Kit. Only Derek's angle allowed him to see it, but there was a definite shift of Jess's weight that brought her closer to the other woman. "Both of you or neither of you."

Ryland nodded his head toward Lord Wharton. "You think his testament of her skills is enough?"

"No, I think my judgment of her skills is enough. I didn't run off to Haven Manor on a whim. I met Kit in an alley off St. James."

The duke's glare faded to curiosity. "What were you doing— never mind. You can tell me later."

"Or not tell you," Kit said with a shrug.

Jeffreys chuckled. "Lady's got my vote."

"All right, then," Ryland said. "Jess, Jeffreys, me, Derek, and Lady Wharton."

"Call me Kit," she said. "I'm hardly going to paint a target on myself by being the only one in the party called by her title."

Jess snickered, crossing her arms and looking so triumphant Derek expected her to cheer.

The duke growled. "Jess, Jeffreys, me, Derek, and *Kit*, then. We leave in the morning." He jabbed a finger toward Jess. "Pack lightly."

Everyone filtered away to prepare for the journey until only Jess and Derek remained in the drawing room.

"Care to help me pack up the drawings and translations?" he asked. It hardly took two people to stack up a few papers, but this might be the last time it was just the two of them.

She nodded and preceded him to the study.

"Once you have the bowl," he said as he put the translated pages in order, "you'll take it to Verbonne?"

"Yes. I don't know what the situation currently is, but if the bowl is all that stands between Verbonne and freedom, then the country should have it." She swallowed. "Then I'm going to try to learn if there was indeed another child."

Derek stopped stacking papers. "You think the other line has a valid claim?"

"No. Despite the possible birth of another child, I think the crown belongs to those with a true attachment to the country. One could argue that Queen Jessamine abdicated her royal position when she fled, and any child she had certainly wasn't raised to rule. But if there are others who are truly of a mind to help save Verbonne, that should be considered."

Jess sighed and ran a hand over the cover of the diary. "The country was in chaos when I was a child, probably quite a bit more so than I knew. The continued war would have only weakened it. It needs all the supporters it can get. If the question of blood is answered and settled, then maybe everyone can focus on developing a vision for a future Verbonne together."

Derek's heart pounded and his fingers tightened until the papers in his hand started to wrinkle. He could see himself in that future. Verbonne was rich in culture and history; it was in their blood. They would want to preserve that, wouldn't they? Build upon that tradition again? He could help.

With a shake of his head, he released his grip and smoothed the notes. One thing at a time. They had to find the bowl, get it out of England, find her brother, and establish a renewed government. *Then* he could see if the idea of more time with Jess still made him as excited as the prospect of free rein of the British Museum on a clear sunny day.

⚔

Because a duke caused a stir wherever he went and Jess looked a lot like her mother, whom Lord Bradford and possibly others had seen, Kit and Derek went in to make arrangements for rooms at the inn in Kettering.

That left Jess alone in the carriage with Ryland. She'd avoided being alone with her friend and mentor, knowing he'd seen her at her most vulnerable. Could he still prod at her weak spots?

"The last communication I received was that your brother was still arguing his claim to the throne, even though he had not presented an artifact, diary, bowl, or otherwise. A distant cousin has come out of hiding as well." He paused. "There could be others who are still keeping quiet."

Jess wasn't about to build up that sort of hope. "There's no need to try to build castles on clouds, Ryland. News of one survival is enough to keep me focused."

They fell silent again until Ryland said, "What will you do?"

Why did people keep asking her that? "You say that as if there's a choice."

Ryland slid across his seat until he was directly across from her, their knees almost touching as both of them leaned forward to look out the carriage window. "There's always a choice to make."

Jess sent him a quizzical look. "You mean like you did?"

"There was no choice in holding the title, but I had a choice on whether or not to live it. I chose not to for a long time."

"Are you glad you claimed it?"

"Yes," he said without hesitation. "It allows Miranda to be in my life, allows me to help my country in a way that will continue through peace and war and old age."

Jess couldn't quite grasp being in such a position. She'd been on her own for so long that such a deep connection to an established group was hard to fathom. Then again, what would she do in Verbonne? Her brother would be the one ruling the country. She would . . . what? Renovate the palace?

Ryland continued, "There's something freeing about it, too, living in the light. I spent so much time in the shadows I think I'd forgotten what it was like not to hide. Remembering that it wasn't just about the end but how you got there was becoming harder."

That was something Jess understood all too well. She knew how to hide, how to run, how to cling to the dark. Ryland had always known that one day he would return. Jess hadn't. She'd always thought that one day the dark would simply swallow her whole. One day she'd step a little too far into the shadows and disappear.

And no one would notice or care.

Remembering the people filling Ryland's drawing room, she had to allow that that last assumption might be the slightest bit erroneous.

CHAPTER THIRTY-TWO

Once the door to the room Jess and Kit were to share latched shut, the viscountess groaned and flopped onto the bed. "I've become spoiled by Graham's carriage. I think he managed to have it sprung on clouds, the ride is so smooth."

Jess crossed her arms and leaned one shoulder to the wall. "You didn't have to come."

Kit's head lifted from the bed, blond hair knocked from its pins and sticking out at funny angles. The glare on her face was serious. "Yes, I did. I could not let you go into this alone."

"I'm not alone."

She waved a hand and flopped her head back down. "Those men don't count. Well, Derek does, obviously, but those other two treat you with the delicacy of a stone."

There were so many ways answering that sentence could come back to bite Jess that she sidestepped it entirely. She didn't want to talk about how coddling her during the war hadn't been an option, or how often she'd been on her own, and she certainly didn't want to discuss why Derek treated her differently.

Before Jess could redirect the conversation, Kit said, "This is what you were running from that night we met, isn't it?"

When had all the people in her life become so incredibly astute? Or had they always been, but she hadn't let them in enough or listened to them enough to tell?

"We thought the war was ending," Jess said, "which meant political lines would be drawn, much like they are being drawn now. I didn't know where Verbonne would fall, if it hadn't already disappeared."

She hated talking about this, hated how much of it was still rooted in the childlike fear she couldn't shake. "All I knew was the man who'd come that night had been British, and his anger had been personal. Ryland was moving about in society again, so his home was no longer a safe place. I look like my mother. And if that man had managed to come back to England . . ."

From what she knew now, though, that man had already been here and had likely been traveling to France and back with the smugglers. When this was over, Ryland would pass the slides and the other information to the Home Office. The question was whether Lord Bradford was a traitor to the Crown or to Verbonne. Could one be a traitor to a country he didn't belong to?

Jess crossed the room and placed her valise on a table before digging through it and pulling out a dark dress. "While I appreciate your concern for my delicate sensibilities," Jess said, giving Kit a pointed look over her shoulder, "that's all you're going to do. You aren't pulling out your cloak and skulking around with me."

"Ha!" Kit lurched into a sitting position and pointed a finger at Jess. "So you admit you intend to skulk about."

"Of course." Jess rolled her eyes. "How else am I to learn anything?"

The truth was that the whole way to Kettering, while everyone in the carriage had talked about methodical plans, Jess had been feeling every additional mile. She was at least two days' ride from the coast. If she found the bowl, she wasn't waiting. She was running and taking the first boat across the water, whether by fair means or foul. Verbonne, France, Belgium, it didn't matter to her where it landed as long as she was on the continent and out of Lord Bradford's reach.

"I didn't come for your reputation," Kit said. "That's probably already murkier than I want to consider. I came because you shouldn't be alone. I know it's different here, with all of this, but you didn't leave Daphne and me alone when life was difficult and you could have."

"Haven Manor was a good place to hide," Jess said.

"Do you really believe that's all it was?"

Did she? Yes. No. At first. Jess squirmed and avoided the question. "I'm not alone. I've acquired quite the collection of guard dogs, remember?"

"They—we—are simply worried about you. We *care*." Kit dragged out the last word like she expected Jess to flinch from the statement.

Inside, she did.

"I know," Jess said. She wished they wouldn't, though. All of them were taking a risk by being here. Derek's family didn't even know he was on this adventure. How would they ever understand if something happened to him? Had he even written them in the past month? They'd already shown signs of worry when she'd met them. Would one of them go to Haven Manor, only to find it uninhabited by anyone other than servants?

Jeffreys didn't have a family, but he'd never convince Jess that he didn't have a fondness for Ryland's little girl. He probably slipped the child treats and was already planning grand London adventures for when she was older.

"I think you're lying," Kit said, rolling over until she could climb off the bed. "I don't think you have any idea how much people care for you."

"Apparently enough to leave a husband, a wife, and a child waiting to see if and when they return." The jab was unnecessarily harsh, but Jess wanted Kit to step back, to be a little bit angry. Just because they cared about her didn't mean she deserved it, didn't mean they should risk their safety.

"Graham knows I owe you my life."

"You don't owe me anything," Jess said, draping the dress over the back of a chair and digging in her valise, even though she was just moving the same four items around in the depths of the small bag.

"You mean I could have gotten out of that predicament on my own? Here I thought that thug had only run away because you threw a knife at his feet and said the next one was going to be aimed higher." Kit giggled. "I borrowed that line once, by the way."

"You only said it because you missed," Jess said, having heard the full story of that night from Graham.

Kit shrugged. "It worked."

"You'd have talked your way out of it eventually."

Kit shoved Jess's valise to the floor and plopped herself in the chair so that Jess was staring down at her. "Maybe. Maybe not. That's not the point, anyway. The point is, you laid into me for walking alone in that area at two in the morning even though you were doing the same thing. Even then, you were looking out for those weaker than yourself."

"I'm not a martyr, Kit. I don't have a noble goal like you and Daphne." Jess stepped back but didn't turn away. If Kit insisted on having this discussion, Jess would give it to her. Jess would let her see it all.

"Just because it isn't organized doesn't mean you aren't helping people. You do little things in the moment. I see it all the time." Kit grinned. "You care about us. Admit it."

Was that all Kit wanted? Jess had admitted it to herself a long time ago, and even though it had made her vulnerable, she hadn't been able to deny it, nor truly regret it. "Yes, I care."

Kit's face grew serious. "We care, too. You matter. You're family. We love you."

Jess turned away. "Derek said love requires sacrifice."

"'Hereby perceive we the love of God, because he laid down his life for us.'"

"Are you quoting scripture to me?" Jess asked, one side of her mouth tilting up.

Kit laughed. "Of course. You don't think I say 'hereby perceive we' in normal conversation, do you? In any case, Derek is right."

Kit crossed the room and gave Jess's shoulder a slight push. "It's why we put up with you, you know. It's obvious you love us even if you don't say anything. When you love someone, you sacrifice for them because they mean more than you do."

Jess did love them. She wanted them all to live happier, better lives.

They'd all gotten there. Kit was with a man who made her smile and was no longer trapped by guilt and obligation. Daphne was starting anew, reunited with her father and fulfilling a mission that made her heart sing, with a man who appreciated her uniqueness. Ryland and the others were building their lives. It was easy to see his household was a happy one.

Jess certainly didn't want them throwing those gains away for her sake.

She shook her head and looked Kit dead in the eye. "Don't love me, then. I'm not worth it."

Whatever Kit was going to say was cut off by a knock on the door. Jess went to let the servant in to set up the dinner they'd ordered. As soon as the servant left, the men joined them to plan their next steps. They had a bowl to find and a country to save.

Then Jess would disappear again.

Kit was right. Jess loved them all, and she loved them too much to keep weighing them down.

⁂

While Kit changed into her night rail behind the screen in the corner of the room, Jess donned her dark dress and then climbed into bed, pulling the covers up to her chin and closing her eyes.

She waited while Kit blew out the candle and got herself situated, then waited some more while Kit's breathing evened out and the moon rose.

The evening had been full of discussion about the paintings and examination of the diary notes. With nothing obvious and the sun setting, they'd all agreed to start the search in the morning.

Only Jess wasn't waiting. No, nothing was obvious, but nothing was ever going to be obvious. It was going to be like everything else so far. She was going to chase after the next idea and hope to stumble across what she needed as she went. It'd been a life philosophy that had worked well for her so far. Why stop now?

Once the inn had quieted, as much as an inn ever did, she slipped from the bed and crept to the door, avoiding the squeaky floorboards she'd discovered earlier in the day. The door felt a bit more jammed than it had earlier, and she had to tug at the latch to get it to open.

The reason spilled into her room and blinked up at her.

Derek, dressed in a black jacket and brown trousers that looked appalling together but were probably the darkest clothes he'd packed, propped himself onto an elbow and rubbed at his eyes.

Not wanting to wake Kit, Jess nudged him until he rolled back enough for her to step out of the room and shut the door behind her.

"What are you doing?" she whispered.

"Knowing you," he answered as he stood. "Where are we going?"

"You're going back to bed. How did you ever get out of there without Ryland noticing?"

"I told him he snored and I was going out to the barn to sleep with Jeffreys."

If Ryland had believed that, Jess would eat her knife case. She darted a glance around. He was watching from somewhere, but where?

"Shall we?" Derek gestured toward the stairs. "I'm assuming you haven't deduced that the bowl is here in the inn."

Jess sighed. "I haven't determined that the bowl is anywhere. I'm just hoping something will make sense if I walk around town."

"Good thing I wore dark clothes, then. That is the best way to hide in the shadows, isn't it?"

"Dark clothes and stillness," Jess answered with a nod before heading to the stairs.

She should try harder to get rid of him, but since nothing was likely to happen tonight, there wasn't any harm in stealing a few more moments of his company. It was selfish, but she couldn't help it. Did that mean she didn't love Derek? Did it mean she loved him more? Did it mean nothing at all?

Jess needed to find this bowl before it created more questions than she was capable of handling.

They slipped from the inn and walked toward the older part of town. Unfortunately, what had once been older wasn't anymore. The market area showed a great deal of recent construction. Jess looked around and frowned. If they'd made significant changes to the town and buildings in the past hundred years, the bowl might be anywhere. It could be displaying flowers in a local manor house for all she knew.

Near the marketplace was an open area, with a large statue at one end. At some point the statue had probably marked a grand entrance or been surrounded by some type of park, but now it stood awkwardly to the side. Scorch marks on one side of the base indicated a fire in the town's history, explaining the abundance of newer construction.

"What did this town look like then?" Derek murmured.

"We don't even know for sure when *then* is. Only the first diary entry has a date."

"We know when the queen and her party fled the country," Derek said with a shrug. "They had to hide the bowl shortly after that in order to know how to place the paintings."

Jess squinted her eyes until the moonlight created nothing but silvery shapes. She did that sometimes when looking at art with Derek, as if blurring the details would help her see what he saw. It hadn't worked yet, but she wasn't giving up. She could do this. She could forget what was in front of her, forget what she could see, and try to imagine what had been.

"What did the first passage say?" She nearly had it memorized and assumed he did as well. Though the bowl was at the end of their journey, it would have been the beginning of the queen's.

Derek recited the part about hope, despair, and love before continuing, "'Anoint the king and let him rule, these three shall be his crown, and he will usher in a new day.'"

"How are hope, despair, and love a crown?" Jess opened her eyes and frowned at Derek. "That's a weird thing to say, isn't it?"

"It's poetry of a sort, which means everything is symbolic. You can't take it literally."

Jess looked around, but they couldn't see much from the dark alcove they were tucked into.

Suddenly, Jess felt incredibly foolish. What had she been thinking? What did she think she would do even if inspiration suddenly struck? The pavement around her was empty and cold, the houses quiet and dark. Piles of boards and stones proved the town was moving on from its prior devastation, meaning the bowl was likely lost and she'd never know it because she didn't know whether or not she was checking in the right place.

Whatever had been here when The Six had come through was disappearing. Jess looked up at the statue of some ancient king and gave him a nod. *You're lucky you're too big to tear down or you'd be next, old man*, she thought.

Despite the fact that this was a fruitless endeavor, she wasn't ready to go back to the inn yet, wanted to spend these last moments with Derek, collect these last memories. She had to believe that somehow she would find the bowl tomorrow and make a run for it.

Perhaps it was time to do like Ryland always said she should and send up a prayer or two. It was certainly getting to the point of her not being able to handle the situation on her own. It was going to take a miracle to find the bowl.

"If you were going to hide something, where would you put it?" Derek asked.

Jess turned her head toward him. "What do you mean?"

"Where would you hide something?"

Leaning back against the stone wall of the alcove, Jess looked about the market area and considered the question.

Over 150 years ago, a desperate, loyal group had entered this town and decided where to hide something. If she'd been one of them, what would she have done?

"It would have to be somewhere that would last a long time," Jess said.

Derek nodded. "At the time, the Holy Roman Empire was weakening, but Leopold the First's hold of his family lands wasn't. They'd know that, at best, it would be years before someone came to retrieve the bowl."

"So somewhere that something could remain hidden for years, possibly even decades, through tragedy and weather and people and growth." She nodded toward the scorch marks. "Not somewhere that could burn down."

Derek nodded.

"It would have to be somewhere I knew I would be able to get back to," Jess added, following the idea now. "I might bury it, but that's risky. All it would take would be someone building on top of it to endanger your hiding spot."

"I didn't bring my shovel, so that's good."

Jess blinked and choked back a laugh. Had he just made a joke? She grinned as she continued musing. "If it might have to stay hidden beyond my generation, I'd avoid buildings. Whoever owns them later might renovate or ban you from the premises."

"That takes out a lot of places, then."

It didn't leave much, that was sure. She dropped her head back against the wall and closed her eyes. Where *would* she hide something for an extended period of time?

When she opened her eyes again, all she could see was the top of the statue and the upper floors of a building across the street.

She picked her head up and looked at the statue again. Where would she hide something? She'd hide it somewhere that was too much trouble to tear down.

"Derek," she said over the excitement building within her, "how large would the head be on a statue that size?"

"It depends. Some of the great Italian sculptors actually made the head and shoulders bigger so the statue would look proportionate from the ground."

"Make a guess."

Derek tilted his head and considered the statue before making a circle with his arms. "Probably about this big. Maybe a touch bigger."

"That statue. When was it built?"

"That's impossible to say from this angle. I'd have to look at the details and—"

"Old, though, right?"

"Based on the way the town has grown around it, I would say yes."

These three shall be his crown.

It was the right size. It was the right shape. It was, possibly, the right age.

If she was wrong, this was going to be very embarrassing, but if she was right—and she really did think she was right—then Jess had found the bowl.

CHAPTER THIRTY-THREE

A brisk night wind blew through the market, cutting through Derek's trousers and ruffling the tails of his jacket. He followed Jess's gaze up to the statue. What was she thinking? Did she recognize the man? The pose? Was it some memory from Verbonne?

He opened his mouth to ask, but before he could she was sliding her spencer jacket off her shoulders and shoving it into his arms. The leather harness that held four of her knives came off next. She slid one knife free and then dropped the harness into his arms as well.

"What are you . . . ?" Derek trailed off because she had already left their little alcove and was clambering up onto the plinth of the statue.

One boot wedged into the folds of the king's robes, then another stepped on the thigh of the leg propped on a rock. Soon her hands were gripping the statue's shoulders, and her head appeared over the top, knife clenched between her teeth. A few more moments and she was clinging to the back of the statue like a young child. She hooked one leg over the top and then was sitting on the shoulder, hugging the statue's head, one leg exposed from boot to knee.

One very shapely leg exposed from boot to knee.

She took the knife and began banging the top of the head with the handle, giving Derek something other than her leg to look up at.

Dull thuds rang through the market.

As much as Derek wanted to drag her down from the statue and ask her what in the world she thought she was doing, his time might be better spent watching for anyone else who might want to come along and do the same.

After tucking the mass of knives, leather, and fabric under his arm, he set up a pattern of looking from street to alley to house to Jess and then back around again.

On his third glance up to Jess, which felt like hours later but couldn't have been because the partial moon still shone down on them, a thin piece of statue flaked away, revealing a glint of metal. It was difficult to drag his eyes away and look around the area once more. On his return to Jess, she'd exposed another portion of metal.

He could see the shape now. The crown of the statue was a bowl turned upside down and covered.

Curiosity overwhelmed him, and he darted out of the alcove to pick up a fallen piece of statue. Thin stone with a mixture of stucco and plaster underneath. There was likely a simpler way to remove it from the statue, but Jess wasn't going to wait around for Derek to figure it out.

Over the thuds and grunts Jess was sending about the area, another sound emerged. The rattle of wheels.

"Jess," Derek hissed, but she was too focused, having just managed to get her knife below the edge of the bowl. The stone casing was falling away rapidly now. Another few minutes and the bowl would be free.

The question was if she could get it free and get away before whoever was coming their way arrived.

The best thing Derek could do was hide so that she didn't have to worry about him as well as herself. He darted back to the alcove just as an old carriage turned the corner. It had once been a grand vehicle, but time and use had left its mark.

Derek nearly choked as he got a better look at the carriage. He knew that carriage. It drove straight toward Jess and the statue, as if that had been its destination all along.

A man climbed out, older and with a slight limp. He made his way to the base of the statue and looked up at Jess. "I couldn't have trapped you better if I'd planned it."

Jess looked down at him, somehow managing to smirk even from her crazy perch atop a piece of marble. She pried one more piece of stone loose and flung the piece at the man.

He stepped back just in time for it to land at his feet instead of on his head. His face was turned away from Derek, but the sneer was clear as he looked up at Jess. "This is the bloodline that I am to believe is fit to rule my forefathers' homeland? A hoyden willing to expose herself in the middle of the marketplace."

"It's the bloodline that put this thing up here to begin with," Jess said, not pausing in her work. She stabbed her knife beneath one edge of the bowl and started trying to work it free. "How did you know I was here?"

"We've been following your friends since they left Wiltshire. They made it exceptionally easy, though I must admit I was surprised that they all convened at the Duke of Marshington's house. They hardly seem the type to socialize in such . . . elevated levels."

"Yes," Jess said with a grunt, "it boggles the mind that a marquis and a duke might know each other."

Derek shifted his weight. What should he do? If he ran back to the inn, he'd never be able to get help here in time. Besides, he refused to leave Jess alone, even if he was a measly rescue option. If the limping man kept insulting her friends, she'd be throwing that knife at him. Derek had a feeling the only reason it hadn't happened already was because she'd only taken one knife up there with her.

"When the report came to me that you had gotten into a carriage with them and come here, I was surprised. You've managed to avoid notice for quite a while." The man hobbled another step closer, and his horses shifted.

The jangle of harnesses spurred Derek out of his frozen shock. He needed to do something. As amazing as Jess was, she was stuck up on top of a statue. Unless she'd learned how to fly, she was going to have to climb down that statue, and no matter how quickly she did it, that man was going to be there, most likely with a weapon.

"Such a shame you couldn't track me earlier, Lord Bradford. It would have been much simpler to catch me when I was on your property."

Derek cringed at the name but pushed away the fear that rose in him upon hearing it. How did she feel facing the man who had taken and possibly even killed her family? Derek couldn't afford to experience such empathy right now. She needed him to think.

"So that was you at my home. I wondered. I had to act as if it was."

Derek couldn't overpower Lord Bradford. Neither could Jess. Whatever tricks she might possess, her size could only do so much, and she was up there with only one knife that, by now, would be excessively damaged. Even with a limp, Lord Bradford was taller and had the benefit of being a cruel and—Derek suspected—somewhat insane man.

There wasn't anything Derek could do about the confrontation, but there had to be a way he could help. He needed to think like Jess.

Movement. Forget the details and consider the movement.

"Such a shame that you didn't know what you had," Jess taunted. "You could have found the bowl years ago if only you'd known."

"Finding it years ago would have meant nothing. If Napoleon had won the war, my cousin would have been placed in control of the area, as was his right. Since that did not come to pass, now he shall rule the country outright."

"Why is she on top of a statue?"

The whispered voice in Derek's ear almost made him scream. Only a large hand suddenly covering his mouth stopped the sound. The hand knocked Derek's spectacles loose, and he reached up to fix them as he turned to look at the whisperer.

If London could see the Duke of Marshington now, they really would tremble in fright. He was dressed head to toe in black, with a pistol tucked in the waist of his trousers.

Derek peeled the duke's hand from his face and said, "Because that's where the bowl is."

"And the man?"

"Lord Bradford."

Derek looked back at the scene in front of him, gaze trailing from the statue to the carriage. "If we can distract him once Jess gets down, can we make a run for it? There's only one servant, and Bradford limps."

Ryland shook his head. "There's nowhere to run but streets. The carriage will easily be able to give chase before we can get somewhere unless we break into a house. Then we're still trapped."

That made perfect sense. The carriage was also likely where Lord Bradford intended to stuff Jess as soon as she climbed down. The logical thing to do, then, was make sure the carriage didn't go anywhere. If only he knew how to do that.

Ryland apparently had other plans, since he was sliding a knife from his boot. "We'll have to make sure Bradford doesn't go anywhere."

Whatever Ryland intended made Derek's stomach heave. "Is that necessary?"

One dark eyebrow rose and looked at Derek as if he was simpleminded. "Unless you have a better idea."

"There is a closer claim to the throne. A direct line from King Nicolas," Jess called down as she slid the knife around the bowl a bit more, still working to dislodge it from its decades-old perch.

He couldn't watch her now. Derek looked back at the carriage. Could it be disabled quickly and quietly? He didn't know anything about carriages. Well, not anything practical. This was an old carriage, with huge wheels and C springs. None of that would keep the carriage from moving.

Wait. C springs. Derek slid one of Jess's knives from the pouch. Would it work? He didn't know, but it was the only idea he had that didn't involve possible murder, so he was going with it.

"I have an idea."

Both of Ryland's eyebrows shot up now.

Derek swallowed hard and slid a knife from the harness Jess had left with him. Even if his plan succeeded, he wasn't willing to risk that Jess's legs would be able to run. They'd been gripping that statue for a while. "Once she gets down, we'll need to get away quickly. Can you get horses?"

"I can get horses. Jeffreys is already preparing the carriage." The duke paused. "Do you know what you're doing?"

"No," Derek said. "But I think it's better than killing him, don't you? Traitor or not, he deserves a trial."

The duke nodded, but his face was grim. "We'll try it your way. But if anything happens to Jess—"

"It won't." Derek had to believe that, had to believe he'd be willing to do something to keep it from happening. "As a last resort, I'll throw myself on Bradford. Should slow him down a bit."

Ryland shook his head and slipped away.

Derek tried to ignore the continued taunting between Jess and Lord Bradford. He slipped out of the alcove, walking as quietly as possible across the square to the back of the carriage. Two thick leather straps held the body of the carriage to the springs. Would he even be able to cut through them? Only one way to find out.

"Where is your other friend?" Lord Bradford asked. "The one who followed you about my house like a whipped puppy."

Derek nearly fumbled the knife, but he held tight to it and began dragging it across the leather. A fine line appeared, barely breaking the surface. He sliced faster.

"He followed me until I climbed up here. He can't stand the defacement of art, I'm afraid. Doesn't have the constitution for it."

Derek grinned. She had to know how his stomach had turned when she made her first bang against the top of the statue. *Cut, cut, cut.* The knife was finally making progress, the weight of the carriage body helping to stretch the opening he was making. A few more swipes should do it.

He stopped. What would happen then? Would the crash alert them that he was there? Would one strap keep the carriage from rolling?

He turned his attention to the other strap. Best to get it nearly worked through as well. Then a couple quick cuts should have the entire back end dislodged.

"Why does your cousin want to rule a country he's never lived in?" Jess asked.

Derek hacked at the second leather strap. How did she not have the bowl free yet? It had been completely uncovered long before he'd ducked behind the carriage.

"We grew up with the stories of the glories of Verbonne. Then we had to watch from England as your grandfather and uncle threw away everything that had made our legacy great."

"One would think"—Jess gave a grunt—"that you would care more about the country you've been tasked with running instead of one under the care of your enemy during the war."

"My father left me a burden, but my mother gave me a legacy. Once my cousin is in power, I will be able to be a voice of unity between our nations. Verbonne will be a great ally for England, creating a solid port to the continent and opening new trade routes."

Derek used his sleeve to wipe the sweat from his brow. He certainly wasn't cold now.

"Thank you for freeing the bowl," Lord Bradford said. "If you toss it down, I'll be on my way, and you'll be free to climb down at your leisure."

Derek's time was up. Whether Ryland had located horses or not, Derek was going to have to grab Jess and get out of there.

With all his strength he sliced at the leather. One strap pulled free, the sudden weight stretching the other so thin the slightest pressure of the knife started a tear, and in moments the back of the carriage went crashing onto the springs. Derek snatched up Jess's jacket and knife harness, intending to round the carriage and see if Jess needed help.

Shouts rose and a shot rang out before he'd managed to find his footing. Chaos exploded. People started leaning out their windows, lending their own shouts to the ruckus. Two horses burst from an alley to Derek's right.

"Nice job," Ryland said, tossing Derek a set of reins. "Climb on." Then he rode into the fray, presumably to rescue Jess.

Derek wasn't the best of horsemen, but he knew how to ride. He mounted and turned to find Ryland at the base of the statue, waving a pistol in the air as Jess wriggled down and fell across the back of the horse, a large bowl clasped in her arms.

With a shout, Ryland kicked the horse. Derek followed, trusting his horse to follow Ryland's as Derek used one hand to secure his spectacles and the other to try to find a place to tuck Jess's jacket and harness. The jacket probably didn't matter so much, but the knives likely did. He folded up the harness and shoved it in his jacket pocket, squeezing his horse with all the strength his knees possessed. At the moment, that wasn't much. He felt two breaths away from fainting.

As they charged through alleys and toward the edge of town, Derek kept his head down and prayed. He and God had been on good terms since Derek was a young man, sitting for long afternoons with the local priest as Derek examined all the different carvings and artworks in the church.

Never had Derek had to trust Him like this, though. There was something so different about knowing danger existed, about even brushing against it, than there was about living through it.

The horses slowed at an inn on the south edge of town. Derek's legs wobbled as he slid to the ground, but the beaming grin on Jess's face restored a bit of his strength.

"We did it," she cried, holding the bowl aloft. It was difficult to see in the pale moonlight, but the bowl appeared to be some sort of hammered metal, decorated with carvings on the outside and lined with jewels on the inside. Centered in the bottom was a large iridescent opal. The waterstone.

"So we did," he said quietly. He had just enough time to realize the full reality of it before she was there, hugging him with one arm, her tiny body pressed against his side while the bowl jutted into his stomach. He grunted but wrapped one arm around her shoulders to hold her there just a bit longer. His head lowered until his cheek pressed against her hair. The jumping of his insides calmed as he held her and breathed.

A sleepy stable boy came out of the inn's stables and collected the horses as a carriage rolled into the yard.

Before it had stopped rocking on its wheels, the door flung open and Kit jumped out, looking a bit more than disheveled, a dress thrown on haphazardly over her night clothes.

She walked straight up to Jess, ignoring Derek completely while she leaned in to hug Jess's other side. "Thank goodness you're safe." Then she stood back, crossed her arms over her chest, and glared. "I can't believe you let me sleep through the entire thing."

Jess pulled away from Derek but continued grinning. "It all went rather quickly. You didn't miss much."

Didn't miss much? Derek still thought fainting was a very real possibility. He'd never been as frightened as he'd been at the back of that carriage.

"We really do need to get out of here before he manages to follow us," Ryland said, clamping a hand on Derek's shoulder. "Nicely done, but if you're going to faint, please climb into the carriage first. Makes the entire process a bit easier."

Mouth dry, Derek nodded, dimly wondering if he should be offended by the duke's statement, but without Jess's warmth to distract him, he was a little too shaken to care.

CHAPTER THIRTY-FOUR

When Jess insisted on taking the boat on her own and no one else in the carriage protested, Derek's resolve to go with her faltered. Was it the best thing for her? Was insisting on accompanying her for his benefit or hers? At some point he was going to have to believe her when she said she wanted to leave him behind. Since his part really was done now, those farewells might as well be on English soil.

Maybe one day he would get to see France and Verbonne and the rest of the continent that had been unavailable to him because of the war, but that day wouldn't be soon. When he finally managed it, he wouldn't look for her. She'd likely be married by then anyway.

The idea made the prospect of visiting the country a little less appealing. There were plenty of people who never left England, and he could go wherever he wanted in a painting.

No, it was best to say good-bye to her here in . . . whatever town they were in. He'd bounced around the country so much in the past month that he'd lost all sense of bearing.

His one regret was that here at the end they were surrounded by people. He missed the conversations they'd had when it was just the two of them in the carriage, sharing strange facts they knew and asking questions. He knew information from books, but Jess

322

knew life. She'd explained things and saw things differently than anyone he'd ever met.

He was going to miss her.

That was an okay thing to admit. It was natural to miss people who changed your life in some way. Missing her didn't have to mean he wished she'd stayed. He could miss her and still be happy for where life took her.

He could.

Jeffreys drove the carriage straight out onto the dock just as the sun was peeking over the horizon.

"They're still here," Ryland said as he threw open the door. "I've been having multiple port schedules sent to me for weeks. I was hoping you'd make this one." Then he jumped out while the carriage was still rocking.

"Oy there!" a sailor yelled at him as Ryland walked aboard the boat. "We was just taking in the gangplank. We're pushing off."

"I'm the Duke of Marshington," Ryland announced in a clear, authoritative voice that rang down to the dock below and likely across the ship deck. "Where is your captain?"

A man with better clothes and grooming approached Ryland.

"Oh good," Jess said as the rest of them scrambled out of the carriage and Jeffreys handed down Jess's valise and the blanketed bundle containing the bowl. "That's Captain O'Henry. He ferried me more than once during the war."

"You'll have safe travels, then," Derek said. He should hug her or shake her hand. Neither would be appropriate, though, and kissing her hand seemed even more ridiculous. Tipping his hat might work but his hand only encountered his overlong hair. Simply saying good-bye didn't seem enough.

Ryland strode down the gangplank. "Up you come, Jess. He's got to set off."

"Right." Jess looked at Derek, her expression unsure and hesitant. "This is it, then."

Derek tried to say good-bye, but his mouth was too dry. He just looked at her.

"Good-bye," Kit said jauntily, sliding up next to him. "Or fare-well, if you'd rather. You two seem to be having difficulty saying it, so I thought I'd help."

"Right," Jess said again, but she turned and without a word strode up the gangplank, while a sailor came down to do whatever sailors did to prepare a boat to leave.

She was really leaving. Right now. He'd thought they'd have more time.

"She thinks no one should love her," Kit said, sounding matter-of-fact when the words she'd just said should have been anything but.

"What?" Derek asked.

Before Kit could answer, Ryland came up to Derek's other side, pulling out a book Derek knew well. "Think she'll need this?"

The diary. Did she need it?

"I . . ." Derek looked from the book to the ship and then to Kit. "What?"

"Better run it up to her, just in case."

"Right." Because somehow Derek would know how to say good-bye at the top of the gangplank instead of the bottom. And what was he supposed to do about what Kit had just told him?

Ryland shoved the book into his hands and gave him a nudge. Derek shot up the gangplank. He didn't want her last memory of him to be of him gaping at her, unable to say anything. He couldn't have her walking away thinking she was unlovable.

He almost lost his balance as his feet hit the boat deck and his world rocked a bit. He looked around to find her. She'd moved fast once she'd gotten up here. She was nearly halfway across the ship deck.

"Jess," he called. "The diary."

A scraping noise sounded behind him as he ran to hand her the book.

"Derek," she gasped. "What are you doing?"

"The diary. Ryland thought it best you have it, so I brought it to you." Derek swallowed. "And I couldn't let you leave without saying good-bye."

324

Jess took the diary with a groan as she dropped her head forward. With a sigh she lifted it again, her face expressionless. "Save your good-bye. Apparently you're coming to Verbonne."

She pointed behind Derek. He turned to see that the path back to shore was no longer there, and the ship was starting to rock a bit more as she prepared to set sail.

The sailor from the gangway ran up to Derek with a valise in hand. "His Grace said you forgot this."

Derek took his luggage without a word. He'd been had, but he couldn't be mad about it. He was getting to go to Verbonne, getting to spend more time with Jess, getting to support her as she returned home when she thought she never would. Getting to have a conversation about what Kit had revealed.

It was something he never would have had the courage to insist upon, not with Jess so adamant that she didn't want it, but he was grateful for it all the same.

Captain O'Henry came up to them. "Good you both made it. Told His Grace to get you two aboard, that I couldn't hold the ship even for him." The man shook his head, and sunlight glinted off his earring. "His Grace. Still can't quite cotton to calling him that. Imagine all those times I had a duke hiding in my hold and I didn't know it."

"It wasn't really a time for revealing secrets," Jess said tightly.

"No, I guess not." The captain gestured behind Derek. "This isn't really a passenger vessel, so we haven't any cabins, but seeing as it's such a short hop over to Verbonne, you two can rest in my cabin until we get there. If the weather holds and we hit the tides right, we'll be docking tonight. If not, it will be in the morning."

Were Derek and Jess still supposed to be traveling as a married couple? Why else would the captain offer to leave them in his quarters alone? Best to stay with a safe, neutral comment until he knew for sure. "We're much obliged."

"I'm sure your quarters will be far more comfortable than bunking down on the cargo," Jess said with a small smile.

Once in the captain's quarters with the door shut, Jess set her bag down with the bowl on top of it and crossed to the windows that ran along the back of the ship to watch the water. Derek set his bag with hers and moved to stand beside her.

He took a deep breath and admitted, "I'm glad I'm going with you."

Slowly she uncrossed her arms and lowered her hands. Her fingers twined between his and squeezed. "I'm glad you're coming with me, too."

⊰⊱

Jess had moved in and out of many a port in her day. She'd hidden in trunks, disguised herself as a sailor, even slipped over the side and swam to another part of the shore. There was no need for any of that as the boat sailed into Verbonne's port just as the sun was setting. Somehow entering her former homeland like a normal visitor felt a bit less momentous than she'd expected. Certainly less eventful.

"You're free to stay until morning," Captain O'Henry said. "It'll be difficult to find lodging this late."

"I know where we're going," Jess said. She didn't add that she had no idea if they'd be welcome or not. Besides, she liked seeing a place for the first time at night. The darkness gave a certain amount of security, as even people familiar with the town stumbled about at night.

This wasn't her first time here, however, even though it felt as if it were. There wasn't much of the little girl who'd once lived here remaining in the woman she'd become.

"The palace is this way." Jess guided Derek down a wide street. People still wandered about, visiting taverns or walking home from a day's work. No one took notice of two people carrying small bundles and walking like they knew where they were going.

"Will your brother be there?"

She hoped so. She hoped she would recognize him. Would he recognize her? Was it even a possibility? Her features hadn't changed much, but life had changed her. Didn't that type of aging show on a person's face?

"Only one way to find out," she said, trudging up the hill.

"Kit said something interesting as I was boarding the ship," Derek said softly.

"Hmmm?"

"She said you didn't think you were worthy of love."

Jess stopped walking briefly and then shook her head as she moved on. "I was tired. I didn't really mean it."

"Didn't you?" Derek matched her steps and her pace, staying at her side and looking straight ahead. Somehow that made it easier.

"It isn't so much that *I* am unworthy," Jess said with a sigh, knowing Derek would not let this go until he had a satisfactory answer. "It's that . . ." Jess sighed again. How was she supposed to explain this? "You said love required sacrifice. Kit agreed. I'm not worth anyone making that sacrifice."

Derek shook his head. "You're looking at sacrifice the wrong way, then."

They turned a few more corners, and the people on the streets thinned out until they were practically alone, guided along by nothing but starlight and a sliver of moon when the clouds decided to let it through.

Jess guided them into the deeper shadows to avoid suspicious glances. They hadn't seen a bath or even a proper bed in days and were looking more than a little bedraggled.

It was also easier to talk in the darker shadows.

"How is there a wrong way to look at sacrifice?" Jess asked. "It's one person giving up something for another."

He was quiet for a moment, then stopped and turned her to face him. "Why did you leave London?"

Jess frowned. She'd been over this and over this, and as much as she would admit that possibly she'd been a bit rash in making her decision, she didn't regret it because she'd met Kit and Daphne and the others. "I'm not going through that again."

Derek sighed. "I'll rephrase it. Why did you run from London and not from Haven Manor?"

"Because Kit and Daphne needed me," Jess said before she could think about it.

"Did you care for them more than you did for Ryland and Jeffreys and everyone else who worked for the duke?"

"Of course not." Jess would have crossed her arms and glared if her hands hadn't been full. "That's insulting, Derek."

"I have a point," he rushed to assure her. "Staying at Haven Manor sacrificed your anonymity. Would you take it back?"

Jess stood quietly for a moment. Would she? If she could go back knowing that staying would mean exposure, would she still have stayed? Yes. "I couldn't have left Daphne alone like that. It would have killed me to leave then."

"Love is a sacrifice, but it's also selfish, because when you are able to give the other person what they need, it comes back on you, too. Which means you don't get to decide if you're worth it or not."

Jess's throat felt suddenly tight. "We can't have this conversation right now, Derek."

He sighed. "I know, but I felt it needed to happen, and I don't know what's waiting for us at the top of this hill."

"Me neither."

"Shall we?" Derek wrapped his free arm around her shoulder and guided her along the path. "For what it's worth," he said, "God decided you were worth love a long time ago when He sacrificed Jesus on your behalf. If you're going to continue to claim you aren't worth it, you're calling God a liar."

"Ring a fine peal over me, why don't you, Derek," Jess said, forcing a laugh even as the words he'd said punched her right in the soul. They didn't say anything more as they approached the palace, where a guard stood at the gate.

What would Jess say? Who would believe her? In the current uproar, would anyone even believe that she was there to help?

"Feel up for one more adventure?" she asked Derek.

He grinned at her, his teeth white against the darkening night. "Of course."

"There used to be an old gate around the back corner of the palace garden. Care to see if it still opens?"

"If the alternative is explaining to him that two people who look like us should be let into the royal palace of a country in turmoil, yes. I'd very much like to see if the gate works."

Jess chuckled and turned down a small lane. There was a very questionable future ahead of them. She didn't want to walk into it with the weight of their previous conversation on her mind, so she tried to lighten the mood. "Did you think you'd be doing something like this when you answered the call to catalogue the art at Haven Manor?"

"No," he said, his voice solemn. "I never thought something like this would happen to me."

The mood suddenly didn't feel any lighter than it had been. She swallowed around a tight throat. "Me neither."

They continued in silence. She had to try a few different paths to find the one that led from the lane to the palace gardens, but eventually they came to the gate. Vines had grown over it, but she cut through them easily, and soon they were inside the walls.

"There's going to be more guards inside," she said. "Nicolas may not even be here. If his rule is in question, they may not have granted him the palace."

"If he's smart he took up residence anyway. It gives his position credence," Derek added.

"We'll assume he's here, then."

Derek laughed. "How do we find out if that's true?"

"I suppose we ask."

"Why didn't we just ask the guard, then?"

"Because it's so much more fun to ask when you're already inside the house." Jess grinned up at him, but she didn't truly feel that mirthful. Memories were assaulting her the farther they crept into the garden. In the distance, she could hear the ocean on the rocks, could smell the begonias her mother used to cut from the garden and put in Jess's room, could remember what rooms were behind some of the windows.

She extended the hand holding the valise toward him. "Come along."

He wrapped his hand with hers around the handle of her bag and nodded. "Lead on."

They didn't see many guards as they worked their way around to the back of the palace. Was it because of the war? Because Nicolas wasn't the true leader of the country? Because he wasn't here?

If he wasn't here, someone would know where he was, so she simply had to continue with her plan.

Once on the terrace, there were fewer shadows to hide in, so she pushed aside the memories of breakfasts and afternoon teas and started trying every door. Five attempts later, she found one that was unlocked.

"We need something to prop open this door," she whispered, looking around. Once the terrace had been grand, with potted trees and an abundance of furniture. Now it was all but bare.

Derek set his bag down and looked around. "Something small?"

"No, large."

He found a loose stone in the balustrade and brought it over. Jess winced at the removal, but she forced herself to focus. Besides, if the stone had been loose enough to pick up, repairs were already needed.

Watching Jess place the rock in a way that held the door wide open, Derek tilted his head and asked, "How long before they notice?"

"I hope not long," Jess said. "Otherwise I worry greatly for my brother's life."

She grabbed her bundles and entered the house.

Here the memories were more difficult to ignore, partly because the difference was not quite so stark. The interior, at least in this section of the house, seemed to have remained mostly intact. It had been her family's wing of the house, designed to hold advisors and visiting dignitaries.

"The upstairs parlor, I think." Jess led the way up the narrow back staircase that she would creep down when she'd wanted to step outside and listen to the ocean at night.

They'd just entered the room when a shout was raised from the floor below and the sound of footsteps and people yelling filled the corridors. The open door had been discovered.

"Do you trust me?" Jess asked.

"If I didn't I'd have walked away a long time ago."

Jess smiled. "Then let's have a seat."

CHAPTER THIRTY-FIVE

"Where should we sit?" Derek whispered, not seeming a bit concerned with the shouts and pounding footsteps of the guards.

Jess considered the shadowy room. They should probably sit in the chairs, but she wanted him close by. If they were physically threatened, she could protect him, and if her brother appeared, well, that was the sort of thing a girl didn't want to face alone. "The sofa. More maneuverable."

He gave a short nod and they settled themselves in, their bags on the floor at the end of the sofa, and the bowl, still wrapped in its blanket, on the seat beside Jess.

How long would they have to wait?

Assuming the guards were loyal to Nicolas, they would be ensuring his protection first, then begin circling outward, searching the other rooms. If he'd returned to his childhood bedroom, they'd discover them soon. If he'd taken the royal suite, she and Derek might be here awhile.

"This was our private family drawing room," she whispered to Derek. "My mother had another room where she accepted visitors, closer to the front of the palace. Since she wasn't the queen, it wasn't overly formal, but it was used a great deal because she was more accessible than the queen."

At least that was the explanation her mother had given her

seven-year-old daughter. Who knew if it was the truth or not? Jess couldn't remember much of her aunt—couldn't remember that much of her uncle, to be honest. She'd seen more of him in those short months he'd been at the farm than she'd seen of him in the entire eight years she'd lived in the palace.

Jess pointed to the corner. "I was allowed to play checkers and cards at that table over there as long as I wasn't too loud," she whispered. "It's funny how many rules there were about when and where we could spend time as a family until we were forced to live on top of one another in a tiny cottage."

"Survival is a powerful motivator," Derek murmured.

"And an amazing equalizer." Jess had learned so much in that cottage—discovered her ability to pick up languages by listening to them over time, found the difference between quiet and silent, acquired skills like cooking and laundry and even hunting and farming that she'd never have honed living in this palace.

The guards were moving in the corridors again, though not shouting this time. The search had begun. It was only a matter of time now.

Jess dropped her hand to the cushion and gripped Derek's tightly. He squeezed back but didn't say anything.

As the lantern light approached the drawing room door, she squinted her eyes, preparing for the onslaught of sudden brightness when they entered the room. When it came she felt Derek flinch, but he didn't let go of her hand. It helped Jess's smile feel a bit more natural as she turned it on the guards and eased her eyes open.

"How do you do?" she asked in English, using the most cultured tone she could manage. In her ears, it sounded like her mother. "Would you please let my brother know he has a visitor?" She patted the still-wrapped bowl on the sofa next to her. "I've brought him a glad-to-hear-you're-alive present."

The guards stayed in the door, weapons at the ready, lanterns held aloft, and stared. Obviously this had not been what they'd expected to find. Maybe they thought she was the ghost of her mother.

She was fairly certain at least one of them knew English, but she switched to French and repeated herself just in case.

No change in expression. Should she try Dutch? It wasn't her best language, only rudimentary really, but she could probably struggle through a bit of an explanation.

"We've found them," one of the guards hollered into the hallway in French.

More rushed feet in the corridors, and then the guards near the door parted to let another man through, one with an air of authority and strength. The kind that just might stab them first and ask questions later.

Still, Jess smiled at him. "Ah," she said, deciding to stay with French, "you must be the captain of the guard. Very good. Will *you* tell my brother I've come to see him alive with my own eyes?"

The man's lips twisted. "You are hardly the first to claim to be his sister."

Why hadn't Jess thought of that? If he was saying that she was the key to holding the country, then of course there would be other people claiming to be the one he needed. The governments that wanted to absorb the little country had probably even sent some of them.

"I'm very glad to know that you didn't accept those impostors," Jess said, fingers tightening their hold on Derek's. How was she going to convince them? She wasn't ready to show the bowl, not until she was face-to-face with her brother.

"As the story was made up, you are all impostors."

Jess laughed and turned to Derek. "Isn't that funny? What they thought was a falsehood brought out the truth."

Derek's returning smile looked sick. No wonder, as there were at least three weapons still pointed in their direction.

"Which room is he staying in?" Jess asked. "His old one, three doors down on the left? Did anyone ever repair the hole he put in the wall before we left? Or perhaps he's in the royal suite that's on the third floor in the center hall. Is that atrocious bird print still on the walls in that drawing room? He's going to want to change that if he expects to receive visitors there."

The captain's smirk faded a bit, and his eyes narrowed.

"Fetch the king," he told the guard behind him in French.

Was it a good or bad thing that the guard already considered Nicolas the king? If the people did, too, this would be much easier. Surely no one thought Verbonne's port was worth reopening the war. The bowl would merely be ceremony to allow everyone to back away and save face.

It would also convince her brother she was who she said she was if he didn't recognize her.

The guard remained, though only one pistol stayed ready as footsteps trailed off and eventually returned.

The guards parted again, but this time the man who passed through was in a dressing gown, his frown just as fierce as the captain's had been.

He looked like their father. His face had settled into similar lines, his hair was starting to recede from his forehead in the same way, and the shoulders had broadened. He was the picture of their father. "Nicolas," Jess breathed.

Until that moment, she wasn't sure that she'd really believed he had survived.

"My sister is dead. The diary is burned." Her brother's voice was hard and unyielding, and it made Jess flinch as if he'd struck her. Obviously he was not ready for a loving family reunion. "Why you think you can come in here and claim either is a mystery, though at least you look the part. I will know who you are before you die. Did Richard Bucanan send you? England? The German Confederation? Their threats will not work. I will protect this country. I will rule it."

How to play this? If she got angry in return, violence would escalate quickly, and Derek would be caught in the middle. She'd stay seated, stay calm. She'd had a month to consider the idea that she wasn't alone. He'd had five minutes.

"My name is Jessamine Beauchene," she said slowly. "Ten years ago my father shoved me under the floorboards, along with a bag containing a diary and a handful of other family heirlooms. I'm sorry to say I've lost a couple of those over the years, but I still have the diary." She took a deep breath and moved slowly, hoping the flickers of lantern light would disguise the movement of her hand toward the edge of the blanket that was wrapped around the bowl.

"Your name is Nicolas Beauchene," she continued, still moving her hand, "and when I was ten, you hid a frog in my bed, not realizing it wouldn't happily stay under the covers, and you stayed up half the night waiting for me to discover it and threw a temper tantrum like a two-year-old the next morning when you learned it hadn't worked.

"And," she said with emphasis as her fingers hooked the edge of the blanket, "if you're hoping for a peaceful coronation, you might want this."

She whipped the blanket back, intending a dramatic reveal of the anointing bowl. Instead she sent it clattering to the ground. Still dramatic, she supposed, but not quite as elegant as she'd hoped. All last-minute plans couldn't go perfectly.

Everyone reacted to her sudden movement, pulling knives and pistols. Jess jerked Derek down to the floor in case someone chose to fire their weapon, but he surprised her by twisting and landing with her beneath him.

Then Nicolas was down on the floor with them. The bowl lay by his knees, but he wasn't looking at that. He was looking at her, and he looked even more like their father than he had before, so much so that Jess thought her heart might actually hurt to look at him.

He lifted one hand to graze her cheek. "Jessamine?"

Before she could answer, he was pushing Derek aside and crushing her to him in a strong grip. As her brother held her, she felt one more strong squeeze on her fingers before Derek let go of her hand.

∞∞

For the next week, Derek did what he did best. He sat back and observed, giving the time and attention he'd once reserved for the past to the present. He rather thought this was what artists did: observe life, see the lights and shadows and patterns, and then put the heart of it on paper.

Perhaps that had been what was missing when he had tried to paint. He'd been painting what he saw with his eyes instead of his heart. Maybe, when he returned home, he'd give creating art another try.

"Monsieur," one of the guards whispered as he entered the breakfast room where Derek was lingering over a cup of coffee and watching the waves in the distance glint in the morning sun.

"She's gone again?" he answered in French. His French had gotten better the past few days as he'd used it almost exclusively in the palace.

Once the coronation bowl was in hand, things had moved quickly in the palace. Nicolas had already been planning to declare a coronation ceremony and dare the opposing forces to stop him. With bowl in hand, there was little they could do, since they'd agreed to abide by the tradition.

After a day in the palace, though, Jess had taken to sneaking away from her guards on a regular basis. It sent them into a panic, since none of them realized she could do a better job defending herself than they could.

The first time she'd run off, he'd tried to tell them not to worry, but he'd still gone in search of her. Ever since, she'd run away at least once a day. Derek liked to think it was because she missed him, since those times he went to find her were the only moments they managed to talk. Derek wasn't even sure what he was still doing there.

Each day she'd run off a bit earlier. Today she hadn't even made it through breakfast.

"*Oui*, monsieur," the guard said urgently. "His Highness said we were to keep her in sight at all times, but she disappears."

"Yes," Derek said dryly, setting his coffee cup aside. "She's rather good at that. I'll find her."

Even though she never hid in the same place twice, Derek never had much difficulty locating her. All he had to do was pinpoint the bulk of the current activity and then go in the other direction.

Today she was in the portrait gallery on the opposite end of the palace from the ballroom, where the preparations for the coronation ball were taking place.

"You know," Derek said, trying to look casual as he strolled into the room, "this would go much faster if you would just take me with you when you disappear."

She threw him a ghost of a grin over her shoulder. "I'm just trying to give you something to do."

"Have you seen this place? There's enough art here to keep me busy for years. I can't believe it wasn't pilfered during the war."

"My father and uncle hid most of it away in a secret vault underground. It's behind where the dungeons used to be. Nicolas showed it to me a couple of days ago when he talked about making sure the palace was ready for the foreign dignitaries and leaders who will be arriving tomorrow."

Derek leaned against the wall, looking at her instead of any of the paintings. He'd been in here twice already, spending a great deal of time staring up at the portraits of Queen Jessamine and Queen Marguerite. Two women, long dead, who had somehow managed to change his life.

He didn't need to look up at them now, though. Instead his full attention was on the woman who'd had a much more direct hand in altering his future. Eventually he would leave this place, leave her, but he wouldn't be the same man when he returned to England.

"Are the dignitaries going to stay here?" Derek asked. The room he'd been given was functional but hardly impressive.

Jess nodded. "Everything of quality has been gathered into one wing of the palace. The guests will be placed there."

"And where will you be?"

"I don't suppose miles away on a frigate returning to England is a good answer, is it?" she asked quietly.

"Do you want it to be?"

"I don't know." Her gaze dropped from the portraits to him. "He wants me to announce my engagement at the ball."

Derek nearly doubled over in pain as the words slammed into his gut. He'd known he loved her, but until that moment he'd convinced himself it was as one loved a friend or a sister, that he would be happy for her wherever life took her.

He'd been lying to himself.

"To whom?" he finally managed to choke out.

"James Ascot. A distant cousin of sorts who's apparently been living in Germany. Nicolas wants us to marry and act as ambassadors to England. He thinks my connections will smooth the way."

Jess's voice was flat, but Derek's heart felt flatter. Not only would she be married to someone else, but she'd be in England. Within reach but still as far away as the moon. "He's not wrong."

"I know he's not. England would welcome a friendly port here, one they don't have to guard or manage. But Ascot's been in Germany. What does he know of England—or even Verbonne, for that matter?"

"What does anyone know of Verbonne?" Derek asked. "It's a new country, strictly speaking. Your brother may be incorporating traditions and heritage, but he'll be starting from scratch when it comes to governing."

Jess gave a dry laugh. "I'm afraid I won't be much help there. I only know how to break the rules."

Derek hated seeing her like this. Cold. Pale. Tense. If he was going to have to rip his own heart out and leave her, he at least wanted to fool himself into thinking she had a chance to be happy. He wanted to remember her that way. Maybe, while he was still here, he could help her see that she could be content within these walls. It didn't have to be all doldrums and tension.

"Did you play here as a child?"

Jess nodded, a hint of a true smile playing at her lips. "My governess liked to bring me here. She could claim she was teaching me about my heritage, but all she really did was sit in that chair and watch me run around." Her grin grew a bit. "I had a lot of energy."

"I don't doubt it." Derek grinned in return.

"What was your first painting?" she asked, looking up at the wall of portraits again but without the same weight about her as before.

"It was called *Baptism of the Lord*. I used to look at it every Sunday while I pretended to listen to the sermon. The priest noticed and invited me to come in one day and give it a closer look. Then he started explaining what was happening in the painting, what would be happening to Jesus in the days following. I started listening to the sermons after that, but he let me come in during the week and showed me the other art around the church."

"Want to see the first place I ever hid from my governess?" She tossed him the smirk he had grown to find beautiful, and he knew he'd willingly follow her anywhere. He wouldn't have any trouble questioning his loyalties. If she asked him to stay, he would.

She wasn't going to ask him, though, because he wasn't what her family needed. Jess's marriage wasn't just going to be about her. If she was to announce it in mere days, it wasn't about her at all. It was going to be about reestablishing this country.

He still had today, though, and maybe a few days after that. He'd take them. Maybe when he returned home, he'd paint them. "I'd love to." He gave her an answering grin. "Lead on."

CHAPTER THIRTY-SIX

*J*ess and Derek rejoined the rest of the palace inhabitants for luncheon, but it was a strained affair. She would have given almost anything to be back in the portrait gallery with Derek.

She'd have given almost anything to be back in England, truth be told. Guilt turned the food she'd eaten into a rock in her stomach. Shouldn't *this* feel like home now? Did it just need time?

After luncheon, her brother approached her from the other side of the table. She'd seen precious little of him, even when she'd sought him out. On the rare occasion she was allowed into whatever room he was in, he did little more than send her a vague nod and continue about his business.

Most of the time he spoke in Italian, obviously thinking she didn't know the language, as she'd admitted to him that she'd needed Derek to translate the diary for her. That Nicolas didn't want her to know about his plans after the coronation bothered her.

So did his plans.

He spoke often of removing the threat that was Richard Bucanan. Every time Jess heard the name she tried to remember where she'd heard it before. Had Lord Bradford said it? Had she heard it somewhere else?

Beyond that, the tight control he intended to exert over the people was almost oppressive. Given what they had already suffered in their war-ravaged land, was taking even more from them the way to start a new country? Some of Nicolas's advisors, the older ones, had spoken against his plan.

Jess never saw them at another meal.

"Jessamine," her brother said, taking her arm.

Jess sighed. He simply refused to use the shortened version of her name. "Yes, Nic?"

He frowned but said nothing. Either he'd given up on having her address him by a formal title—or at least his full name—or he didn't want to rehash the argument in front of others. "I'd like to speak with you in my office, please."

Jess's eyebrows rose. "Of course." Was he was finally going to talk to her, ask her where she'd been, what she'd been doing? He'd asked nothing beyond how she'd survived the invasion of the farm. His openness about his own story was as absent as his curiosity over hers. She'd learned more from Ryland than her own brother.

They'd never been close, but didn't it matter to him that all they had left was each other?

Once the door shut behind them, Jess jumped in, hoping to have the conversation she'd been wanting to have for the past week. "I was so happy to hear you were alive. Has there been a search to see if any of the others—"

"Mother and Father are dead. I saw the execution records. Our uncle's family as well." He said the words coldly as he sat behind his desk.

"Oh." Jess lowered herself into a chair. "What about the servants and advisors? You survived by pretending to be one of them. Perhaps others did as well."

He shrugged. "If they make their way back here, I'll gladly welcome them, but Jessamine, while you've been living coddled away in England, the rest of Europe has been ripped apart. You don't understand how difficult it's been."

While she'd been coddled in England? Jess gritted her teeth. This was about moving ahead, not reliving the past. "After the coronation—"

"Ah yes," Nicolas interrupted her again. "James Ascot will be arriving Saturday. I'd like you there to greet him. You'll need to hurry your dress fitting along."

He'd brought her in here to talk about dresses and James Ascot? What about them as a family, what about the country? Jess frowned. "My dress fitting?"

"Yes, for the ball. The dressmaker is waiting in your room now."

One of his advisors—she didn't know his name because Nicolas had never seen fit to introduce her—entered the room. He glanced at Jess and began speaking in halting Italian.

It was all she could do not to laugh when he mentioned the risk of *dust* affecting the coronation plans when he likely meant *rain*.

In flawless Italian, Nicolas brushed the problem aside, saying, "I have no concern for the weather right now. I must get rid of the woman's distraction."

He flashed Jess a wooden smile. "Pardon me, dear sister, but I have urgent business."

Of all the moments she'd overheard, Jess wanted to reveal her knowledge of Italian more than ever in that moment. She had no doubt that she was the woman and Derek was the distraction. If Nicolas so much as scratched Derek with his fingernail, she'd show him where he could stick the bowl she'd retrieved.

So far nothing had gone like she'd hoped with this reunion. Nothing had been what she expected. Derek was the only light in her day. If that was taken away, what would she do?

Jess was almost afraid to find out.

❧❦

If someone had told Derek a month ago that he would be in a place like this and wish he could visit with the people, well, one person, instead of inspecting the priceless treasures, he wouldn't have believed it. Somehow, in that short span of time, everything he knew about life had changed.

He liked it.

While he still appreciated the world around him—and he really wanted to know if that painting was by Nathaniel Bacon—he liked the fullness Jess brought to him.

The door behind him opened and he turned from the painting. Had Jess disappeared again already?

It wasn't the guard who had sought him out, though. It was her brother. Derek had seen him only at meals, and never had the man spoken to him. It was as if, in the soon-to-be king's eyes, Derek did not exist. Or at least, he hadn't. Derek was now quite obviously in the forefront of the ruler's mind.

Derek gave his most courtly bow. "Your Highness. May I be of assistance?"

"You can pack your bags." He looked Derek up and down. "Or leaving them behind may be more of a blessing. Perhaps in gratitude for your service we will provide you a new suit of clothing." His eyes lifted to his hair. "And a trim. Either way, there is a ship leaving our port for England's shores Sunday morning. You will be on it."

The coronation was Sunday morning. The ball was Saturday night, a beginning of the celebration that would end in the solemnity of a new king, a new beginning.

And Derek was being uninvited. Though he hadn't truly been invited in the first place.

"Jessamine is needed here, and you are a distraction she does not need. She is grateful to you for your assistance."

The king's words implied that Jess had sent her brother to do what she could not. That showed how little King Nicolas knew his sister now. Jess would never be so cowardly.

That didn't change the fact that the ruler of the country Derek was in wanted him gone.

"I see," Derek said, because he did see what was happening. This king wanted Jess to do his bidding, wanted to give her an order and have her follow it. Derek would wish him luck with that, but he didn't feel the sentiment in the least. Jess should not be a political decoration, and she wouldn't stand for being one long.

Perhaps Derek could give Jess one last gift before he left. "May I offer you a piece of advice before I go?"

"No." The word was cold, succinct, and final.

Perhaps the advice he'd give Jess, then, would be to turn her brother's life into a veritable circus. "I'll go say my good-byes to Jess."

"*Jessamine* is busy. There are final fittings to be made to her gown and then introductions to the arriving dignitaries. As I said, your services are no longer needed. She cannot afford the distraction."

Derek could fight back and argue with the man, but that wouldn't get him anywhere. He would leave on that boat, but he would also see Jess before he did so.

"I understand," Derek said, being sure not to give voice to anything indicating agreement. Jess would let her brother think he was getting what he wanted and then go around him. Derek would do the same.

"Good. The guard will escort you to the docks Sunday morning."

Derek watched the man go. What had he said Jess was doing? Final fittings for her gown? A gown that likely didn't include a short jacket under which to hide her knives.

He had time before he left. He could give her something to remember herself by. She didn't have to reinvent herself to help her brother. After all she'd done for England as herself, her brother was foolish to ask her to change. If at the same time, Derek's gift reminded her of him, well, he couldn't say he'd find that disappointing in the least.

⚇

Something was very wrong. There was an itch between Jess's shoulder blades, which she normally considered a warning from her instincts that she'd noticed something but hadn't understood it completely.

The problem was that she didn't know if the something wrong was going on around her or was simply her. She was already despising the dress she was wearing to tonight's ball. It was heavy, ornate, and nothing like what she would have chosen herself. She hadn't gotten to choose, though. Instead her brother wanted her swathed in three layers of skirts, the outer one so heavily embroidered it could stand up on its own.

Unfortunately it wasn't much worse than the dresses he'd insisted she wear to greet the people who had traveled to Verbonne. Well, the ones *he* greeted. She'd been told to smile and nod and stop fidgeting so much. Considering the only movement she'd been doing at the time was breathing, she had to assume he'd prefer one of Derek's statues in her place.

She knew what he'd done, knew he'd sent Derek away. What she didn't know yet was what she was going to do about it.

When a man with weak shoulders, dressed in the latest fashion, had come through the greeting line, Nicolas had introduced him only as her future husband.

Jess had smiled, nodded, and left the room before going down to the kitchens, where she made Naples biscuits soaked in syrup. The servants gave her terrified glances, but no one said a word. A guard appeared in the door and stood there, watching her in similar tense silence.

There were many factors to consider as she rolled dough and cut out biscuits. She examined every statement, considered every angle. If he weren't her brother, what would she do with the information she had?

When the biscuits were done, she nibbled on one, still thinking. It was only when she swallowed that she realized she'd baked as a form of comfort. It hadn't been torturous or left her wracked with guilt.

She picked up one of the biscuits and stared at it. Cooking had been her refuge at the farm as well; the tiny kitchen was the place she'd been happiest. It had only been when she was running from those memories that she'd hated the room. Had letting the bad memories come, and addressing them, allowed the good ones to linger?

Grabbing a bowl and a square of linen, Jess wrapped up the biscuits. The first time she'd met Derek, he'd complimented her on her Naples biscuits and then proceeded to tell her that adding syrup would make them better. He'd been right, but she'd thrown the first batch she made into the fire out of spite. Would he remember that?

A young kitchen servant with wide eyes and brown hair stood to the side, and Jess called for her.

"Yes, milady?"

Jess frowned. She supposed she was a lady now. Did she have a title? Her father had been a duke, but what did that make her?

Marriage material. A political bartering tool.

She pushed the growing bitterness aside and focused on the biscuits. "I want you to find the man named Derek Thornbury. He's a guest here, though he'll have stayed out of the way."

"I know who he is, ma'am. We've been instructed to stay away from him."

Of course they had. "Well, I'm changing your instructions."

"But they came from the king, milady."

He wasn't actually king yet. Jess couldn't stop the unkind thought, but she didn't voice it. Instead she asked, "What's your name?"

"Maria, ma'am."

This girl had been staring at Jess the entire time Jess had been in the kitchen—not in horror but in fascination. Jess knew a kindred spirit when she saw one. This girl knew the art of breaking a rule or two.

"Ever wanted to be a lady's maid, Maria?"

The young girl's eyes widened. "I work in the scullery."

"Not what I asked."

The girl nodded. "My mother taught me how to sew. I was going to be a seamstress, but her shop was burned."

Jess didn't have to ask how the shop had burned. Outside the palace walls, it was obvious war had been here, even if Nicolas wanted it to look like the country had moved on. He was doing everything he could to make Verbonne look as splendid as it had once been, to prove it was a phoenix rising from the ashes.

He was almost more concerned with the appearance of it than

how it would actually happen. And that was what had been bothering her that she'd been unable to pin down until now.

All of Nicolas's plans were surface. Nothing was mending the country.

She'd have to deal with that next.

"Well, I am in need of a lady's maid, and I find I don't want a normal one. Do you want the job?" Jess was going to scream if she had to spend one more morning getting dressed by the insipid women Nicolas had assigned to her.

"Yes, ma'am," the girl whispered.

"Fabulous." Jess handed her the bowl of biscuits. "That means you answer to me, and I protect you from everything else. Your first job is to deliver this bowl to Mr. Thornbury. You won't have to tell him where it came from. He'll know. Then meet me in my chambers."

A short time later, Maria had done so, though she'd come to the chambers with a smirking housekeeper in tow. The stiff woman obviously expected Jess to deny that she'd promoted Maria to such a lofty position, and Jess had gotten great joy in setting the woman right.

Then she sent everyone else out of the room. It had taken Jess and Maria a bit of doing to figure out how to get into the dress, but they'd gotten to know each other while they did it. The more Jess learned, the more confident she felt in her choice of her new maid.

Now, two hours after Jess had left Maria straightening the bedchamber, she wished there'd been a way to bring the girl to the ball. At least then there'd be one friendly face.

"There you are," her brother said in her ear. "Why do you keep slipping away from where you're supposed to be?"

"Perhaps because we have a different opinion of where I should be," Jess bit out, tired of scraping to him in reverence. It wasn't her. She couldn't continue doing it.

"We are the survivors of war, Jessamine. We represent that Verbonne will be a survivor as well."

"How is that going to happen, again? All of this sparkle isn't going to sustain a people."

Nicolas's eyes hardened, though he kept his face neutral. No one could know the brother and sister were fighting, after all. They were the representation of all that was good in Verbonne. Anyone who implied differently would be silenced.

Jess frowned and said in fluent Italian, "What you're doing is wrong."

His eyes widened and then narrowed. "I'm the king, Jessamine— or I will be by this time tomorrow. I get to decide what is wrong."

No, he didn't. Such a mentality had been destroying kingdoms and families and lives for all time. If Nicolas were going to continue down that path, Jess couldn't be a part of it. In fact, she was going to do anything she could to stop it.

Knowing he was watching her, she moved deeper into the party, maneuvering herself to a point where she could slip from the ball-room and out into the garden. She needed to think, and she didn't need to have to remember to put on a show while she did it.

CHAPTER THIRTY-SEVEN

*J*ess went out to the rocks, to the same wall Queen Jessamine had been standing on in the painting. In the glinting starlight, peaceful waves kissed the edge of the wall. No storm brewed in the ocean now.

The ballroom behind her was another matter.

Across those waters lay England. A country she'd served, lived in, grown to love. Behind her was Verbonne. The place of her birth and her heritage, known to her by distant memories and old stories.

She was supposed to love Verbonne as much as, if not more than, England, but all she could find in herself was the satisfaction of a job completed and the desire to leave it behind as she'd done all the others.

"I thought you'd make your way out here eventually." Derek's voice broke her trance and brought a smile to her lips before she realized it was forming.

"Were you waiting for me?"

"Yes." He came and stood next to her, shoulder to shoulder, looking out at the water. "You'll have the guards in a panic. Again."

Jess grimaced. "I know."

She glanced at Derek. His coat looked a little worse for wear for all the travel he had done lately, and his trousers were loose. A far cry from the carefully lit palace behind her.

Considerably more real as well.

Her glance moved up to his face, but it wasn't hidden by a swath of too-long hair anymore. "What happened to your hair?"

"Your brother so kindly offered me the use of his barber. A new suit was delivered to my room, too. I haven't decided if I'm going to wear it."

She frowned. "Grow your hair back."

"I will," he said with a laugh. He gestured to the palace. "Looks like quite the party."

"You should have been invited," she said. "The coronation would be considerably more perilous if not for you. It might not have even happened at all."

"They don't see it that way."

"Well, I do." She crossed her arms over her chest. "I'm not returning to the ball without you."

His laugh rolled over the rocky coast, but it had an edge of sadness to it. "You say that as if it would be some magnanimous sacrifice on your part. Yet here you are, already having chosen to abandon it by your own choice."

"I can't be what they want me to be," she said quietly. She had finally found a role she couldn't wear.

Derek turned his hand over and gripped hers, the heat of his palm seeping through her satin glove.

Satin. Of all the ridiculous fabrics to put over one's hands. Satin practically screamed ornamental. Pretty. Useless.

His thumb tracked back and forth across her hand, calming her as he had on their voyage across the water. "I've seen you become fifteen different women in the time that I've known you. From a street urchin to an old hag to an elegant lady with money to burn. You can be anyone you want to be."

"For a time, yes, but this"—she flung her free hand out to indicate the palace—"this is forever. At the end of the evening I won't be shedding this dress and running off into the night with a piece of information that will change the course of a war or a country. I'll be taken to a room I don't feel I can breathe in, and tomorrow I'll be wrapped in more fine clothing and expected to do it all over again. I'll be Lady Jessamine for the rest of my life. And I don't know who she is."

"Who do you want to be?"

She wanted to be Jess. She wanted to go back to England and tease Daphne and match wits with Kit. She wanted to see how Reuben and Sarah and the other children from Haven Manor grew up. She wanted to watch Ryland become a father who frowned at young men in a ballroom. She wanted to see if Martha learned how to make bread that didn't break a tooth.

She wanted to spend more time with Derek, wanted him to keep challenging her to rethink how she saw things, including herself.

None of those were here.

Here was Verbonne. Here she was Lady Jessamine, and what she wanted didn't matter. That was something she'd learned from Ryland, and even from Kit and Daphne's new husbands. Being an aristocrat—a good aristocrat, anyway—meant the country was more important.

Even Ryland, for all his unconventional and scandalous ways, had done what he'd done for the good of England. He'd been willing to sacrifice his life and his title in the name of king and country.

So had Jess. She'd spent years putting herself in danger on behalf of England. Part of her would still be willing to do so, though with a bit more trepidation than she'd done before. There were people she loved now, whereas before she'd thought all the people she loved were dead. Still, saving England would mean saving the people she loved, so she'd do it again if she had to.

All she felt when she considered Verbonne was guilt. An overwhelming, soul-crushing guilt because she wasn't enthusiastically willing to make the same sacrifice for the country of her father, of her birth, of her childhood.

"I don't know my brother anymore. We're strangers."

Derek's grip tightened. "As were we once. And I think, well, I'd like to think that we became friends as we worked toward our goal."

Jess swallowed. Yes, they'd become friends. And more. He'd

challenged her like none other, while accepting her for who she was. He'd offered to teach her without condemnation or belittlement. He'd let her lead when her abilities were stronger than his, then forced her to acknowledge when there was something she just might not be capable of doing. He'd distracted her at times when nothing else had ever broken her concentration.

He'd made her feel alive.

Without him, would she become one of the walking dead, those going through the motions while the life inside them faded?

Maybe. But that was her problem to deal with, not his. She should let him leave thinking she would be fine. She wanted him to remember her well.

She wanted to ask where he would go, what he would do, but she already knew. He would finish the job at Haven Manor and then move on to the next. Like her, he wouldn't be the same, but he would continue.

"You're leaving in the morning," she said.

"Yes. I wondered if he told you."

"Not intentionally." She shrugged. "He speaks in Italian. Or at least he did. Tomorrow it will probably change to Spanish." Her eyes glinted. "I speak that language, too."

Derek's response was a chuckle. "You've been chasing this moment a long time, Jess. Whether you admit it or not, you kept the diary in the hopes that this would one day be the result." Derek dropped her hand and wrapped an arm around her shoulders.

"It's not what I hoped it would be," Jess admitted.

"No." He took a deep breath and continued, "You still found what you've been running to. Or from. Either way, for the first time in your life, you aren't running."

"What are you saying, Derek?"

"Don't start running again. If you decide to leave, do it through the front door. No matter how difficult you may find it, this is your family. You lost them once. Don't throw them away now that you've got them back. It might be work and it will never be what it was, but it could be beautiful in its own way."

"You're asking a lot of me." She'd run from everywhere she'd ever lived. Never once had she said good-bye.

Until now. Until him. She was saying good-bye to him, and it just might kill her.

"I know you can do it. You've had your time in the shadows. God has brought you into the light. Maybe it's time to try living there for a while. You might find that you shine."

Living in light. What a concept.

Derek grinned, then whispered, "'No man, when he hath lighted a candle, putteth it in a secret place, neither under a bushel, but on a candlestick, that they which come in may see the light.'"

Jess laughed, a free laugh that felt lighter than anything she'd done since arriving in Verbonne. This was why Ryland still read the Bible and sought God when circumstances were going well, why Daphne insisted on reading it to the children every night, how Derek had managed to find faith even in his calm, orderly existence. It wasn't about protection from danger—it was about life.

Somewhere along the way she'd absorbed more of that than she realized.

That was how she knew Nicolas's plan was wrong.

There'd been a story Daphne read about two kings or a king and an advisor or a cousin. She couldn't remember that part, but she remembered the king was Rehoboam and he'd wanted to lay a heavy yoke on his people to show them his power. The other man said not to. And then there was the time when Jesus said His yoke was light.

She didn't have the details, needed to spend some time looking for them, but she knew enough to know Nicolas was wrong.

"I have something for you," Derek said as he took his arm from around her and reached into his coat. He passed her a bundle of fabric.

She unrolled the linen to discover it covered a layer of leather—a long strap that would wind securely up her leg and a shorter strap to keep the flap close to her leg.

Three knives lined the bundle.

"You don't have to stop being yourself," he said. "You shouldn't. Just as your brother isn't the boy you remember, you aren't the girl you remember. I think that's a good thing."

"I can't tell you good-bye, Derek."

Telling him good-bye was wrong. Even if that wasn't in the Bible anywhere, she knew in her heart that she should not be saying good-bye to this man.

"Then don't. Walk away and leave me here. Pretend this is where I stay. Stand here whenever you need me. Think of me, talk to me. I'll be just over those waters. I'll hear you. You won't be alone. I promise, Jess, even if you forget who you are, I never will. When you need reminding, stand here and remember."

Her eyes burned with tears that she refused to let fall. Hidden in those floorboards, she'd been too afraid; then she'd been too determined to prove herself. After that, it had been about protection. Now there was no protection left. Derek had shattered her defenses. She would have to rebuild them now, but she'd do so with him on the inside so that she would never forget.

She stepped forward and put her hand on his shoulder before leaning up on her toes and placing a gentle kiss on the corner of his mouth.

"Until the next time, then," she said with a shaky smile, letting her fingers trail down his arm as she walked away, maintaining contact with him until the very last moment.

⚬⚬

Jess paused in the final shadows, pulled off her gloves, and knelt to affix the sheath he'd made to her lower leg. It gave Derek peace, seeing her walk forward with a piece of him at her side. No one would see it beneath the skirts of the bold dress, but Jess would feel it. That was what mattered. It would be a shame if the Jess he'd come to know was relegated to the past like an old painting.

When the pale shine of her hair had disappeared and her dress was visible only in his imagination, he turned away. His small bag was already packed and waiting for him.

King Nicolas had made arrangements for him to leave in the morning, but Derek refused to live at the mercy of others anymore, so he'd made his own arrangements. He would be boarding the ship tonight. With any luck, he'd sleep through the shifting of the tide and the boat's departure.

He could pretend that Verbonne and everything in it was a dream.

The sense of importance at the palace didn't quite extend down to the dock. If anyone he'd passed knew they were officially crowning their king in the morning, they either didn't care or had left it to think about tomorrow.

The ship was mostly cargo, with a handful of small, basic passenger compartments. It didn't take Derek long to settle into one. He didn't need to unpack, knowing he would only be on board for a matter of hours.

From his narrow bed, he could see the stars in a cloudless sky but nothing else. He took off his jacket and shoes but left the rest of his clothes on as he lay down. Everything he had was already rumpled beyond redemption. Sleeping in it wouldn't make a difference.

He would go to William's home when he docked in London and get cleaned up. Then he would go back to work. He would teach and study and, yes, paint. He would busy himself with the same life he'd had before he met Jess.

He wouldn't be the same man, of course, but he was rather looking forward to that part.

The stillness of his body and the motion of the boat finally lulled him to sleep, despite the turmoil of his mind. As his eyes drifted shut and lost view of the stars, all he could think was that when he woke, it would all be over.

He couldn't find a bit of joy in that.

CHAPTER THIRTY-EIGHT

*J*ess stole into the ballroom behind a server holding a tray loaded down with some sort of stuffed pastry, like a miniature meat pie. Her stomach clenched at the idea of eating, though she wasn't sure if it was in hunger or fear that she might choke on anything she attempted to swallow.

There was no reason for her to hide. She was supposed to be an honored guest of this celebration. Still, she found herself clinging to the edges of the room, moving slowly from shadow to shadow until she'd made her way to an area behind where her brother was accepting the congratulations of foreign dignitaries.

A woman stood by his side, a bland smile matching her patient and emotionless eyes. Likely Charlotte, whom Jess hadn't met yet and Nicolas hadn't told her about, but whom one advisor had mentioned was to be the future queen.

It was good for a new king to have a queen, she supposed, but she couldn't see any particular love between the two of them. Love probably hadn't been on Nicolas's mind when he had proposed the marriage. It certainly hadn't been on his mind when he'd arranged hers. Not once had he taken into consideration the fact that she loved another.

Jess paused. Well. She rather wished she'd fully realized that fact a few hours ago. She might have been able to convince Derek they should both be on that ship.

The tight leather surrounding her calf helped Jess breathe as she stood near the window, observing the party. It also berated her for the cowardice she was giving in to, remaining unseen despite the brightness of her dress.

A movement beyond the windows caught her attention. Had another guest been lured to the dark gardens for a moment of peace?

She cupped her hands around her eyes and stepped closer to the glass to see better. The figure wasn't dressed in evening wear, and he wasn't heading to the gardens but to the ballroom doors where Nicolas was holding court with a circle of powerful men.

Doors the guards weren't paying any attention to. Honestly, whoever trained these men was an imbecile.

Jess shifted a bit closer to her brother before kneeling and gently lifting her skirt to remove a knife. Right then, she wasn't Lady Jessamine, wasn't nobility, wasn't even an attendee at the ball.

She was Jess.

As the man approached the door, light from the ballroom illuminated his features. He wasn't a guard, nor was he dressed like a guest. His face was hard and angry, clearly one of an enemy.

An enemy headed directly toward her brother.

She mentally paced out the distance between her and the door the man would soon be entering, calculating how hard she'd have to throw the knife and how many revolutions it would make.

Another half step forward. She could stop him with a knock to the head by the hilt of her knife. No one needed to die tonight.

He wrenched open the door.

She screamed, hoping everyone would freeze, just for a moment, and then she sent the knife flying. The hilt smacked the man in the side of the head, and he crumpled to the ground.

Jess rushed forward, reaching the man at the same time as Nicolas's guard. She placed her foot against the man's throat as she bent to scoop up the knife, shoving the ridiculous skirt to the side with a low growl. The man wasn't moving, but she wasn't taking any chances.

"Who is he?" she asked the guard.

"Richard Bucanan, the man who would claim King Nicolas's right to the throne," the guard answered, obviously responding to the authority in her voice before realizing whom he was talking to.

"Jessamine," her brother hissed near her ear. "What are you doing?"

"Some people say thank you," she murmured. "Do you have a containment cell somewhere?"

"Of course I do," Nicolas said.

"Then I suggest you put this man there until we know more."

"We know all we need to know."

"Do we?" Jess kept her voice at a whisper as she gestured toward the man, the knife still in her hand. "He doesn't have a weapon, brother. He was angry, yes, and no doubt looking to stir up trouble, but if you even try to claim this as an assassination attempt I will refute you from the rooftops."

Nicolas's eyes narrowed. He'd become a hard man over the years, and Jess didn't really blame him for that. She'd lost her family in one fell swoop. He'd lost everything over the course of many long, tortured years.

He'd had to be hard. He'd survived, but Verbonne would not if he was going to run a country as another harsh dictator. That was something Nicolas hadn't apparently learned yet.

"Perhaps," he said, "I should have you locked away as well."

"Please do," Jess said. "Let us see what sort of loyalty that earns you from a people who have only known betrayal and war."

His gaze dropped pointedly to the knife in her hand. "Where did you get that?"

"It's mine. You aren't the only one who had to learn to survive."

They said nothing, two people who shared blood and a handful of memories but precious little else, staring each other down in a crowded ballroom.

Eventually Nicolas realized people were watching him, and the man beneath Jess's foot was stirring.

"Take him to the dungeon," Nicolas declared loudly.

The guards jumped forward. Jess waited until they had a good hold on the man's arms before removing her foot.

As everyone watched the man being dragged from the room, she knelt and put her knife away. It wasn't quite as convenient or subtle as the set of sheaths at her back, but it would do.

When she straightened, she found Nicolas watching her instead of the commotion. "I think we should talk, sister of mine. There are clearly details you haven't been telling me."

"There are questions you haven't been asking." Jess tilted her head. "In light of that, I suggest you refrain from making any announcements about me tonight."

They stared at each other a moment, but he said nothing more, simply turned his back on her and restarted the dancing.

Jess wanted to leave, wished she could be anywhere but there, but she spent the rest of the evening dancing and smiling and laughing at the ridiculousness of anyone thinking they saw her do anything spectacular.

As everyone made their way out to catch a few hours' sleep before the coronation commenced, Jess waited and rolled her head around in an attempt to loosen the tension.

"You've been keeping secrets from me," Nicolas said behind her when it was only them, a handful of guards, and the departing orchestra.

"Hmmm, yes. You should rethink one of your advisors. Charles. If you truly want to be a free nation, he's not going to support it."

Nicolas scoffed. "How would you know that?"

"Because he told that other man, Francesco Bianchi, that Verbonne would be better suited as a member of the German Confederation."

"Francesco Bianchi doesn't speak English. He rarely speaks French. How would you know what they said?"

"*Parlo italiano, ricordi?*" Jess said, rolling her eyes at his apparent short memory.

Nicolas glanced toward her leg where the knives still sat snug against her calf. "Ah yes. When did you learn Italian?"

"I perfected it in Italy. Don't ask me when. Life sort of blurred together for a while there." She wasn't about to spill her secrets before Nicolas spilled his, not when he was the one with the power in the room. Or so he supposed.

Nicolas's scowl darkened.

"Don't say anything you will regret," Jess warned. "You don't know everything. Probably don't even know half of what you think you know."

"This conversation isn't over," Nicolas said.

But maybe it should be.

As Jess walked back to her room, she thought about love, thought about Derek and what he'd said about her and her brother and Verbonne. What he'd said about love and sacrifice.

If she loved her brother, should she be willing to sacrifice who she'd been for him? For the country?

That didn't sit right, even though people she trusted and admired had all said love was a sacrifice. Derek had said something about need as well, that Jess had sacrificed because Kit and Daphne needed it. What was the verse Kit had quoted?

"Hereby perceive we the love of God, because he laid down his life for us."

God had given the sacrifice she needed, not the one she'd asked for. That was the sacrifice love demanded. It wasn't sacrificing to make someone else happy; it was sacrificing to provide what they needed.

Her little jaunt through her memories had jarred something else loose. She now remembered where she'd heard Richard Bucanan's name.

Thirty minutes later, Jess was in one of her own gowns and making her way to the dungeons. A guard sat at the entrance to the area but not directly by the cell. A rock thrown down a side corridor got him to abandon his post to go investigate.

Nicolas really was fortunate no one had decided to assassinate him yet.

She crept into the dark, dank passage carrying a lantern partially covered with a piece of black cloth, and made her way down the cells until she found the prisoner. There weren't many cells, perhaps a half dozen, but he'd been placed as far away from the guard as possible.

The man blinked at her, raising his arm to shield his gaze from her pointed light. "What do you want?"

"Keep your voice down unless you want them to know you have a visitor," Jess whispered, adjusting the cloth so that barely any light from the single candle within the tin lantern illuminated the area. She sat on the floor outside the cell and waited for the man to join her. He was older, though he looked spry in the way that men who made a living from the land tended to be.

He watched her awhile but finally moved forward and sat across from her. "Who are you?"

"Good. Smarter question," Jess said. "I'm the reason the left side of your head is probably a bit tender right now."

The man lifted a hand to rub at the side of his head.

"I'm also the sister of the man being crowned as king." Jess took a deep breath. "Now I've told you my identity. You tell me yours. Who are you?"

"Richard Bucanan."

"So they say. You don't want the crown."

He looked at her in shock for a moment. "I . . . no, I don't, not really. No one believes me about that. How did you know?"

"Because you tried to tell England about the paintings. If they'd listened, everything might be a bit different this weekend." Jess wasn't sure if she wished things were going differently or not. She still wanted this country to be free, for the people to rediscover the culture they loved, but was this the best way?

"How did you—"

Jess swiped a hand through the air. "You are the one in a cell. I get to ask the questions."

The man grunted.

"Why are you here?"

"I don't want to rule the country, but I don't want to see it die."
He sighed, and his head drooped forward. "It meant a lot to my
grandfather. He was nearly obsessed with it. I never understood
why. He was born in England, lived there his entire life."

"Who were his parents?"

"A painter named Dominic and a woman named Nicolette."

Relief rushed through Jess. There had been a child. A girl child.
She would bet anything Nicolette had been named for her father,
Nicolas. "Continue."

"My grandfather would talk about growing up among the paintings, about the stories told by his mother. By the time the stories
made it to us, they were little more than fables."

"Why are you here, then?"

"Because my family devoted their lives to that fable. My aunt
married a nobleman to try to gain us more power. It was practically a disease among them, these stories, this . . . this . . . vendetta.
My whole life I'd been told it was the destiny I was born to. My
cousin even committed treason for it."

"I've met him," Jess murmured. "He doesn't like me much."

Bucanan shook his head. "He doesn't like anyone. I kept quiet
about it at first because of some sense of loyalty, but it's gotten
out of hand. He's emptied his coffers in an attempt to restore our
power in Verbonne.

"Before I came over here," Bucanan continued, "I left a parcel
of information with a magistrate who didn't seem afraid to pros-
ecute aristocrats."

"Good." Jess would send word to Ryland. The codes in the
magic lantern slides might help seal Lord Bradford's fate. "Now
tell me why you're here."

"Because Nicolas sent men after me. I never bought into the idea
that I should have the crown. Perhaps it was the war, perhaps it
was the idea of being royalty instead of just nobility, but whatever
it was, Bradford became obsessed. The more I denied wanting it,
the more he pushed, and the more he did on his own. I didn't know
if he'd try to make a claim of his own, so I told him I would."

"Nicolas learned of that, I assume."

"Maybe. Or maybe he assumed I held my cousin's fixation. Honestly, my only concern was that Nicolas take Verbonne and make it the fable my grandfather believed in. He doesn't seem to be doing a very good job yet."

No, he didn't. Jess had yet to see the makings of a good king in him. "Tell me what you think he should do."

⬥⬥

Derek was ecstatic to have had a bath and a night in a comfortable bed, but other than that, he wasn't very happy to see England.

When he went down to breakfast, Ryland was waiting on him.

"I could have sworn I'd gone to William's house," Derek said, seating himself and thanking the servant who immediately brought tea and food to the table.

"You did," Ryland said. "I'm infringing on his hospitality."

"How very ducal of you."

"Not feeling very favorable toward the aristocracy right now, are you?" Ryland chuckled.

No, Derek wasn't. Because if Jess had been a normal woman, she'd have been able to come home with him, he'd have been able to court her, and his heart wouldn't currently be sitting somewhere at the bottom of the English Channel.

"I've several estates full of art," Ryland mused. "I never really thought of having it catalogued, but it seems like a smart assessment." He leaned forward and braced his elbows on the table. "I wouldn't have to be in residence while you worked, if you preferred it that way."

A drop of tea splashed out of Derek's cup as he set it down. It spilled onto his serviette and spread slowly through the fibers. "I've been thinking of trying to paint again."

Why had he admitted such a thing? It wasn't as if he could take up some sort of artist residency somewhere. He still needed to work.

"Even better." Ryland sat back in his seat. "Miranda has been

364

telling me that being a patron of the arts would make me more refined."

Derek felt a grin building. "You want to be my patron? You don't even know if I have any talent."

Ryland shrugged. "I have a few sketches in my possession. They look good to me."

"Why?"

"Because I had a horrible family. I couldn't protect them, not from themselves. So I made myself a family."

"You collected people."

Ryland winced. "Seems mercenary when you say that."

"Not really. People care for their collections—restore them, nurture them, protect them. All in all, it's rather a good bit more noble than collecting art." And whether he knew it or not, the duke had passed that on to others. Wasn't that what Jess was doing now? Starting her own collection that comprised an entire country?

Derek sat back and looked at Ryland. "Why me?"

"Jess is mine. By extension, now so are you."

"And Daphne and Kit?"

Ryland nodded. "Them too. I like Chemsford. Parliament will be better off for having him in it. Wharton, too, one day. His father's a good man."

Derek opened his mouth to turn down the offer, but then he stopped. It was a job. A good job. One that would allow him to explore painting a bit as well. Did Derek want to work with a daily reminder of what he'd lost? It would be painful, yes, but then again, he was going to hurt no matter where he was.

From a career perspective, this would put him in a good place. Between the duke and William, he'd have references to one day land a prestigious curator job or perhaps a position with the Royal Gallery.

"I'd like to go home first. See my family. Finish at Haven Manor."

Ryland nodded and picked up the paper. "You know where I live."

"Here, it would seem," Derek said, a genuine, easy grin breaking through.

Ryland chuckled. "You're going to be all right, Derek Thornbury."

Derek certainly hoped so.

❧❧

Though the coronation was beautiful, Jess had to fight to stay awake. She'd stayed up all night taking the measure of a man she'd been told to fear since childhood, a man who, it turned out, was also a victim of Lord Bradford's obsession.

The truth was that while the past colored the future, the people living in the present still wielded the paintbrush. They could change the course they'd been set on. All that was left was for Jess to decide how to tell Nicolas what she'd done.

She'd let him become king first. It was only fair.

The anointing of Nicolas's head drew a large cheer from the gathered crowd. The sermon from the presiding priest drew a cheer from Jess's heart. She was listening differently, now that she'd realized how important it was to seek God in the quiet times in order to know what to cling to in the chaos.

When the crown was placed upon the new king's head, the crowd's cheer was deafening. It was the cheer of a people who'd only heard stories of being their own government, of controlling their own destiny. Tomorrow, the work of forging ahead as a reborn country might frighten them, but today they were excited.

That was as it should be.

Other things would soon be as they should be as well.

"Maria." Jess turned to her lady's maid, who was sitting next to her in the royal box, despite the glares of the other dignitaries and noble ladies. "How do you feel about England?"

CHAPTER THIRTY-NINE

*D*erek took a month to collect his belongings and finish his report for William. When he felt that putting it off any longer would be insulting, he returned to London and to Montgomery House.

"We've had a room set up for you. Miranda's sister said it had good light for painting," Ryland said after Derek was shown into the study.

"I'm afraid I'm going to have a slight delay before starting work for you, Your Grace." Derek shifted his weight but tried to stand tall and confident.

Ryland raised an eyebrow in inquiry.

"I did a lot of thinking while trying to tell my family what I've been doing."

"I can imagine how well that went," Ryland said with a slight laugh.

Derek had to admit there'd been a great bit of scoffing, particularly from his older brother. "Yes, well, it helped me come to a conclusion." Derek took a deep breath. "I don't want my life to be a tragedy."

Ryland stared at him for a few moments. "I'm sure that statement makes sense on some level, but I don't see it."

More than one painting had been born of sorrow and loss. Derek had spent a lifetime studying them and admiring them, even going so far as to revere them. Living such a story was far less pleasant than looking at it on a gallery wall. The duke wasn't likely to understand that. But the nice thing about his life as opposed to a piece of art was that Derek still had the ability to change it.

"I need to make a trip across the Channel," Derek said, instead of trying to explain his thoughts.

"You might want to wait on that," Ryland said, holding up a piece of paper. "Apparently Jess sent me something and meant to arrive before it, but her timing was a bit off and she's going to be a day or two late."

Derek's throat went dry. Had Ryland been in communication with Jess this whole month? Had she married the man her brother wanted her to? Was she happy? "She's coming here?"

"So it would seem. Why she would send something instead of bringing it herself is somewhat baffling."

"Oh." Derek shifted his weight. He'd been so set to leave here and go to the docks, discover the fastest way he could travel to Verbonne. Jess was one step ahead of him, though. He should probably get used to that if he wanted to keep her in his life. "When does that say she'll get here?"

He flipped the letter over. "It doesn't say, though the delivery is supposed to arrive today or tomorrow, so likely a day or so after. There's also a drawing on here. I'm not sure if it's supposed to be a duck or a horse."

Derek leaned over the desk. "Are you sure it isn't a flower?"

"I'm not sure she didn't hand the quill to a toddler. You're the art expert." Ryland tossed the paper down on the desk. "Your bags have been taken up to your room if you want to go freshen up."

"I told them to leave them at the door," Derek said. "How would they know I'm now staying?"

Ryland pointed at the study door. "It's open. I've only expressly forbidden eavesdropping near the bedchambers, my private parlor, or when I'm in a room with the door closed."

Sure enough, a maid popped into the study. "Your room is ready, Mr. Thornbury. Would you like me to show you?"

A few hours later, as they were sitting down to dinner, the echo of the brass knocker on the door could be heard throughout the public rooms of the house.

Ryland frowned. "It would seem Jess's delivery is a bit insistent."

Derek abandoned his plate to make his way to the front hall, curiosity overtaking his manners.

The last thing he expected to see when the butler opened the door was King Nicolas.

"Who is that?" Ryland asked, coming up to stand beside Derek.

Before Derek could answer, the king made to push past the butler, pointing an angry finger at Derek and preparing to yell.

Until he had the air knocked out of him as the butler flipped him onto his back. "I didn't say you could enter, sir."

The two guards who had been standing behind the king rushed inside, only to find two maids pointing pistols in their direction.

Ryland crossed the hall and waited for King Nicolas to catch his breath and climb to his feet.

"I am the king of Verbonne," he said angrily.

"And I'm an English duke," Ryland said dryly. "Should we test who really has more power right now? Given that you're standing in my home, I'd think twice before you answer."

Miranda looked over the scene and sighed. "Jess sends the absolute worst gifts."

※ ※

This was what happened when Jess tried to make a plan instead of just barreling through one item at a time.

Still, she wouldn't trade the past month. It had been necessary. As much as she knew she didn't want to live in Verbonne, she also knew she wanted it to thrive. She loved it, in a way, and it had needed a month of her time. That was all that had been needed to put a few plans in motion to keep her brother in check while he realized the world wasn't at war anymore.

One of those measures had been breaking his former greatest enemy out of a rather poorly guarded dungeon and taking him on a tour of the country.

Bucanan was now fully prepared and equipped to be Verbonne's ambassador to England. Or at least their advocate. She wasn't entirely sure how citizenship worked in a newly established country, or whether Verbonne would be diplomatically recognized. Still, if the country was going to survive on its own, it needed an ally as powerful as England.

Since England would benefit as well, it shouldn't be that hard to convince them. As long as she could convince Nicolas without Ryland killing her.

How long had he been here? A day? Two?

Was he even still here, or had Ryland thrown him out? Nicolas was a king, after all. That would gain him a bit of respect, wouldn't it?

She knocked on the door to Ryland's London home. Depending on who answered and how mad they were, there were several things she could say.

Every thought she had in her head disappeared when Derek opened the door.

He was grinning at her. His hair had grown and now flopped across his forehead again. His spectacles were a bit crooked, with a smudge high up on one lens, and Jess was convinced that never had a man looked better. Well, objectively speaking, there were several better-looking men, but she preferred seeing this one.

"You've really done it now, haven't you?" he asked.

"Probably," Jess answered, her lips forming a grin of her own.

Derek pushed the door open and granted Jess and Richard entrance. Once they were standing in the hall, Derek looked back and forth between the two of them. "You aren't pretending to be married to him, are you?"

"No." Jess lifted her chin in triumph. "I've a proper lady's maid now."

Richard snorted. "I don't think hauling a scullery maid out of the kitchens counts as proper."

"Sounds like a proper lady's maid for a cook," Derek said.

This time Richard laughed outright. "She said the same thing."

"Must make it true," Jess said. "I'm assuming my troublesome brother is here?"

"Yes."

Jess bit her lip. "What has he said?"

"Nothing much. He said he came to talk to you—not a duke and certainly not a professor."

Jess frowned. "But you aren't a professor."

"I don't think he cares."

"Well, he needs to learn to." Jess crossed her arms over her chest. "People matter. I've been trying to tell him that all month."

"He said he hasn't seen you in a month."

"He hasn't. I've been sending him letters." She stopped and looked up at Derek. "I thought about writing you letters, too, but I hate writing and I knew I'd never send them. I wanted to see you when I told you I loved you."

Richard coughed. "Is there a drawing room? Parlor? Maybe I should just step back out onto the street?"

"Drawing room is through that door. The good brandy is in the lower part of the Chinese cabinet behind the vase of purple feathers," Jess said, waving her arm to one side of the hall. Knowing how Ryland's house worked, she pitched her voice a little louder. "If someone hasn't already told Ryland I'm here, please do so, and have my brother come to the drawing room as well."

And through it all Derek grinned. "Am I allowed to say I love you, too, now?"

Jess heaved a sigh of relief. "That would be greatly appreciated, yes."

Derek took her hand in his, sending that familiar and now welcome warmth running up her arm. "I love you." He squeezed her fingers. "Now can we please unravel whatever you've done so we can have a proper conversation about what that means?"

"I don't know what you're mad about," Jess said, letting her brother realize the full force of her abundant confidence. The man looked a little bit lost in the face of it.

"You disrupted the entire country," the king growled.

Jess sighed. "I did no such thing."

Although she rather had. As the entire story was revealed, Derek had tried not to laugh. Ryland had no such restraint, until his wife bobbled her teacup and spilled a bit on his leg. Jess had turned the new little country on its ear, and Nicolas had been forced to accept it or admit that his own sister had undermined his rule and his guards couldn't find her.

"You swear to me that you never left Verbonne's borders?" Nicolas asked.

Jess rolled her eyes. "What would be the point of that? Richard needed to get to know Verbonne through something other than stories. For that matter, you and I needed to do the same. That's why I sent you the letters."

"You sent me taunts," Nicolas growled.

"And it made you travel the country and meet your people. They were very appreciative of that, by the way."

Derek marveled at Jess's ingenuity. Wherever she'd gone, she'd sent Nicolas a letter. He would chase after her, but instead of finding her, he'd be surrounded by his subjects, forced to play diplomatically nice and live up to the stories Jess had told about him just before he'd arrived.

"Yes, yes, I talked to everyone. I would ask them if they'd seen you. They said they had and then proceeded to show me their businesses and families instead of telling me where you'd gone. One old lady tried to teach me to knit."

Jess leaned toward Derek. They were already sitting scandalously close on the drawing room sofa, but he didn't push her away. "That reminds me. I made you a scarf."

Derek sputtered a laugh into his hand. Never again would his life be dull. The boys who had teased him in school, the men he'd known since, none of them would ever believe that the perfect woman for him would be anything like Jess. He wouldn't have believed it either.

Thank goodness God thought bigger than he did.

"You have to admit," Jess said to her brother, "you know Verbonne better than you did before."

Nicolas grunted and folded his arms over his chest.

"As entertaining as this is," Ryland said, "why send him here?"

She motioned toward Richard. "To meet his new English ambassador. It seemed safer to do it here."

Nicolas frowned. "He cannot be our ambassador. He is not Verbonnian."

"His cousin is being tried as an English traitor," Ryland chipped in. "He may want to change nationalities."

"You need England," Jess said. "Your plan to place the people under military rule and fairly well force them into slavery is wrong and foolish and the fastest way for Verbonne to end up right back where it was—at the mercy of whoever feels like overpowering her."

"How did you know about that?"

Jess waved a hand about. "I speak French, Spanish, Italian, Russian, German, Dutch, and enough Chinese to probably get myself through a town without getting killed."

"Honestly," Ryland said, "you're better off not saying anything in her hearing you don't want understood. I'm fairly confident she could spend a month with my daughter and become fluent in child-speak. In fact, please do. I'll pay you to interpret."

Derek had spent a bit of time with the little one. He had thought it was because the child wasn't his that he couldn't understand her. He hoped Jess's language skills would extend to their children, whenever they had them.

The idea of having children with Jess had him pulling her a bit closer on the sofa.

"What language I speak is not the point," Jess said. "It's time to make friends, gain allies, and focus on rebuilding your people. Verbonne doesn't need bigger borders or a stronger army. England just defeated the army that defeated the army that took over Verbonne in the first place. Just make friends with the Prince Regent so they come running to save you next time."

Ryland winced. "It doesn't work that way."

"Essentially it does," Jess said, "and you know it."

Nicolas and Richard stared at each other across the room for a very long time. Even Derek was growing uncomfortable.

"Do you think we should leave them to talk it out?" he asked Jess.

"Yes." She stood abruptly and moved toward the door. "Whatever they do now is up to them. I fell in love with Verbonne and her people. I'll be happy to help however I can, but I also love England. I have a home and family here." Her eyes met Derek's. "My future is here."

"Well, I wouldn't mind traveling." Derek grinned. "There's a great deal of art to see."

Ryland shook his head and moved to the door as he looked to Richard and Nicolas. "Don't kill each other. I'm putting my butler at the door."

Nicolas groaned.

As Jess and Derek followed Ryland, Nicolas called out, "Just one question. What in the world did you draw at the bottom of the letters?"

Jess frowned. "It was supposed to be a person."

Derek threw his arm around her. "I think in the future I'll do the drawing while you do the talking."

"Sounds like a plan to me."

EPILOGUE

ONE YEAR LATER

*J*ess didn't care for the massive number of people pressing in on her or the decided lack of exits available from the top floor of the Royal Academy, but she was ecstatic that one of her husband's paintings was hanging on the wall for all these people to admire.

It was her, though no one would know it. She was painted from behind, her hair flowing down her back, face lifted to the sun. Yellows and golds flooded the canvas. He entitled it *Girl in the Light*.

It had taken Jess a while to convince Nicolas that she would not be participating in the politics of Verbonne. No matter how he tried to entice her, all she saw was more games to play, more darkness to navigate, and she refused to be that person anymore. She'd lived too many years in the shadows to step into them again, now that she'd learned what it was like to live in the light.

She wasn't running anymore. She wasn't hiding.

It felt wonderful.

Jess and Derek did travel a bit, but they'd settled back at Haven Manor. The cottage they were building approximately halfway between Haven Manor and Marlborough was almost finished, and Jess couldn't wait to move into it. Even though she'd be frequently making the walk to Haven Manor to teach the women how to cook and protect themselves, she would have a space of her own to build a family and a future, to have roots.

She had a closet now, instead of living out of a trunk.

The kitchen still made her sad on occasion, but most of the time she allowed herself to remember Ismelde's happy smile and the way she sang as she kneaded bread. Derek was painting and doing occasional work at Oxford, though he was going to start teaching at the local school in Marlborough the next year. Maria was still her lady's maid and enjoyed sewing with the women at Haven Manor. Martha had chosen to live a simple life in order to raise her little boy and now worked for William's new factory.

So much was going on around them, and instead of just watching, Jess and Derek were right in the middle of it. Their lives had purpose and peace, two things Jess had never realized she needed.

Derek came up to her and stood beside her, looking up at the painting. She lifted her hand to subtly twine their fingers together.

"You did that," she said, referring to far more than the painting itself.

"No," he said. "I just helped you see it."

Author Note

While the timeline of Napoleon and the remains of the Holy Roman Empire are accurate, the country of Verbonne and its inhabitants are fictional. As an amalgamation of several bits of histories from several different countries, the country is not based on any one single place. Fournier and The Six are also fictional, so sadly no one will ever see their stunning and remarkable paintings. The other works and painters mentioned in this book, with the exception of the statute in Kettering, are real, though.

Acknowledgments

*M*any years ago, what sometimes feels like a lifetime ago, I wrote a book called *A Noble Masquerade*, and during one particular scene, I needed a secondary character. In walked Jess. She was supposed to be little more than a prop, a character I used to get something done, but she turned into so much more. I fell in love with her as I wrote her, and then she and the readers demanded she have her own story.

I had the most amazing fun writing this book, and the first group I have to thank for it is the readers who insisted Jess needed more. I completely agree.

There were a few more people who made this story possible as well.

I'd like to thank Van Gogh. I am not much of an art lover, but the one painting that does hold special meaning for me was done by him. That connection inspired much of Derek's love of art. Thank you to my extended family for letting me drag you all to the Museum of Modern Art while we were in New York so I could see *The Starry Night* in person.

Huge thanks go to Robin, Athena, and Peri for their assistance in helping me understand how Jess could learn and use so many languages. It is a skill I don't possess but find truly amazing.

Particular thanks goes to Paty Hinojosa for helping me translate the Italian and to Melodee for my Russian.

More appreciation to Raechel Lenore for sharing her knife-throwing prowess. Since that's another skill I don't possess—and not one I'm willing to learn by trial and error—your knowledge was essential!

Lastly, to my family, my agent, and everyone else who helped me with the creation of the HAVEN MANOR series, I couldn't have done it without you. To God be the glory!

Kristi Ann Hunter is the author of the HAWTHORNE HOUSE and HAVEN MANOR series and a 2016 RITA Award winner, an ACFW Genesis contest winner, and a Georgia Romance Writers Maggie Award for Excellence winner. She lives with her husband and three children in Georgia. Find her online at www.kristiannhunter.com.

Sign Up for Kristi's Newsletter!

Keep up to date with Kristi's news on book releases and events by signing up for her email list at kristiannhunter.com.

Also from Kristi Ann Hunter

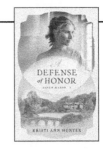

Far away from London, three young women establish a home for children to protect them against society's censure over the circumstance of their birth. But each woman also has secrets of her own and will have to choose if guarding them closely is worth risking a surprising love.

HAVEN MANOR: *A Defense of Honor, A Return of Devotion, A Pursuit of Home*

You May Also Like . . .

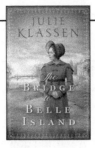

While Benjamin investigates a mysterious death, evidence takes him to a remote island on the Thames. There, Isabelle is trapped by fear and a recurring dream about a man's death. Or is it a memory? When a second death brings everyone under suspicion, and the search for truth brings secrets to light, she realizes her island sanctuary will never be the same.

The Bridge to Belle Island by Julie Klassen
julieklassen.com

Gray Delacroix has dedicated his life to building a successful global spice empire, but it has come at a cost. Tasked with gaining access to the private Delacroix plant collection, Smithsonian botanist Annabelle Larkin unwittingly steps into a web of dangerous political intrigue and will be forced to choose between her heart and her loyalty to her country.

The Spice King by Elizabeth Camden
HOPE AND GLORY #1
elizabethcamden.com

In the midst of the Great War, Margot De Wilde spends her days deciphering intercepted messages. But after a sudden loss, her world is turned upside down. Lieutenant Drake Elton returns wounded from the field, followed by a destructive enemy. Immediately smitten with Margot, how can Drake convince a girl who lives entirely in her mind that sometimes life's answers lie in the heart?

The Number of Love by Roseanna M. White
THE CODEBREAKERS #1
roseannamwhite.com

⬧ BETHANYHOUSE

More Fiction from Bethany House

After facing desperate heartache and loss, Mercy agrees to escape a bleak future in London and join a bride ship. Wealthy and titled, Joseph leaves home and takes to the sea as the ship's surgeon to escape the pain of losing his family. He has no intention of settling down, but when Mercy becomes his assistant, they must fight against a forbidden love.

A Reluctant Bride by Jody Hedlund, THE BRIDE SHIPS #1
jodyhedlund.com

At loose ends in 1881, Cara Bernay befriends a carefree artist, the brother of the handsome but infuriating Henry Burke, the Earl of Morestowe. Recognizing the positive influence she has on his brother, Henry invites her to accompany them back to their estate. When secrets on both sides come out, Cara devises a bold plan with consequences for her heart.

The Artful Match by Jennifer Delamere, LONDON BEGINNINGS #3
jenniferdelamere.com

In spring 1918, British Lieutenant Colin Mabry receives an urgent message from a woman he once loved but thought dead. Feeling the need to redeem himself, he travels to France—only to find the woman's half sister, Johanna, who believes her sister is alive and the prisoner of a German spy. As they seek answers across Europe, danger lies at every turn.

Far Side of the Sea by Kate Breslin
katebreslin.com

❖ BETHANY HOUSE

CPSIA information can be obtained
at www.ICGtesting.com
Printed in the USA
FSHW021543241019
63355FS